Lighthouse Paradox

D1329976

D. Ann Kelley
James G. Kelley

Lypton Publishing, Peoria, IL

Lighthouse Paradox

First Edition
Copyright © 2004
Printed and bound in the United States of America

Library of Congress Cataloging-in-Publication Data

Kelley, D. Ann & James G. Kelley.
Lighthouse Paradox

1. Mystery 2. Great Lakes 3. Theft

ISBN   0-9752780-0-2
LCCN 2004092006

10 9 8 7 6 5 4 3 2 1

Dedicated to Susan Kelley

My loving wife... JK

My favorite mom... DK

Acknowledgements

First, we would like to thank Merlin and Lorna Kelley, as well as Josephine Tischer, for their original account of the 1959 plane crash near the lighthouse.

To Terry Pepper of the "Seeing the Light: Lighthouses of Lakes Michigan, Superior, and Huron" at www.terrypepper.com/lights, for his monumental help in finding the exact dates the original plane crash at the lighthouse took place; Jim Hammond from Cape Cod for his outstanding assistance with the details of the Piper Supercruiser and radio communication; Master Plumber Tom Ellis for his descriptions of plumbing procedures and other help; and Chippewa County Deputy Sheriff Jerry Brown for his technical description of police procedure that would take place on Drummond Island (any variances from actual procedure were done for the purpose of plot and are completely our responsibility).

To Brian White, Doug Didia and Mackenzie Sand of Quintek Productions for the cover artwork. To Leigh Tye for her editing.

To the staff of the Lake Superior State University KJS Library, Bayliss Library (in Sault Ste. Marie, MI), and International UFO Museum and Research Center Library (in Roswell, NM) who were all very helpful in our research. We appreciate The Sault Evening News for their permission to reprint the original letter left in the lighthouse.

To Norm Young, LaRae Dorman and Holly Rairigh for putting up with our constant book-related discussion, and for their ideas. We greatly appreciate the people of Drummond Island and the customers of the Book Nook and North Haven (www.drummondrentals.com) who have shared our excitement for seeing this book come to print.

Last but certainly not least, we would like to thank Susan Kelley for her unending support and encouragement during our writing, her valuable opinions, and her enthusiasm for seeing our goal come to life.

PROLOGUE

The black and white four-by-five told the story.

The candid shot of the soldiers had been taken by a journalist trying to capture the quieter moments of the Korean War. The men appeared homesick, scared and weary. One of the men told the group a story from home and they were all caught smiling or laughing. It was a rare moment for them, and yet it was defining. Lost innocence was etched around their eyes and showed in their faces. Their manner reflected the dark lessons they learned while defending a nation. In the shadows of war, they became brothers far closer than those of birth. Placed in the same squadron, they leaned on each other: *trusted each other*. They were inseparable or so they had thought. Three days after the picture was taken, the group lost half of its members. Eight had become four.

Turning the picture over in his hands, he couldn't help but wonder why he hadn't been among those who were killed. After all, he was the only one who *deserved* to die. His betrayal was total. Even worse, he couldn't bring himself to confess the truth. He just waited for the day when someone would find out what he had done. He knew judgment would come.

He was right.

One

NOVEMBER 23, 1953 5:33 PM

The hangar at Kincheloe Air Force Base (KAFB) was large, cool, and drafty. The wind coming from the northwest rolled across the plains of Saskatchewan and Manitoba, crossed the vast openness of Lake Superior and pounded the northern coastline of Michigan's Upper Peninsula. Kincheloe was a hell hole of a place to be stationed since winter temperatures often dropped into the double negative digits, but remarkably, three of the four officers huddled inside the hangar chose KAFB in order to remain together after surviving the Korean War.

The wind roared against the sheet metal of the hangar, unfurling a loud rattle to which the men had become accustomed. 2nd Lt. Cal Johansen, a pilot, leaned back in the cold metal folding chair, his posture held as rigidly as the five cards clenched in his right fist. He dragged hard grey eyes over the features of his opponents. Over a half month's pay sat in the center of the card table, taunting the two pilots and their radar officers who hovered around it. The men were playing five card stud with nothing wild. Holding a full house of sevens and jacks, Cal knew he would win.

1st Lt. Neilson cleared his throat. "Come on Cal, throw down."

Cal grinned. "I'm going to raise the ante."

Before anyone could protest, the shrill scream of the alarm ripped through the hangar swiftly. 1st Lt. Neilson and 2nd Lt. Appov leapt from their chairs, knocking them over as they rushed out of the hangar, followed closely by Cal and his radar officer. Neilson's fingers moved adeptly to fasten his flight jacket as he ran, carefully moving from foot to foot over the snow patched ground. Near their planes, the ground crew assembled in quick order.

"Neilson. Appov. You're clear as soon as you're ready."

"You'll get your instructions in the air. Johansen, Lewis, stand by."

Neilson rushed up the flight ladder, securing himself into the cockpit. Appov strapped in behind him. Air Defense Command Radar detected an unidentified target over Lake Superior.

In moments, the F-89C all weather jet interceptor taxied down the runway and smoothly ascended into the heavy grey sky.

"This is Kincheloe Air Force Base Tower. Climb to 30,000 feet. The UFO is moving west—northwest out over Lake Superior. You are cleared to fly west and to descend 7,000 feet. Bend east—northeast at a steep descent to make contact. Move to identify and intercept. This is not a drill. Repeat: This is not a drill." The ground controller articulated the coordinates provided by Truax Air Force Base in Wisconsin, and Neilson confirmed them as he gained altitude and increased speed.

Appov squinted his eyes, suddenly troubled. "What the hell is that?"

Neilson shifted all of his energy into controlling the plane, flying at over 500 miles per hour. His control panel seemed skewed. His body felt uneasy. His pulse hammered in his head, his throat, behind his eyes.

The last radar contact was at 8,000 feet, 70 miles off the Keweenaw Peninsula and approximately 150 miles northwest of Kincheloe Air Force Base. On the ground, the commander of KAFB, Lt. Col. William Robertson entered the control room with powerful strides. "What in hell is going on up there?"

The young man sitting at the radar screen gave him all the information he had. "Truax reported an unidentified flying object in restricted air space over the Soo Locks at 17:37, Sir. At 17:40, an F-89C was launched to intercept and identify the aircraft. The bogey was intercepted 150 miles northwest over Lake Superior. At that time the two planes, our F-89C and the unidentified craft, merged into one."

Robertson held up his hand. "Merged?"

"The two radar blips became one on the screen. Truax then reported that the planes had disappeared, or rather that they were no longer on the screen."

"Continue." The order was a sharp snap, forcing the answers to come faster.

"Sir, neither 1st Lt. Neilson nor 2nd Lt. Appov have responded to our hailing. We've alerted both the U.S. and Canadian Coast Guard as well as the Royal Canadian Air Force. A second F-89 has been sent to the last known location to look for the missing jet, or possible wreckage."

No new information or wreckage debris would ever be found. The disappearance of two officers under his command would haunt him for the rest of his career and beyond. The United States Government would claim a mid-air collision with a Canadian DC3 had taken place. Later, they would change the facts and name the plane an RCAF C-47. The Canadians would deny this. In 1961 and again in 1963, the National Investigation Committee on Aerial Phenomena (NICAP) denied that any

Canadian plane was involved. The USAF would respond by claiming 1st Lt. Neilson suffered from vertigo and crashed into Lake Superior. The radio communications between the pilot and radar control were never released. Speculation of all sorts would surface, including the belief that the officers and jet were taken by the UFO, a spacecraft from some other world.

Lt. Cal Johansen would demand answers, and be given bureaucratic run around. The cold fact crawled into his belly and remained: eight had become two.

TWO

"Mayday, mayday. Piper 1274 Whiskey is going down approximately 3 miles south by southeast of DeTour Passage." Lee DeForge's voice shook; his palms were damp with sweat. He expelled his breath in a loud gush. No one was responding. Somewhere, someone should be listening. Snow swirled around the plane, confining his vision to a frosty blanket of white. Ice cake crunched into ice cake beneath him. Waves rocked between chunks of ice. Wind ripped across the surface of the plane pulling it up, pushing it down, slamming the nose from side to side. His voice quaked while fear erupted inside him. "Mayday, mayday. Piper 1274 Whiskey has lost engine power and is going down in water approximately 3 miles south by southeast of DeTour Passage."

Lee's heart slammed against his chest, his blood boiled in his veins as he guided the stick shift between his legs. He tried the electric control panel once more. *No response. The plane was not responding.* The realization gripped his mind and spurred him toward full blown panic. He'd have to crash land somewhere below. His typical finesse with the stick shift was replaced with panic stricken jerks. Piper responded by swinging wide of the desired path. Lee's shouted curse filled the cockpit. Somewhere his mind revolted at living through Korea only to die short years later in the miserably cold north. *There, in the distance, a lighthouse.*

Guiding the plane despite his racing heart, he aimed to land it as close to the lighthouse as possible. It was his best shot at survival. Lee picked his spot and nursed the plane closer and closer. The plane, however, was unwilling to carry him the last distance. His attempt to hold the plane in the air a bit longer resulted in the wings stalling and the plane dropped vertically before Lee leveled it out.

The plane bumped and jarred its occupant in its final descent. Lee cracked the door open before the wheels touched the water to make sure it wouldn't jam shut in the landing. In its last seconds of flight, the plane careened to a jerking halt on open water. Frantic, Lee exhaled as he patted his pocket confirming that his possession was still safely tucked in the fabric. Breathing deeply, he pushed himself out of the plane onto the wing, biding his time against the mere moments of flotation left in the Piper. An iceberg slid up against the plane just below the left wing. Throwing a worried glance over his shoulder, he realized the cockpit was filling with water and if he was going to survive, he needed to move now. Adrenaline pulsed through his veins as he lurched onto the ice. He balanced his body to keep the berg from tipping him into the water. Frozen, he watched the Piper Supercruiser tumble below the ice, the plane's impact caused tremors in the surrounding cakes. Cracks continued to spider across the snow covered ice, and Lee's stomach pivoted, bile rushing to his throat in horror. He needed to move. Quickly! Lee's flight instinct kicked in, albeit retarded with shock and cold, but his legs were moving now. The lighthouse he aimed for on his descent, towered in the distance. His only thought was to get there.

Balancing his weight carefully, he dodged thinner pieces and stepped in the center of tilting ice planes. Frigid water rushed over his soft leather boots. Shivers raced through his lean frame. His teeth clanked erratically. Finally, his foot reached a floe still large in size. The spaces between floes were lengthening, and Lee had no choice but to wait. The wind shifted to the northwest and the cake beneath his feet drifted toward the lighthouse.

Lee braced himself against the roll of the waves and allowed himself to feel grateful. It was just the sort of thing that he needed to have happen. He patted his chest pocket beneath his jacket once more feeling the weight he carried still secured there. Exhaling deeply, Lee focused his thoughts. He'd make it to the lighthouse. He'd strip his clothes and build a fire. The lighthouse would have some sort of food provisions. Land was only a few miles away. Someone would rescue him. Of course, *then there would be questions*. Lee quieted his worry and concentrated on survival. He'd worry about facing questions later.

The wind bit into his cheeks; his toes were completely numb. Waves of shock and exhaustion poured through him. He relaxed his legs a bit just as a wind gust bumped him into another sheet, making him slip. Gaining his feet, terror gripped him, as the ice splintered and cracked beneath him. Water edged its way to the surface, and Lee abandoned all caution and ran toward the lighthouse.

When the ice completely gave way he was separated from the steel rungs leading upward to safety by 40 feet. The water assaulted his body with thousands of needles piercing his skin and shooting pain up and down his spine. Training alone had him arching his arms and kicking his legs in a desperate attempt to reach safety. He *needed* to make it to the lighthouse; everything he wanted, everything he was, his *very life* depended on it. Desperate as cold engulfed him, sheer will caused Lee DeForge to grasp the icy steel railing and heave his shivering body out of the water.

Three

APRIL 11TH, 1959

Newspapers were filled with the story.

The Coast Guard had found a logbook in the DeTour Reef Lighthouse with a letter written by Capt. Lee DeForge. He detailed his crash landing, his failed attempts to signal for help, and his final decision to leave the lighthouse and head for land. Upon finding the logbook, the Coast Guard renewed their search efforts to no avail.

Eight had become one.

Four

"City and state, please," the operator intoned.

"DeTour, Michigan."

"For what listing?"

"The DeTour Reef Lighthouse." Richard DeForge spoke clearly.

"One moment, please." Soft keyboard tapping was audible through Richard's cell phone. "I'm sorry, Sir. I don't see a listing for that. You're trying to reach a lighthouse?"

"Yes. Search for just the word lighthouse."

The request was met by further clicking. "There are no listings, Sir. Is there anything else I can search for?"

"Uhm… try the DeTour Chamber of Commerce."

"Ah…" The operator clicked over to the automated system. He quickly hung up and dialed the number provided.

A chipper voice filled his ear after the first ring. "DeTour Village Chamber. How may I help you?"

Richard cleared his throat, grasping for a fictitious name. "Hi, my name is Jim Staley and I'm planning a vacation to the area. I'm wondering if you could help me."

"Sure. What would you like to know?"

"Well, my wife loves lighthouses and..."

"Oh, well, Detour's a great place to visit then. We have the DeTour Reef Lighthouse just off our coast."

"Really?" He controlled his voice to convey the appropriate amount of enthusiasm. "Are there tours?"

"Oh... well, no. The DeTour Reef Light Preservation Society is currently working on it. They're completely renovating the interior as we speak."

"Renovating? What exactly... like new paint?" He pressed.

"Oh, no. Everything is getting redone. The construction crew started over a week ago. It's going to be beautiful when it's finished and they'll definitely have tours when it's done, just not yet. Mr. Staley, why don't you give me your address? I'll send you a brochure on the lighthouse along with some other information about the area to help you plan your trip."

"Oh, well... let me talk to my wife, and I'll get back to you. She might want to wait until she can go on a tour. Thanks. B'bye." Richard clicked off his cell phone. "Shit!" His expletive filled the air as he continued to mutter to himself, thoughts whirring through his head as he dialed another set of numbers.

"Clover Real Estate," a familiar voice answered.

"Hey, Jean."

"Oh hi, Richard. How are you doing?"

"As well as can be expected, you know. What's going on there?"

"It's really hectic. Bill and Dale moved the big meeting up to next Friday. Frankly, they're a bit concerned that you haven't returned to the office yet."

He grimaced. "Next Friday? Why the rush?"

"They're giving us a two-year exclusive deal on a 120-unit condo complex. If we sell an agreed number of condos per year, we'll get a two-year extension. Two percent of every sale is yours if you sell them or not. You need this. Bill and Dale need this… Hell, I need this. Dale's worried you're going to screw it up."

"First of all, Jean, the deal is mine to screw up. They wouldn't even know about the damn deal if it wasn't for me."

"Yes, but you haven't closed it yet, have you? The longer you stay gone, the more nervous everyone becomes."

He said nothing, used to Jean's comments on his poor behavior. Richard frequently found great real estate deal prospects, and just as frequently didn't follow through on them. "Well, I'm afraid I'm going to be a little later than I planned."

Jean inhaled sharply. "Oh, God. They are not going to be happy. You just can't continue to do this to us."

Anger seeped through his voice. "Dammit, I can't help it. There's something I have to do and it's going to take a few more days. You can just tell them…"

"What? Tell them, what?"

With a deep breath, his tone softened substantially. "My father just died, Jean. Do you think I made that happen to take a couple days off?"

"You've been gone for two weeks. Where do you have to go that's so important?"

"Michigan," he bit out, instantly regretting it. "Listen, Jean. I gotta go."

"Just make damned sure you're back by Thursday. If you're not here, you might as well not come back."

"Don't worry, Jean. I'll be back. Tell Dale and Bill I'll be back no later than Wednesday night and will call. I won't let you down."

"You better not," Jean sounded doubtful.

"I won't," Richard reassured her, before clicking off the phone. His mind quickly turned to all the things he needed to do before leaving. The lighthouse being unexpectedly renovated increased the pressure dramatically. If he didn't go now, he'd probably lose his inheritance forever. It could be discovered at any moment, Richard thought. For all Richard knew, minutes might make the difference between recovering his inheritance or not. He checked his watch, 4:58 PM. He needed to finish packing; purchase an atlas and gas; and grab some sandwiches. Richard could be on the road within the hour.

Five

TODAY

LAST FRIDAY OF APRIL, CURRENT YEAR

7:30 AM, DRUMMOND ISLAND

From space, the Gem of the Huron appears to be a strangely shaped emerald hued with deep white pockets and surrounded by the most brilliant of sapphires. From the Drummond Islander IV, one of two car ferries that traverse the St. Mary's River continually, the island is somehow more magnificently appealing. The one-mile journey provides visitors and locals with a southern view of the DeTour Reef Lighthouse and a first meeting with the shallow calmness of Lake Superior's neighbor, Huron.

Rich green foliage provides the home for roaming bear, playful deer, and twelve hundred island residents that call this place *home*. The second largest freshwater island in the world, Drummond stretches approximately 20.5 miles in length, and is 13 miles wide. Over fifty percent state owned, winding trails lead to wild, natural beauty: it literally calls to the adventuring nature of tourists. Bordered on two sides by Canada, Drummond possesses over 140 miles of coastline and the Harbor Island National Wildlife Refuge off its northern coast.

It's isolated mystique draws as many as seven thousand visitors during any given summer weekend. Those who visit either fall in love with the lapping waves, laid back culture, and reminder of an earlier time or feel isolated from the fast-paced activity of city life. Those who love it, spend their entire lives trying to find a way to make Drummond Island a permanent feature of their lives. Those who live there, struggle to find a way to support themselves financially.

Inside a trailer leftover from the early 70's, just off of Johnswood road, an alarm clock sounded. Barely conscious, Joe's body curled tighter, attempting to block the intrusion. The wailing cry slid through his new defenses and aggravated his sleep. He concentrated on willing the noise away. The droning siren gained volume as its' persistent squeal smacked of sharp nails being scraped down a blackboard. Unable to block the sound, Joe's eyes ripped open, blinding him with the searing light of day. His eyes slammed shut, seeking reprieve. The noise triggered a blurry image. There was a reason for it, Joe thought groggily. Reality coursed through his system miserably: It was only the alarm clock. He shivered as the inhuman guttural groan of a wounded animal filled the air around him. If he kept his eyes shut, the beast would pass him by. Painless slumber evaded him, and with a scowl, Joe realized he was the beast.

One long pale arm darted out from under the pile of blankets, swatting at the bedside table. The vexing noise persisted, forcing his head up, his eyes open. The bright green digital numbers from the opposite end of the room teased him. Defeated, he started to raise his body but was slammed back to the pillow by needles shooting into his skull. The pain was a hangover the size of Harbor Island, something that would eat four extra strength Excedrin tablets as a snack and still evoke hell. It was the kind of pain that would keep a man in bed for half a day. Joe had earned it.

He decided to kill the clock and then kill the bastard who placed the infernal device on the far side of the room.

Stumbling out of bed, a string of curses filled the trailer as he tried to find a clean space of floor to stand on. Bare feet landed on a balled up sweatshirt that seemed relatively safe. Hammering at any sanity he possessed, the noise persisted, forcing him across the room. Behind him, a figure curled under the blankets and moaned softly, burrowing deeper under cover rather than emerging. Wide-eyed and dumbfounded, Joe observed the small movements closely. Completely covered, there was no way for Joe to discern who was in his bed. Shivering, Joe looked down, and gasped. He was naked as a jay bird. "Well, hot damn." He muttered in a quiet whisper.

Puzzlement replaced vengeance and, rather than beating the alarm clock senseless, he paused his left arm mid-swing, and shut the clock off with his right hand instead. Trying to flip the switch with his bad hand this early in the morning would only frustrate him. His arcing gaze moved from one wall to the other. The rapid movement caused him to stagger, birthing a new life and death quest to locate the Excedrin. Like manna from heaven, the Excedrin bottle was already right next to the clock. Vaguely, he guessed he probably thought of that last night.

After drinking a hefty quarter of his paycheck, he barely stumbled out of the Northwood and made it home after closing. He had no recollection of hitting on someone or bringing anyone back with him. Images of friends coming home with him filtered through his thoughts. Joe squinted through the dirt streaked glass, noticing his truck outside, but didn't see another car to give him any more clues. Joe frowned thoughtfully, Pete's words ringing in his head: he *needed* to make it to work on time.

Joe curled his toes into the brown and orange shag carpeting and swallowed several pills. Carefully sidestepping heaps of dirty clothing, crusty dishes, empty beer cans, and sports magazines, he stumbled into the living room. Half naked women posed, pouted, and preened from posters covering the drab wood paneled walls. Managing the pain, Joe couldn't help but give the ladies a little smile. Even though his body screamed in protest, Joe was proud of himself for getting up. It was a new day, another opportunity. He staggered through the living room. Couches were auspiciously vacant of the usual friends' sleeping bodies. After heavy drinking, friends often camped out rather than head home. Tripping over dirty plates and empty pizza boxes, Joe stumbled into the bathroom. He swiped the stiff crumpled towel from the bathroom floor, figuring it was clean enough and cranked the hot water full blast.

Impatient, he hopped in rather than wait for it to warm up. Shivering as the cold spray rolled off his body, he congratulated himself on waking. It may not have been the right move to go directly to the bar after Pete's lecture on his performance, but Joe felt like shit and needed some relief. He intended to stay a couple hours and duck out. A couple hours had turned into a long evening and an even bigger bar tab. It had also apparently turned into an overnight entertainment. Scalding water began to pour from the spicket, burning his back. Glancing over his shoulder, he noticed new scratches. With a burst of realization that made his head ache, and his stomach roll, he remembered who he had taken home. Shame colored his face, his hands moved the washcloth over his body with vigor. He had reached a new low. His mother thought he had hit the bottom of the barrel when she last visited his trailer, but it had taken Joe a few more months to really fall from good grace. There was no going back now. When his mother heard who he had been with, she was bound to blister his ears. And she would find out. There were no secrets on islands. Joe groaned. He was destined to be lifelong trailer trash. Refusing to dwell on it, Joe cheered himself up by counting the positive notes. He was awake, and he was going to make it to work on time, which meant he would keep his job. Fate hadn't been decided yet. There was still time to change things.

Smiling to himself, Joe cranked off the water and stepped out of the shower. He wiped off the steam covered mirror with the towel, and evaluated his appearance. His blond hair was a bit long for his taste, and he raked it back with his fingers. Blue eyes were clouded with his hang over, but they were clearing. His tan seemed to darken every day, what with working outside and spending so much time in the sun. Joe skipped the rest of the pep talk in the interest of getting on with his morning tasks, and dried himself off.

Marci, commonly referred to as the town mattress, was a difficult sort of character. She was kind and bubbly, a real sweetheart one moment, vengeful the next—and always seductive. Rumor carried grotesque stories about her that even made Joe blush. Joe shook the thought off and concentrated on the positive. Hopefully, he could get dressed and head off to work without having to talk to her. They had always gotten along well enough, but he had never been one of her conquests before. Joe was suddenly in the mood to clean house. Pete was right, there needed to be some serious changes. He'd make it to work on time today. He'd go to the bar tonight, but on Saturday he would go home early and gather his cans, clean his place.

Hurrying his step, he shuffled awkwardly back through the trailer, avoiding debris on the floor and bumped into the orange counter overhang that separated the kitchen from the living room. Marci's naked body stretched languorously on his bed, in full view, very much awake and bright eyed. She might be a skank, but she certainly was a looker, Joe thought, disgusted with himself but not disgusted enough to take his eyes off her body.

"Hey." Marci smiled and kicked her legs over the side of the bed. "Do you usually parade around naked, or are you just trying to excite me?" Marci purred, leaning back suggestively.

Joe laughed, in spite of himself. "Good time, Marz, but I have to go to work."

"You're not so bad yourself, Joe. We should do this again sometime." The bleached blond pulled on the small strappy thing she had worn to the bar the night before. Joe thought it was a shirt, but it really didn't cover much of anything. "Cook me breakfast?"

Joe guffawed and pulled his eyes away from her, finding some semi-clean clothes of his own. "How can you think of eating this morning after drinking so much last night? Not on a bet. Besides, I have to get to work."

"You're feeling it, eh?" Marci nodded, slipping on the mini skirt. "Well, I'm going to find something to eat before I go home."

Joe raised an eyebrow, speculating. "Sure, but I didn't see your car here. Don't you need a lift?"

"I'll walk," she said, agreeably.

Joe looked her half naked body over and shivered from the morning coolness. Spring had taunted summer weather early on but had cooled right off again in the last few days. "In that? You'll freeze."

"Actually, I'm planning on visiting a friend on the way home." She giggled. "I'm sure he can warm me up."

Joe tried not to cringe and finished dressing. "Sure. Well, I'm gonna pack my lunch and take off. Eat whatever you can find."

The mustard-colored refrigerator creaked open, displaying two Pepsis, salami and cheese, and two pieces of leftover lasagna his mom gave him. Tossing the hard salami and a block of sharp cheddar into his cooler, he grabbed the colas and crackers and headed for the door without bothering to say goodbye.

The temperamental truck roared to life with a rumble. Affectionately known as "the rust bucket" to friends, it actually seemed in fine order for a change. Joe smiled to himself, pleased that something else had gone right this morning. He peeled out of the driveway and turned the radio volume down.

Of course, the truck couldn't keep up its reputation as a piece of shit without actually breaking down on the way to work. The pick up's loud sputter and dying cough mirrored Joe's sentiments exactly. Pete would not tolerate another broken car excuse. He had made it abundantly clear: Joe would arrive at work precisely on time, or he needn't bother arriving at all. Now, he almost wished he had taken Marci up on her morning offer. Or at least he could have filled the cooler with beer, had he not drank it all the night before. He was going to have a hard time finding another job. Peering under the hood, Joe's thoughts ran wild. Contractors talked at the coffee shop, and he knew he already had a reputation of being late to work or of not showing up at all. Pete had run a risk hiring him in the first place, feeling bad for him since Joe's accident in high school. The highly skilled football quarterback had blown every chance he had to go to college while driving home intoxicated after a post-game party. With a dragging leg and lacking coordination in his left arm, what other contractor would give him a chance? Construction was, at times, in the detail work, he knew. Aggravated, he slammed the hood back down. "What the hell am I going to do now?!" Life just didn't cut any damned breaks for hometown heroes turned gimp.

Six

NEW YORK STATE, CURRENT DAY

In the countryside of New York, nestled between Batavia Air Force Base and East Pembrooke, stands a two story, white 1900's farmhouse. Urban sprawl crawled right up next to the large rolling yard but hadn't yet replaced the old country charm of the leaning white picket fence, oak tree in the front yard, and the remnants of flower gardens along the cracking pavement walkway.

The home was purchased in 1951 by Howard and Lenora Baker after Howard's retirement from the Philadelphia Mint earlier in the year. They purchased it as a way for them to be closer to their only child, Carol. Their daughter married a pilot, Lee DeForge, who was stationed in Batavia and announced that she was expecting their first grandchild. Lenora would remark in later years that it was the best decision of their life and was thrilled that they moved fully just before the baby's birth.

In 1959, when their grandson, Raymond, turned eight, separate tragedies left Raymond without either parent. Raymond moved to the white farmhouse to live with his grandparents. Eventually inheriting the house as Howard and Lenora's only descendent, Raymond spent his life there. When Ray married, his wife moved into the memory laden house with him, where they raised their two children until the divorce. Two months earlier, Raymond DeForge passed away. Community members rarely saw him outside the liquor store in the last years of his life.

Despite the sadness lingering from her father's death, Beth DeForge couldn't stop herself from smiling. The furry gray squirrel playing in the rain soaked road forced her to stop the car and wait. She rarely waited for anyone, but today she was in no real rush to face the latter part of the house cleaning project. A moment of sunshine in what was bound to be a dreary day, she mused, checking the tidiness of her clipped blond hair. The mammoth task of sorting through her father's personal effects weighed on her heavily. Guilt drained her of energy when she made the funeral arrangements. She had been asked what type of service her father would have preferred, and she realized she didn't have any idea.

Of course, her mother never wanted Beth and her brother, Richard, to spend time with their father after the divorce. She thought Raymond was a bad influence on the children. Beth suspected the reasons were a little more personal than that, but she didn't challenge her mother. At twenty three, Beth was disappointed in herself to know she hadn't even really tried to keep in touch with her father after she moved out and went on to college. Her mother's influence lessened with each year out of the house and yet Beth never brought herself to seek out her father. Of course she had been busy with nursing classes, working, and a social life—but these were excuses.

It was disconcerting to realize that she knew so little about someone who was half responsible for her own behaviors and characteristics. Her father's will entitled her and her brother to equal shares of everything he owned. The home they spent their early childhood in, even though it was barely recognizable now, was the biggest asset and the most daunting task. Her brother, who had been very little help during the funeral plans and showed no interest at all in the people who attended the service, transformed entirely with the reading of the will. Beth wanted to take a deep breath and allow the home to sit for a spell without making decisions. Richard demanded it be cleaned and put on the market immediately.

Cleaning out her father's house with Richard really hadn't been that bad of a deal. Her brother and she rarely spent so much time together since she went away to nursing school, and he always seemed to be busy selling one piece of property or another. Richard lived and breathed real estate or so it seemed, as he always used it as an excuse not to get together with her. Then again, if Beth wanted to be honest with herself, she'd admit there were just as many excuses from her side as there were from his. It wasn't really much of a bonding experience, but it was kind of nice to go through her father's belongings with someone rather than facing it alone.

Lisa, her closest friend from school, became an unexpected source of aid and joy. Lisa's lively spirit eased Beth's grieving and stopped her from resenting Richard's attitude. When Lisa realized the magnitude of the chore ahead of her friend, she insisted on accompanying the siblings and lending a hand. Richard, on the other hand said plainly that he wasn't going to spend time grieving a man that he really didn't know. Beth smartly chose not to get into any more "feeling" conversations with her older brother—they always turned into arguments. Richard thought their parents were jokes: Their father lost in a bottle and their mother consumed by bitterness. Beth viewed them as two people who just weren't right for each other. She figured they weren't all that different from hundreds of other couples that got together for the wrong reasons. Beth shook her head, reminding herself of the tasks at hand.

Keep for ourselves, give to goodwill, or throw in the dumpster had been the three main decisions they had had to agree about over the course of the week. Unfortunately, most of the household items belonged to the third category. Raymond DeForge hadn't done much to maintain, clean, or update the house in the many years since the divorce. Beth suspected the neglect had started some time before that. Her mother had often used his neglect of life as a main reason for why she left him. The only thing Ray spent time on was drinking, and his propensity for the task had been the ultimate cause of his early death.

Bringing her car to a stop, Beth forced herself to stop analyzing something that was done and over; that she couldn't change. Attempting to see the beauty of the spring day, she exited her car gracefully and tried to envision the happy family that had once lived here. Beth saw it for what it was: an old house bearing many secrets. It still needed a lot of work.

While Beth, Lisa and Richard had been working on the inside, they hired a couple of summer kids to scrape the paint off the house, which was almost complete. Rubble that once littered the yard had been cleaned up; freshly mowed grass showed promise. Beth's arrival this morning was a few thousand percent happier than her arrival the first morning. After all, they would finish up the indoor cleaning today or tomorrow. Waste Management would pick up the over-flowing dumpster, and they planned to load up and drop off the Good Will boxes today, so they'd be set. Her uneasiness about selling the house was gradually replaced with sound agreement with her brother's plan. The funds generated by the quick sale of Raymond's car paid for a good portion of the clean-up costs. A little extra investment in a paint job and a couple of simple repairs and the place would be, in Richard's estimation, quite sellable. Sliding her key into the lock, Beth postponed her actions when she heard the blaring radio of her friend's car pull up. She leaned against the door jamb and waited for Lisa to join her.

The Oldsmobile's door whooshed open, and Lisa squeezed her ample body through the opening. Red hair was gathered together in a haphazard ponytail that bobbed as she balanced a boom box and six pack of Coke on a thick, outrageously curved hip while slamming her car door. They

were a stunning contrast. Lisa was leviathan and dramatic. Beth
was average in height, coloring, and physique. Lisa was decked
in a wild flower pattern muumuu. Beth, on the other hand, was
dressed down from her typical standard, but the soft blue
lounging outfit was coordinated perfectly, her socks folded over
expertly, blond hair done in a tidy clip. Lisa looked messier at
this moment then Beth probably would at the end of the day.
Their dynamic differences had made them fast friends in
college and great friends still. "Good morning!" She called out.

Lisa smiled, waving. "Hey kiddo! Are you ready to hit
it again today?"

"Sure am." Beth quickly moved aside to let Lisa follow.

"I thought Richard was going to move these last night."
Tapping one of the boxes, she gazed up at Beth. "Speaking of
your brother, is he here?" Lisa craned her head glancing down
the hallway.

"Nope, he's not here yet. He wanted to move the boxes,
but I didn't let him. He looked really tired so I insisted he go
home and turn in early."

"Where do we start?"

Beth chewed on her lip, thoughtful. "Well—the sorting
is done everywhere except the kitchen. The windows still need
to be washed in the back bedrooms and the floors should be
vacuumed. We're going to have the carpets steamed but it'll be
better if we take the rug sweeper to them first."

"Perfect. Mindless chores for me in the morning! I'll
get right to it." Lisa enthused. Flipping on the boom box she
had toted with her, she cranked the volume to an acceptable
level and flitted to the back rooms.

Beth smiled, ignoring the small sparks that shot from
the base of her neck down her spine. The kitchen cabinets were
her priority today, and she wasn't going to waste time worrying
about her neck. Richard had reported his completion of the attic

quite cheerily yesterday afternoon so they were really quite close to being done. She turned on the gas stove and filled the blue speckled tea kettle with water from the faucet. Surveying her leftover tea selection, she was disappointed to realize she only had two bags left. She decided on black currant, wrinkling her nose at the orange spice.

She had been pleasantly surprised to find several items and likenesses that she didn't know she had in common with her father. Most surprises, however, were in the way of ancient, molded and corroded items, along with a long dead mouse caught in a trap never found. Ray had been a tea drinker as well as a booze drinker. He used the same sort of toothpaste and actually watered a few plants. The similarities ended almost exactly there. He wasn't a collector like Beth, unless she counted his vast collection of empty Jim Beam bottles and he certainly didn't enjoy variety. He had a gross supply of plain Lipton hot tea bags, but no flavors. Of course, Beth knew her genes from Raymond's side of the family were passed almost directly from her grandmother, Ray's mother. One of Beth's favorite possessions was a photograph of her grandparents, Carol and Lee. Beth looked just like Carol, down to the smallest detail in an uncanny sort of way. Her father had always told her that her mannerisms were just the same from what he remembered.

Bringing cleaning and sorting to mind, Beth poured the hot water for her tea and set to her tasks, smiling at Lisa's singing that was clearly audible above the radio. When Richard finally got to the house this morning, they would have already made great progress. Glancing at the clock, her lips turned downward. *Where was he?*

Seven

Kate Dombrowski's eyes shifted to the large grandfather clock in the dining room, as she turned down the heat on the eggs with her left hand and poured coffee with her right. It was exactly the right time to wake Pete. In 45 minutes she'd wake up the kids, who'd be anxious to mark another day off the calendar in their efforts to finish the last few weeks of school before summer break. Pregnant women, Kate thought smugly, were notorious for bad memories—but Kate's schedule hadn't been thrown yet. Everything was exactly on time, just like Pete liked it. She tightened the loosening sash of her yellow terry robe and marched up the stairs.

Pete stared at the ceiling, listening for the door to quietly open. Kate's smile eased his mind by degrees, but he couldn't bring himself to smile back.

"G'morning, Babe," Kate called. "I didn't realize you were awake. Why didn't you come down?"

Pete said nothing, but rolled toward her on his side, studying her mussed hair.

The stiff posture and the tight set of his mouth paused her normal morning dialogue, and she sat beside him. Worry lines creased his forehead, and his eyes drooped with exhaustion. "You didn't sleep much, did you? Are you worried about the job?"

Pete's sigh filled the room. His glance averted from her eyes down to her terry covered tummy, that he knew was just starting to show the signs of the baby. If she wasn't pregnant, he'd tell her. He'd just lay back and unfold all of his worries. Kate was a great listener. He rolled to the side of the bed and shook his head.

"Oh, no you don't." Kate grabbed his hand as he stood. "Don't even think that you're not going to talk to me just because I'm pregnant. Don't insult me."

"Kate…" Pete's voice trailed off. "I don't want you to worry. It's just a job. The doctor said…"

"That's it, isn't it? You're worried about me being pregnant again. Pete, the miscarriage was over a year ago. I'm going to be just fine. We'll have another great, healthy kid that will…"

Pete resented her blasé attitude and interrupted, finishing her sentence. "That will cost a fortune in diapers, and food, and every other damned thing!"

Kate's expression softened considerably. "Remember when we were pregnant with McKenzie? We worried so much. You were laid off, I was waitressing, and we were barely making ends meet for us, let alone a baby. Now we have McKenzie and Kyle, and we always seem to make it work. It'll be just fine. We might have a tough time, but we'll get through it. Look at how much more we have, at how much better we're doing now then we were then. We have this beautiful home that you built for us and the business…"

"Kate, when you have more—you have more to lose. I never should have taken this job. This damned lighthouse project will take up my whole summer, and I'm not sure I bid enough. The crew…" He rolled his eyes and sighed again. "Gary shows up everyday but his top speed is second gear. Bob's there but I'm sure he's the first to slack off when I have an errand to run. Billy's such a damned kid and has such a temper. He works four out of five days and then thinks he's doing me a favor by showing up that much. Joe shows some promise but he's drinking his paychecks. He comes to work hung over, late and sometimes not at all. I hold up the boat to wait for him and Billy, and the whole crew slows down. It's just... a never-ending battle." Pete dropped his arms to his side in defeat. "Yesterday, I was so pissed off that I lectured Joe and Billy for the better part of an hour on getting their lives together. If one of them is late today, I'll have no choice but to fire him—and I really don't want to do that. But I'll have to. I have to start making an example of someone."

"Joe will have listened, honey. He'll make it to work on time. He respects your opinion, and he'll do better. He's a good kid, Pete." Seeing that her words had little effect, Kate stood next to him and wrapped her arms around him. "Honey, it's going to be okay. I know it."

Pete couldn't help but frown. Her faith in him was overwhelming and scary: he couldn't allow her to believe that everything was just fine and dandy. "You know, it's easy to say things are going to be okay. You're not the one out there needing to yell at slackers and keep the men going. You're not the one who has to figure ways to cut cost and deal with assholes."

"I am in too good of a mood to have this argument with you this morning," Kate retorted. "I am just trying to help. There's no need to be rude, hon."

"Sometimes the truth is rude whether you like it or not. It's not easy. The travel time back and forth to the lighthouse is a killer. We're always needing materials and if I send one of the crew, they'll take three times as long as I would and bring the wrong stuff back. If I go, the crew stops working or slows down until they see the boat pull up. It's ridiculous. It won't just magically be okay. Sometimes I think you just expect that I'll wave a wand and magically provide us with what we need. It doesn't happen that way!"

Kate's eyes lowered, her face coloring slightly as she

pulled away from him.

"You have demands. This family has demands. It's hard to provide them when I'm dealing with shit," Pete raged, rummaging through his closet for work clothes.

Kate opened her mouth to deny any new demands but Pete cut her off. "Wallpaper for the nursery, new carpeting in the living room, a new car... and don't forget about the baby! Don't you think that adds pressure to my life?"

Kate looked away, shaking her head. "Go eat your breakfast. It's getting cold."

Pete grabbed her arm before she walked away. His voice softened but still resonated firmly. "Kate, you wanted to know why I have trouble sleeping. If you didn't want to know, you shouldn't have asked."

Kate took his hand away from her arm. "If you're so concerned about money, why don't you let me get a job? I'd be happy to go back to work."

"No." His tone was final.

Kate pulled away from him, tired of fighting. "Eat your breakfast. You won't like it cold and if you don't eat, you'll become more of a grouch for the crew—and unbearable by the time you get home tonight. I made egg salad sandwiches for your lunch. Your box is in the fridge," Kate paused before entering their bathroom. Pete thought she looked like she wanted to say something, but she continued on. Resigned to the day, he trucked downstairs in search of food.

Eight

Joe slapped the palm of his hand against the steering wheel. Attempts to revive the rust bucket were futile. The clock was ticking, and a car had yet to pass. He hopped out of the truck, beginning to despair. "I'm always gonna be trailer trash," he bemoaned to himself. His mother was going to be so upset with him. He hoisted himself on top of the hood and stared mindlessly into the forest, almost missing the blue Tracker driving by. He waved his arms frantically and to Joe's jubilation, the Tracker's brake lights lit up and the SUV careened in reverse.

Joe grabbed his cooler from the front seat and approached the woman in the driver's side. The brunette rolled down her window expectantly.

"Hey there... I know you don't know me, but I have a huge favor to ask. My truck just choked and I'll be fired if I don't make it to work on time. Is there anyway you can give me a lift?"

"Well... I was actually on my way to..."

"Please. I'll do anything to make it up to you, but I have less than 10 minutes and I need to keep this job." Joe paused, and smiled in attempt to be charming. "Please. I promise I don't bite."

Brushing a fallen strand of hair behind her ear, she

consented. "Okay. Hop in."

Joe rushed around the front of the truck and waited for
the woman to move a camera bag and box of film off the seat
before swinging in. "I have to meet a boat at Ft. Drummond
Marina."

The brunette looked at him somewhat blankly. "Is that
the one down in Whitney Bay?"

Joe arched an eyebrow. "Yeah. You're new here then?"

She shrugged. "I guess you could say that."

Joe's eyes squinted speculatively at the strange answer.

She laughed under the scrutiny. "I'm not trying to be
vague. I haven't been here since I was a little girl, that's all.
And since I moved my stuff here, I've been busy so I haven't
driven around much."

"Welcome to Drummond."

She rewarded him with a full smile.

"Am I keeping you from something important this
morning?" Joe asked.

"I was on my way to the hardware store. There are
some things I need that they didn't have when I was in the
other day. The manager told me the truck comes in on Tuesday
and if I wanted something they didn't have by next week, I
better get the order in this morning." She smiled. "I'm sure the
fifteen minutes or so won't hurt."

"You sound like you think that's funny." Joe laughed at
her humor filled tone, then pointed at Whitney Bay Road so she
wouldn't miss it.

Nodding, she signaled her turn indicator and moved
across the road, over the bridge. "I guess I'm not used to being
in a small town yet or island for that matter." She shrugged.
"Do you work on a boat?"

"Nah. I work for Dombrowski Construction. I have to

meet a boat to get to the job we're working on. We're doing the lighthouse renovation," Joe replied.

"Oh. I didn't realize it was being worked on." She paused, glancing at him. "Do you like construction?" She asked as she rounded the final curve before the marina.

Joe frowned, hesitating.

"Did I ask the wrong thing?"

"I guess I've never thought about it before." He shrugged. "It pays the bills, so yeah, I guess I like it. Listen, I really appreciate your help. My boss doesn't like excuses."

"No problem," she responded, slowing the truck to a stop. Surprise arched her eyebrows. "Is that new?" She pointed to the store with large windows facing the docks.

"Yeah. They built it a few summers ago. There are groceries and snacks, a few gifts, and marine stuff."

"Hey, I really appreciate you helping me like this. I owe you."

"Don't worry about it."

Grinning, Joe hopped out of the Tracker and grabbed his cooler, with a final wave tossed back over his shoulder. "Have a good time at the hardware," he called. "Spotting Pete near the boat, he quickly turned his mind to the job, careful to start the day off on the right foot. The last thing he wanted was to get to work on time and then get fired because he wasn't focused on the task at hand. He walked quickly but carefully, not wanting to draw attention to his dragging leg, just in case the woman glanced his way.

"Hot damn, studly!" Bob called out, swinging his tool belt off his shoulder. The girl pulled her vehicle up to the store and walked in, unaware of her new admirers. Bob whistled shrilly just after she stepped in, beyond hearing range. "Now, if I am thinking proper this mornin', I know I saw you leavin' the bar with that fine ass, Marci, last night. Unless my eyes are lying, I can almost swear that wasn't Marci giving you a ride to work. Looks like Joe got some serious play. Everyone knows how good Marci is… and I bet you got more than just a ride to work from that sweetheart." Bob said, grandly gesturing toward the store.

Pete grinned. "And he still got to work on time! How do you do it? One last night, and one this morning!"

"Or maybe boss, it was two last night," Bob countered, placing his hand over his heart. "Damn, and Marci's ass is enough to put me in shock. She walks into a room and I just need to sink my teeth right into her and hang on for the ride. Congrats on that score, Kid."

Pete rejoined the razz session, waved to Gary, who walked down from his car. "And what about that little Willis girl that works at the store? She has her eye on you too. She's no Marci, but she's cute. And hell… who can tell in the dark anyway?"

Bob threw his head back and shouted with laughter, causing Pete to chuckle quietly.

Heckling, Bob elbowed Joe a bit. "What do you eat? Viagra or something to keep up with all that?"

"Shit, Bob. Joe's only 21? 22? When you were that young you could have kept up with them too." Pete rebuked. "Thank God, I'm married. If Joe is getting all those women, just think of how many I'd be taking home with me."

Bob and Gary looked at each other smirking, before roaring with laughter, while Joe blushed. "Think what you want, guys." Frowning, Joe realized he didn't know the brunette's name and kicked himself mentally.

Changing tone, Pete commented, "Its 8:28. Billy has 2 minutes to get here, or we're leaving him. And if we leave him, he loses his job—which means" Pete swatted Joe's arm with a glove, "that you'll get promoted."

Joe did a double take, making sure Pete was serious. How about that, he thought cheerfully: from certain unemployment to a promotion.

"Well, if I were a bettin' man, I'd say Joe's in for a promotion then. Billy left the bar in terrible shape last night. He got into it with some asshole I didn't know, and got punched in the gut, and I bet he's sportin' a black eye too. I saw Sheriff Cole at the bakery this morning and he filled me in. He got called out, so it must have been serious."

Pete grunted. "It's no excuse. Billy knew the next person late to work would get fired. He should have gotten his ass to work."

"Maybe he was hoping Joe wasn't going to make it either." Bob remarked.

"To be honest, it was a close call. If that honey hadn't stopped and picked me up, I would be grass. The rust bucket died on my way here." Joe hopped onto the boat and settled down for the ride.

"I think I'm going to make your promotion contingent on a few changes, Joe." Pete checked his watch. "8:32." He stepped on board the boat himself, followed by Bob and Gary and nodded for Bob to start it up. "Billy just lost his job."

Joe frowned. Billy was, however pathetically, in worse shape than he was. He felt bad for Billy, but thrilled for himself for slopping into a raise.

"Your two dollar an hour raise is dependent on two things. First, you gotta buy a better car—and I mean ASAP." Pete paused, sure to let that sink in. Joe nodded. "Second, since you're taking Billy's job, you have to find a replacement for you."

Joe leaned back, thoughtful.

"That's how I do it. You better make a strong effort to save money for a car right away and no raise until you find a replacement. Got it?"

"Got it." Joe yelled over the engine, his grin spreading from ear to ear.

Nine

The blue speckled tea kettle screeched, bringing Beth's head out of the kitchen cabinet with a start. She slowly gained her feet and stepped around the butcher block to get to the obnoxious kettle. She was on her second pot for the day and she needed it. Years of grime and dust rested inside the cabinets, and she was determined to have them sparkle before she was done. The kettle's whistle signified time for a break. Pouring hot water into a cup she had prepared, she noticed a slight tingling sensation again. She worriedly scratched at the back of her neck, wondering about what could be wrong. The last tingling sensation occurred a few months before, which would have been about the time her father realized he was dying. She was worried, and her naturally intuitive nature couldn't allow her to ignore that Richard had still not returned.

"Did I hear a whistle?" Lisa called.

"Yep. Break time." Beth dipped the bag up and down in the small porcelain pot.

Lisa pulled a bottle of Coke from the refrigerator. "Still no Richard, hey?" Absently, she gazed out the window, as if expecting him to appear.

Beth shoved aside a stack of cleaning rags and sat at the dining table. "It's really strange. He's been so helpful this week."

Lisa scowled. "Yeah, but it's just like him to do something unexpected. Look at how he behaved during the funeral." She shook her head. "The man should be stretched on a wrack for the way he treats you, the way he behaves."

"Oh, Lisa. Stop being so dramatic." Beth laughed.

"Did he say anything yesterday about not coming in today?"

Beth ran through the events in her mind once again. "No. He seemed edgy, almost preoccupied." She shrugged. "I just kept thinking he was tired. He really wanted to get those boxes out of the house, but I was exhausted and I would feel terrible about making him do it by himself."

"He'll turn up then." Lisa scrutinized Beth carefully for a moment. Beth had been rubbing her neck for minutes. "You're having those feelings again, aren't you?"

Pulled out of her thoughts, Beth realized Lisa was talking to her. "What?"

Lisa sat down beside her. "Your neck. It's tingling, isn't it?" Lisa was well aware of Beth's sensitivity. Becoming friends with Beth had inspired Lisa to read all about the paranormal. Beth usually denied or ignored the feeling, but over the years she had told Lisa all about it.

Resigned, Beth nodded. "It's been acting up since yesterday afternoon. Little sparks here and there. It's getting worse though."

"Do you hear any voices?"

Beth rolled her eyes. "Really, Lisa. Don't be absurd." Beth shrugged again. "You know what I really need?"

Lisa laughed. "I know that look. You want pizza."

"You could go get us one." Beth gave her a pouty face. "Pretty please with sugar on top?"

Nodding, Lisa assented. "I need more Coke anyway." Standing, she grabbed her cell phone from the counter and headed for the door. "The usual?"

"You got it." Beth pushed her impatience behind an enthusiastic smile, while trying to mentally hurry her out of the house. She had ignored Lisa's inquisition about voices, but Beth was definitely feeling that she was being led.

She waited, drumming her fingers on the table top until Lisa was finally inside her car. Slowly, stretching her limbs and quieting her mind, she stilled until she became acutely aware of the direction coursing through her body. Led back to the stairs reaching up from the hallway, she felt the undeniable tug to go up the stairs. As a child, she had hated the attic. It was always dark and hot, and her brother was always finding some new prank or scare tactic to try out on her. In her childhood nightmares, the attic was a home for demons and spirits. The few times Beth had overcome the fear and climbed the stairs, she had experienced any number of unusual feelings. Her awareness of spirits and heightened version of a sixth sense were breathed to life by some bizarre force that Beth identified as coming from the attic.

By the time she reached college, it had become something of a joke. Every test that wasn't completed to her expectations was blamed on the attic. She was surprised to find the same torrential emotion bubbling close to the skin when she returned with her brother and Lisa. She had visited her father after the divorce, of course, but she had never quite felt its presence as strongly as she did now. Therefore, Richard had been assigned the task of cleaning the attic. Slowly, she focused on remaining calm and ascended the stairs.

The attic was an oven, but a clean one. Cleared out and cleaned from top to bottom, nothing remained on the floor. There were no artifacts for her to examine, and Beth felt like a fool. Feeling dismayed at the effort and incensed to believe an old spirit was luring her to something important, she twisted sharply in her hurry to rush down the stairs as quickly as possible. Several steps through her descent, Beth was enveloped in a circle of air that gushed around her, halting her movement. Her body jolted and quivered as she was overcome by the sense of severe cold. Overwhelmed, Beth's vision faded as her body crumbled softly to the floor.

Ten

Standing sentry at the mouth of the St. Mary's River, the most widely traversed waterway in the world, is the DeTour Reef Lighthouse. It is located south of the DeTour Passage, between the eastern end of the Upper Peninsula of Michigan and Drummond Island. Since its opening, the lighthouse has served as a traffic regulator and guardian of vessels traveling through the area.

The 60 foot square, 20 foot high concrete, steel encased pier stretches from an estimated 24 feet of water, and provides a solid base for the 63 foot Art-Deco-style lighthouse. With the focal plane at 74 feet, the lighthouse can be seen from a distance of 17 miles. Comprised of three distinct white walled levels and a red roof, it contrasts sharply with the Huron's clear blue water and land mass background for easy visibility. Built in 1931, the original project took 327 working days and a cost of $140,000. The lighthouse's function has changed over the years, a result of Coast Guard budget cuts, maintenance problems, and technological advance. Today, the lighthouse is leased by the DeTour Reef Light Preservation Society whose primary goal includes returning the lighthouse to its original splendor.

The employees of Dombrowski Construction focused on the second and final phase of restoration: the interior. At the waters' edge, seventeen vertical rungs embedded in concrete at the center of each wall form a ladder and provide four distinct options for the crew to dock their boat near. Cranes, conveniently located in opposite corners (Northwest and Southeast), are attached to booms and can be pivoted to load and unload materials from a barge below.

Since the crew didn't need to load or unload materials this morning, they had taken direction from Pete and moved to complete their assigned tasks. Bobby and Joe were focused on the second level up from the concrete deck or the keeper's quarters. They worked side by side in the small bathroom, with Bob working on the bathtub and Joe working on the sink: everything needed to be removed so the plumbing fixtures could be replaced.

Cast iron sink pipes, Joe discovered, were heavy. Joe set them in the waste pile, severely annoyed by the sharp pains that traveled down his left side. Returning to the bathroom, he swept out the floor area, finally finished with the destruction phase. All of the tear-down elements had to be finished today, come hell or high water—and if they weren't, Pete had said he just might consider firing the lot of them. The bathroom materials would arrive Monday morning. Joe didn't need any more motivation to move quicker, although he was sure he wasn't part of the problem. Thoughtfully, he paused, clenching and unclenching his hand. It was definitely getting stronger, he mused. Pete had been right about construction helping him regain strength, although it was costing his body in the short term. By the end of the day he was going to *need* to stop and get a beer.

"Joe! You about finished? It's lunch time!"

Joe gathered the last remnants with the industrial sized dust pan and yelled back in response. "I'm comin!" Tossing the debris in the bin, he wiped the sweat off his brow. "Warm, isn't it?"

"Well, my goodness, our boy is working hard after all!"

Bob shouted with laughter. "Much more difficult than that running around on the field, isn't it?"

Joe forced a smile and retrieved his cooler. "Been a long time since I played ball."

"Ah, shit. For me it'd have been like yesterday. You graduated before the accident, didn't you?" Bob fetched his sandwich out of the cooler.

"No. Fall of senior year is when it happened. I haven't played since." Joe shrugged off the memory, attempting to focus on something more positive.

"Damn shame," Bob muttered.

"Well, now, it's all what you do with it." Pete offered. "Take Billy, for example. He's strong and capable, but lazy. He's a better than average carpenter. Hell, he comes by it naturally enough. He just doesn't give a shit. It's just easier for him to sleep in. He could do really well for himself if he'd learn how to reign in the temper and make it to work."

"And if he got out of the bar a little earlier," Gary muttered.

Pete narrowed his eyes at Joe. "I'd pay attention to what's happened to Billy, Joe. He may bounce back from losing this job just fine, but Drummond's only so big. Eventually there aren't going to be any more doors that open for him with jobs. He's building a bad reputation."

Joe nodded, realizing the truth to Pete's statement. "Yeah, I know what you mean. Honestly, it's fun to hang at the bar—but it's starting to wear on me. My friends come home from college, and all they want to do is party. It gets old after a while. I am going to try shaping up some. I'd like to clean up my trailer. And I'm gonna buy a new car!" Joe raised his voice and nodded to Pete, emphasizing the last. "It's time I took on some responsibility for my life." Joe wasn't bothered by the laughter that statement caused. He held up his hands in mock defense. "I know, I know. I sound like my mother."

"Well, parents often know the right way." Pete commented, supportively.

Bob guffawed. "Shit, boss. You're just trying to make yourself believe you're still smarter than your kids."

Pete chuckled at that one and opened his pail. As usual, Pete's lunchbox was filled with good looking offerings from Kate's kitchen. She always gave Pete sandwiches on homemade bread, a thermos of soup, and a piece of pie. Kate even sent cookies for the crew sometimes. Pete threw his head back and laughed at Joe's pitiful expression as Joe dug out the salami and cheese from his own cooler. "Hey, maybe if you clean up your life, you'll find a good woman like my Kate, and you'll get better lunches."

Joe was torn between laughter and tears. "There are no other women like Kate. Kate's perfect. She's a great mom and a great cook. You got the last one, Pete."

Pete smiled, thankful for his partner. Maybe she had been right this morning. He hadn't had to fire Joe, and the progress was moving along steadily for a change.

Finishing up with lunch, Pete reminded the guys about which tasks were important to get done. Joe began with the second sink.

Eleven

Beth awoke with a start, her face dripping water. Lisa hovered over her, giving her cheek small slaps, an empty cup in her hand. "What the hell, Lisa?"

"I couldn't get you to wake up…"

Beth clipped the tirade teetering on her tongue when she looked into Lisa's face. A mixture of panic and concern laced through Lisa's eyes, her face contorted with worry. Struggling to sit up, her back muscles whined considerably from the stair it connected with. "A cup of water in the face was really the way to go." Beth muttered, using her shirt sleeve.

"What happened? Did you fall down the stairs? Have you taken to fainting now? When I left, you were fine. Why are you on the stairs?"

Beth shook her head, confused beyond thought. "I don't know."

Lisa noticed Beth's eyes shift down and quirked an eyebrow, hands on hips. "Try another tune."

Beth rolled her eyes. "Okay. I was feeling the tingling sensation, so I ventured up the stairs."

"It must have been strong." Lisa murmured, encouraging her to continue by squeezing next to her on the step.

Beth nodded and scooted over, making room. "I've been feeling it all day. It just keeps getting stronger and stronger. I went up the stairs, but there isn't anything up there, so I came back down. Well, I started to," Beth qualified. She wiped absently at her eyes. "It was incredible. I was here or maybe a step higher." Her eyes danced, reliving the experience. "I froze up."

"What do you mean? Were you scared?"

"No, no. I mean, I *was scared*—but this was physical. I just couldn't move. There was this air that circled around me. I felt like my body was being squeezed like a sponge. I must have fainted." Shaking her head, Beth leaned her head onto Lisa's shoulder.

"Do you think it was your dad?"

Beth contemplated for a moment, finally shaking her head. She had always felt that her grandmother was with her, but she couldn't be sure. "No. I don't know what it was."

"Whoever or whatever it is, you have to go back upstairs. Something's there. It has to be."

Slowly, Beth nodded. "Yes, I suppose you're right."

"Of course I am. Who says this force would let you go down again anyway? We should just go and get it over with."

Beth winced. "You have that look in your eyes."

With a blasé expression, Lisa mocked innocence. "Whatever do you mean?"

Beth smiled. "Okay, let's do this."

Intrigued, Lisa nodded, ignoring the uneasiness that was written on Beth's face. "We'll do it together," Lisa offered, standing tall. She helped Beth up and gave her a little nudge. "Come on, Beth. No time like the present."

The tingling sensation increased dramatically; her neck felt as if it was waking up from a long sleep. Experimentally, she stopped and stepped one foot up on the staircase toward the attic. The sensation lessened. She stepped upward again, and the sensation lessened further.

Trusting her body, she turned around and finished the three steps to the top. Moving her eyes from corner to corner of the room, she took in everything. The room was approximately twelve feet in width, running the full length of the house. The eight ten pitch allowed about six feet of safe walking area before she'd have to worry about bumping her head. Cheap wood panels covered the slanted walls, the floor showed early memories of her brother's rough-housing, and probably their father's before him. A two-foot square slide window was positioned mid-level on the side opposite the stairs. It allowed barely enough light to illuminate that side of the room, casting the stairs in shadows. Beth couldn't fathom why she should be standing there, but the tingling was beginning to feel more like an ache.

Lisa threw her hands into the air, breathing loudly. "Well, I don't see anything. Do you feel anything?"

"Mmm-hmm." Beth chewed on her lower lip.

"What are you feeling?"

"Lisa, shush. I'm trying to concentrate." Moving toward the window, she stepped out away from the wall and gazed out at the lawn. Surprisingly, her brother must have cleaned the glass, she thought with an automatic smile. It looked better than many of the windows she had seen downstairs. It may be that she was supposed to see something only visible from this angle, she considered.

Slightly irritated that the view from the window offered no revelations in the clear view of the freshly mowed lawn and dumpster, she fanned her face with her hand and turned around. Leaning her head lightly against the cool window, her eyes roamed over the attic space, dissecting it as if it were a puzzle.

Inhaling deeply, Beth wiped away the sweat forming on

her forehead with her shirt sleeve and calmed herself. She studied the floor, the knee walls, the ceiling. Running her fingers through her hair, she decided she was never going to find whatever she was looking for and moved toward the stairs, haphazardly turning in the corner to march down. Lisa's called warning was seconds too late. The thud was heard before felt, pain throbbing dully through Beth's brain. "Shit!" She exclaimed, sharing her frustration with the attic. She lowered her body to the top step and dropped her head into her hands, rubbing the bruised spot.

"Damn. Sorry, Beth. I thought you were going to hit it just as you did." Lisa apologized.

Beth gazed off, absently dealing with the pain. "I'm losing my mind." The harsh whisper echoed lightly against the wall.

The room divided into patches of murky light and almost complete darkness. The lighting fixture above didn't work and the window was small. There was a two-foot section of space cast almost completely in shadow that ran adjacent to the stairs, only easily visible from the top of the staircase. Before, when standing there, Beth had concentrated on the steps rather than on looking at the wall. Sitting on the stoop, her eyes drifting without real focus, her eyes rested on that spot.

"Oh my goodness!" She exclaimed, standing in a hurry. "Look!"

Lisa's eyes followed the direction of Beth's but she saw nothing. "What?" Barely visible, a small section of paneling was slightly disjointed from the wall.

Careful of the low ceiling near the knee wall, Beth crouched to examine the paneling. Upon further inspection, it was obvious that this particular piece concealed a cubbyhole type of storage area. Carefully, Beth pulled the slightly stiff door out away from the wall and was immediately rewarded with a diminishing headache.

Beckoning her was a dark green wooden chest. The locking mechanism didn't seem to work, or regardless lay open. Overwhelmed with curiosity, Beth gingerly lifted the top back, smiling at the squeaking hinges. Scrawled in black ink were the words *Carol DeForge Effects* on a manila envelope. "Bingo." Beth murmured. "It's Grandma's."

"Do you think we should take it downstairs?"

Relief poured into Beth's face. "Yes. Absolutely."

Twelve

"This is disgusting." Joe grumbled from his position on the exact opposite side of the wall that contained the plumbing for the bathroom. In the lighthouse, to conserve plumbing fixtures, the kitchen and bathroom were constructed along the same wall with the sinks back to back.

Bob raised an eyebrow, as he worked to remove the cupboard doors from the units to be sanded down. "Are those pipes covered with that orange shit, too?"

"Yes. It's gross. I'm already covered in this sludge from the bathroom sink. This is just nasty." Joe muttered to himself, cranking the pipe wrench.

"Quit your bitchin' Barber, you sound like an old woman," Bob teased, glancing over his shoulder. "You're gonna have to use the saw on that one too, I'll bet."

Sure enough, the corroded cast iron came apart under the pressure of the reciprocating saws-all. "Hell." Frustrated, Joe scooted closer to the pipe. With deliberate movements, Joe angled the tool against the pipe. He'd be damned if he had to ask for help. Completing the cut, he leaned his body awkwardly under the sink and examined the pipes. "There's something in here."

"In the drain pipe?"

"Yeah." Joe reached his hand inside the pipe but couldn't reach the object.

"Well, what is it?"

"I don't know."

"It's probably silverware. In the old days, silverware was lost down the drain all the time."

Joe tried thumping the side of the pipe, attempting to shake it out.

"That's not working," Bob chided, intrigued. "Cut the pipe."

"One sec." The pipe curved in a laying down S, with the object blocked by the bottom of the first curve. Joe raised the saw and cut smoothly through the pipe. Following the slice, he moved the saw to the other side of the curve, intent on removing the entire segment. When he finished, he shook out the stubborn object, surprised to see three grime covered cylinders slide out.

"What the hell?"

Joe wiped one against his pants, leaving a nasty streak. "Old paper? Oh, no shit."

"What is it?"

Carefully, Joe unfolded the crumpled edge and peeked inside the tube. "Pennies," he said, shaking one out.

"Pennies?"

"Wheat pennies." Joe shrugged, examining the back of one. "Old ones."

"I think those are worth a few cents a piece. That'll add to your new car jug, Joe."

"Why couldn't they have been dollars?" Joe grumbled. "Why the hell would anyone put pennies in a drain pipe?"

"Must have been some construction man's idea of a joke."

"I'll split 'em with you." Joe offered.

"75 cents? Call it your lucky day. A raise and a free soda and candy bar."

Joe snickered. "Where the hell have you been? It costs more than that to buy a soda and snack."

"I know." Bob shook his head sadly. "I remember when candy bars were a quarter. The good old days."

"Old timer," Joe murmured, earning a swat from Bob's outstretched arm. Chuckling, he turned back to finish removing the piping.

"I've got this wallboard ready to go to the trash. When you quit foolin' with that pipe, lets haul this shit down to the barge."

Joe nodded. "Ready." Joe heaved the basin into his arms and followed Bob down the stairs and through the screen doors out onto the deck. They fastened the material to the palette attached to the winch, and Bob slowly lowered the mechanism while Joe climbed down the side of the lighthouse to grab and unhook the lowering palette from the barge. When they had finished the task, Bob stared out into the water while Joe climbed back up.

"Shit, I'm glad we don't have to work out here forever. Can you imagine being a keeper and hauling ass up and down everyday?"

Bob chuckled. "The keeper? It was manned by a couple of guys in the Coast Guard."

Joe conceded. "Yeah, but I still wouldn't want to be out here with one or two other guys for weeks on end. No women…" He shuddered, craning his head back to look up at the ten-sided glass walled lantern room. "It's really something but I wouldn't want to live here."

"It has really come a long way. It looks so different than it used to, doesn't it?" Bob returned.

"Yeah, the windows are actually uncovered now. It's neat."

"These skylights in the floor here, are amazing." Bob led Joe over to the 3 by 4 foot glass block window in the floor. "They had them covered up for years because it was easier and cheaper to cover them than fix them when they started leaking."

"Not to be stupid, but it's basically just to let light in to the basement, right?"

"Yep." Bob nodded, took a good look at Joe and chuckled.

"What?" Joe asked, then looked down at himself. "Damn. I look like I fell into a sewer."

"You sure do," Bob agreed.

Pete swung out around the door, face slightly reddened. "What the hell are you guys doing out here? You should be finishing up on the bathroom, not taking in the sights! I expect some work to get done. Do you have any idea how far behind we are?! I want to have all the demolition done by Monday, so we're ready to clean up."

Bob held up his hand in protest. "Boss, we got the bathroom done."

"Then you should be starting on the kitchen!"

"That's done too."

Pete stopped, evaluating Bob's face. "Well then, you should be hauling out the trash. We have to get this whole place cleaned up..." Pete grinned, when Bob held up his hand again.

"That's what we're doing, Pete. We got all the bathroom stuff and kitchen stuff down onto the barge. We also moved that pile you and Gary made earlier. It's all ready to go."

Pete paused, startled. "You have it *all* ready to go? How is that possible?"

Bob tipped his head back and laughed, enjoying one-upping Pete. "It's Joe, over here. Ever since you gave him that raise, he's been asses and elbows. I'm really getting tired of it. I think you should make Gary work with him."

Chuckling, Pete nodded. "Good job, guys." Pete scratched his head, wondering what to have them do for the remaining two hours. He wasn't anticipating having all this work done already and he wouldn't have materials for a new project until Monday. "I tell you what. Sweep up those areas real good and give me ten minutes. I'll run you guys back to Drummond. I'll leave the barge and bring the boat back, 'cause Gary and I still have a couple hours left. But you guys get it all unloaded into the dumpsters and you can go home."

Joe's eyes widened. "You're letting us go early?"

Bob's mouth dropped open. "It is our lucky day!"

"I want a nice job with the unloading though. Don't leave anything behind."

Bob saluted, mocking. "I'm sure we can handle it."

Pete's face sharpened. "Just because you did a good job today, doesn't mean you're out of the woods, Joe. And you too, Bob. We're behind because the whole damn crew has a hard time making it to work. You need to get your asses out of the bar. You're wasting your lives."

"Yes, Dad." Bob affected a whiny voice. "But it's really all Joe's fault. I normally only spend Friday and Saturday night in the bar."

"Weren't you in the bar like four nights this week, Bobbo?"

Bob squirmed. "Normally, just two."

"It's still two nights too many, Bobby." Pete rubbed his palms together, thrilled when he found a good button to use. "How are you ever going to find a good woman, much less hold onto her when you spend all your time at the bar? Kate never hung out at the bar."

"He's got you there, Bob," Joe piped in. Bob rolled his eyes but grinned despite himself. Everyone had a half crush on the boss's wife for her cooking ability plus other attributes. Bob thought she was a genius in the kitchen and didn't mind ribbing Pete about keeping on his toes to keep her.

Thirteen

"Let's cut into the pizza before we get into this box, hey?" Lisa offered.

Nodding, Beth pulled plates from a partially packed box. "Good idea."

Reverently, Lisa lifted the cardboard lid. "Oh God. Nobody makes pizza like Floe." She pulled two slices from the box and set them on Beth's plate, handing it back to her. She took a large bite herself, and groaned. "This is incredible."

Beth grinned. They had been eating pizza every other day since they were lured into the diner during dinner time. "Pepperoni, ham, and mushrooms. Perfect."

Beth exhaled slowly, accepting the soda that Lisa handed her. Sipping the sweet liquid, she pulled the manila envelope and papers from the case. The first item she confronted was her grandmother's death certificate. She read aloud absently. "Carol L. DeForge. Female. Date of Death: April 8th, 1959. Age: 35."

"Shit, she was young!"

Beth nodded. "I know. Richard says that she died because she just couldn't bear to live without her husband. But that's not true: she died of breast cancer."

"Your grandpa died before your grandma?" Lisa

furrowed a brow, confused.

"He disappeared. He was flying north to see a friend and he never got there." Beth shrugged. "They think he crashed somewhere along the way. It was stormy."

"Wow. Your dad must have had a helluva time, what with his parents dying so young and so close together."

Beth frowned. "Yeah, he must have. He didn't talk about it much though."

"But you weren't really around much, were you?" Lisa questioned gently.

"That's true," she conceded. Setting aside the death certificate, Beth was intrigued by a leather bound volume. As soon as she picked it up, papers slid from its grasp onto the table. She glanced at the black and white photograph and moved to the opened envelope sent by the Sault Ste. Marie Coast Guard.

Lisa picked up the photograph. "One of these guys must be your grandpa, hey?"

Beth looked at the photo again, her eyes scanning the eight faces. "This one, I think."

Lisa nodded. "What's that?"

Puzzled, Beth pulled the letter out, and read aloud.

"Dear Mrs. Lee DeForge:

I am writing with regret, to inform you that the search for your husband has been called off. After days of what resulted in being the largest manhunt in Michigan history, and the dispatch of 50 planes to scour the area in search, we have covered the entire Lake Huron coastline with absolutely no evidence of your husband's crash site or location.

In response to your earlier inquiry concerning your belief that your husband was being transferred to KAFB, I can confirm that we have no such record of an impending or possible transferal.

It is the belief of myself, as well as the belief of the US Coast Guard, that Captain DeForge perished in the February 22nd crash. I am deeply sorry for your loss, and on behalf of the United States Air Force, allow me to extend our sincere condolences.

Sincerely,

Lt. Col. William T. Robertson

Commander, Kincheloe Air Force Base

Beth set the letter on the table carefully. Her pale face and blue eyes met Lisa's in shock. "That had to have been terrible for her."

"It must have been terrible for your dad, too. Look at the date! Just think, a couple months later, she died." Lisa placed another slice of pizza on her plate. "What was that about a transfer? Your grandfather was moving?"

Beth rubbed her forehead. "I remember hearing that he had to be transferred, but they were giving him some options. I think he was going up to check it out. He had a friend there or something."

"Yeah, but this letter says there wasn't any record of it."

"They did things differently back then, Li."

Lisa was unconvinced. "I think it's fishy."

"It might be, but let's see what this is," Beth placated. A photograph of Carol and Lee, just after Raymond had been born, was right inside the volume. Beth rubbed her neck with her left hand and flipped it open. "Lisa, it's a journal."

"Gram really was like you, wasn't she?" Lisa smiled, looking over Beth's shoulder. "What does that say?"

"The Last Diary of Carol Lenora DeForge." Beth's eyes glistened, and to Lisa's surprise, she set the book back on the table. "I'm not sure I should read this."

"What?! You have to read it. Who else is there?"

"It's like invading her privacy or something," Beth countered.

"Beth, you're her only granddaughter. You've said yourself that your dad always used to say you were just like her. What possible harm could it do?"

Beth remained silent for a moment, finishing her pizza slice. "Can you imagine writing that? *The Last Diary...* it's so final. So sad. How could she have known it would be her last journal?"

"She knew she was sick, right? I mean, she knew she had cancer." Lisa offered a comforting hand.

"You know what's going to be in there, don't you? Worry. Her husband had disappeared a few months before her death. I bet it's filled with misery." It made Beth sick to think her grandmother had to go through sickness and the loss of her husband.

"She wrote her thoughts down, knowing somewhere in the back of her mind that someone would read them eventually. It's your responsibility to read it, Beth. You're the only one who would really appreciate it."

Beth sipped the soda, hesitating. "I suppose you're

right."

"Of course, I'm right." Lisa nodded, cleaning up the table. "Now, buck up. Take a few deep breaths and finish your pop. You're going to read that and I am going to be right here with you."

Beth smiled, winsome. "You're a lifesaver, Li."

"If you mean I'm a big round sweetie, you're absolutely right." Lisa cooed, enjoying Beth's laughter.

"I want to call Richard though. It's noon-ish and he's not here yet. It's just ridiculous. Anyway, he should see this."

Lisa nodded, handing Beth her handbag. "Good idea."

Beth pulled the cell phone from her bag and hit the speed dial key for her brother. The scratchy voicemail recording rang in Beth's ear. "This is Richard DeForge. Leave a message and I'll get back to you. Thanks."

Beth cleared her voice. "It's Beth. I've been cleaning all day and am wondering what happened to you. I found some of Grandma's stuff. Call me when you get a chance. It's important." Beth clicked off the phone and glanced at an expectant Lisa.

Lisa recognized worry in her face. "He must be off doing a real estate deal or something. I'm sure he's just fine."

"Do you really think I should read this without him?"

"Would he wait for you?"

Beth hesitated. "Good point." She cracked the journal open, waiting for Lisa to settle beside her.

Fourteen

THE LAST DIARY OF CAROL LENORA DeFORGE, ENTRY ONE

I'm scared.

There is no word of Lee yet. I can't quite believe he's gone, and yet, I don't believe I'll see his return. My body aches. Doc Morse told me today that I don't have much time left. Not much time. Not enough time to spend with my son, to teach him about life. My parents will have to do that. I went and saw Dad and Mom today. Dad seemed...relieved. It upset me and I cried. I couldn't tell if he was relieved to be rid of me or relieved that Lee was gone. He loved Lee... so I don't understand. I wish I could ask him. Maybe, it's just me. Dad couldn't have been relieved. It upset him when I cried. Mama's just stricken. It doesn't make me feel any better.

Poor Ray. He misses his Dad, and I don't know what to tell him. Do I tell him his father is dead? What if he's still alive? Is it wrong to hope? Is it wrong to give up? All I know is that I love that little boy. He keeps asking when I'll be done being sick. I just don't know what to say to him.

It was so hard to carry him inside me. I worried about how I would feel, how Lee would feel about him. I was so scared. More scared then I am today. When he was born—the only thing I knew was how very much I loved him. Ray, if you read this, I want you to know that I always loved you. I will always love you. So much. Poor little Ray. He reminds me of his father.

God, I miss him.

I can't think of that just now.

All this time, all my life… I have taken so much for granted. And now the doctor says there isn't much time left. My little, darling boy will be left without a mother, without a father, if Lee doesn't turn up. I fear that he won't.

Somehow, I feel as if I am receiving my due. My father once warned me about reaping what I sow. I keep hearing his words play over and over inside my head.

I don't know why I continue to write. I'll probably burn this, but writing helps, somehow. God, I never did many of the things I wanted to do. I'm thankful for my boy though. What would I have done without him? I made the right choice. Lee's a good man. But what choice did I have? I must cook dinner now. Mama said I should keep the daily routine. I'll make Ray and I dinner and then I'll read to him. Will he understand?

I overheard Dad tell Mom that he's thankful he did the right thing. What right thing? I wish I could challenge him. I wish he would talk to me. He worries about money since he retired. He always worried about money though. I can't share his joy in the little things. I have a hard time feeling joy at all. At least I'll be in heaven soon. But what if I don't make it there? I bet Dad doesn't think I will. I have been such a chore for him. I don't know. Dinner now. It'll be okay, if I stop worrying. For Ray's sake. I need to give him good memories.

Fifteen

"Oh, boy." Beth wiped her dampened eyes with her shirt sleeve, letting the diary fall closed. "She was so torn up, wasn't she? Her parents weren't helping. Her husband was gone... it's just so unbearably sad." It was the only conclusion Beth could draw. She wrapped her arms around herself, trying to relieve herself the shivers that coursed through her arms.

Lisa tapped the table, thinking. "I think there are layers to this."

Beth watched Lisa's wheels turn, realized her friend was coming up with a theory. "What do you mean?"

"I think there's something going on that she's not saying."

"Like what?" Beth frowned. "She was dying, Lisa. It makes sense that she would ramble about her fear. And I really don't want to read this anymore. It makes me feel bad that I didn't know. Dad must have had an awful time of it."

Lisa hesitated, but pressed on. "What was the issue between her and her father?"

"I don't know."

"Your dad never mentioned anything about it?" Lisa persisted.

Beth considered it. "My parents divorced when I was

eight." She shook her head. "I don't remember him ever saying anything about it. The only thing Dad ever said about Great-Grandpa was that he had provided for him. It ended up driving my father a little crazy. His grandpa used to talk about how he had something valuable for him. He died in a car accident just a few weeks after Grandma Carol died. Dad always said that he would find whatever it was eventually. Honestly, I don't think he tried very hard though. Dad liked to talk about finding the fortune more than actually searching for it. I think he thought it would just be delivered to him one day."

Lisa pondered, slightly confused. "Wait a minute. You mean to tell me that Lee, Carol, and Carol's father all died close together?"

Beth nodded.

"I guess bad things really do happen in threes," Lisa muttered. "He didn't know what this thing was?"

"I don't think so. Dad never said what it was. He always told Richard and I, when we were little, that is, that once he found it, we could buy a nice new house and have more toys and stuff." Beth shook the memory clear, her voice became wistful. "Mom hated him for that. She said it was foolish to fill our heads with silly dreams."

"He must have believed it. But he never found it, hey?"

Beth shrugged. "Not if his lifestyle was any indication. His savings account surely didn't show for much. And he hadn't done a thing to this house in a long time."

"We need to read more."

"No." Beth held up her hand, stopping Lisa from protesting. "I just can't, Lisa. I'm tired and I'm worried about Richard... and I need to get away from this for a little while."

Lisa smiled, understanding. "Tea would make you feel better."

"I don't have any more. The last packet was orange

spice, and I even drank that earlier." Beth pouted a bit.

Lisa laughed when Beth wrinkled up her nose. "Let's get out of here for a while. We'll go down to Floe's Diner and have a tea. What do you think?"

"Great plan. Best plan all day, Li."

Sixteen

"I can't believe that Billy got fired today!" Joe shouted over the roar of Bob's engine and music combination as he jumped into the jeep.

Bob cranked the country station down. "What?!"

"I can't believe Billy got fired today," Joe repeated.

Bob barked with laughter in response.

Joe's eyes darted sharply at the driver. "You'd probably be laughing if it was me without the job and Billy sitting here, wouldn't you?"

"Hell yes, I'd be laughing at any ass dumb enough to lose their fifth job in as many months. But Billy wouldn't be wasting his time worrying about what you're gonna do now, eh."

"It was not his fifth job. It was his third job since last spring," Joe defended.

"Whatever. You shouldn't be wastin' your time worryin' 'bout him. Would you rather it was you?"

"Hell, no." Joe shuddered.

"Then don't worry about it, Kid. Count yourself lucky that you got your job. Billy lost his job cause he was too much of an asshole to get to work on time. Same thing would've happened to me or Gary if we didn't take our jobs seriously.

Let it go." Bob cranked the music up again, and then cranked it back down as Joe signaled at the approaching party store.

"Stop here. I want to grab some suds."

"And after all that lip about changing your ways during lunch…" Bob taunted as he slowed the jeep to turn in.

Joe smiled sheepishly. "Get off my case, man. It's Friday. I can drink on Friday." Joe swung out of Bob's jeep, leaving Bob to wait. He popped the door to Wazz's Party Plus open and held it for a woman returning cans.

"Hey, Joey!" Tami Willis called from behind the counter. "Just getting off work?"

Joe grinned, following the can lady. "Yes, I am." He quickly moved down the aisle, trying not to incite more banter from Tami.

"Are you going out later?" She persisted, pinching her cheeks and running her hands through her hair when his back was turned.

Joe laughed, in spite of himself. "Hell, yes. It's Friday."

"Of course," Tami called. "The bar? Or are you going to roll out to the beach later? I haven't heard anything else is going on."

"I really don't know, Tam. I think I'd rather be indoors though. It's still a little cold for a bonfire at the beach." He already got ragged enough about her during work; the last thing he wanted was for Bob to come in and see them chatting.

"Well, I guess I'll see you later then, eh Joe?" Tami inquired.

"Maybe later." Joe shrugged, turning away from her again. Tami was called up to the front by a customer, leaving Joe alone before the beer cooler.

"So, you kept your job today?"

The inquisitive voice snapped him out of his thoughts

about avoiding Tami. Seeing that it was the woman from this morning, loaded down with pretzels and a six pack of Corona, he turned and smiled.

"Or you fell into a big puddle of something nasty?"

Joe glanced down confused and realized he looked terrible. He grinned sheepishly. "I kept my job, thanks to you." His praise was met by her slight shrug, and intrigued, he wiped his hand on a clean section of his pants and stuck his hand out. "I'm Joe Barber. I'm sorry I didn't introduce myself this morning."

She moved the six pack to an alternate hand and reached out for his hand. "Jill Traynor," she replied meeting his eyes. "Nice to meet you." She turned to head down the aisle, assuming the conversation was over.

Joe had another idea. No longer interested in the cooler, he called out. "How 'bout I buy you a beer?"

Jill turned and gave him a small smile, holding up her six pack. "I already have some, but thanks."

He chuckled, shaking his head. "No, I mean at the bar. It is a Friday, after all." Sensing her hesitation, he persisted. "I'd like to pay you back for the ride this morning."

"By asking for another one?" She challenged, humor spilling from her voice. Of course, Joe's truck was still parked on the side of the road, exactly where he left it. Any trip to the bar would have to be taken by her car.

"Oh, come on. One drink. Unless you've got someone waiting for you or plans or something..." While waiting for her to decide, his eyes roamed over her, appreciating.

Jill was a looker. Thick dark hair fell back, away from a flawless cream-colored face. Her eyes were mammoth and strangely colored—green and gold, almost. They sat above a slightly freckled pert nose and a mouth that would drive a man insane. Her body was long, she was just an inch or two shorter than Joe, and trim. Snug fitting jeans and the simple white t-shirt she wore showed off slight curves and a casual demeanor. Her toes stuck out of the sandals she wore, free of polish. She was definitely a looker, but so different than Marci, Joe thought. Marci was always decked out in make-up and catchy clothes, with every ounce of her screaming *woman*. Jill wasn't "done up" but she was just as striking with her dark hair and sparkling eyes as Marci was with bleached hair and bedroom makeup. She bit her lower lip in thought, and Joe realized she was probably going to say no.

"What the hell." Jill finally responded, amused at Joe's perusal. "Sure, I'll go."

Surprised, Joe let out a breath he hadn't realized he was holding. "Great! But, I wouldn't mind cleaning up first."

"Do you need me to give you a lift somewhere?"

"Nah. One of the guys from work is outside. Can I meet you at the bar… say in thirty minutes?"

"Sure. I have to run down to the hardware again anyway. Do you want to meet at the Northwood or somewhere else?"

"The Northwood's fine."

"Okay, I'll see you in 30 minutes."

"Just wait outside for me if I'm a bit late," Joe said, smiling over his idea. He didn't want anyone moving in on her while she waited.

"I don't wait for anyone," Jill winked, pivoting away from him toward the counter.

Joe's smile lit up his face. He concentrated on keeping his pace steady through the aisle, his mind in the clouds. He barely even realized he bumped into Tami.

"Ow! Watch it, Joe!" Tami rubbed her nose.

"Shit. Sorry, Tam. I didn't even see you there." He smiled and edged past her, whistling.

"No, you wouldn't." She muttered, watching him jog out of the store, empty handed.

"What the hell? Where's the beer?" Bob yelled.

"Change of plans."

"Huh? Oh… I see." Bob's voice dropped to a conspiratorial whisper. "You're gonna take the Willis girl up on her offer, eh? Good man. I'd do just the same."

"Asshole. No, I'm not doing anything with Tami. Lay off." Blue eyes rolled at the thought, while he waited for Bob's chuckles to subside. "I need you to drive me to my place and give me a few minutes to change my clothes. I have to be at the bar in 30 minutes."

Bob lifted an eyebrow, questioning.

"I'm meeting Jill there."

"Jill? Who's Jill?"

"Remember the woman in the truck that gave me the ride to work?"

"Oh." Bob scratched his head, nodding. "Well, we're wasting time then. Get in."

Seventeen

Squinting at the sun, Beth rubbed the back of her neck. Richard's cell phone was an extension of his hand. If he wasn't answering it, nor returning her call, there were only two possibilities. He was in trouble, which Beth hated to consider or he was avoiding her. Beth locked and shut the car door, careful to sidestep a puddle, while she contemplated both options. If he was in trouble, she should have been told. There was no reason for him to be avoiding her. Obviously, he could expect her to be a bit miffed that he hadn't shown up today, but he finished his tasks and Beth wouldn't have been too hard on him. He even cleaned the window, she thought, a smile lightening her features as she swung open the heavy glass door to the diner. She held it open for Lisa, who was dawdling to gaze at a brightly colored spring flower.

"Hi Beth! And hello again, Lisa." The rotund waitress waved them in, grinning merrily. "How was the pizza?"

Lisa licked her lips. "Delicious."

"And how's the cleaning going?"

Beth sat at the Formica counter. "Oh, we're getting it done! Actually, we're on our own today. My brother seems to have gone up in smoke."

"Oh? He's disappeared?"

Beth shrugged, uncomfortable with the word. "He

didn't leave a note or anything, and he didn't show up today...
I'm not sure *disappeared* is the exact word I'd use. But I
definitely don't know where he is."

The waitress scrunched up her face in thought. "He was
in yesterday evening for just a few minutes. He picked up a
couple sandwiches to go, and looked like he was in a hurry."

"What time was that?"

"Oh... 5:30-ish? Maybe even quarter to six. I think he
was going on a road trip."

Beth perked up. "Oh?"

"How do you know that?" Lisa asked.

"He brought a road atlas in with him, and was
highlighting it. I can't imagine he does that just for fun, can
you?"

More confused than she had been moments ago, Beth
frowned. "Thanks for your help."

Reaching into her purse, Beth pulled out the phone and
dialed the office number. Light static rippled through the phone
line. "Clover Real Estate. This is Jean. How may I help you?"

"Hi Jean, this is Beth DeForge, Richard's sister."

"Oh, it's good to hear from you. How are you doing?"
Jean's warm voice helped Beth smile.

"Quite well, under the circumstances. Have you heard
from Richard at all today?"

"Not today, Beth, but I did talk to him yesterday
afternoon." Jean replied. "He said he would be traveling to
Michigan for a few days. I'm not sure when he'll be back, but
he indicated he'd return Wednesday evening. I'm sure he'll be
back by Friday, though, because we have a meeting then."
Jean's tone succeeded in masking her worry.

"Michigan? Did he say what the trip was in regard to?

Did he say he was doing something with real estate? Or working on a new deal?" Beth grasped for straws.

"No, he didn't leave me any details, Beth. I'm sorry. I know that it wasn't work related, and he told me it was important. In fact, he said it *couldn't wait*." Jean offered. "I'm sure he'll call again, would you like me to have him call you?"

"I would, yes. Thanks Jean." Beth clicked off the phone, frowning. "I just don't get it."

"Do you think it has anything to do with your dad?"

"How could it? Logically…"

"Logically, it's pretty coincidental that Richard just took off for Michigan right after he cleaned the attic. I do not believe in coincidences. It must be related. What are you *feeling*? Any sensations?" Lisa lowered her voice.

"Oh, Lisa, nonsense." Beth rolled her eyes, moving to what was troubling her. "I think you might be right about that Coast Guard letter."

"You think Richard saw it," Lisa conjectured.

"That's the tough part. Yes and no. I can't imagine him being in the attic and not seeing the hatch."

"We had to really look for it though."

"Yes, but, the panel was ajar. I think he got into the box… but I'm not sure he saw the diary."

"How could he have seen the letter without the diary? Beth, it was laying right on top of the book."

Beth shook her head, feelings and logical thoughts at odds with one another. "Richard has been notorious for looking on the surface of things. But if he had seen it, I think he would have shown it to me."

"Even if he had seen it, what difference does it make?" Lisa questioned.

"Maybe he… oh, never mind."

"What?"

"No, it's stupid." Beth was caught in Lisa's demanding gaze. "What if he wanted to go look for himself?"

"Look for what? Your grandfather's body?" Lisa was horrified. "After all these years?"

"I told you it was stupid." Beth shook her head, failing to evict the imagery that had taken root within her mind.

Eighteen

Quinn McCord leaned against the bar at the back of the room and surveyed the crowd. His angular face, clenched at the jaw line, appeared carved from granite. Steel eyes surveyed the room from above a once broken nose. The well worn and faded Red Wing jersey stretched across his torso, revealing solid strength that was just daunting enough to have tempers, normally piqued by excess drink, quieted with one cold glance. Tonight, he was damned well tired of Billy's wailing.

The dark wood counter stretched nearly the entire length of the bar, preceding glass bottles of liquor, mirrors, and shelves containing various glasses. One pool table stood near to center with the standard stained glass light fixture dangling above it. A juke box flanked the north wall near the door. Mixed and matched battered tables were smattered throughout. Strings of Red Wings hockey flags dangled from the rafters. Beer advertisements decorated the stained wooden walls. Deer heads older than Methuselah stretched toward the ceiling from the walls. They were in terrible shape, but they boasted large racks. Quinn nodded at a regular who sat in front of an electronic card game machine, pushing in quarters, and winced as Billy started up again.

Just after noon, the poor guy had come into the bar with the intention to drink away every last dollar he had. With each additional drink, his conversational tone had become more strung out, more self-pitying. In all honesty, Quinn assumed he'd have run out of money hours ago, but friends and other patrons were buying Billy round after round. He speculated that they felt sorry for him and were trying to ease his pain. Quinn had been cutting him some slack, because it wasn't everyday that a man lost his job. Well, in Billy Spindler's case it was frequent, which made it even worse. Every lost job translated into a few more jobs that he wouldn't be able to get, and Billy had been going through quite a few of them this year. Everyone said the same thing, when he actually got to work, he was a half-way decent worker.

Wiping down the bar, Quinn glanced up at the television sporting the latest Red Wings news. As always, they had made it to the playoffs again, so the bar was bound to be increasingly busy on game nights. Aggravated by the loudmouth, Quinn spared a glance toward Billy and raised a signal for the waitress to cut him off. Billy had begun telling bar patrons about what kind of an ass Joe was and how there was some big conspiracy in stealing Billy's job. If Billy didn't pipe down, Quinn knew Billy would be forced to start shit with Joe tonight. The bar had been filled with rowdy behavior last night, and he was damn well determined to make it through this one without incident. Consumed in his tasks of keeping the place organized, he didn't notice the customer that slid up to the bar until he heard her purring.

Marci leaned over the counter, licking her lips. "Hey, Quinn."

Although Quinn barely spared her a glance, his deep voice rubbed up against her. "Hey, Marz. The usual?"

"No, not tonight. Unless you feel like buying me a drink?" She preened, perching on the end of a tall barstool. She lowered her voice, not waiting for Quinn's response, not expecting one. She opened her purse and pulled out a pack of smokes. Quinn reached over and fluidly lit her cigarette for her. "Thanks. You know, it's quite a shame that we don't spend more time together." She dangled the tip between two darkly painted lips.

Quinn ignored that last statement and began pouring an order the waitress brought him. Marci feasted her eyes on his graceful movements; understated masculinity. Her gaze roamed past him, traveling around the room, taking in the occupants, the conversation. "Did Billy lose his job again?"

Quinn nodded, tossing a towel over his shoulder. "He's blaming Joe."

Marci looked at Quinn quizzically, flicking ash into a tray. "Why?"

"Joe made it to work. Billy didn't." Quinn shrugged.

"That's shitty. It's not Joe's fault." Marci smiled. "I'm surprised Joe made it to work at all."

Quinn responded with a grin. "Yeah, I saw you leading him away last night." Quinn was called to the other side of the bar and returned a few moments later.

"I doubt he'll even look at another woman now."

"Just where you want him, right? Now you can get busy making three other guys totally crazy over you and snag Joe again just as he's about to lose interest."

"Just three other guys? You don't give me much credit, Mr. Bar Man," she quipped.

Quinn laughed and moved back down the bar. Workers were starting to roll in, ready to party away the weekend. When he returned, Marci had finished her cigarette and began scouting her night's prey. She hadn't moved yet, but she was looking. The intent on her face almost made her look feral, Quinn thought with a grin. The swinging door caught his eye, and his attention was soaked up by the entry.

Marci was saying something to him, but his attention

was focused on the woman who just entered the bar. "Quinn! Are you even listening?" Marci whined.

"Yep." Quinn snapped back quickly. "But you couldn't have given Joe as good of a time last night as you thought."

"Why is that?"

Quinn gestured toward the door, watching cold calculation flood into Marci's features. Marci looked up and quickly spotted Joe's companion. She shot a look over her shoulder, questioning. "Too early to be a tourist, isn't she?"

Quinn nodded. "She doesn't look like a tourist, she's too comfortable." Quinn's eyes darted over to Billy. "Ah, shit." Quinn pulled the phone from under the counter and handed it to Marci. "Call Deedee, will ya? Tell her she needs to come pick Billy up. Shit's about to fly, and he already got a warning from Sheriff Cole last night."

"So, have you been here before?" Joe had cleaned up considerably and had made it back to the parking lot at the Northwood just in time.

"When I was little, we use to eat in the restaurant side all the time. But I haven't been here since I came back, and I've never been in the bar side."

"You're in for a real slice of Drummond Island then. It's an experience." Joe gestured to an empty table. "What can I get you from the bar?"

"Corona."

"What are you? A one drink woman?" Joe teased, recalling the six pack that she had just purchased.

Jill rewarded him with a charming smile. "Why settle for anything less than the best?"

Joe chuckled and turned away from the table, completely unprepared for a fist landing in his gut, knocking him off his feet. He looked up to find his assailant looming over him. Jill scrambled to her feet instantly.

"Get up, gimp. Stand up and face me." Billy taunted. "Or I guess dumb ass pricks who date bimbos and steal their friend's jobs are suppose to crawl around on the floor!" He didn't even see Jill's hand before it cracked across his face.

Shocked, Billy stared at this new foe. "What the hell?"

Jill ignored Billy and thought better than to try and help Joe up. Joe struggled awkwardly to his feet, his face flaming red. "What's your problem, Billy?"

Billy pulled his fist back, but was caught fast by Quinn's firm grasp that hauled him back. Drunk off his ass, Billy struggled in vain. Even if he had been sober, Quinn was a good half a foot taller and thick with strength. He was also quicker. Billy was no competition and realized it. Sensing Billy's anger fizzling out, Quinn released him. "You've had too much to drink, Billy. You need to go home."

"Hell no, Quinn. My fight's not with you." Billy rubbed his stung cheek. "It's not with you either, you little bitch."

Joe connected his clenched fist with Billy's face, sending waves of pain through his arm, into his shoulder. He groaned low in his throat.

"Dammit, Joe. Back off." Quinn barked. Grabbing Billy's arm with force, he walked him outside.

Dragging his left leg in pain, Joe escaped to the bathroom.

"Deedee's coming to get you, Billy. You need to go home." Quinn stood beside him on the step in silence until he could see the car he was looking for. "There she is. You okay?" Red faced, Billy mumbled a response.

Quinn returned to the bar, grateful that Deedee lived a short bit away and always got there quickly. Locals, sensing the entertainment was over, had already shuffled back to their pre-fight positions.

"Shit, this is better than a hockey game—there's a fight every night, hey Quinn?" One of the local's yelled, getting a nod in response.

They were still chatting about it. Noticing Joe's absence, he figured he should do what he could to smooth the situation over with the new date. He was completely unprepared for the cool glance that she cast over him. "Nice slap."

"I shouldn't have hit him."

"No, you shouldn't have," Quinn agreed, watching her eyes fill with gold anger. *Too bad Joe found her first.*

"I defended myself."

Quinn shook his head at her misunderstanding. "Billy wasn't talking about you. You just happened to be with Joe at the moment."

Her chin tilted saucily. "You should have been keeping a better eye on your customers, *at the moment*. Doesn't anyone get cut off when they've had too much?"

Quinn grinned, terribly amused to have someone throw his words back at him. Rather than waging a verbal war with this nameless wonder, he nodded toward the waitress. "I need to get back to the bar." He slipped past the bar however and headed for the bathroom. Joe was splashing water on his face: contorted with pain. Quinn lost his smile quickly. "Man, what can I do? Did Billy get a good punch in?"

"No. I did." Joe blew out a breath, angrily rubbing his arm. "I punched him with the wrong damned arm."

"Do you need some aspirin?"

"I already took some pills." He nodded at the bottle he had placed on the sink.

Quinn slanted his eyes, quizzically.

"I carry them with me." Joe shrugged. "Is Jill still out there?" He imagined her leaving quickly.

Quinn hadn't known Joe still took pills for his injuries from the accident. It shook him to think he was still in enough pain to warrant a prescription. He usually hid it well. "Yeah. She's quite the woman." Quinn leaned against the sink, trying to ignore the nagging voice that was telling him to get back to the bar. Failing, he guided Joe back out. He lowered his voice as they stepped back into the barroom. "Did you see her slap him?"

Joe grinned. "Wasn't that great?"

Quinn laughed, agreeing. "You better get back to her."

"I'm gonna need a couple shots," Joe groaned putting the bottle back in his pocket. "I don't really want her to see me take them. Pour two shots of Jack and leave them on the counter. When I come up to get our beer, I'll drink them then. I need them for the pain."

Quinn didn't like that idea but said nothing. Joe must have suffered the combination of drink and drugs before if he took them regularly enough to carry them along everyday.

Joe's leg dragged a bit, but at this point he wasn't in any shape to stop it. He shrugged, somewhat sheepishly. "You're still here."

Jill smiled, pulling her hair away from her face in an absent gesture. "You're not boring, anyway."

Realizing Jill wasn't running for the door eased Joe's reaction. "I'm sorry about Billy," Joe began, but Jill held up her hand, stopping the apology wordlessly. "Still want that drink?"

"If you're still buying, tough guy," Jill teased, turning away from him to find her table.

Joe tossed back the two shots waiting for him at the bar and tried to shake off Billy's anger. Marci scooted next to him, touching his arm gently. "Are you okay?"

"Yeah, I'm fine. Billy's just a little pissed about losing his job I think."

"Deedee will take care of him... that is, if she'll still keep him around after being fired again." Marci shook her head, her eyes moving back to Jill. "Well, if you want some company tonight, give me a call, okay?" Marci winked, peeling off the bar stool. She moved past Quinn, making sure she brushed up against him.

Quinn smirked at Marci and slid around the backside of the bar after serving drinks. "Billy has been drinking since lunchtime, Joe. He was feelin' bad about being fired."

"It's okay." Joe shrugged. "I just wished he hadn't yelled at Jill."

"She slapped him," Quinn said, still impressed. Most women around here just took that kind of behavior. Jill was a treat, he thought, allowing his gaze to land on her.

"I think she thought he was calling her a bimbo."

"Yeah, I got that impression. Billy must have seen you leave with Marci last night."

Joe nodded. "Grab me a Corona and a Bud, hey Quinn?"

"Speaking of the girl, am I going to get an introduction or what?"

"Hell no! If I introduce her to you, I'll never get her to go out with me again." Joe protested, laughing.

"I don't think you'll have that problem. She doesn't seem to like me much." Quinn shrugged. "I think she thought I was too easy on Billy."

Joe grinned, grabbing the beers. "That's not such a bad thing, man." He twisted through people and tables to get back to Jill. Joe held out her beer, which she accepted.

"So what was that all about?" Jill asked.

"Billy lost his job today," Joe swigged back on his beer. "I would have lost mine if you hadn't come along, but he blames me for it."

"Why does he blame you?"

Joe shrugged. "He needs to blame someone."

"Great. So I helped you become Mr. Popularity with a psycho?" Jill chuckled, leaning back against her chair. Before Joe could respond, she changed the subject. "I bet this bar has all kinds of stories, doesn't it?"

Sitting down, Joe nodded. "Oh yeah. People have driven their jeeps, snowmobiles, and motorcycles into this place. One woman stripped off her clothes a couple seasons ago. Guns have gone off." He shook his head, remembering. "Crazy stuff."

Jill's face lit up with surprise. "Jeeps? They drive jeeps right into the bar?"

Joe chuckled. "I've seen it happen."

"It definitely has character." Jill pushed the lime wedge through the neck of the bottle. She met Joe's interested gaze.

"So tell me about you," Joe prodded. "What brings you here?"

"It's kind of a long story," Jill warned.

"It's not even dinner time yet, we have all night."

Laughing, Jill contemplated the best way to begin. "Do you know Clark and Arlene Eby?" When Joe nodded, she continued. "They were great friends with my grandparents and talked them into buying a summer home here a long time ago. I use to come up with them every summer. In the beginning, my parents worked hard and barely vacationed, so I vacationed with my grandparents. Since I was an only grandchild, I was spoiled rotten." Jill smiled, caught in a memory. "After my parents passed away, when I was still quite young, I lived with my grandparents, and continued to vacation here every summer.

My grandpa got sick about six years ago, though. After he passed away, Grandma didn't want to come without him. She passed on a few months ago, and left me the house here."

"I'm sorry." When she said nothing, Joe realized she probably didn't want to talk about it. "Are you just vacationing for a little while then?"

"I don't really know." Jill frowned, uncomfortable. "My parents left me a little money in a trust, and I don't work a normal job so I don't have any specific time that I need to leave."

"How do you *not* work? Are you in school?"

"I have been to many different schools." She laughed suddenly. "I probably sound like a slacker. I'm a photographer. Or at least I am trying to be one. I've studied all sorts of photography: forensic, nature, portraiture, architectural. I love it all. I even enjoy industrial stuff. And so far, I love being here. I start the day with a list of projects that I want to get done on my grandparents' house... or my house rather, and I end up sitting on the deck taking pictures of the sunrise, or some bird I see flying about, or a pretty flower."

Joe was enchanted. Her eyes lit up when she spoke, shining that unusual color that he had noticed earlier. Her laughter was like a soothing harmony. "That sounds pretty great."

"It is. It just doesn't do that great a job of paying for anything besides the film right now. I often pick up side jobs to get by. Actually, I'd like to find a job—nothing too major, but if I spend any more time by myself in that house, or out in the woods, or on the water, I think I'll go crazy before long." Jill laughed, sipped her beer. "Once in a while I get a job doing pictures for an insurance company, but otherwise it's been pretty thin so far. I haven't talked to any of the insurance agencies around here yet."

Joe swirled the beer in his mouth, considering what she had said earlier. "You don't have *any* family?" He had family members all over the Upper Peninsula and especially on Drummond Island.

"I have an uncle in Florida. Grandma left him the house downstate and the majority of their retirement fund. I'm using the money they left me to fix up the house here. It needs a new deck and it has a bunch of little problems that I'm going to work on. Right now I'm wading through five solid years of dust."

"And mouse shit, probably."

Jill bubbled with laughter, nodding enthusiastically. "The first purchase I made was for mouse traps and D-Con. I've been patching little holes." Her voice trailed off. "So, tell me about you. Why are you here?" She turned his question back to him, tipping up her bottle.

"It's home," Joe said simply.

"What makes it home?"

"Well, I grew up here. My family is here. My parents and some of my uncles and aunts live here. My sisters are both in school down state, but they'll come home next week for their summer break. I like it here. I know everyone, and they all know me." Joe shrugged.

"And I know that you work construction," Jill provided.

"Yep. In fact, I got a raise today."

"Well, congratulations. That's great!" She clinked her bottle to Joe's.

Joe beamed, brushing his hair back. "I'm going to get a two dollar an hour raise, but it depends on a few things first."

"Like what?"

"I need a new truck and..." he cut his speech off at Jill's shriek of laughter. Momentarily, he had forgotten the reason for their meeting this morning. He watched her tip her head back, her hair fall back from her face, as she laughed with amusement. He couldn't help joining her in laughter, feeling unashamedly pleased that his truck had died.

In the usual manner of Friday nights the Northwood slowly filled with more people interrupting their conversation with greetings yelled at Joe. Gradually, Joe let the tension that Billy had stirred up leave him. He allowed himself to be overwhelmed by this new person who stood true to her intentions and indicated that she didn't want to spend the whole night in the bar. To his own amazement, he asked her for a ride home when she said she was leaving. For the first time in ages, he walked out of the bar before dark.

Nineteen

Beth rested her head on her cupped hands, leaning onto the counter, trying in vain, to clear her thoughts. With Lisa off to see a movie, the house was quiet, giving Beth a chance to go over her feelings. Her brother had run off somewhere and although logic would have steered her in another direction, she was beginning to feel that his disappearance had something to do with their father's death, and more specifically, their grandparents. She couldn't come up with a reason to satisfy her intellect, but in her gut, she knew Richard would have told her if he was leaving to do something work related. He wouldn't have told her if it was something she might question or disapprove of and Beth was usually able to tell when he was lying. He might have just wanted to avoid talking to her, she thought.

Magnetically, the diary pulled her eyes back to it. The answers could be written neatly in that book and the mystery easily solved. Still, Beth hesitated. Pulling the clip out of her mussed hair, she dragged her fingers through it as she leaned back against the kitchen sink. At some point, she would have to read it. Beth thought about calling her mother and then laughed out loud. Beth's mother was a bitter woman who wouldn't be attached to the sentimental pages of a diary. No, Mom was definitely not the person to call. Beth's thoughts swirled, her mind waged arguments for and against, until her head hurt.

What possible harm could there be in reading it? It was the same reluctance to accept her paranormal experiences that had Beth avoiding the journal. Somewhere inside her, she knew her grandmother was with her... and yet, she continued to deny it. Her mother hadn't believed in spirits and had always discredited Beth's experiences as being impossible– figments of her imagination. Throwing her hands in the air, Beth gave in.

She grabbed one of her friend's colas and settled at the dining table. She needed answers, and she was confident that her neck was going to continue to ache until she got them.

Twenty

Joe was in shock. He still couldn't get over his spontaneous decision to leave early. He had been in the bar every Friday for the last few years and now he was cleaning his trailer, whistling. Rather than just take the phone number she had given him and stay at the bar, he asked her to give him a ride. His mother was going to be thrilled when she heard he made it home once before the bar actually closed and kicked him out.

The pained moments were forgotten as he moved awkwardly between the pizza boxes, loading the junk that littered the floor into garbage bags. Joe grinned, thinking that he had never met anyone quite like Jill. She seemed to be totally different from Marci and the girls he typically associated with. She was witty and reminded him a little bit of Kate. Her face took his breath away, and her body didn't quit: She was gorgeous. He relished his thoughts of Jill with newfound pleasure. If she took one look at the inside of his trailer however, he was sure she'd never want to see him again, and therefore, he was cleaning. He fingered the slip of paper in his pocket and opened it up to glance at her scrawled print. With a burst of energy, he confronted his nervousness with a shrug and picked up the phone. She answered on the second ring.

"Hello?"

"Hey, Jill. It's Joe." He cleared his throat. "Uhm, I'm just calling to see if you'd like to ah… help me with my truck tomorrow."

Jill's laughter bubbled through the phone line, making him smile. "Oh? Should I bring a tool kit and wear overalls?"

He chuckled at the image. "Well, I need to get some stuff out of it and if I can't get it started, I'm going to have to tow it to the garage."

"I thought you were going to take it to a scrap yard."

"Actually, I think I can sell it. It's got some decent parts. Some high school kid might want it for something." Joe grinned into the phone. "If you help me, maybe I could cook you dinner."

"Can you cook?" Jill teased.

Joe laughed. "Well… I can burn a good steak on a grill."

"That sounds great. I can make a salad or something. Actually, we can have dinner here after we're all done. I just bought a grill… it's one of the few kitchen type tools I know how to use. Plus, I can pick your brain about my deck."

"Your deck?"

"You said you built quite a few decks last summer, and I think mine might need to be replaced. That way we'll kill two birds with one stone."

"Great. What do you think about picking me up around noonish, we'll work on my truck, grab some groceries and head to your house?"

"Sounds great. I'll see you then." Jill smiled. "I'm glad we ran into each other at the party store."

Joe beamed. "I had a good time." Joe set the phone down, but picked it back up just as quickly. It was time to enlist help. The phone rang three times before his mother answered.

"Hello." Mary Barber's voice was warm, welcoming.

"Hey, Mom."

"Joey, how are you? You didn't lose your job today did you? I heard that Pete had been in an ugly mood."

"I got a raise."

"You did? Good for you! That's wonderful!"

"And I need some help." Joe just imagined the look that crossed his mother's face. He could almost hear her expressions, he knew her so well. "I am cleaning my trailer and I thought, if I bought you some laundry soap, I could talk you into helping me with my laundry."

"There must be some static in the phone, sweetheart. Could you say that again?"

Joe laughed, good spirited. He enunciated his words, teasing. "I am cleaning my trailer."

"Are you feeling well, son?"

"Mom! I'm serious. I need help."

Mary chuckled. "So am I."

"What's wrong with cleaning?" Joe protested.

"Is this a thorough cleaning? Are you going to remove those, um… unframed pictures on your walls?"

Joe grinned at the naked women displayed in his living room. "Yep." His mother had been trying to get him to take those down for over a year.

"Wow. There's got to be a reason for all this."

"Well, there's this girl…" As soon as the words left his mouth, Joe groaned at his stupidity. He should *not* have said that.

"Oh? A girl? Anyone I know? She must be special." Her voice rose an octave with excitement.

"No, you don't know her. And no, you can't meet her."

"Well, you have to tell me something about her. Where did you meet her?"

"My truck died on the way to work this morning, and she gave me a ride."

"Aw, a nice girl. What's her name?" Mary smiled.

"Jill Traynor."

"Is she a summer girl?"

"Mom!" Joe was done with the questions.

Mary laughed pleasantly. "Okay. If you bring me your laundry, I'll give you a hand."

"My truck's still on the side of the road, Mom. I need you to come get it," Joe explained. *"Please."*

"Okay, okay. I'm on my way."

"Oh, Ma? I need to borrow your vacuum too," Joe added.

"Anything else?"

"No, I can handle the rest."

"Joe?"

"Yeah?"

"I like this girl already," Mary replaced the receiver with a grin.

Twenty-One

The Last Diary of Carol Lenora DeForge, Entry two

I haven't written in a while, but I need to write today. I got a letter today that said they've stopped looking for Lee. I tried explaining it to Ray, and I think he understood. I don't quite know what to do now though. It seems like it's not really happening to me. It's sort of the same way I felt when the doctors told me I have cancer. What should I tell friends when they call? Should I have a memorial service for him? I'll ask Dad.

I don't know how to tell Ray about his father or even if I should tell him. I have been thinking about writing a letter to him. Of course, I could just leave him this diary. It is hard to admit to my child that I failed from the beginning. Should I tell him the whole story or just the basic facts? I owe it to him to help him understand. My breath catches even as I write this. I haven't spoken about it in ages so why should I feel okay with it now? God, please don't let my son hate me.

Lee was a born salesman, so the military snatched him up for these recruiting trips all the time between missions and duties. When he went away, I was lonely. Not that it is any excuse but it was a miserable time. I didn't have many friends at the base, so when I found someone I could talk with, I latched onto him. Over the weeks we filled a place for each other, loved one another. I would count the days to Lee's next trip and when he left, I would enjoy every minute with my lover. Eventually, I became pregnant. I wanted to believe that it was Lee's child, and he was so excited, so happy to become a father.

Lee had no idea about any of it. I knew in my heart that I was not carrying Lee's child. I couldn't tell him. I just couldn't bring myself to tell him because he loved the idea of being a dad so much… I didn't want to hurt him. I did tell my lover though. Reluctantly, he said that he wanted to do what was honorable. He wanted to be a part of the baby's life. I knew that he offered brave words, but he wouldn't have wanted to go through that. Who would? I couldn't let him sacrifice his friendship and his career for my mistakes. He had a bright, promising future before him. I only had one choice… I had to let him go. I told him that I didn't want to leave my husband and, as far as I was concerned, the baby was Lee's. I told him that I loved Lee. I made him promise me that he wouldn't tell anyone, especially my husband. I was testing him.

If he had really loved me, he would have argued or insisted that he tell Lee the truth, he would have insisted upon marrying me himself. I saw the relief in his eyes and I knew the truth. I knew I would see it if he didn't really care about me. Had he argued or tried to convince me that he was serious, that he really cared about the baby, I would have relented. He didn't try to talk me out of my decision so I stayed with Lee, plagued by the guilt that I had betrayed him.

When Lee was sent to Korea, I grieved. I was comforted by my son, but I could no longer be with my lover or lean on my husband. When I told my lover I was pregnant, I knew that I would never be with him again. When Lee went to Korea, a deep part of me wished in a small way that he wouldn't come home. Maybe then, my lover would be with me and become a part of his son's life. When half of his friend's passed, my heart broke inside of me and I wept with guilt. How could I have been so selfish?

I think this sickness, this cancer in my body, just might be God's way of getting even. When Lee returned from the war, broken from the loss of his friends, his brothers as he called them, I welcomed him as a hero should be welcomed. I loved him, and I set aside my yearnings. Raymond was the only thing that got him through. It would have been fine if Raymond had looked like me. It would have been okay, acceptable. Lee's suspicions grew as Raymond looked more and more like another. My father wasn't any help. Damn him. It wasn't his right. It wasn't my father's right to cast shadows on my fidelity. Why didn't he just talk to me, his own daughter if he had suspicions? Was he ashamed of me?

I loved Lee, but my heart belongs to another—to a man who has moved on, and probably has children he can claim as his own. I miss Lee, and I worry for him, and I pray that he knows I loved him. In my mind, he was Ray's father in every way that counts — a father supports and loves his child, as Lee most certainly did.

I'll find a way to tell Ray about my indiscretion. I just don't know if I should tell him who his father is. Does it matter? Thank God, Dad doesn't know who he is. He would have made his life hell, and if I have held onto anything through this life, it was my love for him. You won't hear it from anyone else but me, because I have never told a soul. I'll have to consider it more fully.

Twenty-Two

SATURDAY MORNING

Kate snatched the last pancake, with a daring smile tossed at her husband. Pete laughed good naturedly, without challenging her. His wife ate voraciously, and he knew better than to stand between her and breakfast. He enjoyed watching her lather peanut butter on it, then cover it with applesauce. Pete had always found his wife fascinating, even after all these years. "So, how did the doctor's appointment go yesterday?"

Kate had been in the Soo until late, grocery shopping and seeing a movie after her appointment. "Uhm, it was okay," she muttered, avoiding eye contact.

"Kate." The tone was a warning.

She frowned into her coffee cup which was filled with milk. "The doctor's worried about the baby." She paused, her throat constricted. "He wants me to come in every two weeks. He doesn't want me to work at all... no laundry, no excessive stair climbing, no mental stress." She met Pete's eyes; his concern overwhelmed her. "I think the doctor's wrong though..."

"Kate, you're going to follow the doctor's orders." Pete took her hand in his, met her worried eyes. "I'm really sorry, honey."

"But you're too busy to do the housework and whatnot... and..." Tears filled her eyes before Pete went to her, wrapped his arms around her.

"Babe, we'll hire a housekeeper. I don't ever want you to go through losing a baby again."

"We don't have the money."

"Baby, we'll make it work." Pete wiped away a tear resting on her cheek. "There's something else bothering you, isn't there?"

Kate's frown deepened a bit. "I got a letter from Blue Cross yesterday. I don't really understand it, but it says something about the lapse that we had last year." Crocodile tears fell freely from her eyes. "Because we didn't pay our bill one month last year..."

"Did you call the insurance office?"

Kate nodded. "Yeah, but nobody was in."

"Don't worry about this, Kate. I'm sure we can work it out. Please don't spend your day worrying about this. Now, promise me you won't."

"Let's not talk about this now, Pete." Kate shook her head at him, a small smile forming.

"Okay. The kids are going to get home from Mom's and if they see you crying, McKenzie will surely start up her antics and Kyle will be miserable."

The chuckle rumbled deep in her throat. "You're good for me, Mr. Dombrowski."

"I could say the same thing about you, Mrs. Dombrowski." Pete leaned forward, kissing her softly. "Now, there must be something else we can talk about. Were there any messages?"

"The Hillers called." Kate forked off a large bite of her pancake, popped it in her mouth.

Pete raised an eyebrow, in question. "The Hillers?"

"Mmmm." She rolled the morsel over in her mouth, savoring the combination of flavors .

"Katie?" He received a grunt. "The Hillers?"

Finishing the bite, she explained. "You did a small pole barn for them two or three years ago." She refocused on the pancakes in front of her.

"Oh, yep. Older couple, down in Bass Cove?" At her nod, he continued. "Okay. What did they want?" The Hillers had been good paying customers, if he remembered correctly.

"A new deck."

"Really?" Pete frowned. He was short on workers, now that he had fired Billy. "Did they say what size or anything?"

Kate shook her head. "No. I told them that you would give them a call or run out there. Do you think you can do it?"

"I could have if I still had Billy. Maybe Joe has found someone… I'd hate to turn down some fast money."

"I can help, Dad!" McKenzie, their eleven year old daughter, offered as she bounced through the door.

Pete beamed at her, ruffling her hair. "I'm sure you could, sweetheart, but you've got school. Did you have fun at Grandma and Grandpa's?"

Kate smiled at their interaction and listened attentively as Kyle filled her in on the progress he had made with his video game. A loud knock sounded from the front door. "Honey, was that the door?"

Pete stood up with a light groan and shuffled toward the door. He pegged the man that stood on the other side of it as a total yuppie or some sort of salesperson. He held up his hands before the man could speak. "I have no need to buy steaks, or a new vacuum, or insurance, so I'll save you some time."

The other man shuffled, fidgeted a bit. "Actually, I'm not here to sell anything. I'm looking for Pete Dombrowski, the contractor?"

"That's me."

He held out his hand, offering. When Pete shook it, he continued. "I'm Richard DeForge. I was in Wazz's earlier and I heard you were looking for a worker."

Pete raised an eyebrow. "Have you ever worked construction before?"

"Not since high school but I've worked in real estate and I understand the process. I'm a quick learner, and I'll do anything. I heard you were working on the lighthouse—and I'm a big fan of them. I'm trying to move, but I need to make some money in order to do that... and this area is just beautiful." Richard paused, realizing he might have laid it on a bit thick.

Pete eyeballed the man thoroughly. No matter how ill-fitted to carpentry this new man seemed, Pete needed workers. "I tell you what. I'll give you a week trial at a shit wage. If you prove to me by the end of the week that you have what it takes, I'll make you a full time part of the crew and give you a raise in pay."

Richard considered, nodded. "Sounds good."

Pete grinned, shaking the man's hand again. "Come on in. You can give my wife the information she'll need to put you on the payroll." Pete turned leading the way back through the sunny yellow kitchen. "People call you Dick?"

Richard winced mentally, but nodded. "Sure."

"Great." Pete gestured to Kate. "This is my wife, Kate. Kate, this is Dick..."

"DeForge," Richard supplied.

Pete nodded. "Dick is going to join the crew, babe."

Kate smiled. "Well, that's perfect timing! Let me go get the paperwork."

Twenty-Three

To Joe's surprise, his mother had completed and delivered three loads of the Mt. Everest size pile of laundry that she had helped him scoop up from his floor the day before. She had plunked them in his living room before he had even awakened, taking advantage of the fact that, like most islanders, he never locked his door. There were a variety of items, accompanied by a small note with instructions. Two bathroom rugs that he recognized from his parents home were freshly cleaned and among the linens. In the note, she told him to put them in the bathroom and hang the two matching towels over the bar. Pleased, Joe had complied with his mother's advice. Standing in front of the mirror, his toes were warmed by the soft fringe of the rug. She washed his light blue shirt first because it was a good match with his eyes, and the girl might find him a bit cuter. Joe had rolled his eyes, but in the end, went with the blue shirt. He combed his hair and inspected his appearance critically. He didn't look as good as his trailer, but he was passable.

He had spent all evening, and into the wee hours of the night, cleaning. His dishes were washed, his rugs were vacuumed, all the trash was gone, and he had even dusted. The wall paneling looked a bit bland, but his mom had commented that it was refreshing. She had brought a plant with her, and put it in his living room, assuring him that it would impress any girl. Usually grimy windows were now clear and, for lack of a better method, he had run the vacuum hose over his curtains to get rid of the cobwebs. His place hadn't looked so good since the day he moved in. And he had done it by himself. He was really proud. His mother had wanted to stay and help him but Joe had insisted that he do it alone. Joe realized it was time to make a change in his life, and cleaning his place was just part of the bigger change. Of course, on some level, he knew Jill was a part of it. He had even persuaded his mom to accept money for laundry soap. To Joe's embarrassment, the woman had teared up. Shaking the image from his mind, Joe nodded at his appearance and set out to wait for Jill in the living room. He didn't have to wait long.

The dark steel door was open, allowing the living room to fill with light through the screen. The brunette poised her hand as if to knock but grinned when Joe waved her in. Today, she was a real vision. Her hair was freely flowing around her shoulders, contrasting with the cool green color of her t-shirt. Blue jeans covered her legs, leather sandals reflected her care-free nature. Her green eyes were enhanced by her clothing and by her welcoming smile.

"Hey, Jill. Come on in." Joe stood awkwardly.

"Hi, Joe." Jill angled into the living room, her eyes sweeping over the trailer walls and furnishings.

Joe grinned. "It's not much, but it's home." Her eyes caught everything, observed small details.

"It suits you."

"It does?" Joe had always thought of it as temporary, old, outdated. The loud colors never bothered him, but he never gave it much thought.

Jill didn't bother reaffirming, but rather leaned into Joe's CD tower, examining his titles.

"Would you like something to drink?"

"Pepsi?"

"Coming right up." He swung around the countertop, grabbing a glass from the cupboard, watching her inspect his plant. He almost hooted with laughter. *Thanks Mom,* he thought.

"I can't believe you have such a healthy plant. I can't grow the damn things at all," Jill commented glancing around the room, noticing lighter sections of paneling that must have held prints or posters at one time.

"Actually, I can't really grow them either. My mom gave me that one," Joe confessed, chuckling.

Jill rewarded him with a full smile. "Is she trying to domesticate you?"

"It's more like she's trying to marry me off."

"Ah." Jill accepted the glass of ice and a can of Pepsi without further comment.

Joe arched a brow at her lack of response, worried that he had said too much. "I just mentioned that you were helping me with my truck and Mom drew her own conclusions."

"So, we're going to get your truck moved and then get some groceries and have dinner?"

"That's the plan if you're still up for it. We should decide on what we're going to make though."

"We? I thought you were cooking me dinner," Jill teased, taking a swig of pop.

"I said I would take care of the steaks and you said you could make a salad or something. When we get done with the truck we can stop by and see what Sune's has for vegetables."

Jill nodded. "Okay, but I'll warn you that my salads are heavy on the green peppers and light on the onions."

"Sounds good." Joe grinned. "We could get some of those buns in a tube."

Jill grimaced. "It sounds so tasty when you say it that way, but I love those things too. When I was little, I use to try funny ways to pop them open and then take pictures of the dough."

Joe wrinkled up his face. "Odd," he said, deciding not to ask.

Jill laughed. "Do we need to get anything for the truck?"

"Like what?"

"Tow rope?"

"Oh. Nope, I have everything we'll need that way in my truck. I'm ready to go whenever you are."

"I'm ready. Although, I admit, hanging out with you is really slowing down the progress on my house."

"Well, I'll make it up to you by looking at that deck for you tonight." Joe inclined his head toward the door. "Let's get going."

Twenty-four

Beth had tossed and turned all night. Her grandmother, the woman she felt connected to above anyone else, had betrayed her husband. Could her real grandfather still be alive? It shook Beth's reality to the core. Lee was not her grandfather. Had her father known he was illegitimate? Beth didn't think so. Raymond had idolized his parents. He lived with his grandparents after his mother's death, and in Grandma Carol's diary, she said that no one knew who the father was. Beth reflected upon the two diary entries that she had read, unable to go further. Grandma Carol had commented that she might not deserve to go to heaven, which she must have thought because of her infidelity. Lisa would argue that cheating really wasn't that big of a deal anymore. Times, Beth contemplated, had certainly changed. It was almost too much to think about, and yet, Beth couldn't stop thinking about it.

Beth paced the floor. She checked her cell phone: No new messages. It was already Saturday and she needed to return to work on Monday. She moved through her morning rituals with all the attention of someone watching paint dry. When Lisa arrived thirty minutes later, she was shocked to find her friend on the couch.

"Beth, what's wrong?"

"My father's a bastard."

"What?! What did you find? What did he do?" Lisa was inflamed on her friend's behalf.

"No, I mean literally." Beth shook her head, her thoughts deadened. "Grandma cheated on her husband. Lee isn't my grandfather."

Lisa sank into the couch next to Beth, stunned. "Wow."

"Exactly." Beth rested her head on the back of the couch. "I don't even know who I am anymore."

Lisa smiled, in spite of the situation. "You make that sound like it's the end of the world."

Beth's smile touched her eyes. "It was just a shock, you know. I mean my grandmother had an affair. Grandparents are supposed to be sweet and innocent, and grandmas are supposed to make cookies and be loyal. My grandmother was an adulteress."

"This is more than just an affair, Beth. Your grandmother actually had a child by another man while married. That's a pretty big deal."

Beth nodded her agreement. "I can't even imagine what she must have gone through. She was convinced that she was going to hell. Can you imagine how she felt when she got sick?" Beth shivered involuntarily.

"You finished the diary then."

"No. I just read another chapter. Every chapter is just so…"

"Emotional?" Lisa supplied.

"Revealing." Beth took a deep cleansing breath. "I really need to get back to work. The Salvation Army is coming for those boxes today."

"Don't you want to talk about it?" Lisa inquired.

"I don't really have anything to say. It's surprising, but it doesn't really effect my life too much; and yet, I am so shocked by it. I wonder if Dad knew," Beth sighed.

"Did Carol say who your grandfather is?"

"No. No names."

"Beth, he could still be alive."

"I know. I did the math last night. So what?"

"You could have other family. Uncles, aunts, cousins. It's worth looking into."

Beth shook her head. "Why would I want to wreck someone else's life?"

Lisa rolled her eyes. "You're being a bit dramatic. It's not like you're looking for new siblings. This was a generation ago. Times have changed. If your brother read this, he's probably already searching. Don't you want to know who he is?"

"How? How would he know where to start?" Beth pursed her lips in worry. "There's absolutely no way of finding him."

Lisa rolled her eyes. "Are you for real? Carol might tell us who he is in the diary. And even if she doesn't, this is the information age! There are hundreds of ways to begin. Beth, it happened right here. There are probably answers right here in this community. It might not be too hard to dig up some information such as who were your grandparents' neighbors or friends. Hell, if you have a box of pictures somewhere, the answer's probably right before your eyes."

"Why would Grandma take a picture of a man she was sleeping with?"

"You're missing the bigger picture." Lisa growled with frustration. "Beth, do you really think your grandmother was a floozy?"

"All evidence points to 'yes.' Hell, read the diary. It's written in black and white."

"I'm talking about the kind of woman that goes into bars and hunts up different random men to take her home when her husband's away."

Beth hesitated, considered. "No."

"Exactly!" Lisa pounced on the agreement, rushing her voice to get her reasons across before Beth interrupted her. "If she had an affair with someone, it had to have been someone that they spent time with. It was probably a friend of Lee's or someone she went to high school with or a neighbor. Hell, it could even be someone who was in the military with your grandfather. I'm thinking they tried to stay away from each other and just keep it friendly, but passion drove them to each other. It has to be someone close." Lisa bounced to her feet, pacing, as ideas burst forth. Beth knew Lisa's argument made sense; she just needed to admit it.

Reluctantly, Beth nodded. "You're probably right."

"Of course."

"So, pull out the picture books and we'll get cracking."

Beth stood abruptly. "Okay, but I need to get this stuff done. First, I'll take this box out to the dumpster. Then we'll find the picture books. I think Richard put a box of them in the back bedroom with the stack of stuff we want to keep, if you wanted to look for it…"

"Actually, I brought that tea that you like so much with me, so I'm going to make a pot. You go take the box out, and when you come back, we'll find them together."

Twenty-Five

Jill pulled the camera and box of film off the passenger side of the Tracker and watched as Joe swung into the seat.

"Do you always travel with a camera?"

Jill laughed. "I never know when I'll see something really neat. On my way here this morning, I got some really great shots of deer."

"If you're taking pictures of deer, you'll be using rolls and rolls of film everyday on the creatures," Joe teased.

"I didn't say it was just any old deer," Jill retorted. "It was a mother and two babies. Their little spots were perfect and the sun was shining through the trees just right... a little fog hugged the ground. It's definitely going to be a keeper."

Joe smiled at her enthusiasm. "So, do you do the whole darkroom thing?"

"Yes. I rarely trust someone else with my film, but there aren't any darkroom's on Drummond. I'll have to rent time at the newspaper in the Sault or something." Jill's face took on an expression Joe hadn't seen before. "My God," she whispered. "Is that a bald eagle?"

Before Joe could respond, Jill was pulling the Tracker off to the side of the road. "There are two nestled in the tree there. Do you see that other one?" Joe pointed.

Jill nodded sharply and pulled a bag from the backseat, quickly changing lenses. In seconds the camera was to her way of liking, and she was leaning out the window bracing her arms against the sides to capture a clear shot. She snapped two before the eagles took flight and two more as they were arching into the partly cloudy sky. To Joe's utter shock, she climbed up and over the door, out onto the roof of the vehicle.

"Did you get it?" he called. His question was met with a loud "hush." Oops, he thought, Jill must be in the zone.

Moments later she slid back in through the window. "Okay, you can talk now."

"Did you get it?"

Jill beamed. "Fantastic shots, I think. It's amazing how much good stuff I've taken since I've been here. I have shots of owls, blue heron, deer, and now eagles. Plus countless other tree and flower shots." Jill set her camera by her side and shifted the car back into drive. "My agent is going to be thrilled."

"You have an agent?"

"Yeah. He sells my work for me, or tries to anyway." Jill gave a short mirthless laugh.

"Really? Have you sold much stuff?"

"Some. My pictures have appeared in six, or no, seven magazines. One of my pictures is in a calendar. One's part of a post-card."

"Is it all nature stuff?"

"No, not at all. My agent also knows a freelance writer who has me take pictures to go with his work. He writes mostly architectural articles, so those pictures are of interesting houses. But I only get to do that when the house is near me, or if I'm willing to travel. I think I like nature photography the best because it's more challenging. I can't control the owl's movements; I have to wait for the head to turn just the right way because it's animate. A building just stands there and needs the right angle, the right lighting."

"My dad feeds a bear, if you'd like to get some shots of her."

"Seriously?"

"Yep." Joe grinned, enjoying her expressions. "Are these for an assignment?"

"No."

"What are you going to do with all of them?"

Jill considered the question for a moment. "Joe, is there something that you ever did because you had to? Not for money and not because someone else wanted you to—but just because it was in you to do?"

"What do you mean?"

"I take pictures because that's what I do. From the first time I picked up a camera when I was eight, I was drawn to photography. Somehow, I knew that my greatest joys would be wrapped up in film. If I didn't have to do anything in this world, I would still take pictures just because I love it. It's more than love." Jill searched for the right words. "It's like air to me. For me, a paycheck at the end of a good run is a bonus... but I don't take the pictures just to get a meal out of them. I take the pictures because I *need* to. If I have the opportunity to sell them, that's great." She spared her eyes from the road for a moment and took in his face. In her mind, her memory snapped a picture of its own. "Are you that way about something?"

Impressed, Joe leaned back and thought about his own life. "When I was in school, the only thing I cared about was football. I lived and breathed sports. I had college recruiters talking to me in my junior year and coaches lining me up for better things, but none of it mattered compared to the rush of just being on the field."

"What happened?"

"I was in a car accident. After a game one night, we were partying out at the Bald Knobs. We were drinking pretty seriously but I thought I was good enough to drive home. I spun off the road and into a big tree. The car actually got wedged between two real big ones. I wasn't wearing a belt or anything and my left side got pinned and crunched a bit." Joe shuddered, purposefully lightened his voice. "Anyway, my football days were done. I still do these therapy exercises for my hand." Joe flexed his hand, the memory bringing back aches of longing. "Just stupid."

"That sucks."

Joe was pleased with the statement. He hated looking into the faces of pity and couldn't stand people who tried to make him feel better. It was why he spent most of his time in the bar, why he hadn't cared too much about losing a couple jobs; he was trying to break the 'poor Joe' attitude. Jill did neither of those; she listened and understood. Shaking himself out of the memory, he realized they had reached his truck. Jill drove ahead of it and did a U-turn to bring the Tracker out in front of Joe's truck, so they could use the Tracker to tow the truck in.

Joe hopped out and kicked his tire lightly by way of greeting. "Hey, Rust Bucket."

Jill pulled the camera out, inspired by a man who talked to his vehicle. She leaned against her vehicle and waited. Joe turned around, an easy grin lighting up his face, his youth caught as Jill snapped the shutter.

"Hey! I thought you were going to help me. Less steak for you."

Jill hooted with laughter, sticking her tongue out at him. She replaced the lens cap and set the camera on top of the truck. "What do you want me to do?"

He pulled out the tow rope from the back of his truck and tossed her an end. "Secure that end to your vehicle."

"I can't believe you carry tow rope around with you." Jill mumbled, completing the task.

"You should see what else I have in here."

She placed a hand on her hip, saucily. "Oh yeah?"

Joe chuckled and crooked a finger at her, watching her saunter over to him. He pointed down into the back of his truck, slid his arm around her lightly when she moved closer to look. Jill's gasp was music to his ears. Jumper cables, windshield fluid, a spare quart of oil, duct tape, bailing wire, flashlight, spare tire, tire iron, flares, silver blanket (exposure), bag of salt, and a first aid kit stared up at them. "For my 21st birthday, my friends threw a big bash—and they all went together and bought me this stuff." Joe grinned sheepishly. "I have a bit of a reputation for my truck not working real well."

Jill laughed. "I bet. Why haven't you gotten a new one?"

Joe grinned. "Too much time in the bar? No, actually, I've been saving for a new truck." He angled his head, gesturing inside the beast at a light blue water jug _ full of change. "I just haven't gotten one yet."

Jill's mouth dropped open. "Man, that's a lot of change."

"Yeah, there's probably close to a thousand dollars in there. I have a reputation for collecting change too. The guys on the crew are always giving me shit about it. It's amazing where you'll find coins though."

Jill arched an eyebrow, amused.

"I've got the guys trained to be on the lookout now. Hell, we even found a buck fifty at the lighthouse the other day. At the bar the other night, I found a toonie right beside my truck."

"What's a toonie?"

"It's a two dollar Canadian coin. The one dollar coin has a loon on it, so everyone calls it a "loonie." When the two dollar coin came out, everyone just called it a toonie."

"That's neat. I've never heard that before."

Joe laughed, looking into her eyes. The green irises were filled with rich gold, sparkling with life. The amusement slid from his face slowly. Tentatively, he brushed a locket of hair back from her eyes.

"Joe..." The word was a breath.

He stopped her from moving, by holding her arms gently. "No, let me say something." He breathed once, gathering courage. "I've been with quite a few women. Most of them were just for one night, but you're different. You're smart and you're funny... and I know I haven't known you for very long, but I like being with you. You're not all done up and yet you're so..." He ran his fingers through the dark brown hair, touched her face softly. "You're just so damn beautiful."

Her eyes widened in surprised delight, color danced into her cheeks at the compliment. She leaned back against the truck for support, breathless. "Wow, you don't waste any time."

It was all the encouragement he needed. He captured her face lightly in his hands and lowered his lips to hers. Gently, Joe pulled her closer to him, wrapped his arms around her. He had thought of this moment constantly since he met her. He expected her to be warm, and soft, and amazing. She was more incredible than he imagined. Long moments passed before he slowly completed the kiss and leaned away from her. Finally, he found someone that he might be able to be with, that wanted to just be with him. He left his eyes closed, enjoying her body next to him.

The honking jeep hauled him back to reality and had Jill pulling away from him. Bob hung his head out the window and whistled without slowing. "Uh oh," Jill laughed. "We've been caught."

Joe grinned, not wanting to move. "Looks like."

"Ah… maybe we should get moving."

"Alright, if we must." Joe sighed. "You know, everyone's going to start talking about us now."

"Why? Because some guy saw us kiss?"

"No, you don't understand yet, but if you stay here long enough, you will."

"Don't understand what?"

Joe shook his head, thinking of the right words. "Small towns have secrets, islands have none."

Twenty-Six

Beth heaved the box into her arms and made her way through the screen door out to the dumpster. She was forced to set the box down to open the creaking lid. Papers, unsettled by the air flow scattered across the nearly filled dumpster bringing an old manila envelope to Beth's attention. Without thinking, she picked it up and examined it. The return address was the Sault Ste. Marie US Coast Guard. It was bent and crinkled with age and with the evidence that it had carried something substantial. Beth peeked inside the edge, smiling at the appearance of a letter. She heaved the box into the dumpster, closed the lid, and returned to the house. "Hey, Lisa! I found something!"

"Huh?"

"I found a letter in the dumpster." Beth unfolded it carefully. "It's from the Sault Ste. Marie US Coast Guard. It's dated April 11th, 1959."

"59? Wasn't that the year your grandpa crashed?"

"It was the year Lee crashed, yeah." Beth nodded, reading.

"Dear Mrs. DeForge:

On April 9th, during a routine check of the DeTour Reef Lighthouse, we discovered a logbook with a letter written by Capt. Lee DeForge.

The evidence coincided with the details in the letter to substantiate the probable event that Capt. DeForge crashed near the lighthouse, and in attempt to survive, entered the lighthouse and signaled for help.

The Coast Guard has since searched the surrounding area again for any sign of your husband, to no avail. It is our belief that Capt. DeForge attempted to make his way from the lighthouse to land and did not complete the journey. Enclosed is the logbook we found. We offer our deepest sympathy for your loss.

Sincerely,

Capt. Gerald Givens
US Coast Guard
Sault Ste. Marie, MI"

"You've got to be kidding me!" Lisa exclaimed. "He crashed at a lighthouse?"

"According to this letter, yes. Why would this be in the trash?"

"And where is the logbook?" Lisa piped in.

Their eyes met, with their voices sounding in unison, "Richard."

Beth's frown creased her face, gave her undue age. "I wonder what it said."

Lisa was caught in her own thought track. "I wonder what Grammy Carol must have thought. It would have been horrible to see that right before her death."

Beth raised an eyebrow, questioning.

"Didn't she die in April?"

Speculating, Beth dug through the stack of papers on the tabletop until she retrieved her grandmother's death certificate. "April 8th."

"She didn't know they found him."

"They didn't find him! They found a logbook entry."

"Same thing. It proves that he crashed, and it pretty much proves that he died," Lisa argued. "Carol died without knowing. Richard must have found this and taken the logbook."

"If it was still there to begin with," Beth retorted but silently agreed with her friend's assessment. "Why would this make him leave though?"

"It doesn't matter why, it matters that it did. I'm sure that Richard is headed to this place, wherever it is."

"Why would he take the logbook and leave the letter?"

"He didn't leave the letter. He threw it in the garbage. How could he have ever figured that you would find it there?"

"Good point." Beth agreed, shuffling her thoughts. "I don't even know where this place is."

"Somewhere in Michigan."

"Michigan's pretty big."

"I have a road atlas in my car. Do you want to look for it?" Lisa offered.

"Yeah."

Lisa returned moments later with the atlas. She spread it out and flipped the pages to find Michigan's maps.

"Get your head out of the way, Li."

Lisa moved her head back. "I don't see it."

"Look at the legend. Look for Kincheloe Air Force Base, look for DeTour, look for…" Beth paused glancing at the letter. "Sault Ste. Marie."

"Got it! Sault Ste. Marie, so DeTour must be…" her voice trailed off momentarily. "There it is. DeTour Village and off the coast is the DeTour Reef Lighthouse! It's right here on the map."

Beth whistled. "That'd be a long trip."

"You could take I-90 all the way to Niagara Falls and cross into Canada. Drive up and around through Canada."

Beth groaned. "It'd be a seriously long trip."
"Not if you have company."

"What?"

"I'll go with you."

"I haven't even said that I was going," Beth argued.

"Beth, you know that's where your brother went. He must have gone there. And if he went there, he must have had a reason. I think it's a good idea to go find him." Lisa hesitated. "But what if it's just typical Richard?"

Beth frowned, considered. "It feels different this time, Li. It feels bad."

"Well then, I am definitely going with you."

"You have to go back to work."

"So do you."

"I can get out of mine though, you can't." Beth pointed out. "Besides, you have a big test on Wednesday."

"Shit." Lisa grumbled. "You still need to go though."

"There isn't any absolute proof that he went to this lighthouse," Beth muttered. "But it might be worth checking out."

Twenty-Seven

Jill drove the Tracker slowly into the Marathon station. "Joe, it looks closed."

"Yeah, it's cool. He sees my truck all the time. We'll just unhook it and leave it here." He was already hopping out, moving to unhook the tow cable. When they had the tow cable returned to the steel box and the truck settled, Joe indicated they were finished.

"We have to grab your jug of money still."

"Nah. It can stay in the truck."

"Joe, you didn't even lock your doors. We can't just leave it there. Someone will take it."

"No one will touch it."

"We can't leave it here," Jill insisted.

"I suppose that's the city girl in you, isn't it?" Joe ruffled her hair, teasing. "All right then, we'll put it in your Tracker, but I'll need help carrying it."

Jill nodded, opening the backseat door for them. Joe made the pretense of moving the jug to the edge of the door, thinking that she wouldn't be able to lift her end anyway. Without a groan of protest, the jug was suddenly up and moving, with Joe being dragged along by her momentum.

"Damned thing should have handles," she muttered.

Joe grinned, his arms wrapped around the bottom side of the jug. With an extra push of effort they plunked the change in Jill's Tracker. Jill covered it up with a jacket that had been in the backseat while Joe laughed at her. He eyeballed her for a moment, exhaling deeply. "You're tougher than you look."

"I've changed my mind. There might be a million dollars in that damned jug. New car money? Hell, it could be new house money." Jill guffawed. "It's heavy but it was worth it to move it." At his incredulous expression, she persisted. "Well, don't city people come to vacation here?"

"Sure." His easy agreement placated her.

"One of them could take it," Jill argued.

"Nah. We don't get those kind of people here. But if it makes you feel better to have it moved, I'm happy." He chucked her chin lightly with a curled hand.

"Well, you might have money to burn but I wouldn't want to lose it." Jill slid back into the driver's seat as Joe climbed in beside her.

"You're the one with the working car and house on the water who doesn't really work, Ms. Traynor."

Jill laughed at the formal use of her name. "A working car and house on the water costs money, Mr. Barber. And it's not that I don't work, I mean I *do* take pictures. I just don't have a nine to five job."

Joe arched an eyebrow, speculatively. She was strong and obviously motivated, just maybe, he thought. He considered the ramifications for a moment, as Jill pulled into the grocery store lot. "Do you want a job?"

"Well, ya, of course. I can get by for a time, but I'm never going to get my house projects done without a paycheck. I've been avoiding looking for one, because I don't want to work with tons of people or waitress or anything like that." Jill opened her door, but waited for him.

"How do you feel about working construction?"

"What would I have to do?" Jill countered.

"Errands mostly. Can you drive a boat?"

Jill rolled her eyes. "I'm not a complete city girl. Grandpa use to take me fishing all the time."

"I think the job might work for you then. You'd have to drive the boat back and forth, running to the hardware for supplies, keeping the tools organized, and doing a lot of clean-up."

"Your boss is looking for a new worker, though? Because I don't want you to go beg a job for me or anything," Jill stated evenly.

"He is. Actually, I don't get that raise I told you about until I get a new truck and a new worker for the crew. It can be really physical, but I think you might like it." *What would it be like to work with her?* Joe wondered.

"Well, it'd be really good to learn more about it in general. My grandparents' house, I mean *my* house, needs quite a bit of work."

Joe hesitated, hauling himself out of the car. "There's just one thing."

Jill matched his pace toward the grocery store. "What's that?"

"The guys are kind of… crude sometimes."

"My best friend is a firefighter who kick boxes so I can handle tough guys. I'll be just fine."

"How did you ever manage becoming friends with a firefighter? Do those guys normally associate with picture people?"

"First of all it's a she. Carly's as tough as they come; brutal, even. Say the wrong thing to her and prepare to lose your teeth."

Joe chuckled.

"I wouldn't be laughing, Joey. She's showed me some moves," Jill teased.

Nodding, Joe opened the door to the store for her, adding, "I'll remember that."

Twenty-Eight

SUNDAY MORNING

Whoever was touching his face was about to get slapped. He came up with a start, snarling. "What the hell?!"

"Joe honey, are you okay?"

He squinted, rubbing his eyes. "Ma?"

Mary Barber breathed a sigh of relief. "Alice got home from college last night and she told me that she didn't see you at the bar. Are you sick?"

"What time is it?"

"A little after eight," Mary brushed the hair out of his eyes.

Joe groaned. "Mom, it's Sunday morning." He wanted to weep. "What are you doing here?"

Mary ignored her son's questions and touched her hand to his forehead. "You don't feel overly warm."

"Mom! Why do you think I'm sick? I'm not sick," Joe pulled away from her, disgruntled.

"Last night was Saturday."

"And your point is?"

"You're always at the bar on the weekends. Alice just knew she'd be able to see you there. She was a little worried when you never showed."

"This island!" Joe vented. "I can't do anything without you knowing about it. Hell, everybody knows about it."

Mary sat on the edge of his bed, still concerned. "Did you go to a party or something then?"

"You make me sound like an alcoholic. No, I was home at a reasonable hour and I went to sleep."

"Sleep? Oh… you mean you had company." Mary frowned, realizing she could have walked in on them. Slightly embarrassed, she continued. "You should really get to know someone before you have relations with them, son."

"Dammit, Mom! I went over to Jill's for dinner. We cooked, we ate, we sat out by the water and talked, and then I came home alone. Period. Not that it is any of my sister's business." *Or yours*, he thought, but wouldn't say it.

Mary responded with momentary silence. "She must be really special."

Joe let the frustration roll off him with a deep breath, allowing Jill's face to fill his mind. "She is really special."

Mary grinned, showing the same full smile her son had inherited. "When do I get to meet her?"

"You don't." Joe grinned, seeing his mother's wounded expression. "Although she is the type of girl I would introduce to the family."

"Well, that's something."

"Thanks for the laundry, and the plant, and stuff. She actually noticed."

Mary giggled like a school girl, delighted. "I knew she would. Are you going to spend the day with her then? Maybe you could come over for lunch or dinner."

Joe bolted upright. "Shit! Oops, sorry Ma. I forgot that I hadn't looked at her deck. I told her I would yesterday, and when we got out there, I completely forgot about it. I should call her."

"Deck? Deck of what?"

"On her house."

"She has a house?" Mary's mouth was quizzical, her expression serious. "How old is she?"

"Twenty-two maybe? Something like that." Joe leaned back on his pillows, realizing his mother wasn't going to let him go anywhere until she had sucked him dry of information. She'd be pleased if she thought it was his idea to tell her. "Okay, okay. I'll tell you about her." Joe rolled on his side.

"First tell me how she has a house. I thought you said she was a summer girl."

"Her grandparents were friends of the Eby's, you know, down on Cream City Point?" Mary nodded for him to continue. "Well, her grandparents bought a house here, and Jill's parents died pretty early on, so she moved in with them. So... when they came up for the summer, she came with them. Her grandmother died a few months ago and left her the house here. It's a cute place, but it needs some work."

"Poor girl. She doesn't have any brothers or sisters?"

"No. Her only living relative is an uncle. He lives in Florida or something like that." Joe shrugged. "She's a photographer... you should have seen her taking pictures of these eagles yesterday. It was really great."

"Is she pretty?"

Joe said nothing for a moment, his eyes shifting around the room with his thoughts. Finally, they rested back on his mother's. "Yeah, she's pretty, smart... and different. She's not like," his speech fell away, a small smile crossed his face as he stared at the floor. "She's not like other girls."

Mary leaned back, watching her son's expression shift subtly. She had never seen him this way before. He looked softer, happier... *in love*. She realized Joe was becoming a man and changing right before her eyes. For the first time in years, her normal worries drifted away. Her son was going to be *okay*. She cleared her throat quietly. "Did you tell her about the bear?"

"I did. I'm sure she'll want to shoot it."

"Shoot it?" Mary was horrified.

"Take pictures of it, Mom. Geez."

"Oh, right." Mary stood, slowly. "I'm happy for you, honey. And I want to meet her. Sooner rather than later. It would do you good to come see your sister too. You haven't seen Alice in months."

Joe nodded. "Okay, but first I'm gonna call Jill."

Mary grinned. "I'll just let myself out. Oh, I put some of my blueberry muffins in your fridge."

"Hooya!" Joe raised his arms, a throwback to his football days, in delight. "Tell me you made them this morning and I'll love you forever."

Mary laughed, thrilled to see her son in an upbeat mood. "You'll love me forever."

Clad only in boxers, Joe jumped out of bed, scraped past Mary, intent on devouring the lot as he rounded the corner into the kitchen. "I bet Jill would just love one of these. She can't cook very well either."

"I'm gonna let myself out, Joe."

"Actually, do you think I could borrow your car Mom?"

"When are you going to buy a new one for yourself?" She countered.

"Soon. Please let me take it." Joe gave her that I'm-your-little-boy pout that she was helpless against.

Mary melted, relenting. "Okay, but you'll have to drive me home." Joe grinned all the way to the telephone. He punched the numbers in from memory and rolled his eyes at his mother's expression.

Jill answered quickly, breathlessly. "'Lo?"

"What were you doing?"

"Oh, hi. I was just about to go take some pictures of this turtle that I found. What are you doing?"

"My mom just dropped off a pan of blueberry muffins that she made this morning, and I thought you might like one. Also, I forgot to look at your deck yesterday."

"Okay, do you mind if I come get you after I'm done with the turtle?"

"Actually, I'll borrow my Mom's car so you won't have to."

"Great. I'll see you in a few minutes?"

"Yeah."

"If I'm not inside, I'll be near the shore photographing my turtle."

"Your turtle? Your flowers, your deer, your eagles. Pretty soon, you'll be calling it your island." Joe teased, laughing.

Jill smiled. "That wouldn't be so bad, would it?

"Nah. It wouldn't be bad at all."

"I'll see you in a few minutes."

"'Kay." Joe replaced the phone with a cheesy grin splashed on his face and faced his mother's raised eyebrows. "Never mind, Ma."

"Do you want to take a shower?"

Joe nodded, caught in the midst of a loud yawn. "Do you want me to run you home first?"

"No. I wanted to water your plant anyway. Go ahead."

Twenty-Nine

Nestled on a 200ft wooded lot on the south shore of
Drummond, Jill's home was a one story, 960 sq. foot house
built in the early 60s. Joe had recognized it last night as being
one of the first wave of summer residences that was built for
year round use. Before then, summer places weren't winterized
against the cold which would make them impossible to live in
during the colder months. The home style was a dark stained
wood with simple, basic windows flanking the wood & glass
back door. Stained to match was an old outdoor shed that
predated the home by several decades to his estimation. Joe
was still amused that she called the door facing the turnaround
the 'front' door. Last night he had explained that islanders refer
to the front side of their homes as the side facing the water, and
the driveway side as the back.

The back door was blazing open this morning, so Joe
pulled the screen door handle back and stepped into the
kitchen. It was definitely an efficient home, even if it was a bit
small to Joe's way of liking, but it seemed to suit Jill perfectly.
The house was designed well. Her prints and keepsakes created
a warm atmosphere. The walls throughout the home were pine
that had been light at one time but grew steadily darker with
age, providing a cozy atmosphere. The bedrooms were close
quarters, with the master bedroom offering a clear view of the
water.

She had colored the bedroom with matted and framed photographs that she had taken on a high school trip to Yellowstone. She had decorated the living room the same way. A photograph of her, as a baby, with her parents warmed the wall of the living room. The fireplace stood on the wall facing the water, centered between large French windows that reached nearly floor to ceiling. The fireplace was comprised of split hardheads which added to the ambience of the room. The five inch thick mantle, cut from the center of a pine tree, gave it Drummond Island character. Above the mantle was a quilted wall hanging that Jill had told him her grandmother had done for her. The piecework fabric depicted a brown haired girl leaning into a camera in front of a sunrise. Joe had loved it the moment he laid eyes on it and Jill had wistfully told him that it was her most cherished possession.

The living room was actually combined with the kitchen and dining room. The dining table was small and scarred, the kitchen was cheerful but built for efficiency. Hardwood floors met homemade pine cabinets, topped by a commercially made butcher-block style countertop. Her bright white microwave stood out against the varnished pine that had darkened over time. He speculated whether or not she had used the aged gas stove. He set the plate of muffins on the counter and avoided stepping on the freshly washed, dried, and vacuumed brightly woven rag rug. The night before it had been hanging over the back railing and Jill had amused him with her tales of hosing the mice shit off of it. He would have tossed the thing, but Jill was determined to keep it.

Beyond the window on the left of the fireplace, the front door was open. Realizing she wasn't in the house, Joe slipped through the front screen door and made his way over the deck down to the rocky shore. It took him several minutes to spot her. Joe's stomach rolled. The woman had climbed up a tree and was now leaning drastically away from it to capture something's image.

Not realizing that she had an audience, Jill wrapped her denim clad legs around the tree and arched her body to achieve just the right angle she was looking for. The brown long sleeved t-shirt had her partially blending in with the surroundings. Her hair was pulled back so that it didn't distract her. Below her, Joe held his breath as he saw what he thought were two snowy owls perched in another tree. They almost looked stuffed unless the viewer noticed the slight rustle of feathers, the occasional movement of their heads. He listened as Jill took her camera through the motions as one of the owls lifted its wings for flight. The second followed it and Jill began her descent.

"The owls are gorgeous! Are they nesting?" Joe called out.

Jill grinned down at him, craning her neck, climbing down. "I'm not sure. To be honest, I've never seen a pair of owls like that. I can't wait till I see the prints from it."

She lowered her foot to the ground and turned to smile at Joe. "What? No muffins? I'm starved."

"Inside." He took her hand as she made her way over the rocky ground. "My mom's muffins are really good."

"She brought them over this morning?" Jill inquired.

"Yeah, she heard that I wasn't at the bar last night and she got worried."

Jill stopped, eyes widened in surprise. "How could she possibly hear that this soon? And why would she be worried that you *weren't* in the bar?"

Joe laughed at her, pulling her along after him. "She was probably worried because I usually close the bar. She thought I was sick or something. News travels really fast here."

"Wow." Jill picked up a muffin and handed one to Joe.

"What?"

"I've never had to account to anyone that way."

"That must have been wonderful," Joe thought aloud.

"No, not quite," Jill shook her head. "My grandparents were great but they were older and they just kind of let me do what I wanted to. I had a penchant for returning at odd hours because I'd be working with the newspaper or hiking. They just got used to me. I think having a mom like yours would be amazing. For you to just know that somebody loves you so much… it must be the best kind of feeling."

Joe paused, let the blueberry linger in his mouth before swallowing. Finally, he nodded. "Honestly, it annoys me a little. But I know that my mom means well. She just feels the need to stop by, or lecture, or whatever if something's not up to her way of thinking. One time, when my trailer was really messy, she refused to come in for a month, thinking that I would clean it up." Joe shook his head, caught in the memory. "It didn't work. I wasn't ready to change."

"She sounds like a great mom." Jill smiled, tasting her muffin.

"She is."

"This is incredible. She makes them from scratch, hey?"

"Yeah. She doesn't do anything out of a box." After Joe swallowed his bite, he gestured outside. "Let's take a look at the deck."

"I'm a little nervous that you're going to tell me the whole thing needs to be replaced. I really don't want to undertake that kind of a project so soon, but I don't want to just leave it either. I've been walking on it since I got here but the boards don't feel right."

"Don't be nervous. We'll know in a few minutes."

"Do you need me to do anything?"

"Nope. It won't take me very long."

Jill nodded. "Sounds good. I'll put some coffee on and be right out."

Joe mumbled to himself as he crawled under the deck. He tapped and pulled at various boards, testing them.

Jill was perched behind the screen door, waiting. Impatient, she rocked back on her heels. "What's the verdict?"

Dusting himself off, he stood and stepped up onto the deck. "Good news and bad news."

"Shoot."

"The good news is that the deck is salvageable. The main structure and joists are fine. The bad news is that it needs quite a bit of work." Joe pointed to one board with a grimace. "See the hole in that one." He waited for Jill's nod. "Someone put their foot right through it because it got punky. The two right next to it and those," he said, pointing again, "all need to be replaced. The steps going down are rotting because they weren't put on blocks so the crossers need to be replaced. Some of the railings are loose in a few places but I think we can fix those with lag bolts. But there's another problem."

"What is it?"

"These boards are made from five/quarter pretreated lumber. They don't make this stuff anymore, so we'll have to replace the boards with cedar."

"Won't that look bad?"

"Nah. I think we can stain the cedar green to match the other boards. When we're all done, we'll put a wood sealer on the deck to stop this from happening. That's most of the reason why it happened in the first place; it hasn't been sealed in years."

Jill's face fell. "It's going to take me all month."

Joe chuckled, brushing her hair out of her eyes. "After we remove these boards, and get the materials, we can do this in a day."

She looked at him speculatively. "We?"

"Well, I have a little trade for you. I'll help you fix your deck and next Saturday you can take me to the Soo so I can buy a new truck. Afterward, I can take you out to dinner and a movie."

"That sounds more like a date then an exchange."

"Whatever it takes to get you to say yes." Joe's face lit up when he offered her a full smile. "Do we have a deal then?"

With eyes twinkling, Jill accepted. "We have a deal."

"If you grab me a piece of paper, I'll write down a material list for you. Then we'll go see if they have what we need."

"Will the lumberyard have this stuff?"

"Actually, we're going to a local mill. It'll take a week or so but we can get them started. The boards will need to be planed down so it'll be easier to get them there. On the way back, we can stop by my place and grab some tools and then we'll come back and tear up the bad boards. You'll have holes in your deck for a while and you'll have to watch your step but we'll put it all back together next Sunday."

Jill returned moments later with paper and pencil. She hesitated, her thoughts spinning audibly. "You don't have to help me with this though. I'd take you to the Soo anyway."

"I would be happy to help you." Joe touched her chin lightly, tilted her head toward his and kissed her. "It'll be fun."

Thirty

The grim gray road spoke of the journey ahead. Already weary of the journey, Beth knew she hadn't even begun the first real leg of the trip yet. Dark clouds rolled overhead splattering the car with droplets, while Beth felt herself begin to lose focus. Her senses had calmed to a dull ache, her thoughts were beginning to blur.

She was on her way to Ithaca, New York: home. The trip was actually going to set her back by several hours but was for the ultimate best. In order to make the journey to DeTour Village to find her brother, she wasn't going to be able to return to work. Since she hadn't held the position for long, she thought it was best to talk to her boss in person, and drop off some of the things from her father's house that she had gathered to keep. This way she could spend the night in her own bed, do laundry, take care of any mail or E-mails that might have arrived, and repack for the new trip. She made a mental note to stop at the pharmacy and have a prescription refilled, pondered whether or not she should visit her mother.

Tomorrow morning she would head for Michigan.

Thirty-One

Monday Morning

Joe struggled with a yawn as he pulled the seat belt over his lap and secured the metal tab at his side. "Did I mention that you needed to bring a lunch with you this morning?" He glanced at Jill pensively.

"No, you didn't. I remembered that you had a cooler with you the day I dropped you off. So I brought one."

"You remembered that?"

"I'm observant. Sometimes it's a curse. My mind is always filled with these little details that I notice. I have a hard time flushing them out of my thoughts," Jill shrugged.

Joe nodded, wondering what else she had noticed, what had caught her eye about him. He sat with his thoughts, allowing comfortable moments of silence to pass as the Tracker ate up asphalt underneath them. He looked over, humorously seductive. "I thought of you this morning."

"Oh yeah?"

"I caught a mouse," Joe deadpanned, remembering the stories she had entertained him with the evening before.

The declaration caused Jill to hoot with unexpected laughter. "That's great! You have no idea how many of those little buggers I've caught since I've been back. I haven't seen one in days though."

"You're going to have the same kind of problem come fall though, you know."

"What do you mean?"

"When it gets cold the mice will want to climb back in. They'll want to spend the winter where it's warm."

"No way. They can't."

Joe chuckled at her seriousness. "Yes, they will."

"No, I mean they *can't*. I plugged the holes."

"With what?"

"Steel wool and canned spray foam. There is no way those little monsters are getting back in. The guy at the hardware set me right up with what I needed and told me how to do it. I went all the way around the base of the house with the stuff and I even put D-Con out underneath. They're *not* getting back in." Jill was adamant. "Once I get the bugs gone for good, I'll be good to go."

"How much stuff did you buy for the bugs?" Joe slanted his eyes at her.

"Lots. Terro, ant traps, Raid spray. You name it, I got it." Jill grinned, slowing her car as it rounded the final corner.

The blue Tracker pulled into the parking lot ten minutes before the boat was scheduled to leave for the lighthouse. Pete and Gary had already arrived and appeared to be shooting the shit with some tourist. Joe gestured toward Jill as he slung his tool belt around his hips. "Hey, Boss!" Joe called out, waving.

Pete signaled for him to come over. When they were within talking range, Pete tapped his watch and clutched his chest with affected shock. "You're early. You're never early."

Joe laughed. "It's all Jill's fault. Pete, this is my positive influence and your new employee. Jill Traynor, Pete

Dombrowski." Pleased with himself, Joe leaned back grinning. "I got a replacement for Billy, I'm getting a new truck on Saturday, and now I get a raise. Hooya!"

Pete raised an eyebrow and chuckled awkwardly, looking Jill over. "I got a replacement for Billy too. Joe, this is Dick DeForge."

"Glad to meet ya, Dick." Joe stuck out his hand, meeting Dick's softer grip. "This is Jill Traynor. And this is Gary, one of the guys," Joe added helping to welcome the new guy.

Greetings were exchanged all around followed by a lingered glance between Pete and Joe. Pete shrugged, "It's okay. It was your job to bring someone in and you did." Pete met Jill's eyes. "Joe did tell you that this is construction, didn't he? This isn't a job most young ladies aspire to."

"I spent yesterday afternoon tearing up my deck, sir. I can handle this job. Joe said it would be mostly errands and clean up, but he said I'd get a chance to learn."

"You want to learn construction?"

"My grandparents left me a house that needs some work." Jill smiled before adding, "Construction's expensive, so I'd rather learn how to do it myself."

"Bite your tongue, woman." Pete chuckled deeply, looking Jill over, contemplating. He had never had a female employee before, but this one had spunk. "I'll hire you on one condition."

Jill raised an eyebrow, waiting.

"Don't ever call me 'sir.' The name is Pete, or 'hey you,' but not sir. You make me feel like an old man." Joe laughed at this and waved to Bob who was approaching more quickly then usual. "And don't take any shit from anyone. Now, you and Dick are new on the same day—so you both take orders and directions from everyone. I expect a fair day's work for the pay, and I expect you to show up on time. The first day you don't make it to work on time you lose your job. At the end of the week, if you're both still around, I'll give you a raise. Any questions?"

Jill shook her head, Dick mumbled 'no.'

"I'll need you to stop by my house some time this week and give your information to my wife. Social security number, address, and stuff like that. It wouldn't hurt to call Kate, Joe, and remind her that you just got a raise." Pete offered him a wide smile, with a wink in Jill's direction. "You never know, I may forget to mention it to her."

Joe chuckled, signaling Bob over. "Bobby, this is Jill Traynor. Jill, this is Bob."

Bob let his hand linger in hers and chuckled. His eyes roamed over her body, stopped in her eyes. "I'm going to be thinking of reasons to get to work earlier and earlier if it means I get to work with you."

Jill widened her eyes with affected innocence. "I'm glad you think I'll make a good carpenter, thanks."

Bob shook his head, grinning. "You're too fast for me."

"Just wait until you see what I can do with a hammer," Jill countered.

Bob laughed and slung his arm around her shoulders. "Come on, Jilly. Tag along Dick, I'll show you the boat."

Pete shook his head. "Gary, take Dick and Jill over to the boat and start loading the barge. I need to talk to Bob and Joe for a minute. This weekend I got us another job. It's a decent sized deck out in Bass Cove. I thought I'd send you guys out to work on it."

"Actually, Pete, if it's just the same... Jill is a damned good worker, and she'd like to learn more about decks specifically. It'd be real good if you'd let her come too."

Pete shook his head. "I can't spare three of you from the lighthouse. I could send just you and Jill."

"Just me and Jill?" This raise really means more responsibility, Joe thought, surprised.

Bob howled. "Ha! Little jack rabbit Joe wants to be paid to play with his woman."

Joe rolled his eyes. "No, it's not that. Jill and I work well together. I just didn't think you'd let me run something like that."

"Damn, Joe. How many decks have you helped me build?"

"Lots, but you were always right there."

Pete eyeballed him. "Can you handle it or not?"

Joe hesitated for the barest of moments. "I can handle it."

"Between the sheets, maybe." Bob shook his head, needling. "Bad idea, Pete."

Pete entertained Bob's idea and thought to mention the rules. "Don't even think that I'm paying you to score, son. Find your own time to do that. It's lucky that I'm hiring your little minx in the first place. I can't keep her on if the work suffers."

"If you're worried about me and Jill, send her with Bob to do the deck and I'll stay at the lighthouse. I don't need to work with her. She wanted a job somewhere, and I needed to find a worker." Joe kept his voice casual. "I just want her to be able to learn about deck construction."

Bob leered. "Hell, yes, send her with me. That's a great idea. I'll make her do all the bending and the…"

Pete shook his head, chuckling. "No, she can go with Joe. But dammit Joe, you keep your hands off of her on my nickel."

Joe nodded seriously.

"Pete… maybe you don't remember, since Kate's pregnant and all and probably a little moody, but you didn't get much out of that promise. There are lots of things the kids could do without Joe using his hands."

Pete rolled his eyes. "Bob, go replace Jill at the barge, and dammit, clean it up a little. We don't need to scare her away in the first fifteen minutes. Joe, the two of you can head right out there. I have the directions and address for the house in the truck so you won't miss it. I also have a drawing of what the new deck will look like. Let's go look at it. It'll be easier for you to understand it, if you can see it."

Joe followed Pete to the truck, listened to his instructions carefully. When Joe agreed that he understood, Pete lowered his voice. "Joe, I know this out of the ordinary, but I'd like you to stop in and check on Kate. I don't want you to tell her about this, it's just that I'm worried about her. If she needs anything hauled, or anything at all, just go ahead and help her out. Maybe Jill would throw in some laundry for her or something. Take as long as you need, and just write down the time you head out to the deck job."

"No problem, Pete." Joe's forehead creased with worry. "Is the baby giving her a tough time?"

Pete nodded somberly. "The doctor's worried about her exerting herself too much. I'm worried that she won't listen to his instructions and just go on with her routine, thinking she can handle it. I've had a talk with the kids, but…"

"It's cool. I'll call you on the cell and let you know how she is."

Pete exhaled, relieved. "Good. That works. Thanks Joe. You can take my truck and drop Jill's car off by the house. I'll get a ride back with Bob. Tools are in the back. The materials will be delivered from the lumberyard before noon, but just focus on the tear down. If you have any questions, just call me. If you want to stop by after work, or hell, just give me a call— tell me how the day went."

Thirty-Two

Kate greeted the pair with an easy smile and waved them in. "Hey, Joey." The bright yellow sundress accented her long hair, her petite frame. Bare feet peeked out at them and Kate matched the cheerfully painted toenails with a welcoming smile.

Joe smiled at the pet name. Jill stepped in behind him, surprise coloring her face. "Kate, I'd like you to meet a friend of mine, and one of your new employees, Jill Traynor. Jill, this is Kate."

Kate offered her hand, which Jill accepted warmly. "Are you surprised that I'm Pete's wife? Don't feel bad. Most new workers are. I think they expect a contractor to be married to someone with some strength."

"Katie has strength alright, it's just not in her arms," Joe teased.

Jill grinned, liking her already. "I never would have guessed that you're pregnant if Joe hadn't told me, but I don't doubt your strength."

Kate patted her stomach lightly, her face contorted in a look of horror as an idea filtered through. "Pete didn't hire you to do cleaning did he?"

Joe laughed at Jill's mirrored look of horror. "Nope. Jill is going to be working construction. I brought her in as Billy's replacement. We're going out to do that deck job today."

Kate nodded, relieved. "Well, that's something. That man is just paranoid. He sent you to check in on me, didn't he?"

Joe shrugged, sheepish.

"Well, you can have a little snack on the way out then, can't you? Iced tea and oatmeal cookies? I baked them last night."

"We'll sit and have a snack only after you give us some chores. Do you need laundry hauled downstairs?" Joe's concern was evident in his gaze.

Kate started to shake her head, and Jill stopped her by gently placing a hand on her arm. "It's my first day at work, and if you don't give us some chores Pete might not be too happy with me. I'd feel better if you'd let me do something because I'd like to keep this job. I don't think he was too thrilled about hiring me."

"Oh, that's right. That other man got a job from him the other day too." Kate arched an eyebrow at Jill's determined gaze. Joe leaned against the counter, waiting to see how Kate would refute Jill's argument to help. Kate was stubborn as a mule, Pete often commented. Something changed in Kate's eyes, and to Joe's amazement, she nodded. "There are two laundry baskets full of clothes downstairs that I need up here to fold. And there's laundry in the bathroom hamper that needs to go down. Joe, why don't you go grab the mail for me? And Kyle's bicycle is out in the middle of the driveway again. He says something's wrong with it. Could you look at it and put it back in the garage?" Joe nodded, rushing off. "Oh yeah, Joe!" Kate yelled after him. "Pete is grilling burgers tonight, so could you scrape down the grill?"

"Yeah, I'll clean it up!" Joe called.

Kate smiled while patting her stomach and said more to herself than Jill, "Then, we can sit and have a snack. Junior needs to eat."

"Do you know if it's a boy or a girl?"

Kate's eyes twinkled. "No, not yet. We haven't come up with any names either."

Jill grinned. "So, where's the laundry?"

Kate led Jill toward the bathroom and held the door for her. "To tell you the truth, I'm surprised that my husband did hire you. He doesn't like me to be around the guys too much because of their language so I'd think that he would take one look at you, since you're so pretty, and recommend that you work somewhere else." Kate rested her face in her palm and sighed.

"I don't mind the language at all. I can do the job, and I told him so. If he's not assured, he can always fire me. But he said he'd give me a week."

No longer interested, Kate changed the subject. "How long have you been dating Joe then?"

Jill came up with a startled expression. "Well, I met him a couple of days ago. I don't know if I'd call it dating yet. I'm really just getting to know him."

Kate led the way to the stairs and leaned against the banister while Jill made her way down. "I've never quite seen him so taken with a girl before. I mean he dates and everything, but he wouldn't have helped one of them get a job." Her voice raised a bit as Jill disappeared from view momentarily. She smiled as she saw the younger woman come back up the stairs. "He's a real doll, isn't he?"

Jill responded with a question. "You've known each other a long time?"

"Honey, on this island everybody has known everybody for a long time. Joe's been here since birth, and I've been here

longer than that. His mom is just a wonderful lady. I use to
baby sit him and his sisters when he was really little." Kate
hesitated for a moment, leading them back to the kitchen.

"You barely look old enough." Jill laughed at Kate's
expression.

"Oh, honey. You really do want to keep your job. Trust
me, I'm older than I look. I have an eleven year old daughter, a
son and another one on the way—I'm old enough." Kate's eyes
sparkled. "It's my small size and, of course, the hair. I keep
thinking I should cut it, but I never end up doing it."

Jill's eyes rested on the other woman's cheerful face. "I
can tell that Joe really admires you."

Kate winked. "If there's anything you want to know
about him, I wouldn't mind dishing."

"Thanks. I'll keep that in mind. So, that's how Joe
started working for your husband then? Because you're close to
him?"

Kate shrugged. "Do you know about the accident Joe
was in?"

Jill nodded. "Yeah, he's told me about it briefly. I don't
know the small details, but I think I get the picture."

"Joe tried working other jobs, but he wanted to make
more money. This is his first carpentry job, and I think he likes
it. He almost lost it a few days ago though... he has a hard time
getting up in the morning when he spends most of the night
before in the bar."

Jill nodded. "I know. I gave him a ride that morning.
That's how we met."

Kate's laugh was loud, contagious.

Jill rubbed her ear, grinning.

"Well, Joe could use a little good luck. I'm glad fate
brought you two together." .

Thirty-Three

Pete leaned back against the wall, regaining his breath. Bob had loaded too much material onto the winch the last time, so Dick and he had pulled the last load bodily onto the deck, then hauled it onto the grated catwalk just inside the lighthouse's storm doors. Bob and Gary had both moved on to the next job, while it had taken Dick moments to steady his pulse. He leaned against the railing, gazing at the floor below. Steel grated flooring bordered the level in a pathway, arching over a large room positioned in the concrete base of the lighthouse.

Pete looked the younger man over. He had a good fifteen years on the kid, and he hadn't been beaten up by the haul. "Come on, Dick. We're burning daylight."

Richard staggered up the staircase to the living quarters behind Pete. "What is it that we're working on? Are we working on the bathroom or kitchen at all today?"

Pete motioned him to follow, while he squeezed past the packaged windows leaning against one wall of the hallway, into the dining room, and finally the kitchen. Doors were propped open with blocks for easy movement. "The deconstruction is all finished here, but we'll need to make some repairs to the cabinets. We've already removed the doors. New paint and new countertops will make them look a whole lot better. We're saving the sink, but the faucets were shot so we have new ones here, in this… shit! I brought up the wrong crate. Listen, run down to the catwalk downstairs and bring up the other box that looks like this." When Dick hesitated, his attention still on the place where the sink obviously had been, Pete snapped his fingers.

"Oh, right." Dick muttered, moving out of the kitchen to complete the order. His footsteps slowed as soon as they passed through what had once been an office. His eyes skimmed walls and spaces looking for hiding places. He dawdled until he heard Pete's yell. "Move your ass, Dick!"

When Dick returned, Pete grabbed the crate from him quickly. "What are those big boxes in the hallway?" asked Dick.

"They are brand new replacement windows for these," Pete responded, gesturing to the two windows in the kitchen. His gesture widened to encompass the walls and the rest of the room. "I have sub-contractors to do the electrical work but we'll be doing the rest in here and throughout the lighthouse."

Richard nodded, brushing past the windows and the patchy, peeling walls with disdain, focusing on the sink area. "So, who had all the fun ripping out this old plumbing?"

Pete gave the younger man a sideways glance, surprised at the attempt to learn about the job and the coworkers. "One of the guys."

"Did they find anything in the sink?" Dick was insistent, even as he helped Pete tote a crate over to the work area.

Pete crooked an eyebrow. "Why would they find something?"

Dick shrugged, off-handedly. "Interesting stuff gets lost down the drain all the time."

"Not any more. They put traps or screens to stop silverware from getting caught in there. Although my wife loses spoons into the garbage disposal once in a while." Pete shuddered. "It makes a helluva noise."

"The sinks in this lighthouse must have been really old though, right?"

"Yeah."

"They wouldn't have had those screens or traps then, right?"

Pete nodded. "You're right, but it's beside the point since nothing was found."

Dick rephrased his earlier question. "So, you took the pipes apart yourself?"

"No. I told you that one of the guys did."

"Which one?"

Pete scratched his head, pulling out materials, half listening to Dick's attempted conversation. "What the hell... oh there it is."

"Pete, which one?"

"Oh, ah... Gary, I think." Pete handed Dick a box of new kitchen cupboard handles. "I want to get all the supplies we could possibly need out here. I've been really careful to think through every detail. For example, that countertop was selected by the DRLP society members. It's a unique size, and it took several weeks to get it made to fit so it had to be ordered a long time ago. Those little details trip up the job if it's not well thought through. It's the side trips to the hardware that really kill the budget," Pete nodded to emphasize the importance, chattering on to Dick.

Realizing he was expected to comment, Dick swallowed audibly. He hadn't been listening to Pete's rambles at all. He was focused on getting Gary alone to discuss the plumbing. He needed to find out from him directly if there had been anything found in the pipes.

"Gary looks like he needs help."

Pete arched an eyebrow as Gary struggled with bringing one of the countertop segments through the door. "He can handle it."

"If he drops it, or damages it, you'll be set back weeks, won't you?"

"Yah, okay. Gary! Set that down and grab Bob to help you with that." Pete called. Dick rolled his eyes inwardly, annoyed that the plan didn't work. *Patience*, he reminded himself, was going to get him the answers he needed.

Hours later, just after lunch, Dick was granted his opportunity. Bob popped his head into the kitchen, calling for Pete's help with some other task. "Dick, give Gary a hand here. Just do what he tells you."

Pete followed Bobby into the keeper's room just as Bob slid the new molding out of the box. "It's the wrong stuff isn't it?"

Pete examined it closely. "Nah. It's just not stained. We were told that it would come to match this shit here." Bob waved toward the molding that didn't need to be torn down and replaced. "It needs to be considerably darker."

Pete nodded, glancing at his watch. "Why don't you take the boat in for the last load? Run to town and get the stain you need."

"Sounds good, boss." Bob gained his feet, brushed his pants off. "How do you think the new guy will work out?" He asked, his voice lowered.

Pete shrugged, contemplating. "Hard to say, really. He seems easily winded, but that should fade in time." He turned to continue on the task at hand but turned back. "Bob, why don't you call my cell phone before leaving the hardware? Just in case we need something else."

"No problem."

"Actually, we should make a habit of doing that. I need to cut time out of this job anyway that I can."

"Over budget?"

Pete nodded, "Get moving, Bob. We're burning daylight."

"All right, John Wayne." Bob teased, slipping out the door. Pete was a big Western fan, often mimicking John Wayne's accent. Once in a while, one of the guys ragged on him for it.

Across the lighthouse, Dick waited for the right moment to bring the drainpipe up again.

Thirty-Four

Joe wiped the sweat from his forehead and took a deep, cooling breath. They were making excellent time on the tear down. They had spent the day working solid hours, making headway, energized by each other's company. Joe was proud of himself, thrilled that it hadn't been too difficult to keep his word to Pete. Jill did things efficiently, worked diligently. Gladys, the home owner, provided them with fresh glasses of lemonade at every turn.

Jill flexed her arm, to Joe's amusement. "You know, if I keep at this construction stuff, I am going to be built by the end of the summer. I can just feel my muscles growing."

"Maybe you can take on your friend eventually."

"Ha! It would take more than muscles. I've never seen her lose a fight. She has lost fights before but I didn't see them. I just helped her deal with them afterwards. She hates losing."

"How long have you known her?"

"Five years?" Jill asked herself, nodding in answer. "A little over five, maybe. We were roommates' during our freshman year of college."

"I thought you said you didn't really go to school." Joe countered, carefully prying a board up with a crowbar.

"Well, I didn't graduate with a four year degree or anything, but I definitely went to school." Jill spared a glance over her shoulder. "What are you doing? Why are you being so careful with that?"

"Tell me what this is made from," Joe requested, laying the board atop another that he had separated from the pile. They had backed Pete's truck up to the edge of the deck. All the rubbage was heaved directly into the truck, while Joe set the salvageable boards in a separate pile.

"It's the same thing my deck's made of, isn't it?"

"Yep. You need eleven good boards. I think we might be able to get that many out of this deck. Some of these are in good shape." He winked at her and then concentrated on his work.

"Can we just take them?" Jill thought the scenario sounded a bit underhanded.

"They'd be going to the dumpster anyway. Pete won't mind a bit."

"Wow. That's really great. What about the ones we ordered yesterday though?"

"I know the guy real well. I'll just call him and tell him what happened. He'll be cool, don't worry about it."

"If you keep this up, I'm going to have to buy you dinner." Jill smiled, re-energized in her task. Peaceful moments passed before she bumped into her next question. "Why didn't you ever try school?"

"I'm not smart enough." Joe thought about that for a moment, tossed the board into the pile at the foot of the deck. "Maybe it just wasn't for me."

Jill nodded, accepting. "Where did you work before here?"

"I worked at the lumberyard in summer breaks during high school. After school, I worked at the golf course mostly. I had shorter run jobs with other places, but mostly the golf course." He pried another board loose. "What kind of jobs have you held?"

"Mostly odd jobs, or assignment type jobs. I worked for a newspaper for six months though, taking pictures and running errands. That got me a job taking forensic pictures for the local PD. I did work for a little pizza place for a summer. It went under, though."

Joe grinned. "Couldn't cook, hey?"

"I did okay. My grandma got sick, and I quit so I could take care of her." Her voice quieted. "I took small jobs after that, but nothing with regular hours. I attended seminars and week-long classes every once in a while. I did a study of my grandmother in different kinds of lighting. That's one of the ones I sold to a magazine. My agent fell in love with it."

"Do you have a copy?"

"Yeah. I have files filled with negatives and prints that I've done. My agent stores quite a bit of stuff for me because I haven't landed anywhere yet. He says I need a bigger selection, which is part of the reason why I'm out at all hours grabbing new images. I may bring more of it up here, but I have a list of projects that I want to get done first. If I end up staying here for more than just the summer, I'll want to turn the back bedroom into a darkroom. Or maybe even the little shed out back. Would it be hard to run electricity out there?"

"No, not at all, but I don't think you'd want to use that building. That thing's really old, Jill. It might be pretty dilapidated structurally. The roof didn't look so great on it." Joe glanced at his watch. "I have an idea."

"Shoot."

"Well, it's almost lunchtime. Typically, we'd just stop what we're doing and eat, but we are really close to having this thing disassembled. If we work until we have this ready to go to the dumpster, we can eat in the truck on the way over. When we get back, we'll load the rest of this stuff in the truck, with your boards on the bottom so we don't throw them away. Then we can start putting the new deck together. I think we can get a good portion of it done."

"Sounds good. But what exactly goes into that?" Jill asked, continuing with her task.

Joe added another good board to Jill's pile. "First we mark out where to put the joists. See that tree?" He pointed at a tree until she nodded. "We're going to build the deck out so it goes out and around it. We'll use two by eight, on sixteen inch centers for the floor joists. They support the floor boards of the deck. They're also attached to the four by four posts that set on top of concrete blocks that go to the ground. When we get the support structure built, we can put the floor boards on top and then see if they'd like some built in benches or chairs."

"There's quite a bit to this deck stuff." She rubbed her sun-pinkened nose.

"Yeah, like railings, stairs, and sealer. We also build decks with hot tubs and even gas or charcoal grills. We can build them around trees, with or without benches and flower boxes."

Thirty-Five

"Did you find anything when you took the plumbing apart, Gary?" It had taken Dick two hours to work the conversation around to the sink pipes, and he viewed himself as a skilled communicator. Gary was not a talker. At very best, the man shook his head or nodded and sometimes downright glared when Dick spoke.

"Huh?"

Dick repeated the question, enunciating each word and yet keeping a bland, careless expression pasted to his face.

Gary grunted.

Lost at what the sound meant, Dick envisioned himself throttling the man if he didn't get a clear answer. Maybe he should try a different tactic. "My great grandmother once lost her diamond engagement ring down the sink drain. My great grandpa had to tear it all apart and get it out, and the next damned day she did it again. It was the running joke of my family forever. It's become legendary in the town even. It's interesting what kind of stuff ends up in sink drains."

Gary didn't acknowledge Dick's speech.

"I was just thinking that maybe something like that could have been found in one of the sinks' drains here. Did you find anything in the drain?"

"Shit, how would I know about that? Bob tore apart the plumbing." For Gary, it was if he had spoken a novel.

Dick was torn between being absolutely frustrated and totally relieved that he had finally been given another direction in which to look. Dick grabbed the edge of the window, repeating the process that he had been helping Gary with all afternoon. The replacement windows were made to match the originals. In the end, it would be difficult to tell which ones were new.

Across the lighthouse, Pete was just about to start muttering about Bob taking so long getting the materials when he heard the boat pull up. He slid through the door and glared down at Bobby as he climbed his way up with a sack hanging from his back. "Dammit, Bob. What took you so long?"

"Take a look at the boat I came in. There's trouble with the motor on the other one. I had to wait until the guy got back from his lunch break to help me out with it and try to get it fixed. In the meantime, we're gonna have to use this one here. Thank God we got most of the materials in already."

Pete raised an eyebrow. "Is it serious?"

"Nah. It just needs a part that they didn't have, but it won't be hard to fix. Sorry, Pete."

Pete waved it off. "Well, it's quitting time by now." He held the door for Bob and called for the others. "Come on, guys. It's time to pack it up and call it a day."

Dick breathed a sigh of relief. The men gathered their lunch pails and traversed the ladder back into the boat. Bob sat up at the front of the boat with Pete, leaving Dick to sit by Gary.

"I gotta leech a meal off my mom or something tonight. You know, my birthday's tomorrow. It should be good for a free meal a day early shouldn't it?"

Pete nodded, chuckling. "Yeah. Remember, this is only Monday. Just because it's your birthday doesn't mean you can be a slacker and not show up to work for the rest of the week."

"Boss, you know I always get to work on time. I'm just gonna go out and drink a little tonight and quite a bit tomorrow, but I'll still make it to work." Bob turned toward the back of the boat. "I fully expect you guys to show up for my birthday and buy me a beer." Gary grunted and Dick nodded.

"Ah, shit!" Pete exclaimed. "I forgot to scrape the damned grill and Kate wants me to cook tonight."

"Kate will have it all clean for ya, won't she?"

"No. I told her she better not lift a finger. She needs to rest."

"Yeah right. I got a twenty saying it's clean when you get home," Bob taunted.

"Shit, Bobby! Didn't you just say you were going to bum dinner and hit everyone up for free drinks? If I won, what would I get? An IOU?" Pete chuckled. "Anyway, what do you take me for? I wouldn't take that bet because I know you're right."

Bob's face was brightened by the full spread grin. "I always am, boss."

Thirty-Six

Quinn wouldn't be human if he didn't appreciate a show.

Marci stretched her body against the pool table, purring seductively, putting on a little entertainment for Quinn and the patrons. She wore a shirt, if it could be called a shirt that was nothing more than material draped across her chest held by taut strings tied at her back. Her pants were molded to her body, and once again, she had the attention of every man in the bar. She brought the pool stick up to her chest, gyrated teasingly against it, catching Quinn's gaze and throwing back a playful wink. The man hovering over her was a fisherman and one that she had taken home in seasons before. She gave him a flirtatious twitch of her backside and sauntered up to the bar. She flipped a cigarette out of the pack and leaned forward to let the bartender light it for her.

Quinn smirked and flipped the Zippo open. Jumping to life, the flame licked the end of the cigarette. "Got your hooks in the fisherman early tonight, hey? I'm surprised you didn't wait and see who else would show."

Marci lifted her shoulders delicately. Her eyes never left Quinn's. "If you'd ever let me, I'd sink my hooks into you." She accented the comment by keeping her eyes on his, inhaling deeply.

"That wouldn't be nearly as entertaining as watching you in action every night. Why this guy?" Quinn questioned. The bar was slow tonight; he had time to chat. "He doesn't look like your normal selection."

"He's married and he's good to me."

Quinn swallowed the ice cube he had been sucking on. "No kidding?"

"It's so much easier to be with men who don't have the icky notion that there should be a relationship. Some men don't have to be pressured into buying a woman gifts." Marci smiled, at Quinn's amused expression.

"Unreal." He leaned forward, conspiratorially. "Is he any good though?"

Marci shuddered. "A lady never reveals such things." She leaned forward, inhaling from the cigarette deeply. "So, whose the loner over at the table there?"

Quinn shook his head. "I don't know. I haven't seen him in here before."

"He's cute."

"Well, maybe he'll be in tomorrow," Quinn teased.

Tami moved right past Marci and sat down. "Hi Quinn. How are you tonight?"

"Better, now that I've seen you." Quinn grinned at her, tossed the bar towel over his shoulder. "How are you?"

Marci simmered. For all the pseudo-sexual encounters she had shared with Quinn, and all the seductive gestures she had used on him, he never asked about her person, how she was, what she did that day. Quinn never even touched her. This damned pale-faced brat always had him going the extra mile.

"Not bad. The day flew by since we were busy at the store. Joe said he was probably going to stop by later, and I know Alice is home now, so I thought I would come by too."

Tami blushed at the mention of Joe's name. She had adored him since high school, and she talked Quinn's ears off about it regularly.

"Do you want the usual, Tam?" His eyes were comforting, friendly.

She nodded, slipping out of her jacket.

Marci's eyes narrowed. "So, you're not even going to say hi to me?"

Tami glared at Marci. "Leave me alone, Marci." Quinn slid her drink across the counter to her, winked.

"Ouch. Where'd all the hostility come from?"

Tami sipped from her drink and ignored the other woman.

"You'll be singing a different tune when your dear Joey comes in, won't you?" Marci kept up the stream of chatter, the innocent tonal quality of voice. The change in Tami's expression had Marci gloating. "So, you've heard that I sunk my nails into Joey, hey? Its too bad that he's seeing someone now. Couldn't get him yet could you? My, he is worth getting too." Marci looked down her nose, laughed haughtily. Her voice eased up considerably as she exhaled. "You could have had him if you had lightened up a little. You're such a prude, Tami."

"Just because I'm not sleeping with every man who walks in here doesn't mean there's anything wrong with me." Tami retorted, her cheeks on fire. Quinn was called out to the floor by one of the patrons.

"Oh, Joe and I didn't do too much sleeping."

Tami focused on the mirror behind the bar, wishing Marci would just go away. The action incited Marci to move in closer, drop her voice low. "When you're in bed at night, all alone, what do you think about? You could have had him. Why can't you realize that? Joe's a child's game."

"Don't you dare say anything about him," Tami fumed.

Marci made sure Quinn was well out of ear shot before she continued. "Do you think about me having sex with Joe? Do you see us tangled up together? Does it burn your throat? Do you cry?" Marci taunted, pushing just because she could. To her satisfaction, tears gathered in the younger woman's eyes, and she smiled knowing that she had succeeded in getting a reaction from her. "You could have had him, so many times, had you just said something. I'm not your competition, Tami. You don't need to fight me. I certainly didn't want him the way you do. Fight the new girl, she's in your spot."

While Marci kept up the banter, she plotted her next move, surveying the new meat she had asked Quinn about, like a wolf hunts her next meal. The fisherman was totally engrossed in his game and not paying attention. As Tami wiped away her tears and Marci lost interest in her, Dick rose from the table and approached the counter.

Marci pouted for him, sultry. "What can I do for you?"

The question caught Dick off guard, but he regained his composure when he noticed the bartender's amusement. "I work for Dombrowski Construction. A guy called Bob said he was coming out drinking tonight, since tomorrow's his birthday, but he's not here. Do you know him?"

"Sure do. Bobby's usually just a weekend drinker, but if tomorrow's his birthday it makes sense."

"Do you know where I can find him?" Dick's eyes barely left the stunning woman before him. He had never seen someone so blatantly sexual. He cleared his throat, tried to concentrate.

"Chuck's." Her voice was breathy, bedroom style. She had him cold, she mused. Too bad she already had plans.

Dick raised an eyebrow. "Where?"

Marci licked her lips. "It's another bar. If you take a right out of the parking lot and just follow the road for a few miles you'll run into it on the left." Her directions were accentuated by her subtle movements atop the barstool. "I'd join you, but I already have plans."

"Maybe some other time then," Dick quipped. "Thanks." He turned, and with a quicker step, headed out the door.

Tami sneered. "You're a real slut, Marci."

"As opposed to being a fake slut?" Marci softened her expression and kissed the top of Tami's head in a maternal way. "There, there, Tami. Don't cry." She slid off the stool, tossed a kiss at Quinn, and patted her fisherman's bottom.

Quinn raised an eyebrow, sliding back behind the bar. Marci was the most entertaining person, he thought to himself. Tami's head was resting in her hand, and the poor girl looked tired. He ruffled her hair affectionately, trying to get her to pick up her head. "Tam tam, Joe's here," he whispered. Noticing fresh tears, he grimaced. *Not again*, he thought miserably. "Tami, what's wrong?"

Tami shook her head. "Nothing. I'm fine, really. Just a little spat with Marci. She can be such a bitch."

Quinn bit his lower lip to stop himself from saying something crass. "Tami, you have to let Marci roll off you. She doesn't mean half of the things she says."

"That's where you're wrong. I think she means everything she says." Tami wiped the tears away with the back of her hand. "I'm fine, really."

Joe grabbed the door behind him before it could swing wide. He entertained the idea of turning around and going home when he spotted Tami. He had waved to Marci on the way in, thankful that she wouldn't be there, but now he had to deal with the other side of the female spectrum. If Marci was the worse kind of wolf, Tami was the most impressionable kind of sheep. Joe sidled onto a stool and nodded at Quinn, as he smiled at Tami.

"Bud, Joe?"

"Nah. I'll take a bag of pretzels and a Pepsi."

Beside him, Tami raised her eyebrows at the change in behavior. "How's the lighthouse going?"

Joe shrugged, oblivious to the look in Tami's eyes. "Jill and I worked on a deck job today, so I really don't know."

Quinn passed him his order, his jaw dropped. "Jill's working with you now? Construction?"

Joe nodded, ripping open the bag. "Yeah. We got a lot done today."

"Where is she?"

"At home."

Interrupting Joe's munching, a familiar voice shrieked from the doorway. "Joey!"

Joe was pleased with himself for not groaning. He slid off the stool and welcomed his little sister with a warm hug. "Hey, Ali!"

Alice giggled, pleased. She glanced to Joe's side, taking in Tami's presence. "Hi Tami. Hey Quinn." Her eyes brushed past Tami quickly and lingered a bit on the bartender who she dated off and on.

"You look good, Alice." She did. Quinn looked over the changes with a grin. Alice's hair was cut short, the blond brought out with highlights. Her face was fixed artfully; the red shirt hugged her curves. "Welcome home."

The blond beamed. "Thanks. You too. Look good, I mean."

Joe cleared his throat, throwing a warning look at Quinn.

"I came here looking for you last night, but you weren't here, Joey." She assessed her brother carefully. "Something really has changed."

Joe rolled his eyes at the perusal. His little sister was becoming more like their mother everyday. Of course, she really wasn't little anymore, he reminded himself. She had just finished her first year of college, and the year away from home showed in her eyes, her demeanor. "I was at home. You could have found me with a phone call."

Alice perched on the stool beside her brother. She pulled Joe's drink away from him, taking a sip. "My God, it's Pepsi!"

Quinn chuckled behind the bar as she raised a hand to his forehead, feeling for temperature. "Are you sick?"

Joe leaned his head against the bar and groaned. He turned toward Tami. "Save me," he whispered.

Tami grinned, placing her hand delicately on Joe's shoulder. "It's okay, Joe. She means well," she teased.

"This girl must really have made an impact on you," Alice muttered. "I don't remember the last time I saw you without a drink."

"Oh, come on. You haven't seen me since Christmas."

Quinn laughed. "She has a point, Joe. You've definitely been behaving differently."

"So where is wonder woman?"

"Huh?"

"Wonder woman? She-woman? Super woman? The woman who has tamed the untamable? I think her name is Jill the Amazing, or Jill the Incredible. Too bad your name isn't Jack. Jack and Jill. Get it?"

Joe laughed heartily, enjoying his sister's antics. "I missed you, sis."

"I missed you too." Alice smiled sweetly, before winding up again. "But stop avoiding the subject. I have to meet this dream lady. Mom talks about her non-stop. She interrupts Dad and me with some new little theory or detail about her every time we try to talk about something else. I have to meet her! Mom's never talked this way about anybody. She must be really special. She is here, isn't she?" Alice spun around on the bar stool, studying the occupants carefully.

Joe shook his head. "Mom's never even met her."

Alice was taken aback by that comment. "She described her to me in detail. How does she know all this then? And why haven't you introduced her?"

Joe shrugged, frowned. "Mom would drive her crazy with questions and you know it. I don't want her scared off just yet."

"Well, come on. Divulge. I want details."

"She's female. I like her." Joe smiled, thoughtfully summing it up.

Alice was shaking her head before he finished. "Don't think you're getting away with that. I'll get the answers out of you eventually."

"So, have you been dating anyone?" Joe arched an eyebrow at Quinn, reminding him wordlessly about the last time they discussed the verbose blond. Joe had made it clear that he didn't want Quinn seeing her.

Quinn rolled his eyes in response, grinned at Tami.

"Yeah, but nobody great." Alice crooked her head around her brother at the wide eyed brunette who was between Joe and Alice in age. "How have you been, Tam?"

Tami smiled. "Good."

"Are you still working at Wazz's?"

Tami nodded. "I commute to Brimley two days every week for classes, but other than that, I'm here. Do you like school?"

Alice bubbled like champagne pouring into a flute. "I love it. I love my classes, and my professors are cool, and it's so nice to live in a big building with people the same age. There's always something fun going on if you know where to find it."

Joe grinned, happy for his sister. He leaned back and listened to her tell stories of school, glared at Quinn good naturedly when he showed too much interest, and enjoyed his friends.

Thirty-Seven

Finally, Beth was back on the road and on her way to DeTour Village. Her mother had told her she was on a wild goose chase, which had made Beth regret stopping in and letting her know her plans. Even the name of the town didn't sit well with her. People often drove in the wrong direction and ended up lost when detouring from the right path. To her dismay, Canadian Honkers had been flying overhead giving her great imagery to lead her thoughts. Beth had barely been working her nursing position for four months and already she was becoming a burden. Thankfully, her supervisor had understood, but Beth wasn't confident that her leniency would continue. Beth asked for an open window of leave, and she would report in as soon as she had a clear idea of how long she would need. The supervisor had told her she could float her for another week, but after that it was going to get tricky. Her tone made Beth nervous.

Concerned, Beth had called Lisa, and it had taken her friend a while to convince her that this was absolutely where she needed to be. There was no other destination that Richard would have chosen to Lisa's way of thinking. It was obvious that he had taken the logbook, and that was proof positive that he was investigating this lighthouse. If Beth wanted to stop worrying about him, she needed to go figure out what had happened there and why her brother had taken off. Nothing short of understanding would clear her mind, Lisa argued. Beth refuted her friend's logic by spending hours placing calls to Richard's friends, his real estate office, his cell phone, again attempting to locate him or any trace of him to no avail. She filed a missing person's report with the police department and made inquiries after car accidents. Since Beth admitted that Richard had told his secretary he'd be gone, the police weren't real enthusiastic in helping. She had delayed leaving from home until Monday evening when she had exhausted her efforts to find her brother *again*. Beth had stopped Lisa from accompanying her, which was a small note in Beth's favor. She loved her friend dearly, but Lisa's personality was a bit too voluminous for a long car ride and honestly, Beth had no idea how long she'd need to find her brother.

It was as if the man had just disappeared, leaving Beth with a vague notion of how her grandmother must have felt when Lee vanished: lost, frustrated, and worried. It seemed that once again this unknown lighthouse would play a role in the DeForge family. *Why had Richard really gone? What was in the logbook?* All she knew was that when she found him safe and sound wherever he was, she was going to make his life a living hell for worrying her like that.

Beth shook her head to clear it and refocused her energies on driving. Attempting to view the dark clouds as nothing but quirks of Mother Nature, she tried to abandon her most pressing fear: last night she had dreamed of her brother surrounded by a pool of blood.

Thirty Eight

"It's 12:30," Gary answered, glancing at his watch after leaning his edge of the window against the wall.

"Great! I'm getting tired of these damned windows. Lunch time!" Bob hollered, with a haphazard grin thrown towards Pete. "Right?"

Pete chuckled, then ribbed. "Man, you'd think somebody made you boss. You don't think that when I'm signing your paychecks though." Pete noted that Gary had already moved toward the table. Beside him, Dick sat his tools down. "Hold up on that, Dick. Let's finish this one before we take a break."

Dick grumbled wordlessly and resumed the task of putting up the sheet rock. *This was taking too long.* Every attempt to get closer to Bob had backfired. Now, he was stuck working with Pete, who hauled ass. He wasn't used to this physical work and he needed to get it done. The green colored sheet rock was heavy, and they had been working with it all morning. He had been forced to listen to Pete drone on about all sorts of useless information. White sheet rock was normal, and the green stuff they were using today was moisture resistant. In the lighthouse, it was all green, but typical homes would have mostly white with green possibly used in bathrooms and kitchens. Richard had sold homes for years without knowing the construction details, so what point was there in learning now? The only thing he had to understand about real estate was money. What he really wanted was a drink.

Unfortunately, he had just picked up cola to go with the sub he got at the party store. He didn't figure Pete would think too much of him bringing something with some kick to work. Dick's arms ached as he held the piece still, waiting for Pete to finish nailing it into place. Finally, Pete finished and backed off.

"Come on, Dick. Let's eat."

Dick scooped his brand new cooler off the floor near his coat and took a seat next to Bob. "Happy Birthday, man."

Bob raised his glass. "That's right but you can save your wishes and put it into a drink tonight." Bob's eyes swept over the others, grinning like a banshee. "I expect everyone to be there. You too, Pete."

Pete chuckled. "Well now, I don't…"

"I've been with you the longest of anyone here. Twenty minutes and a drink can't hurt anything. Katie will love to come out and you know it."

Pete leaned back and grinned. "We'll see about Kate, but I suppose I can stop in and get you a drink."

"You guys too." Bob gestured to Gary, who grunted, and Dick. "I expect you both there with loaded wallets."

Dick grinned. "Are you going to the Northwood or Chucks?"

"The Northwood to start, but we'll see what happens. I plan on getting some dinner and going straight to the bar. Maybe seven o'clock. Early. A man only gets to celebrate his birthday once a year. Am I right?" He elbowed Pete, grinning.

The voice of reason, Pete spoke up. "You know, its only Tuesday. I fully expect you to show up to work tomorrow and on time."

Bob rolled his eyes heavenward. "Get real, Pete. When was the last time I was late? You can count on me to be here."

"Without a hangover?"

Bob guffawed. "That's a bit much, boss. I'll be here, but don't expect me to be alert."

"Listen, if you get shit faced, you might as well take the whole damned day off. In fact, just go ahead and take the day off. You won't be worth a shit anyway."

Bob winked broadly. "With pay?"

The cell phone rang, startling him. "Shit. It must be Kate." He hurried to his feet and across the room where his cell phone rang from inside his coat pocket. Pete reached inside the tweed lined jacket and flipped the switch to accept the call. "Hello?"

"Hey, hon."

"Kate, are you okay?"

Kate's smile reached through the phone link, comforted her husband. "Of course, I'm okay. I'm sorry to bother you but I just got a call from Paul Lincoln. He wants you to build a garage for him, and he wants it done right away."

"Right away?" Pete remembered Paul well. He had built an addition onto his house the year before. Paul had talked to him about building a small pole barn, but it sounded as if the project had gotten bigger.

"He and his wife are up today and tomorrow. They have the money so they want to get moving on it. I told him you would definitely want to talk to him. I hope I said the right thing. He's in a rush because there's a hardware downstate going out of business and he can get cheap stuff. Did I do the right thing?"

"Yep, Katie. You did fine. Call him back and tell him I can be at his house in about an hour. I'll have Bob run me back to the marina."

"Ask her about going out tonight!" Bob called.

Pete rolled his eyes. "Bob wants to know if you'd like to go out to the bar for a little while tonight. It's his birthday."

"Oh, hon. I asked Mom and Dad over for dinner already. I forgot all about it, but you can go. Tell him he can come over for dinner some night this week, and I'll make him a cake."

Pete groaned. "Kate, it's really not necessary."

"Peter Dombrowski, you tell Bobby he's welcome any time."

"Alright, alright. But you shouldn't be having company anyway. I don't want you to exert yourself."

"Pete, I'm just making a casserole. Mom's bringing a salad and rolls. It's no effort at all," Kate reasoned.

"I'll tell him. Was there anything else?"

"Nope. See you later, hon. I love you."

"Me too. Thanks, Kate."

Three pairs of expectant eyes lingered on Pete as he replaced the cell phone. Kate rarely called as Pete hated interruptions.

"What's up, boss?"

"Dick, can you drive a boat?"

Dick shrugged. "I've never done it, but I could learn."

Pete frowned. "Nah. Bob, I need you to drive me in and then you can drive back the barge. Paul Lincoln wants a garage built and I need to go meet with him right away."

Bob nodded, hopping up. "What kind of a garage? When does he want it built?"

"Does it look like I've spoken to the man about it? Kate just relayed a message. I don't have any details."

"Let's get to it then."

Pete nodded at Dick. "You can work with Gary on the windows. When you get back here Bob, you can replace Dick and then Dick can haul this shit onto the barge. Clean up anything we don't need."

"Did Kate say she could come out?"

"She's invited the in laws over for dinner."

"Pisser," Bob muttered as he threw his jacket on, held the door open for Pete. "This way you can stop by and check on the rabbits too, hey?"

"Good idea. I wanted to poke my head in and glad hand a bit with the Hillers anyway."

"You can remind Joe that I expect to see his ass at the bar tonight."

"Pushy bugger," Pete groaned. He had heard enough about birthdays, free drinks, and getting hammered to last him the year.

"Hey, boss. It's payback time. All those homemade pies that Katie sends with you," Bob rubbed his stomach, grinning. "I might not have that but I am gonna swim in freebies tonight!"

Pete shook his head. "I'll tell Joe, but I don't want you pulling him down with you. Today's not his birthday. A few days on the wagon doesn't prove shit." Pete grunted, concerned. "Not to me."

Thirty Nine

Jill pulled the sunglasses off her nose and squinted up at the darkening clouds. She had been so busy working that she hadn't been paying attention to the weather. They had finished building and attaching the deck frame to the house and were now laying out the top boards.

"Joe, are you gonna grab this or what?"

"Oh, yep. Sorry." Joe took the board from her outstretched arms and moved to grab the next one. "Damn, it's hot today." He used the back of his hand to wipe the sweat away from his forehead.

"It's not really that hot, we're just working hard."

Joe conceded. "Well, I feel hot anyway."

The sliding door above the deck slid open, a white haired head popped out between sheer curtains. "I made some lemonade for you! Oh! You kids have done such a wonderful job! It's almost done, isn't it?"

"Well, we've got a ways to go, but it's coming along." Thankful, Joe reached up and accepted the two glasses of icy tart liquid. Handing one over to Jill, he slurped some from his glass. "Thank you, Mrs. Hiller."

Jill mirrored his actions and plopped down on the grass for a second.

Pete slammed the door to his truck and strode around the corner, lost in his thoughts. Shock caused his mouth to fall open. Gladys laughed openly at his expression. "Why, Pete, you look like you've seen a ghost! Aren't the kids doing a wonderful job?"

Joe picked his head up. "Hey, Boss. What's up?"

"I didn't expect you to get this much done, Joe. This is great!"

"They even worked right through their lunch break yesterday! They've been working so hard," Gladys cooed, bringing her hand to her face. "I've been trying to get them to slow down, but they won't. Every time I look out my window, it looks different."

"Is that right?" Pete shot an inquisitive glance at Joe.

"We ate in the truck on the way to dumping the old material," Joe shrugged.

"Is he treating you alright?" Pete asked Jill.

"Yep, although I must say I'm faster than he is," she teased.

Joe grinned. "What are you doing on the island? Did you run into a hitch at the lighthouse?"

Pete ignored him, grabbed a four foot level out of the truck Joe and Jill were using. He set it carefully on top of the deck, looking closely at the bubble. He grunted and moved around it, testing areas with his weight, evaluating the construction. Jill laughed openly at her boss's behavior and at Joe's concerned expression.

"Did we miss anything?" Joe inquired, annoyed when the question gained more silence. "Are you worried that I can't build a deck or something?"

Chuckling, Pete nodded. "I'm still the boss, kid. Be happy that I trust you to build this without supervision. You're doing a great job. I didn't think you'd be done with the tear down yet, in all honesty."

Joe beamed, the grin spreading from ear to ear. "Yeah?"

Pete eyeballed him. "Yeah. Jill, you must be having a helluva influence on Joe's work ethic here."

Her face lit up with her smile.

"I need to talk to you for a minute though. Why don't you come over to the truck with me?" Jill had scrambled to her feet and moved the next board over to the deck. "Jill, you are entitled to a break."

"I'm fine, thanks."

Pete lowered his voice when Joe reached the truck. "Cut the shit for a minute. How is she working out? Really."

Joe grinned. "Like a charm. She picks me up a bit too early in the mornings, but she's a hard worker. Do you think that I could have gotten so much done if she wasn't doing her share?"

Pete exhaled. "Good, that's what I wanted to hear. As of Monday, she'll be getting her raise and full-time employment."

"Cool."

"And you'll be getting fifty cents more an hour. Impressive work, Joe." Pete thrust his hand foreword, shook Joe's.

His eyes widened in surprise. "Really?"

Pete nodded. "It was only a few days ago that your job was on the line, but I have a feeling that these changes are for the long haul. If you start going back to your old ways, I'll pull the raise though."

Joe shook his head. "No need, Boss. Billy getting fired was a real wake-up call. You don't need to worry about me slipping up any time soon."

"Good. There's something else I wanted to talk to you about though."

"Shoot." Joe couldn't have stopped smiling if he had tried.

"I just came from Paul and Debbie Lincoln's place. We built them an addition last year. Anyway, he'd like a garage built, but we're gonna need to do it in the next three weeks."

"What about the lighthouse? Can we take a break from that?"

Pete shook his head. "No, that needs to go full force."

"Pete, I'm not sure Jill and I can handle a whole garage. I mean, a deck's pretty simple by comparison."

"I'm thinking I'll send Bob with you. I need Gary with me at the lighthouse. There are some projects out there that he's just better at then Bobby. You've been in on two garages, and Bob has been in on almost as many as I have. He could build one in his sleep. I'm sure between the three of you, you can handle it. I'll be popping in, but I have to focus my energy on the lighthouse. Gary, Dick, and I will continue to work out there. I may leave you and Jill to frame in the walls and lay out the trusses. Bobby can come in and help with the roof. When that's done, I can pull him back to the lighthouse and let you finish it up." Pete looked to Joe, gauged his reaction.

Joe rolled the thought over for a moment before responding. "I'll need help with the garage door too. Those things are a bitch to install, and I've never done one alone."

Hearing the response he hoped for, Pete grinned. He knew Joe was ready to take responsibility for the job if he could admit his limitations. "I'll send Gary in to do the door, but you can help him and learn so you can do it by yourself next time."

"Okay, then. I'm gonna get going. Either Thursday or Friday we can duck out to the garage job, and I'll show you guys the plan. I'll give you a call. Keep up the good work." Pete pulled the door open on his truck.

"Wait. Aren't you going to tell Jill the good news?"

"You brought her in, you tell her."

Joe grinned. "Okay." He turned back toward the deck but was stopped by Pete.

"Bob expects you and Jill to be at the bar later."

"It's his birthday today, isn't it?"

Pete nodded. "He'll be damned difficult to deal with tomorrow if he drinks as much as he plans. I told him he could take the day off if he needed to, but that doesn't spread to you. It's not your birthday." Pete pointed a finger at him.

"At least I won't have to deal with him, since we'll still be working on this."

"It's not too late to finish the deck job myself."

Joe laughed and waved Pete off. Whistling happily, he returned to the deck.

"What's gotten into you?" Jill quipped.

Joe's wheels started turning, planning. "Oh, nothing. How 'bout I take you to dinner tonight? Then we can go to the bar and buy Bob a couple drinks. It's his birthday, so everybody will be there."

Jill grinned. "Sounds great. I've never been one to turn down a free meal."

Forty

Joe couldn't believe his luck. Jill had let him drop her off at home and take her Tracker back to his place. He slowed the car sliding down the drive, surprised to see Bob's jeep in his yard. "Hey, Bobby!"

Bobby came out of his truck grinning. "What? No happy birthday tune?"

"Happy Birthday to you!" Joe squealed.

Bob winced, grabbing his ears. "Never mind, man."

Joe chuckled. "What the hell are you doing here?"

"I came to pick you up, take you to the bar for my big celebration. I thought we could grab a burger or something first. Or maybe some fish, down at the Moose or out to Chuck's. We could pick up the ladies on the way."

"I'm sorry, but I have plans."

"Plans?! On my birthday, you made plans! Cancel 'em."

Joe shook his head. "Nope."

Bob wiggled his fingers suggestively. "Oh… those kind of plans."

Joe let that go, gestured toward the trailer. "I'll treat you to a beer now though."

Bob shook his head, gestured to the six pack on the seat beside him. "I'm already taken care of."

"Don't let Cole catch you with that," Joe intoned.

"Sheriff Cole's got better things to do," Bob retorted. "How's the deck job going?"

"Real good. Pete gave me another raise."

Bob's eyes widened. "No shit? How's the girl doing?"

Joe's eyes sparkled. "Really good."

"Yah, I bet the grab ass is going really well. I mean… is she doing any actual work?" Bob chortled with laughter.

Joe sobered. "She's a really good worker. She's green but she catches on quick. Hell, she'll be passing you by in no time." Joe shoved him, joking.

"Ha ha, junior man."

"Not so junior anymore, what with two newbies under me," Joe replied.

"I suppose that's true."

"How is the lighthouse going? Is that new guy worth anything?"

Bob shrugged. "I really haven't gotten a chance to work with him, but he seems alright. He's kind of slow but he should shape up." Bob took a deep swig of beer. "He's coming out tonight."

"I'll be by later. I just have plans for dinner."

Bob nodded. "Bet your ass, you'll be there later. Bob only turns thirty once."

"Does it bother you at all?"

Bob looked toward the darkening sky, shrugged. "Nah." A light mist started falling. "Damn, I better get inside the bar. I'm gonna get soaked."

"Happy Birthday, man. I'll see you later."

"You know it, the night is young and we are gonna party it up."

Forty-One

After working a full day and returning the truck to Pete's, Joe had agreed to return to Jill's in an hour. They had figured it would give them both plenty of time to shower and change clothes for dinner. Ninety minutes later, Joe cringed as he pulled into Jill's driveway for a second time that afternoon. At least his mom had dropped off the rest of his clothes. The dark blue wool sweater was heavy but it was his best one, a Christmas gift from his sister the year before. She always said it was what he looked best in. He was worried it would be too heavy, but the temperature had dropped substantially since work this afternoon. Joe pulled the car next to the house and beeped the horn. Rather than run through the rain, Jill's arm motioned him in.

The house sat a substantial distance from the driveway edge. Jill had plans to have it extended eventually, but her plans hadn't helped him stay dry today. The torrential downpour had soaked his sweater clean through and wrecked his look. Stepping through the door, he quieted when he realized she was on the phone. Warmed by a thick, white robe she twirled the phone cord around her hand, paced absently while she talked or listened.

Joe pulled the soaked wool over his shoulders and laid it over the back of a kitchen chair. The long sleeve shirt he wore beneath it was still reasonably dry. He shuffled his dripping hair back from his forehead, combed through it with his fingers. He tuned out her conversation, amused by Jill's open doors. The rain pounded the shore, the half-complete deck project, the windows. Jill replaced the receiver behind him, moved to lean her head against him and watch the clouds roll over Lake Huron. "It's hard to believe that it was sunny this morning, isn't it?"

Joe wrapped his arm around her. "Who was that on the phone?"

"My friend that I told you about."

"The firefighter-kick boxer?"

"Yeah. Carly wants to come up sometime this summer." Jill shrugged. "We do have a slight problem though."

Joe peered down at her. "What's that?"

"I got a message from my agent. He says he needs to discuss something important so he's going to call me tomorrow morning at nine. He's always super busy so if I don't meet that call, it might take days to get back in touch with him. Do you think we could go into work late and stay after?"

Joe nodded. "Sure. You can have your phone call and just pick me up after. Let's just call Gladys and tell her what we're going to do so she doesn't worry." Joe spied a phone book and flipped through it. "Did he sell one of your pictures?"

"I don't know. Dean never says exactly what he wants to talk about. He rarely calls unless it's something important though. I'm gonna run back to the bedroom and get some clothes on." She gestured to the robe she wore. "I got carried away talking."

Joe picked the phone up and made the call. When he had finished, Jill reappeared. Her dark hair was brushed around her shoulders; faint traces of make-up softened her face. Her daily t-shirt selection was replaced with a mint green button down blouse; jeans exchanged for soft tan wool. A simple gold locket caught the light, glimmered. Joe was undone. "You look great. I've never seen this necklace before, it looks old." He stepped closer to her, fingered the delicate pattern in his hand.

"It's a locket. I don't normally wear it, because I'm always getting into odd spaces and if I lost it I'd never forgive myself. It was my grandmother's." She opened it up for him, showed him the tiny picture of a young couple. "My parents." Clear blue eyes darted from the necklace to her face. She pulled it away from his hand gently. "Are we ready to go?"

"I hope you don't mind, but I laid my sweater on the chair to dry. It's soaked."

"Do you want me to put in the dryer?"

"Actually, my mom's always yelling at me for ruining sweaters in the dryer. She says it wrecks them or something. If it's okay, I'll just leave it there."

"Okay. I have one of my grandpa's jackets in the back bedroom. I'll grab it for you." Jill pulled away from him and fetched the jacket.

Minutes later, the couple was seated in the Tracker, with Joe driving toward town. The downpour had already moved on and left a light misting rain in its wake. When they drove right past the Northwood, Jill's eyebrows shot up, but Joe shook his head at her. When Joe finally pulled the vehicle to a stop, Jill noticed that the clouds had begun to roll away softly, letting the sun shine through in patches. Jill remained silent, staring up at the sky. Joe came around the side of the car, intent on opening the door but she had already swung out.

"You might want to grab your camera."

She grabbed her camera off the backseat. "Joe, what happened to dinner? I'm really hungry."

"We're going to have dinner here. We're celebrating."

"Celebrating what?"

"Be patient, Jilly. The ground's a little wet, so be careful. There's some neat stuff you might want to take pictures of. Have you ever been here before?" He took her hand, led her around puddles.

Jill shook her head. "No. This is Bayside, isn't it?"

"Yep."

"You're actually taking me to Bayside for dinner? Isn't it expensive?"

Joe rolled his eyes. "Just look around. There's an outdoor chapel over here that is just incredible. The original owner had it designed by Frank Lloyd Wright. You'll love it." He led her along the wooded path, holding her hand, pulling her forward when she spotted a cardinal that she wanted to shoot. "You can shoot him on the way back. We're almost there."

Jill stopped mid-stride and gasped with pleasure. "Wow."

Wooden benches faced a tiered, raised platform. Light spilled through the trees onto the altar and bench, against the backdrop of a large stained wooden cross. Ten by ten wood cants reached up to the cross and stepped downward on both sides. Surrounded by woods and nature, with the sound of waves lapping in the distance, and light illuminating some areas and shadowing others, it was an ethereal experience. Speechless, Jill readied her camera just as a bunny hopped onto the platform. She captured many images, while Joe enjoyed her reaction. He spoke in a stage whisper, respectful of the intimacy the outdoor chapel evoked. "It's really great, isn't it?"

Jill smiled. "It's amazing. I had no idea anything like this was here." She held her camera ready and walked through the aisle, gazing all around her.

"The Catholic Church held mass out here a few times when it was first built. They don't do that anymore but there are still weddings out here from time to time." Joe lowered himself to one of the benches and watched her.

Jill pivoted on her heels, met Joe's eyes. She looked through the viewfinder and grinned. Joe looked more than comfortable surrounded by the greenery: He belonged. The foliage seemed to lighten his features; make him more attractive. She clicked the shutter, smiled sweetly.

"I should charge you for that." Joe teased. He stood, held out his hand. "Come on, there's a really great birdhouse that you just have to see."

She put her hand in his and followed him, with a loving glance thrown over her shoulder at the wooded chapel. "Birdhouse?"

"When it was built, it was worth like three thousand dollars. I have no idea what it's worth today. It's right over here." Joe led her around to the birdhouse, tilted her head up to see it.

"Bird mansion is more like it," Jill muttered. Her camera grabbed a few more images before Joe pulled her along after him. They followed the rock path to view the water's edge. The waves rolled through shadows and stretches of sunlight. The clouds were thin in areas, thick in others. The thin places seemed to glow, allow the light through while the dark clouds remained heavy grey. Jill grinned and inhaled deeply. "This is what I love about Drummond."

Joe raised an eyebrow, waiting for her to continue.

Jill gestured toward the water. "It's so soothing and yet so powerful. The water rolls onto the beach, and no matter where I go I know that I'm going to run right into it again. I know that I just have to meet the shore and I'm refreshed, energized. It's almost as if, when I'm here," her voice dropped to a whisper. "I don't have to be anyone else but me; I don't have to worry about what will happen next, or whatever problem is going on. I look at the water, and none of it matters.

"It reminds me how small I am, how tiny my problems are. I wonder how anyone can be here and not fall in love with the island. It's so reassuring to live in a place that has a wall of water separating, surrounding. It's like the bad stuff can't get here. The boundaries are kind of protective, you know? I wonder if people ever think of it, of what makes it different than other places." Jill's eyes fluttered closed and she lifted her palm to the sun, allowing the light to warm her skin, the rolling breeze to muss her hair. She opened her eyes, and turned to Joe, pulling his hand up. "Do you feel that? The life... out there in the water. Here, where the water meets the rock. It defines us; it makes us who we are. This moment, we're islanders. I don't think I ever understood it before. Just think, you've been an islander your whole life." She turned toward him, looked into his reflective eyes. "Do you feel that? The beauty of it?"

Joe's mouth tilted upwards, moved. He had never thought to describe it like that, had never been given the words to say such things. He knew he would never live anywhere else, never feel anything but love and joy about this place. "I feel *you*." He pulled her into his frame, met her mouth with his. The fluid current of the waves matched the energy that passed through him to her as their mouths danced together; as their bodies pressed closer. They leaned into the kiss, reveling in each other's heat, the warmth of their sharing. Eternity seemed to pass, and when Joe slowly pulled away, he was pleased to see her eyes still closed, her breath ragged.

He wrapped an arm around her, gazed at the water that had been a part of his whole life, considered the way he had taken things for granted. "You see things, Jill. You notice things that other people don't see. After the accident, I was so angry that I stopped appreciating what we have here." Joe calmed his breathing, took a few moments to let the waves soothe him. "It's really great, isn't it?"

Jill met his eyes, surprised to see his glisten. "It is. It's laid back and it's wonderful, and it's... it's like another world." Jill leaned into his side, her eyes scanning the sky.

"Joe, look." Her voice was a breathy whisper, her hand gestured in the direction she gazed. On the horizon stretched two parallel rainbows, coloring the sky, intermingling with the clouds.

Joe's grin filled his face. His mother would say it was a sign. "Will those turn out in a picture?"

Jill smiled up at him. "I've already taken one. Here." She touched her temple softly. "I don't need to put it on film. I'll always remember this."

How did I ever get so lucky? Thoughtful, Joe kissed her lightly, thankful for her. He cleared his throat, gestured toward the restaurant. "We should probably go eat."

Jill nodded and allowed him to lead the way.

They began their dining experience in the lounge. They talked about construction and island living and the hardwood floor that graced their feet. They sat by the windows, so they could enjoy the last hour of daylight where they were served drinks before they moved into the dining room.

When their table was ready, Joe was pleased to see that it also sat near the wall of windows facing the water. The table was covered with rich white linen, simple china, elegant crystal. The chairs were rustic in appearance, made from rough wood branches. The fieldstone fireplace roared with life at the center of the dining room, a majestic moose head arched over a mantle, gazed at those who partook below. Pendleton wool blankets draped over log beams, added to the lodgy warmth of the gourmet restaurant. Servers were dressed carefully, refilling water glasses with impeccable timing. The music of loon song and northern birds quietly enchanted them as Jill told him stories of growing up, and listened to his stories.

The ambience was total: folded in their laps were thick linen napkins; glowing at the center of the table was a quaint oil lamp. The senses were celebrated with the atmosphere of a rustic northern lodge, and the tastes of quality cuisine. An appetizer of flatbread with artichoke hearts and a combination of cheeses had been a stellar beginning to the meal.

Joe cleared his throat. Jill stilled, expectantly.

"You wanted to know why we're celebrating," he began. "Pete gave me some good news today."

Jill leaned forward, "What?"

"You're no longer on probation. As of Monday, you'll get your raise. He wants to keep you on full time."

"Oh, great! That's terrific!"

"And he gave me another fifty cents an hour."

Jill beamed, her eyes sparkled. "Way to go!"

Joe grinned. "Do you realize that's $100 a week? I mean, first he gave me two dollars and now another fifty cents." Joe paused, looked down. "I think he's really trying to keep me from slipping. He wants me to get my life together."

Jill looked unsure of what he meant.

Joe crooked his head to the side. "You know, showing up late, drinking too much, keeping a bad truck around." He shifted the subject quickly, not wanting to tell her how poorly he had been behaving. "He told me we're going to be doing a garage job together, but he'll give us more details in the next couple days. Bobby will be with us for the roof and for areas that need three people though. But we can put up with him, right?"

Jill nodded, rosy color filling her cheeks. "I really appreciate you helping me get this job, Joe. I know you must have told Pete I was doing well for him to make the decision so quickly."

"I told him the truth. You don't have to thank me for it."

"Without you I wouldn't have gotten the job though. I appreciate it." Jill reached for his hand across the table, eyed him steadily. "Thank you, for today. I really enjoy being with you."

Joe's eyes flashed with delight. "Me too."

forty-Two

"Hey Quinn, let's have another round over here! Dick's buying!" Bob called.

Nodding, Quinn moved to pour the correct drinks. They had started early. Bob had been getting free drinks from everybody all night, with Dick buying him the most. He had even sprung for a few rounds for the whole crew as well, so perhaps Marci had caught herself a nice one for the evening. Generous, of course, was Marci's idea of nice. Pete had come and gone, grumbling characteristically that the crew better show up to work the next day. Marci had already crawled into Dick's lap once and Quinn wouldn't be surprised if she went home with him tonight. The bar, Quinn thought, was actually pretty busy for a Tuesday. Pete had only been gone thirty minutes, when Joe and Jill arrived. He passed the drinks to the server and waved at Joe. Joe nodded back and walked Jill to the table.

Sitting at the bar, Billy picked up his head, glanced in the direction Quinn waved. "What the hell is he doing here?"

"You haven't made up yet?" Quinn questioned, surprised. Billy and Joe usually did most of their partying together. The petty argument about the job should have ended the day after it had begun.

Billy met Quinn's eyes, shook his head. "He hasn't called me or anything."

Quinn rolled his eyes. "The phone goes both ways, Billy. Why don't you talk to him? You know he didn't steal your job, man."

"Aw, shit. I know. I'm gonna duck out of here. Call Dee, hey? Tell her I'll be walking home, she can come grab me."

Quinn nodded, watched him slip past Joe's turned head and out the door as he picked up the phone.

Jill had settled into the chair, with Joe trotting up to the bar. Joe grinned over the counter, waiting for Quinn to get off the phone. He enjoyed watching Jill joke with Bobby, and get to know the guys. He couldn't quite quit smiling.

"Hey Joe, how's it going?"

"Real good, Quinn."

Quinn eyeballed him. "You look different, happy or something."

"Man, I am. Jill's incredible." Joe lowered his voice, leaned over the counter. "We just got done having dinner at Bayside."

Quinn dropped his voice to match. "Bayside? You whipped out the big guns already, hey?"

Joe shrugged, sheepish. "I wanted to celebrate getting another raise today." He eyed Quinn, speculatively. "I heard you introduced yourself to Jill, hey?"

"Yeah. I saw her at Wazz's. I didn't want her to go on being pissy with me because I didn't cut Billy off the other day."

Joe's attention was caught by the blond who swung out of the bathroom. He grimaced when his sister waved at him.

Alice grinned when she caught sight of him, her eyes surveyed the bar. She mouthed, "Is she here?"

Joe gestured toward the table, obviously putting an effort into smiling.

"Be glad that you celebrated already, now that your sister's seen her." Quinn shook his head, watching the carrot blond rush over to the table. "Good for you, Joe. I'm glad you found her."

"I'll be glad to keep her if she makes it through my sister. Yikes," Joe muttered. "Hey, pour another round for Bob on me. Jill will have a Corona, make mine the usual. And what is Alice drinking? You know she hasn't turned 21 yet, right?"

Quinn rolled his eyes. "Pepsi, Dad." He said, mocking the older brother routine.

"Good. Get her one of those too."

He nodded, assembling the order. "You didn't miss Pete by much, you know. He looked kind of out of it though."

Joe raised an eyebrow. "Oh?"

"Sharper than usual. It's not like I see the guy all that much but I know his usual grumbles and this was different. He was definitely edgy. He asked if you had been in or not; looked like he wanted to talk to you."

Joe shook his head, puzzled. "Hmmph."

Quinn spared Joe a glance, deliberated. "Billy just left, you know."

Joe's gaze brushed the ground. "I feel bad about that. I guess I should talk to him."

Quinn remained silent, slid the drinks in front of Joe.

"Thanks. I'm going to go rescue Jill."

Alice greeted Jill with an outstretched hand and giddy smile. "You must be Wonder Woman, I'm Alice."

Jill picked up her head, shook the younger woman's hand, placed the blond hair and bright blue eyes instantly. Joe hadn't mentioned the feisty girl's name, but she must be his sister. "Actually, my name is Superwoman," she quipped.

Alice threw her head back in laughter and pulled a chair next to her. "My mom thinks you're terrific, even if Joe won't let her meet you."

"Is that right?" Jill crooked an eyebrow, her eyes took in small details. Alice was lanky like Joe, with the same freckles, crystal eyes, and summer colored hair. Her lips were a bit thinner, accentuated by complimentary cosmetics. Her hair was curled, her sweater and jeans chosen specifically for the bar. Designer knock-off boots covered her feet; the leather matched the belt slung around her hips and the hand bag she perched on the table next to her.

Alice's eyes roamed over Jill just as thoroughly as this new woman was looking her over. "You're not at all what I expected." Alice covered her mouth with her hand, surprised to hear herself say something so cheesy. She rushed to explain, "I always expected Joe to go for someone like that." Alice dropped her voice, slanted her eyes towards Marci who leered at Dick.

Jill raised an eyebrow, taken aback. Joe's little sister was blunt as a spoon. "That's right, Mom tells me that you're a photographer."

Joe was waylaid by Bob's insistence that he listen to a new joke and then another, and another. Almost an hour later, he noticed Jill yawn and thought to rescue her. "Okay, Sis. That's enough." He placed his hands on Jill's shoulders, rubbed them lightly. "We both have to work in the morning."

The brunette grinned up at him, pivoted her eyes back to Alice. "It was really nice to meet you, Alice. I can't wait to meet your mom, she sounds wonderful."

Joe groaned; glared at his sister.

"Sorry, Joey. It just isn't fair that Mom hasn't met Jill yet."

Jill stood, excusing herself. "I'm going to use the washroom before we go."

Alice barely waited until Jill was out of earshot. "Joe, she's fabulous. An absolute sweetheart!" she cooed.

"Yeah, she is."

"Mom will go nuts over her. She's just too cool." The Cheshire grin pasted on Alice's face scared Joe a bit.

They exited the bar with Alice on their heels, the crowd having thinned considerably. Dick had been pacing his drinks, carefully loosening Bob's tongue, and retaining his own sobriety. Marci had gotten bored, was throwing herself in front of Quinn, leaving Dick with the opportunity he had painstakingly waited for all night.

"Gary told me that you worked on the sinks at the lighthouse," he began.

"Huh? I'm not at work," he slurred, swaying uneasily.

"No, you're not. Do you remember the sinks, Bob?"

"Sinks? I just wash my face few mins ago," his words ran together.

"At the lighthouse, Bob. I'm talking about the sink pipes. Did you find anything? Like silverwear?" *There was still time to find the fortune and make the meeting... barely enough, but still time,* Richard thought.

"Oh! In the pipes?!" Bob nodded emphatically.

Dick's pulse raced. "What did you find?"

"A buck fifty."

Dick's eyebrow shot up. "One dollar and fifty cents?"

"Nuh-uh. We found pennies. Three rolls of pennies. Some sap's idea of a joke." Bob looked into his empty glass. "I need 'nother drink."

"I'll get you one in just a minute." Dick leaned forward, took Bob by the arm, his heart sinking by the second. "Are you sure that's all you found?"

Bob nodded.

"They're just normal pennies?" Dick grasped for straws.

"Old."

"They're old?"

Bob nodded.

"What did you do with them?"

"Yeah, yeah... uhm..." Bob frowned, unsure.

"Are they still at the lighthouse?"

Bob grunted.

"Where are the pennies?"

"I dunno. The kid found them."

"Kid? What kid?"

"Joe."

"Joe has the pennies?"

Bob nodded, slumped over in his chair.

Dick's eyes widened. "Bob? Bobby?" Lower he muttered, "I can't believe this." Dick slapped his cheek lightly to no avail. "Hey, bartender!"

Quinn rolled his eyes, slid out from behind the bar. "What can I get for you?"

Dick gestured to Bobby. "I think he's passed out."

Quinn nodded, checked the slumped man. "No problem. I'll drive him home after we close."

Forty-Three

Jill slowly pulled away from Joe's embrace. Leaning away from him, her long fingers refastened the buttons of her shirt. "I need to go home." Her hair was mussed, her cheeks filled with color.

Modestly surprised, Joe leaned back on the couch and gazed up at her. Maybe she didn't feel comfortable, he mused. "You know, you can stay," he said tentatively.

The dark haired beauty stood up from the couch and smiled. She leaned down and kissed him lightly. "No, I need to go home."

"I can come with you."

Jill shook her head. Absently finding something else to focus on, she pulled the drapes closed on the windows, helping Joe prepare for sleep.

"Did I do something wrong?" He arched an eyebrow, slightly confused by her behavior. He had thought this would be the night, for sure.

"No, not at all." Finishing with the drapes, she turned to face him.

"Then what is it?"

"I just don't want to rush this." Jill pulled her hair away from her face, looked down at him, and realized he needed more of an explanation. "I don't even know where I'm going to end up in this world."

"The way you were talking earlier, you seem pretty taken with Drummond." He couldn't help the tone of annoyance that had trickled into his voice.

"Joe, I've only been here a few weeks, and I don't want to make quick decisions about anything."

"I don't really think it would be a quick decision. I mean, we've spent a lot of time together."

"And we have all kinds of time to take this to the next level. For now, I'd like to think about keeping my job, getting to work on time, getting my deck fixed, getting some good pictures to sell: simple things."

"I'm not all that complicated," Joe replied.

Jill sighed as she sat back down on the couch. "I don't want you to think I'm going home because I don't want to be with you. I'm going home because I need to think about this."

"I don't understand what there is to think about." Joe realized he was pushing but couldn't help himself.

"Joe, I don't have anybody. I mean, I have Uncle Dave in Florida, but I don't really have anybody else. No parents, no grandparents, no siblings. If this isn't right, I don't want to lose you as a friend. I'd rather we take our time and both be sure this is what we want. Wouldn't you rather be sure?"

Joe groaned, buried his face in his hands. "I suppose you're right."

Jill picked up her head, and met his eyes, leaned forward and kissed him lightly. "Thanks for understanding."

"Don't thank me, Jill." His voice quieted considerably. He reached up, touched her cheek softly, gazed into her gold flecked eyes. "This has been one of the best days I've had in a really long time."

"I had a really good time too." Jill smiled softly. "See you tomorrow, then?"

"Yeah. Come get me as soon as you get off the phone with your agent."

"I will. Good night, Joe."

Joe pulled his shirt back over his head, walked her to the door. "See you in the morning, Babe."

Jill raised an eyebrow, affected a saucy expression. "You'll see me in your dreams," she teased.

"You're right about that." Joe pulled her to him, kissed her quickly, then let her go. "Good night."

forty-four

Exhausted, Beth found a motel and headed straight into the shower.

Her overactive imagination was playing terrible tricks on her. She concluded that it must be the result of fatigue. She would be in DeTour tomorrow and could start searching for her brother then. When she found him, she could lecture him soundly about making her worry, then turn around and go back home.

Beth turned off the water, and grabbed a towel from the hook outside the shower. She gathered it around her body, drying off. Stepping out of the shower, she pulled on a warm nightshirt from her bag and settled on the bed. She dialed Lisa's memory code on her cell phone.

"Luscious Lisa at your service!"

Beth giggled; her first expression of pleasure all day.

"Beth! Hey, how are you doing? Are you there yet?"

"No. I need to take a break, so I have a motel room in Sudbury for the night." Beth shrugged. "I should be in DeTour tomorrow. How was your day?"

Lisa's voice portrayed concern. "Is something wrong?"

Beth rolled her eyes. Maybe Lisa wasn't the right person to call. But at this point, who was? "No, I'm doing good."

"Liar. What's up, Beth? I'm not talking about anything else until we get through this. There's really no point in calling to talk to me if you're not going to get to the rat killing."

Beth shuddered. "I hate that expression; I don't know why you use it."

"Don't think that snapping at me is going to change my mind about this. Spill it! Whatever's wrong is in your voice."

Beth took a deep breath, then conceded, "I've been having visions. Actually, they're not visions – they're flashes."

"Of what?"

Beth hesitated. Lisa demanded, "Of what?"

"Blood, Li. I see Richard. I see a pool of blood on the floor and a body. It's everywhere."

"Oh, God," Lisa paused. "What do you think it means?"

Beth rolled her eyes. "Death. What else could it mean?"

"It could mean that your imagination has run wild. Have you been reading one of those thrillers you like so much?"

Beth glanced guiltily over at the paperback on the bedside table. "That's what I thought at first, but I'm not so sure."

"Listen. Don't worry about it. I know that sounds like shitty advice, but you can't do anything about it right this minute. We're not even sure your brother is in DeTour."

"You're right. It's shitty advice."

Lisa sighed. "Well, maybe you should try to hold the vision."

"Why?" Beth shook her head, appalled.

"To explore it. If you could hold on to it, you might be able to look around, or figure out what's happened, or where your brother is."

"Wherever he is, someone's hurting him."

"Honestly, it might not even be about your brother. I mean, we learned all about this in school. People who have recently lost a loved one often have bizarre visions."

Beth nodded, liking that idea. "Why didn't I think of that?"

Lisa grinned into the phone. "Well, sometimes brilliant friends are good to have around."

Tiredly, Beth sighed. "Well, I should get to bed so I can get up early and get going tomorrow."

"Okay. Rest easy. Call me tomorrow."

"Will do. G'night, Li."

"Good night."

Beth replaced the receiver and glanced around her room uneasily. Although she wrestled with fatigue, she held off for hours before she gave in and settled into bed. She dreamed of blood.

Forty-Five

WEDNESDAY MORNING

The warm, fluffy, clean towel sat on the edge of the still sparkling countertop—so different than the towel he had scrounged off the floor the first day he met Jill. This week he had made it to work both days on time, had gotten another raise, and had enjoyed one of the best evenings of his life. Rather than hurrying from the cold linoleum to the cold spray of the shower, his feet were warm on the brown rug his mom had provided. Even better, he hadn't spent every night in the bar, hadn't suffered the hangovers that he had grown accustomed to. His friends must have noticed the change as well, since they weren't littered throughout his living room as they had been many mornings. He was beginning to enjoy this elevated version of life: clean towels, clean clothes. Of course, he had his mom to thank for that, but he *had* done a load of laundry on his own since she finished the first pile. Proud of himself, beaming like a boy who just learned how to ride without training wheels, Joe looked himself over in the mirror. He needed to get his hair cut, but other than that, he looked as good as he ever had. He was fixing his life, getting it online, behaving responsibly. He was becoming the kind of man that a classy woman like Jill would want to be with, maybe even love eventually.

He tested the water with his good hand. The water was comfortable so he stepped in, humming. This weekend he would buy a new truck. He figured he'd choose a two-year-old Ford Ranger with low miles if he found one he liked. He planned it out in his head, knew exactly what he could afford and how fast he'd like to pay it off. He already started dreaming about setting money aside for land or a home this fall. Paying rent wasn't getting him anywhere and he knew it. Hell, Jill already owned a home. She couldn't attach herself to a loser, and Joe was determined not to be one any longer. His dad hinted at giving each of the kids ten acres—he owned a forty acre parcel along Maxton Road—maybe it was time to start hinting that he was ready. Maybe with a gift of land, he could start building a house as soon as next year. He was thinking of studying for the general contractor's test to get licensed; Bobby had lent him the books and had encouraged him to take the test. Studying was a step in the right direction; it would prove to Pete, and to everyone, that he was committed.

Joe rubbed shampoo into his scalp as his mind bounced from idea to idea about how to better his life and what he could do next. He had continuously joked with Pete that he would never find someone like Kate, but he was sure he had done just that. Jill was a good woman, with the same honesty and fierce loyalty that made Kate special. She was someone his mother would adore. Thinking of his mom, he grinned as he lathered soap in his hands. His mom was always worrying about him, pressing him for details. Alice was right. He couldn't postpone their meeting much longer. He knew he had made progress with Jill and was confident that Mary wouldn't scare her away.

Belatedly, Joe considered their discussion of the night before. He hoped he hadn't pushed Jill too hard. He hadn't really understood how alone and vulnerable she was. He needed to reassure her that he wasn't going anywhere. Even if it didn't work out, Joe thought, they could always be friends. Shaking his head, he let go of his worry and thought of how different they were. He complained about family members

always prying into his business, constantly asking him
questions, and demanding certain behaviors. What would he
have done without them? On Drummond, and probably islands
elsewhere, Joe thought, family wasn't necessarily blood kin,
but those who were there when they were needed. Practically
everyone on the island had stepped up and given a damn when
he had needed them to. They had all looked the other way when
he was less than thankful. Drummond Islanders had raised
thousands of dollars to pay medical bills and help his family
care for him. At times, he had resented their interference. He
had wanted to spend his life sulking about his scarred body and
his shattered dreams. Today, he realized just how lucky he was.
Jill had never known that kind of family, that kind of selfless
love.

He shook the thought from his head as he rinsed the
shampoo. He watched the suds gather at the bottom of the tub
and then chase each other down the drain. Finally, feeling fresh
and clean, he cranked the water off, brought the towel to his
face and began drying off. Lost in his thoughts of Jill, he
stepped out of the shower. With previous women, he had stayed
around only long enough to get his needs met and have some
fun. The dark-haired photographer was different, and she had
been right—he dreamed of her the night before.

By now, Joe realized with some chagrin, Alice would be
chirping away at their mother about meeting Jill the night
before. Mary would be deducing some surefire way to pop over
after work and surprise them with a dinner invitation. Of
course, her attempts would be futile since they were going to be
working late. Joe set the towel on the sink's edge, and combed
the wet hair back away from his eyes.

Joe frowned, hearing muffled noises coming from the
living room. Was Jill here already? Either he had been wrong
about the hour and dawdled too much time away in the
bathroom or Jill's phone call was cancelled and she was now
making herself at home. Wrapping the towel around his waist,

he flipped the light switch off and slid the door open, his eyes adjusting to the darkened living room.

A figure, cloaked by the darkness was huddled over the drawer in his entertainment center. *What the hell?* Since he had started seeing Jill, his friends had stopped dropping by unexpectedly. Joe squinted at the intruder. "Billy, is that you?"

Forty-Six

Although the sun was up, the drapes were still closed from the night before, the door still shut against the burgeoning light of day. The couch where they had come so close to making love still sat exactly where it had been: untouched. The tidy living room was now strewn with debris from an overturned table and the contents of ransacked drawers; the evidence of a struggle. In the midst of what had been the abode of a bachelor, Joe lay curled on his side: the pained form of a man who believed he had understood pain.

He hadn't.

Thoughts and images flashed within his mind. The numb sensation of waking blurred his vision. The startling realization that he had been attacked was swiftly overshadowed by a pitiless and blinding pain inside his head. Opening his eyes slowly, he realized that his eyelids were coated with something sticky. His head rested in the same substance that coated his face. I just need to get up, he thought, but his body didn't respond. Darting his tongue to his lower lip, Joe tasted the unmistakable metallic flavor of blood. He was horrified to realize that what coated his eyes, ran down his nose and pooled under the side of his face was his own blood. Horror escalated to terror.

His thoughts ran wild. He wanted to deny the images pulsing through his mind. His breathing came in thick gasps, severely labored. He needed to warn Jill, get help, stay conscious. He tried to shift his head backward and failed. He willed his body to move, but it remained still. The atrocity of death flooded his awareness. "Oh, God." Terror growled deep within his throat, roared between his ears, within his belly.

His eyes closed, and moments later, opened. He had no idea how long they had been shut, but he knew he had to keep them open. He had to warn Jill. Inky blackness threatened to darken his vision permanently. He dug within his body to find the will to move his hand, trace a message that would offer explanation and warning. Somewhere inside him, inside the man that had wanted to give up so many times during months of rehabilitation, was a man that now fought for seconds of life. His own life; his own blood seeped from his head, trickled down his nose.

The deep red liquid spread outward from his head and with a trace amount of strength he drew his right hand to his side, curved his finger outward. Pain rolled over his body, clutched his hand in spasms. Joe gasped for breath, fighting with every ounce of strength left within him to finish what he had started. His hand trembled with the force of an earthquake as he completed the first letter, moved to the next. His left eye was covered in blood; his right eye struggled against the flow to stay open. The second letter was complete. Joe's hand moved willfully to the third.

The fog threatened his consciousness. He was losing the battle and he knew it. Through the fast enclosing tunnel of darkness, pure white light emerged from its center. Joe struggled to focus on the light and was momentarily blinded by it; but comforted as well. From its core a figure emerged more beautiful than anything he had ever seen. The light embraced her, haloed her, and Joe was allowed a glimpse of her radiance. An angel had been sent for him. Joe forgot his fears and was slowly overwhelmed by the messenger of heaven. With each step she took, Joe experienced the euphoric bliss of receding pain. Calmness washed over him, enveloped him, and Joe reached toward her endless warmth with his soul. With one last twitch of an eyelid, his body stilled.

At that moment, approximately 45 miles northwest, an old man bolted upright in his bed. Judgment had come.

Forty Seven

THREE MINUTES EARLIER

Jill was uncharacteristically giddy. Her apprehension about becoming involved with Joe faded with the news that her agent had sold one of her photos for a magazine cover. Besides that, a card company wanted to purchase three of her wildlife images for a line of cards. The news spurred Jill to tell her agent about the pictures she had taken recently. Her agent had thought that this company might be a good bet for future work. The sale would generate a tidy little sum and would garnish more recognition for her work, which was an even bigger win than the paycheck.

She pulled the Tracker to a stop and hurried to the door, surprised that it was still closed firmly behind the screen. She opened the screen a bit and rapped her knuckles against the cold steel. She waited a moment and repeated the knocking.

He's overslept, she thought. Impatient, Jill pushed the door open and called to Joe. A stench assaulted her. Repulsed, she immediately covered her nose with her sleeve. *What the hell?* Her eyes searched the room, seeking to understand. She moved cautiously, unable to comprehend what she was seeing until her foot touched the thick red substance. The realization hit her like a fist to the stomach. Immediately, she rushed toward Joe, knelt beside him, reached her hand to his throat but stopped. From another time, she pulled a memory, a sentence from another crime scene. Don't touch the body. The impropriety of her thoughts had her stumbling backwards, away from him, struggling with her denial. Her scream caught in her throat, bile rushed to her mouth.

"No!" Her behavior turned primal, her mind fought against reality as the scene registered within her mind. Her scream reverberated off the thin walls of the trailer, escaped into the morning air. Green eyes pinched shut; she turned her head away from him. The mind tries to make sense, the body revolts. *If I go back outside, if I forget about this, it will all go away. I just need to wake up. If I wake up, I'll be safe in my bed at home and this will all go away. This isn't him. This can't be him. He's not dead. He's young, and healthy and alive. This is just a cruel nightmare. He won't die. I watched my parents die, my grandparents die. **He can't die.** This is why I explained it to him, he didn't understand last night and I explained it to him. Surely, after understanding about me, he wouldn't die. He can't die.* "Oh God, please don't let him die." Slowly, Jill opened her eyes, expecting in her chaotic denial that she would be snuggled in her bed. Sobbing, Jill confronted the lifeless form before her and fell to her knees. *He's dead.*

Unbidden, buried memories surfaced. Blood seeped from various cuts in her arms from fragments of glass. Glass was everywhere. The seatbelt held her tightly on her side. Terrified, she screamed. 'Mommy, Daddy, wake up! Get me out of here.' Neither of them had moved and the little girl had screamed again and again. The little girl screamed now, from within the adult, as her parents were replaced with Joe. Now, Joe sat in the car ahead of her, his head slowly turned around, bloody, as it was at this moment, and he winked.

Horror quivered within her body, her limbs. She needed to flee, to escape this hell that was her life. She didn't make it out the trailer door before vomiting uncontrollably. Her limbs shook violently with shock. Her body jerked and heaved with involuntary spasms that ran down the length of her spine, relieving her of any trace of control. Her mind rebelled against the images: past and present.

Several minutes later, when the heaving finally subsided, she stepped around the lake of blood carefully, numbly, and reached for the phone. Mindlessly, she dialed 911. Tears streamed down her face unchecked, unrealized. She sank to the ground on her knees, holding the phone and stared at his bloodied body. Later, she curled on her side and faced him, unable to remove her eyes. "No, no, no." Over and over again the word pounded her skull, wreaked havoc in her stomach. This couldn't be happening.

Numbly, she realized that someone was talking to her. In her left hand the telephone was still clenched. She pulled it to her face. "He's dead. Joe's dead."

"Where are you, ma'am?"

Jill fought for some sense of reason, stilled the fear boiling inside her and got it done. "Joe Barber's trailer. He's dead. He's covered with blood and he's dead." Her voice broke and she sobbed. "So much blood, so much. Oh God. No!" Jill let the phone slip out of her hand, overwhelmed by the sobs that choked her throat, constricted her chest, and hampered her breath. As each new image burned into her memory, moans of grief poured from deep within her body, calling out for help that didn't come. Minutes, she lay motionless, her knees brought up to her stomach, her body curled into a fetal position. Desperately trying to evict the lifeless image, Jill failed in her attempt to deny the heartbreaking reality. He lay there, lifeless: naked except for a blood stained towel caught around a foot. Like every detail that she kept imbedded in her memory, she couldn't shut this one out. Her imagination tangled the bodies of her parents, her grandparents in the blood on the floor next to Joe, mutated the images. Her mother's face replaced his, her father's replaced her mother's—on and on the cycle ran, leaving Jill mindless to anything but gut wrenching pain.

Her photographer's eye snapped new mental images of horror; her breath came in loud, wracking sobs. Minutes fled by in seconds. She retained the presence of mind not to touch him, not to make the mistake that others do when they can't help trying to save someone they know. She had been a part of crime scenes before: she had photographed them. Joe was beyond saving. Rationally, she accepted that. In the next moments however, and in the next years, her mind would whisper to her that he had winked. She couldn't be sure. Blood lay around him in a thick pool, covering his eyes, his head, and his nose. The majority of it seemingly spilled from a large gash at the back of his skull. Grey matter stuck to the side of a blood-splattered hammer behind him.

Slowly, Jill pulled the fragments of reality back together within her mind. She pulled herself upright, belatedly realizing her face was wet. She had been oblivious to her tears. She gazed around the body. Joe was curled on his side. The left side of his face was buried in the crook of his left arm that curled underneath him. His right arm lay outstretched. In the blood, Jill could see that he had written something.

Scrawled messily were the letters "P E," followed by a straight line, an unfinished letter. "Oh, God." The bile rushed into her throat once more as she glanced over to the hammer with Dombrowski burned into the wooden handle. *Pete*.

forty-Eight

Deputy Sheriff Jack Cole deeply inhaled the fresh air, as he stepped outside. He had taken pictures of the scene and surroundings with the 35mm he had in his truck, done a preliminary survey of the scene, and called for the medical examiner and county detective. He continued by securing the crime scene with yellow tape. Once it was obvious that the subject was deceased, Cole dismissed the ambulance. The local doctor, a deputy coroner of Chippewa County, pronounced Joe dead. The doctor now leaned against his car, studying the young woman who remained silent. He tried to talk to her, but she was lost in her own world of grief. Now, Cole and he waited for Sgt. Det. Bishop to arrive with a team of investigators.

Many minutes, perhaps even an hour passed since Jill escaped to sit beside a tree. Her mind refused to engage or recognize the passage of time. A dark, cold, lonely place claimed her mind; silenced her thoughts. She sat immobile, almost as if asleep, but her eyes were wide open and blank. It was as if someone had flipped a light switch and turned the life within her to 'off.'

Studying her from across the yard, Cole grimaced apprehensively. The young woman looked broken, devastated, Cole thought. Regrettably, it was his job to begin the horror of making her replay the nightmare that possessed her. It was not the first time in his career that Cole wished he had chosen a different path. Cole took a deep breath and moved toward her. He didn't recognize her. He approached her carefully, spoke quietly. "Ma'am?"

Jill's eyes flicked toward him in perusal, although she said nothing. "I need to ask you some questions." Cole waited for her response. When she remained silent, he sank to the ground beside her. "Can you answer my questions?"

Jill nodded slowly. "Yes."

Cole flipped open a notebook, and took out his pen. "What is your name?"

Jill leaned her head back, closed her eyes. "Jill Traynor."

"Is that spelled like it sounds? Trainer?"

"T-R-A-Y-N-O-R."

Cole noted the spelling. "How did you know Joe Barber, Ms. Traynor?"

"I was...ah..." She took a deep breath, continued. "I was dating him." Her voice broke. She wished for a cigarette or a drink or something to do with her hands. She tapped them on her leg. Her eyes shed tears sporadically, her lids blinked heavily.

"How long have you known him?"

She cleared her throat. "A few days. Not even a week. Last Friday, his truck broke down and I gave him a ride to work. That's how we met. We've been seeing a lot of each other since then. I work with him. He got me a job with Dombrowski Construction. This would have been my third day."

Cole raised an eyebrow, jotted the information down. "Can you recount the events of this morning, Ms. Traynor?"

Jill nodded, her eyes downcast. "I was on my way to pick up Joe for work. Last night we decided to start work an hour later, because I had a conference call this morning."

Cole interrupted her. "Was Pete going to send a boat back for you?"

Jill shook her head. "We're not working on the lighthouse with the crew. Joe and I are... or I mean we *were* building a deck here on the mainland." Faintly, she remembered someone referring to DeTour as the mainland. She shook her head. "Here on Drummond."

Cole nodded, waiting for her to continue.

"I came over to get him; knocked on the door. He didn't answer, so I just went in." Jill paused, her chin quivered. "He was lying on the floor. I didn't touch him. I knew it was too late." And his eyelid fluttered, Jill thought. Maybe, it hadn't been too late. "I'm a photographer. I spent 6 months working with the local PD where I grew up, doing forensic photography. Maintaining a crime scene's integrity, and not touching anything were the first lessons I ever learned. I tried to make it out of there before I got sick, but I couldn't get out in time." She paused, riveted her eyes to Cole's for the first time. "I'm sorry."

Cole nodded, urging her to continue.

"I wanted to touch him. It seemed natural to go over and try to do something... but I didn't. I knew I couldn't."

"You did the right thing. He was beyond help." So the vomit had been hers and not the killer's. That made sense. Anyone who understood homicide, knew clear evidence was critical. Cole nodded. "Ms. Traynor, what else did you touch?"

Jill closed her eyes, thought back. "I walked in through the front door, so I touched the handle. My foot touched his blood. I called from the phone. I sat on the floor, but I didn't touch the hammer or him..." Her voice broke once again,

trailed off. "I spent a lot of time there the past few days, so
you're going to find my prints everywhere."

Cole nodded, his mind rushing over what he had
learned, piecing together facts. If she had only known him for a
few days, she couldn't be asked about unusual behavior. She
wouldn't know. "Ms. Traynor, I just have a few more
questions."

Jill waited, silent.

"You said that you were going to work late because of a
phone meeting?"

"Yes."

"Did you have that meeting?"

Jill nodded, "Yes."

"Who was it with?"

"My agent. He sells my photographs."

"When did the call end?"

"I'm not sure. I never looked at the clock. When I hung
up the phone, I literally jogged out to my car and came directly
over here."

"Where are you staying?"

"I own a home on Cream City Point road." Jill caught
Cole's surprised expression. "Do you know the Eby's?"

"Clark and Arlene, sure."

"I own the home right next to theirs."

"I will need the name and phone number of your
agent."

Jill recited the information.

"I also need you to stay on Drummond Island. If you
need to leave for any reason, I'd like you to contact me first.
Do you understand?"

"Yes." Slowly, Jill rose to her feet.

"Ms. Traynor, I don't have the materials to do this now, but I know the county detective will ask for your fingerprints."

"Am I a suspect?"

"Not from me, no." Cole smiled sympathetically. "Is there anything else that you think might be relevant?"

Jill hesitated. "Billy…" She thought for a moment, shrugged. "I'm not sure what his last name is, but they fought on Friday. Billy started it. He was drunk and violent. Joe told me that he had lost his job that day and it wasn't that big of a deal… but, it kind of seemed like it."

Cole jotted the note, familiar with Billy's antics. "Ms. Traynor, did Joe mention any problem he was having with anyone?"

"No. Joe never seemed like he had enemies, except for Billy."

"Did Joe refer to him that way?"

"No. He never talked about him at all."

"It may surprise you, but Billy and Joe are—were close friends."

Jill shook her head. "I never saw that, but it's a small town." She shrugged.

Cole observed her candidly as he handed her his business card. He opened his mouth to speak, but was distracted by the battered roar of a car needing a new muffler pulling into the drive. As if on cue, Billy hopped out of the car, wide eyed at the presence of Cole's SUV and the Coroner's vehicle. Cole hurried away from Jill, intent on stopping him. "Billy!"

The young man turned, waved. "What's up, Cole? What's going on?"

Cole countered with a question. "What are you doing here, son?"

"Is Joe in some kind of trouble? Why are you here?" Billy bobbed back and forth, edgily. His eyes darted from Jill, then back to Cole.

"What are you doing here, Billy?"

"I came to see Joe."

"How did you know he would be home?"

Billy persisted. "Where is he?"

"Billy, I asked you a question." Cole braced his legs, clasped his hands together grimly and stared him down.

His eyes shifted downward. "I came to apologize."

"How did you know he wasn't at work?" Cole kept his voice level, stared into Billy's eyes. If Billy had known, so did Joe's killer.

"I didn't. I figured I might catch him here. Joe only makes it to work four days a week if he's lucky." Billy fidgeted nervously. "If he wasn't home, I figured I'd leave him a note."

"What were you apologizing for?" Cole kept his face serious, the expression noncommittal. It would be impossible to get the answers he needed after Billy realized Joe was dead. He needed to hurry through this. Confirming Jill's statement was important.

"We had a fight. What's going on?"

"A fight about what?"

Billy shook, his voice raising an octave. "What is going on?"

Cole had lost him. He softened his expression. "I'm sorry, Billy. Joe is dead."

"Dead?" Billy echoed the word, the meaning not registering immediately. "He can't be. I just saw him last night.

I was coming over to apologize. There must be some mistake."
He looked into the Sheriff's eyes, pleading for him to change
his answer.

"There's no mistake, Billy. I'm sorry."

Billy's face wrinkled up, trying to understand.

"I need you to answer some questions, son."

"No, I…"

"I need your help, Billy."

Absently, Billy swallowed air, nodded.

"Why did you come here this morning?"

"I came to say I was sorry." Tears ran down his face,
blurring his vision. "I got fired a few days ago. Joe and I got in
a fight, and we haven't talked since."

"What day was that?" Cole got out his notebook again.

Billy cleared his throat, his eyes glistened. His voice
cracked when he spoke, "Ah, Thursday, I think. Friday,
maybe." He shook his head. "I don't remember."

Cole nodded. "And you came here because…"

"I felt bad." Billy brought his hand to his head, his
elbow against his chest. "I saw him at the bar yesterday, and
Quinn thought I should talk to him." Pain was evident as he
whispered, "Oh, Christ." Billy's hands trembled; he needed a
drink. Better yet, he needed to drown in a bottle.

"How did Joe live? What did the inside of his trailer
look like?"

"Real bad. Dee refused to go in there most of the time."

"That's what I thought," Cole added, making a note.

Jill walked up behind Cole, overhead Billy's answer. "I
was in it last night and it was spotless," she refuted.

"Joe was a slob." Billy shook his head. "He wasn't a
good housekeeper."

"How would you know? You haven't been in there. I've never seen it anything less than spotless." She spit out the words coldly.

Cole arched an eyebrow at Jill's sudden hostility.

"What do you know?" Billy mumbled, seeking to blame someone. "You haven't been here his whole life."

"I know that you were the last person to fight with him, the last person to physically strike him. I know you haven't been in there in days. Why are you here? Why did you pick this morning to come here?" Jill's bloodshot eyes stared into him, demanding answers, justice. "Where were you last night?"

Cole listened, decided not to intervene unless the argument escalated, using the conversation as an opportunity to learn more about the young woman, possibly more about the situation in general.

"Where was I?!" Billy's voice buckled, as the volume rose. "You think I had something to do with this? Joe was my friend." The wave of pain washed over him, buckled his knees. "He was my goddamn friend! Where were you?"

"If he was your friend, why'd you hit him the other day? Why did you call him a gimp and yell at him?" Jill demanded angrily, needing someone to blame. "What kind of a friend are you? I saw you sucker punch him. I heard the names you called him at the bar. With a friend like you, who would ever need an enemy?"

Her words hammered into Billy's sanity. Overwhelmed, tears poured from his eyes. He sank to his knees, sobbing. "He was my friend," he repeated like a fallen mantra. "I didn't get to say I was sorry." Billy lifted his tear stained face to the sky, and yelled, "I'm so damned sorry."

Cole placed a calming hand on Billy's arm; waved Jill back. Drained, she slouched as she walked away from them, disgusted with her behavior, but unable to make it right. Cole watched her as he comforted Billy. In his gut, he knew that she was not responsible. It was time to send her home. He should keep her until the detective arrives but she needs to get away from this. He motioned for the doctor to help him out and reapproached Jill.

"I may need to ask you a few more questions but I can have someone drive you home now if you like. What is your phone number, Jill?"

"493-5888. I can get myself home."

"Are you sure? You've just been through a terrible shock."

"I can drive, Sheriff," Jill sighed.

Cole looked into her eyes and nodded. "If you think of anything else, please call me." After Jill walked away, Cole turned to the doctor and explained that he needed him to stay with the crime scene while he informed Joe's parents. Too many people already knew and news spread fast. Cole wanted to be the one to tell them.

Forty-Nine

When Cole rolled back into the driveway, he immediately recognized the tan sedan of Detective Bishop and the coroner's car. Cole was relieved the meeting with Joe's parents was over. Seeing Joe's slain body had been horrible, telling his mother had been monumentally worse. Joe was born in the Soo and lived his whole life on Drummond. The Barbers were good people, and he remembered how hard Mary handled the car accident when he told Mary and Tom their son was seriously injured. When Cole knocked on their door this morning, looked into Mary's eyes and told her Joe was dead, he experienced a whole new meaning of loss in her devastation. Thankfully, Tom and another of their children were there. Cole figured they could lean on each other. Shaking the scene off him, he hurried out of his vehicle and into the trailer.

Bishop held an unlit cigarette between his fingers as he scratched his balding head. He stood back away from the body, idly watching the coroner work. A uniformed officer assisted the coroner by gathering samples. The detective stuck out his hand, nodded. "Cole."

"Bishop," Cole said in greeting, as he pumped the offered hand.

"Tell me what happened here."

Cole cleared his throat as he took out his notebook. "I arrived on the scene at 9:45," Cole began, continuing the scenario as it happened, filling Bishop in on the details of finding Jill, Billy's arrival, and what he had learned.

"Where are they now?"

Cole grimaced inwardly. "I have allowed them both to go home."

"I see. It's not possible that they're suspects?"

Cole shrugged. "Billy's an islander. He has a temper. He flies off the handle at times and fought with Joe just last Friday. If it had happened right then," Cole shuffled from foot to foot. "Perhaps, but I don't think it's him."

"And the girl?"

"I don't know her. She just met Joe on Friday. I can't see a motive there either, but again, I don't know her."

"Tell me about that." He pointed with the cigarette.

"I believe that the P E and line, is actually PET, or Pete. Pete Dombrowski was Joe's employer."

"Dombrowski. Isn't that the name on the…"

"Hammer. Yes, it is."

"We've got the murder weapon and a message from the victim identifying the killer: Sounds open and shut. Where is he now?"

"I don't think it's that simple," Cole shook his head.

Bishop raised an eyebrow, condescendingly.

"We don't even know if Joe drew that message."

"You think the killer might have done it to throw us off?"

Cole hedged. "I've known Pete for years. He's a good man. I can't even imagine a motive. He and his wife love Joe."

"Do they love him too much?"

"What do you mean?"

"Could the wife be having an affair with him?"

Wincing, Cole shook his head. "No. I can't see it."

Bishop rolled his eyes. "If the wife was having an affair with him, could Pete be driven to kill in retaliation?"

Cole frowned. "I don't believe that is the case, but if it was… I might be able to see it."

"Well, let's see what we have here. We got the young man that had a fight with him in public…"

"Billy," Cole supplied.

"Right. He has a temper and shows up at the crime scene after Joe should have been to work, with an unlikely story. But you say it can't be him." Before Cole could respond, Bishop continued. "We have a young woman, the victim's girlfriend, who finds the body, has blood on her shoe, but doesn't touch the body. But it's not her!" Bishop waved his hands widely, to dramatize his statements. "We also have P-E-T written in blood, which… oh my, actually happens to be the first three letters of the boss's name. The murder weapon also has this same man's name right on it. And you don't think it could be him either?!" Bishop leaned close to Cole. "You know what Cole, I'm going to let you in on a little secret," he dropped his voice to a whisper. "Someone killed him, and you are not going to eliminate our best three suspects based on your gut!"

Quietly, Cole corrected him. "It wasn't really a T, it could have been an I or an L."

"And maybe it was a T." Bishop rolled his eyes. "Let's go find the wife. Ask her some questions."

Fifty

Using a soft, white dishtowel, Quinn rubbed the watermarks off the wine glasses before setting them back on the shelf. The bar didn't open for another hour, but he was frustrated with a project and needed to get out of his house. The cook was in the restaurant side preparing the lunch menu. He could hear her whistling from time to time but other than the two of them, the place was vacant and a perfect distraction for him. Quinn was annoyed to see Billy push through the front door.

"I need a drink."

Quinn shook his head without turning to face him. "It's way too early for that, and you should think about finding another..." Quinn's words trailed off as he took in the deep, haunted expression, tear stained cheeks and red eyes. "What's wrong?"

"She's sending me to jail."

"Why would Dee do that? You didn't hit her, did you?" Heaven knows why she sticks with you, Quinn thought silently.

Billy was too distraught to be offended by the question. "Not DeeDee. That little...ah," Billy struggled to think of her name. "Jill."

Quinn leaned back, bewildered. "Why would Jill want you in jail?"

Billy brought his eyes to Quinn's. "Oh God, you don't know. It's Joe, Quinn. He's dead."

The glass in Quinn's hand dropped to the ground and shattered, unnoticed. He shook his head, failing to understand. It wasn't possible. "When? How?" His voice cracked on the word as Quinn struggled to maintain his composure.

"This morning," Billy shrugged, wiping at his eyes. "Somebody killed him. I went over there this morning and they were all there: Cole, Jill and the coroner. I wanted to apologize like you said. I wasn't thinking that he'd be at work. I wasn't thinking at all. I just woke up and knew I needed to make it right between us." His voice broke with a sob. He cleared his throat loudly. "When I got there, they wouldn't let me in. Cole started asking me questions. Then Jill started yelling that it was my fault. She'll probably convince Cole that I killed him." Billy wiped at his eyes again.

Quinn leaned against the counter, gripped his hands against the edge. In a few days there would be a funeral. A terrible, tragic funeral, and even worse, there would be no more Joe. "Oh, God. Alice." Quinn shuddered to think of Joe's poor sister of his parents, of Pete and Kate, of Tami. So many people had really loved him.

Billy emitted a low, humorless chuckle . "To hell with it. If I'm going to jail, I might as well drink."

"Why would Jill say you killed him?"

"She told him about the fight, told him that if anyone killed him, it was me." Billy looked to the ground, his voice quieted. "It doesn't really matter. It's not like I can blame her."

Seeing Billy's devastation, Quinn seethed with anger. "She has no right to say anything about you. She's known him, what? A whole week? It hardly makes her an authority. And Cole wouldn't believe that you would do anything to him anyway." Billy and Joe had been life-long friends: together they grew up, graduated from high school, and worked in construction. Quinn watched the younger man break, convulse. "Bitch," he muttered.

"I don't even know how he died. I know there was blood, though. Jill had blood on her." Billy's gaze touched the ground, swept back to the bartender. "Quinn." Billy elevated his voice, pleaded. "*Please.*"

Heartache spilled from Billy's voice, but Quinn stood firm on the alcohol and poured him a glass of water. "Cole is probably going to question you again. The last thing you want to do is start drinking. You need to be calm and clear when you're questioned, Billy."

"Damn it, Quinn. Give me a drink." Billy slapped his hand on the edge of the bar.

Quinn ignored it. "I'm gonna call Dee. You should go home."

Defeated, Billy laid his head back against his arms and wept for his friend, for himself. Quinn offered a comforting hand and blamed Jill.

Fifty-One

Kate turned the oven off and set the non-stick, insulated baking sheet on the stovetop. She was making the boys cookies and feeling bad that she hadn't done it in a few weeks. The doorbell interrupted her progress. With a smile, she set the oven mitt down and hurried to the door. She was surprised to see Deputy Sheriff Jack Cole and another man.

"Well, what a nice surprise. Hello Jack, come on in." Kate was one of the few who called the Deputy by his first name.

"Hi, Kate. I'm not sure how nice of a surprise it is, but we need to talk to you. This is Detective Bishop down from the Sault office."

Kate shook the man's hand and welcomed them into her home. "Well, if you need to talk to me you might as well do it with a cookie. I just pulled them out of the oven. The guys on the crew have been grumbling a bit. Since I realized I was expecting again, I have been slacking a bit on the cookie making. Why don't you both come in, and we can sit in the dining room."

Cole winced at the reminder of her pregnancy as he gestured Bishop to follow him in. The oatmeal and chocolate chip cookies smelled like heaven. The men took a seat at the table and accepted the coffee she offered. Bishop stopped her from getting the cookies. "Ms. Dombrowski, we have some very bad news. It might be better if you sit down."

Kate's head snapped back, her hand shooting unconsciously to her belly. "There wasn't an accident at the lighthouse was there? Is Pete okay?"

"Pete's okay, Kate." Cole kept his voice calm, not wanting to upset her more than necessary. Troubled by her pregnancy, he folded his hands on the table to fill some time.

"One of the children then?"

"No, the kids are fine." Cole straightened in his chair, let his eyes roam a moment. He had read somewhere that it was always best to start with a question you knew the answer to. "Is Pete at work?"

Kate relaxed a bit and sat in the seat that the detective indicated. "Yes. He's out at the lighthouse."

"Is that a big job?"

"Yeah. They leave from the marina at 8:30am, but Pete's usually up early so he can get things ready to go. Sometimes, he goes out and works a few more hours in the evening. Like today, he was up and gone at 7:00am. I didn't even get a chance to make him breakfast." Kate brought her eyes back to Cole's, startled by the intensity of his gaze.

"I don't know how to tell you this. To be honest, I forgot about the pregnancy until you mentioned it."

Kate raised an eyebrow carefully, braced herself. "It's okay, Jack. Just tell me, or ask me, or do whatever you've come to do. I'll answer any questions you need me to, but you better tell me the bad news. Straight out."

Cole nodded. "I need to know about your relationship with Joe Barber."

Shock lifted her eyebrows. "What about it?"

"Tell me how it started, where it is now."

Kate pulled the tie out of her hair, ran her fingers through it. "I started babysitting Joe when he was little more than a baby. I was fourteen when he was born, and I took care of him and his sisters for part-time work all the way through high school. I have always been close to the Barber family."

"And now?"

"He's a good friend. He works for my husband, eats dinner here once in a while." Kate met Cole's eyes, above the coffee mug she had brought to her lips.

"Kate, I need to know if your relationship with Joe is more than friendly."

"More than friendly? You mean, *sexual?*" Aghast, Kate lowered her coffee cup, stared him down. "Is Joe in some kind of trouble?"

Cole ignored the last question. "Is it?"

"God, no. Why on earth would you think that? I love my husband. Pete's my whole world. Well, he and the children, I mean. Why would you think such a thing?"

The police officers exchanged a silent look, nodded. "Kate, Joe died this morning."

"Oh, Lord." Tears sprung into Kate's big blue eyes. Her hand returned to her belly, she brought the other to her forehead. "Oh God, no. Poor Mary. She loves that boy more than life." Kate picked her head up. "Was it... a car accident?"

Cole shared a hesitant look with Bishop, then returned his gaze to Kate. "Joe was murdered."

Kate blinked, shocked. "Murdered? I don't understand. Did he go somewhere yesterday?"

Bishop leaned forward, curious. "What do you mean, ma'am?"

"He couldn't have been killed here. People just don't get killed on Drummond, unless it's an accident. He must have gone somewhere, right? Where did he go?"

Cole fumbled with a way to continue this, undone by the intense sadness that overtook her. It had been a rough day. First Jill, then Billy and the Barbers. Jill had gone into shock. Billy had reacted as if he had been physically attacked. Then Joe's parents and sister. Mary had calmly walked into the next room before losing it, hurling dishes out of cupboards, throwing everything in site, screaming until her husband could bring her down. Alice had rocked her mother and sobbed. Kate Dombrowski had taken it almost better than everyone else. She displayed no intense dramatic outbursts, but her eyes had filled with irrevocable sadness.

"Why would anyone want to kill Joe?" Their hesitation unnerved her. "Jack, spit it out. Say whatever is on your mind." Her mind brought her to the solution slowly. "Why were you asking about our relationship? Do you think I have something to do with it?"

"There is certain evidence at the crime scene that necessitated these questions. We needed to know if you were possibly having an affair with the victim." Bishop leaned back in his chair, trusting the wide blue eyes and crocodile tears.

"I'm sorry, Kate."

"Jack, how could you think that? You know Pete. For heavens sakes, you play cards together. Pete loves that boy."

"We have to follow the evidence." Cole swallowed audibly. "Kate, do you know of anyone who would have wanted to hurt Joe? Any enemies?"

She shook her head. "Everybody loves him."

Cole scratched his head, dismayed. He had gotten the same message from Joe's parents. "Okay. I know this is rough, but I'd like to ask you not to contact your husband. We're going out to question the crew now, and I don't want anyone preparing answers."

Kate nodded, sniffed. "Okay."

"Do they have any way of being contacted out there?"

"Pete has a cell phone, but only the guys and I know the number. All calls come through here, and I have Pete call them back."

"Will you give me that number?"

"Sure." Kate waited for Cole to bring out his notebook and then enunciated each number for him. "I just can't believe Joe's dead. He was so full of life, and he had just met Jill."

"How well do you know Ms. Traynor?"

Kate tilted her head to the side; her eyes followed the sunflower wallpaper pattern aimlessly. "I just met her once, but I liked her. She seemed like an honest person. Joe was quite taken with her."

"Did she feel the same for him?"

"I only met her once, Jack. I have no idea, but I can't imagine her physically hurting him."

"I think we have all we need." Bishop rose from the chair, waited.

"Would you like me to call someone to stay with you?" Cole asked.

"I'm okay."

"Thanks for your time, ma'am." Bishop angled his head toward the door.

"You might as well take a cookie." Kate stood abruptly, as if the domestic chore would somehow ease the lump that had settled in her throat. "I'm sure this has been an awful day for you." She handed each man two cookies and saw them to the door.

When the door closed behind Cole, Bishop grunted. "I should get another wife."

Cole rolled his eyes, waited until they were back in his SUV before saying anything. "What do you think?"

"She wasn't sleeping with the kid, and as far as she knows, her husband is innocent."

"I don't need a recap, I was there." Cole hesitated, blew out air he was holding. "I believe her."

"So do I, but her timetable gives Pete ninety minutes to get it done and get to the job site. The same ninety minutes the kid died in. I'm betting no one was with him, so he doesn't have a reliable alibi."

"If Kate wasn't sleeping with Joe, what would be the motive?" Cole challenged, backing out of the driveway.

Bishop contemplated it, running various ideas through his mind, discarding them one by one. "I don't know."

"Maybe we're looking at it the wrong way."

"How else can we look at it? The kid was an hourly construction worker; he rented a trailer, was nice to his mother, and was seeing a new girl. One day, somebody pops him. Next to the body, are the letters P-E-T. On the other side is a hammer belonging to his boss, Pete Dombrowski." Bishop droned. "His bosses name begins with those same letters."

"It wasn't P-E-T. It was P-E."

Bishop rolled his eyes. "Okay. I guess I'm jumping there. It's P-E and then something."

"It looks a little too packaged, or staged. Too easy."

Bishop shrugged. "These things often are. In most murder cases, the victim is killed by someone he knows."

"Let's not jump to conclusions here. I've known Pete a long time. He's a good man and has a nice family. There's no prior violence or bad behavior. In fact, I have never had words with him as a police officer."

"Good men often do very bad things," Bishop intoned.

Cole remained silent, but mentally reaffirmed that they were looking for someone else.

"Cole, you have to look at the evidence. The evidence points in a clear direction."

Cole conceded with a nod. He wouldn't rule out Pete until after he had looked into his eyes, heard the answers to his questions.

Fifty-Two

Belying the horror within Jill's mind, the overhead blue sky was bright with sunlight. Wrapped in Joe's forgotten sweater, Jill spent the last few hours tossing in bed, still only long enough to stare out of the window, at Lake Huron. The waves rolled onto the rocky shore endlessly, but she didn't hear or see them. She saw Joe; he was everywhere. She tried to rest, to block him from her thoughts and failed. Hunger and a need for distraction drove her to seek comfort at the Northwood. She slouched through the door, absently noticing the emptiness of the room.

Quinn, had slowly simmered since Billy had told him what had happened. Jill's presence was not a welcome addition to his sanity. He had sought someone to blame, and his mind always landed on her. He couldn't help but notice the curve of her body, the graceful turn of her head, as she tilted her face to the floor and slid onto the barstool. His reaction angered him. How could he be thinking about sex at a time like this, he asked himself. Focused on his anger, he approached her coolly. "Can I get you something?" he asked sharply.

Jill's head snapped up at the terse voice. She studied him, taken aback by his latent hostility. "What?"

Quinn shook his head, turned to move away from her.

She repeated the word, insistent.

Quinn hesitated and then pounced. "What gives you the right to blame Joe's death on an innocent bystander? Who the hell do you think you are? You think just because you spent a few days with him, you're some kind of expert?"

"I didn't blame his death on anyone!" Jill retorted, raising her voice a notch. "And how am I suppose to stay out of it when I'm the one that found him? I think that puts me right in the middle of it."

"Cut the wounded act. You knew him, what? A few days? Billy was his friend since birth. How do you think it felt for him to be questioned by Cole? For someone to blame him for Joe's death? Billy had enough to deal with before this." Quinn spat at her, concentrating on the argument, relieving his own demons rather than listening or thinking about hers.

"Oh! And I don't have enough to deal with? You're one to talk. What did you have to deal with? Did Billy come in and cry a bit about his friend dying?"

"You know, Joe was just fine before you came along. His fights with Billy never lasted more than a few hours. You come into the picture, and all of a sudden, it's a different ballgame. You shouldn't have slapped Billy that night, and you shouldn't have said anything this morning."

Exhausted, Jill sighed and quieted for a moment. Finally, she explained, "I didn't blame him. I told the truth. I told the Deputy what I thought was relevant. The only person I have ever seen remotely offensive to Joe was Billy. It's relevant," she repeated, almost to convince herself that it was.

"It's not relevant." Quinn argued, eyeing her coldly. "He just lost his job a few days ago, fought with his friend, and now he has to live with the fact that Joe died before he could apologize. How could you do this to him? You think just because you witnessed some little fight, that you have it all figured out?" Quinn gestured, pointing at her. "You know nothing. Billy was his friend."

"You know, you're right. I haven't been here for very long, and I don't know everything, but there are things that you don't know."

Quinn asked, "Yeah, like what?"

Jill shook her head, silently wishing she wouldn't have said that. Any response, she knew, would sound self-pitying. "Billy wasn't the one who walked into Joe's trailer this morning and found him covered in blood. Billy wasn't the one who had to call the police and tell them Joe was dead..." To Jill's disgust, her voice broke and tears that she had believed were dried up welled in her eyes. She ignored them and marched through her argument before she lost control completely. "Billy didn't watch every person he ever loved die in front of him. Don't talk to me about what I know and don't know, you sanctimonious prick." Jill paused, breathed. "So, I don't know anything? What the hell makes you my judge? I know what I saw, what I've learned." She swiveled off the bar stool, intent to get as far away from Quinn as she could.

Quinn hadn't taken a moment to look at her until she started crying. Guilt rolled in his gut, his thoughtless words slapped him. "Jill, wait." He walked around to face her, cringed at the tears that poured freely. He put his hands on her arms, and looked into her face. "I'm sorry."

"Screw you, let me go." She struggled half-heartedly, her energy sapped by shock and grief. She had no strength to continue the argument, and the fight drained out of her when she saw the concern now evident in Quinn's intentions.

"I'm really sorry, Jill. I had no right to say those things to you. Hell, I didn't even mean most of them. I just needed someone to yell at."

Her lip quivered as the tears turned into a torrent. She nodded, and went when he tugged her toward him. He gathered her into his arms and held her. He stroked her hair and rocked her a bit in the middle of the bar. "Do you want to get out of here? Maybe go drink somewhere else where we can talk or laugh or whatever?" He whispered, gently.

"Don't you have to work?"

"I can make a call."

Being with anyone was better than being alone. At least with Quinn, she wouldn't have to pretend that she felt a certain way, or be friendly when she didn't feel friendly: Quinn had already seen her bad side, she could just be real. Jill nodded against his shoulder. "Please."

Quinn walked her back to the stool, slid around the bar and made the call. Twenty minutes later the pair was on their way to Chuck's. The outdoor/indoor carpeting was right out of the late seventies, the paneling from some time before. Jill's normally photographic mind barely noticed the pool table, billiard lamp, antiquated deer heads. The waitress got their order and shared condolences with Quinn. Customers were teary-eyed, curious, and all wanting to talk about Joe's death. Some were pointing to Jill and trying to get a better look.

"Maybe this wasn't such a good idea." Quinn spoke quietly.

Jill shrugged. "Let's just eat and get out of here." Her eyes had lost the colorful spunk that made them so charming. She looked at him without really seeing him.

Quinn berated himself silently for giving her such a hard time. He had been a real ass, and it really didn't have anything to do with Billy. Quinn realized that Billy was his own biggest problem. As a bartender, people told him their troubles, unburdened themselves to his listening ear over some drink. Jill had become the center of an easy target and right in his line of fire at the wrong time. The smallest thing he could do was help her through this. "I don't know about you, but I could really get drunk tonight. If you would like some company, we could stop and pick up some stuff at Wazz's and go back to my place, or your place."

Jill nodded. "If that's okay with you. I'd rather not deal with a bunch of people."

They accepted their drinks from the waitress, and Quinn asked for the food 'to go.' They made small talk as they waited and fielded questions from other customers about the morning's events. When the food was ready, Quinn hurriedly paid the bill, said goodbye, and rushed off with Jill in tow. At some point, they decided to spend the evening at Jill's, for which she was thankful. They drove to the party store silently. Tami sat outside on a log slab bench and stared up at the canopy over the gasoline pumps. The cigarette between her fingers turned to ash unnoticed. Quinn moved to say something to her but she shook her head not wanting the interaction.

Minutes later they were loaded down with beer and liquor and on the road again. They arrived at Jill's and made themselves comfortable on the sofa. They talked about small things, carefully avoiding Joe's death for a long time. The sun dipped behind the trees and the pile of bottles cluttered the floor around the couch, where they curled comfortably. A stretch of silence had Quinn wondering if what she had said was true, or if she was speaking out of spite.

He turned his head, ran his hand through his hair. "Jill." He waited until she craned her head around to meet his eyes. "Did you mean what you said earlier today? About your family?"

Jill's eyes darkened a bit. "That they're dead? Yeah." She shook her head, in thought. "I'm probably cursed."

"Why do you say that?" Quinn wasn't going to let her say something so extreme and not explain herself.

Jill sighed, not wanting to talk about it – but she had brought it up, she thought. "I was little when my parents were killed. We were on our way to a school play I was in, and running late because I had spilled grape juice all over myself. I'm not sure if they actually ran a light, or just weren't as cautious as they should have been. They crashed into one of those big moving trucks that was speeding through an intersection." Jill took a swig from the bottle before continuing. "I was trapped in the backseat, but I must have faded out for a few minutes because I remember waking up and seeing men with tools trying to take the car apart. I was scared and angry, and I couldn't understand why mom and dad weren't saying anything.

"I went to live with my grandparents after that. They only had two children: my mom, and her older brother. My grandparents sold my parents' house and set up a fund for me. When I was eight, I would ride my bicycle to the cemetery and visit them." She laughed quietly, her eyes filling with gold flecks as she was caught in another time. "I use to take them drawings that I had done and tell them about what I was doing. There was a bright red cardinal that would sit on the tombstone. I tried to draw him, but I could never get it quite right. That's when I got into photography. I grabbed Grandma's camera, hid it in my knapsack and snuck off to the cemetery. I was gone for hours. There were only 12 shots left on the role, so I took my time and got just the right ones. It was dark before I went home and my grandparents were worried sick. They didn't know that I was sneaking off to the cemetery; they thought I was playing in the park with friends. A group of us biked to school together, and afterwards they stopped and played. I went to the cemetery." Jill shrugged. "Looking back, its kind of odd that they didn't pick on me about it."

"What did your grandparents say when you came home?"

Jill smiled. "They must have been panicked, but I came home so excited. I didn't even think that I could get in trouble and I launched into this explanation of what I had gotten and how great it was. Grandma was thrilled to see me so happy… it had been a while, I guess. They didn't yell or anything. Grandpa took me right out the next day and bought me my first camera and a bunch of film, and taught me how to load it properly."

"Did the pictures of the bird turn out?"

Jill nodded. "The film in the camera was black and white, which I didn't know at the time. It made the picture even the more haunting. I wasn't so thrilled with it when I was little. When we got the pictures back, I insisted on going to the gravesite and reshooting the area in color. Grandpa helped me but I never saw the bird again. When I had my first real class, one of our projects was to take a black and white and color something dramatically with a special marker. Like those popular pictures of the little kids... you know what I'm talking about?" Quinn nodded. "Instead of shooting something new, I went straight home and dug out those pictures. I had one where the bird was perched on the edge of my parents' stone, kind of on an angle. I hadn't remembered the lighting and shadows. It really was a great picture, it was just missing something. So, I colored the bird red and I took it back to the teacher. He couldn't believe that I had taken the picture when I was eight. He said it was a masterpiece of skill, or once-in-a-lifetime luck."

"That's incredible." Quinn gazed across the wool blanket at her.

Jill nodded, the somber expression returning to her face. "My grandfather passed away when I was fifteen. By then, we had been spending every summer here and we'd drive up for my spring breaks and what not. Sometimes, we'd go to Florida to visit Uncle Dave, but most of the time we came here."

"How did he die?"

"Stroke. First, he had one that paralyzed his side and stopped him from speaking. Grandma rented one of those hospital beds and had him set up in the living room. God, that was bad. He would try to say something, and would struggle. Grandpa was a talker. It must have been the worse thing in the world for him not to be able to speak. He couldn't write, either. His right hand didn't function at all, so he'd scratch things onto a pad with his left... but, most of it wasn't legible. I'd come home from school and sit with him, try to help him. A few months later, he had one that was fatal." Jill choked back another drink, and swallowed the lump in her throat

"Grandma and I came up here twice after that, but she couldn't handle it. Grandpa had really loved it here. She thought about selling it, but never did. Eventually, I graduated from high school and attended college. The school counselor use to talk to Grandma about encouraging me to study something else. He always said that I had a mind for science and for solving things." Jill shook her head sadly. "Grandma tore him up one side and down the other." She mimicked her grandmother's voice, "If my granddaughter knows what she wants, I'm not standing in her way. And neither are you."

Quinn chuckled. "She sounds feisty."

"God, was she ever. I moved into dorms freshman year. I got an apartment with a friend after that, took an internship with the Daily Journal, which got me into the police department. I loved police work so much that I talked the chief into letting me stay on, and shoot forensic pictures. Crime scenes fascinated me. I learned how to be observant, how to remember tiny details about areas, about people. They teach you to study the four corners of a frame, to make sure you have what you want before you click it off. One of my professor's use to tell horror stories of weddings. I never got into those. I was more into the darker moments, rather than the lighter ones."

"After I went to college, Grandma spent the winter months with Uncle Dave in Florida. Then, this last September she announced that she didn't want to go. She never said she wasn't feeling well but she was just tired of traveling. So we cancelled her ticket, and I spent more time with her."

"You were worried," Quinn supposed.

Jill nodded. "Yeah, I was. One day, I came in and she didn't answer. I found her motionless in her bed. The doctor told me that her body just gave out, just decided to quit." Jill shook her head. "I think she just got tired of living." Jill remained quiet for a moment. Along the story path, Quinn had lightly rubbed her arm, attempting to soothe, unconsciously.

Noticing the motion, she looked away guiltily. "I'm sorry. I must be boring you to tears."

Quinn shook his head. "You haven't bored me."

She nodded, absently tried to pull her arm away.

Quinn held her there, touched her chin gently. "Jill, it's okay to talk about it. It's okay to reach out and share your stories. If you want to talk about Joe, you can. I know he was important to you."

Jill's eyes filled with unwanted tears. She rolled them, angry with herself. "I've been so selfish, Quinn. I'm sorry."

"Selfish? How?"

"You've known him for years. You were his friend. I've known him for a few days. It doesn't give me the right to feel like I'm the only one that's… hurting." Her voice caught, shattered.

"No, you're not the only one whose hurting, but I don't think you really believe that. I think you're just trying to shut it out. It's natural to want to stop living, to want to escape. But, Jill, we are living. That's why we need to talk about it. Denying that he's dead won't bring him back."

Jill voiced the concern that had haunted her for years. "Almost everyone I've ever been really close to dies. What if a little bit of me dies with each person I bury. What if there's nothing left?"

Jill wiped the tears from her cheeks with one hand. She leaned her head back on the couch and looked at Quinn. He continued to rub her arm, lost in her grief filled eyes. Within Quinn, something snapped. The grief rolled to the surface, and suddenly Quinn reached for Jill. He pulled her close, finding comfort in the soft warmth of her body. Passion rose inside of him, and he drew her onto his lap, ravaged her mouth with his. She responded with her own aggression and need to live.

He broke away from the searing kiss, brought her hand to the pulse at his neck. "Do you feel that, Jill?" She looked at him, her eyes clouded. "We're alive." Fresh tears gathered in her eyes, spilled off her cheeks. Quinn pulled her against him, and held her against the grief that coursed through them both.

Fifty-Three

Thursday Morning

Beth stepped out of North Country Sports' and crossed the street back to the corner restaurant's parking lot. The sport shop's owner told her the only people going out to the lighthouse were members of the construction crew working on it, and if anyone else was going out there it would almost have to be through them. Furthermore, the construction crew was Drummond Island based and directed her to the ferry boat. Beth unlocked her car, and hopped back in, parked her car in the line up. Apparently, she had hit it just in time for a boat. She had no more than put her car in park and the cars ahead of her were sliding down the hill at a crewman's waving arms.

The line started to move. Rolling her car over the metal grid and over the gate, she followed the arm directions precisely, stopping when the man signaled her to. She rolled down her window to pay the fare, then hopped out of the car and watched as the gate creaked upward, raising in the same manner a drawbridge would. The ferry was only three quarters full, giving her ample room to walk between cars and lean against the painted steel side, gaze out over the water. In the distance, Beth could plainly see the lighthouse.

Flipping out her cell phone, she dialed Lisa.

"T'sup?"

Beth laughed into the phone. "Good morning, Lisa."

"Hey, Bethy. Where are you? Are you in DeTour yet?"

"I'm on a car ferry, headed to Drummond Island. I can see the lighthouse from here. It looks big. Even if Richard isn't here, Li, it is so worth it. Just to know where Grandpa Lee crashed, to feel the energy."

Lisa grinned. "You're feeling it then, hey?"

Beth inhaled the pure Huron air, enjoyed it. "Am I ever! It's so fresh here... so beautiful, serene even."

"What about the other?"

Beth didn't have to be told what she meant. "Yeah, it's bad still. Yesterday morning was the worst. I actually got sick, Li. The image was so vivid."

"Has that ever happened before?"

Beth was comforted by the worry evident in her friend's tone. "No. What's weird is that I don't think it's my bother I am seeing. I mean, I can't explain it."

"Hopefully, you'll find your brother and find some answers."

The boat bumped against the rubber tire barrier of the corrugated steel dock. "Shit. I have to go, we've made it to the island."

"Keep your head up, Beth. And remember, I'm only a phone call away."

Beth grinned. "Talk to you later, Li."

"'Bye."

Beth hopped back into her car, rolled off the ferry, and followed the road's curve that took the decision of which way to go right out of her hands—there was only one way. She drove after the cars, surprised at the utter lack of buildings. Typically, she thought, towns popped up close to the link to get off the island, but then, very little seemed typical lately.

Fifty-Four

Jill rolled over in bed and groaned at the brightly lit room. She opened her eyes to find Quinn stirring beside her. Frantically, she glanced down, breathed a sigh of relief to find her clothes still on and to see Quinn fully clothed. Quinn winked open one eye, took in her expression. "Hung over?"

She groaned.

Quinn raised himself onto one elbow and leered. "I can make you feel better."

She arched an eyebrow. "Don't even think that you're going to get me to drink one of those special concoctions. No way. What I could really use is coffee."

"Can I take you out to breakfast?"

"Eh. I'm not sure I can handle talking to people right now."

"Hmmm." Quinn thought for a moment. "Well, my jeep is still at the bar, so you're going to have to drive me in anyway. We could stop at the bakery, and I could run in for donuts and coffee, then we can take them to the bar and eat them."

"Isn't the bar closed?"

"Exactly. It'll be nice and quiet."

"Okay, but I need to shower first. I smell like a bottle of whiskey."

Quinn grinned. "I think you may have spilled some on you."

"Hey, listen. About last night…"

Quinn placed his finger on her lip. "Don't." He wasn't about to let her minimize what had happened, or sweep it under the rug, or worse yet apologize.

Jill leaned away, fell silent, made a mental note to bring it up later. She couldn't let him get the wrong idea. Instead of making another argument, she rolled out of bed. "I'm going to go shower then… and try to find some aspirin."

Quinn watched her grab some things out of a drawer and stumble out of the bedroom. He rolled over and peered out the window. It was a gorgeous day even though he doubted many islanders would notice. He wandered around the house, viewing her pictures, trying to figure out how she thought. When she reappeared in much less time than he expected, she looked better—tired, but better.

"I'm ready." A small smile crossed her lips. "Of course, I won't be completely awake until I have cups and cups of coffee in me."

"Let me splash some water on my face and we'll get out of here."

Jill nodded, brushing past him, careful to avoid contact. They couldn't have a repeat of last night. Joe had wanted her to make love with him desperately, and Jill had abstained with little effort. Had Quinn even suggested it, she probably would have given in. Thank God he pulled away when he did, she thought, as she gathered empty beer bottles into her arms.

"Okay, I'm ready." Quinn retrieved his ball cap from the kitchen table, slid it over the dark crew cut hair.

The night's growth had his strong, angular face looking softer, more approachable. Jill cleared her thoughts and grabbed her keys. "Let's roll."

They drove to the bakery in comfortable silence. Quinn parked and went in for food and coffee. Jill sat back and listened to the radio, thankful she hadn't had to go through the night alone. Minutes ebbed away before Quinn returned. Jill drummed impatient fingers on the steering wheel. Finally, he swung out the bakery door, motioning for her to open the car door for him. She helped him get situated, and peeled back out of the driveway.

"You are never going to believe what is going around."

Jill slanted her eyes at him. "What?"

"They interviewed Kate yesterday and insinuated that she was having an affair with Joe."

"What?! That's absurd! Who told you that?"

"Kate's sister was in the bakery this morning. Apparently, Kate was upset and called her. Now it's *everywhere*."

"And they asked Pete not to leave Drummond. Pete thinks he's a suspect."

The blood. "Shit. It's because of the blood."

Jill still hadn't told Quinn many of the actual murder details. "What blood?"

"Joe's blood." Jill shuddered. "Scrawled in Joe's blood, were the letters P E, then a line. At the time, I thought it was a message. It didn't occur to me that Pete could have killed him." Jill shook her head. "Joe adored Pete and Kate. No way."

"Was the line like a T?"

Jill thought about it, saw it in her mind. "I'm not sure."

"Oh, and get this. That Dick guy didn't show up for work yesterday."

"Yeah, but who did? It was Bob's birthday the night before, remember? Everyone was totally hammered."

"Bob showed up. So did Gary."

"And Pete, right?"

"Yep, but Pete left the house at seven in the morning. That gave him ninety minutes before the boat left."

Jill winced. "Pete couldn't have done it. Why would he?"

Quinn stared at her. "Why would Joe have written his name, if he wasn't involved?"

"I thought it might have been a warning."

"A warning for what?"

"I don't know." She met Quinn's incredulous look as she brought the Tracker to a stop. "I don't know," she repeated. "P-E looks like Pete to me. Is there anything else it could mean? Or do you know any other Pete in Joe's life? Something that could be related to his death?"

Quinn pondered the question for a moment. "There's only one Pete that I know of."

"Why didn't Dick show up for work? And who is this guy? He just shows up and wants a job? Who does that?"

Quinn grinned. "Isn't that the pot calling the kettle black?"

Jill opened her mouth, then closed it, conceding the point. "Yeah, I guess I did the same thing, didn't I?"

Quinn juggled the bag and coffees as he climbed out of the Tracker and led the way to the back door. "He was drinking pretty heavily. I think Marci took him home, so I'm betting that he just couldn't get up. He probably didn't have the energy. What do you know about him?"

"Next to nothing. I never worked with him, since I haven't been out to the lighthouse yet. My first days of work were spent building a deck. Joe would have already left if I hadn't had that call from my agent."

"Huh?"

"Yesterday morning. I should have been there at quarter after eight, but the night before, Joe and I decided to go in late. My agent scheduled a 9:00am conference call, so I didn't get there until about quarter after nine or something like that."

"Who else knew that? Did Joe tell Pete?"

Jill followed him into the bar once he had gotten the door unlocked and sat on a stool next to Quinn. "I don't think he told Pete. I know he called Mrs. Hiller, just so she wouldn't worry about us showing up late. I think I was with him the rest of the night, until late. I can't imagine him calling Pete after I left him at two in the morning."

Quinn handed her the large coffee and the donut bag. "Well, one of two things happened: the killer was in Joe's trailer for some other reason and Joe surprised him or he went in specifically to kill Joe, somehow knowing that Joe would be there. I'm guessing it's the first because why would anyone want to specifically kill him?"

"It could be random."

He raised an eyebrow, dubious. "Those kinds of things just don't happen on Drummond. And if random, was it a robbery? Who in their right mind robs someone who lives in a thirty year old trailer?"

"If Joe wasn't the target, and it wasn't a robbery, why would anyone be in his trailer?"

"Lots of people stayed at Joe's trailer. He use to say it was other slobs that cluttered it up, not him."

Jill shook her head at the image. "That's so odd."

"What?" Quinn said with a mouthful, after biting into a bear claw.

"I never saw it messy. It was really clean every time I was there and I don't think anyone stayed over since I met him."

Quinn grinned. "He must have cleaned it for you. And the word got out pretty fast that he was dating a Kate."

"A *Kate*?"

Quinn winced. "Oops, sorry. Joe and I defined women as either Kate's or Marci's. He came up with the scale. He adored Kate. We used them as opposite ends of the spectrum. A Marci is someone you take home from the bar, a Kate is someone you take home to meet the family."

"Well, it's nice to know that he thought of me as a Kate. I really liked her when I met her."

"You know, Billy probably stayed there more than anyone. Technically, he lives with his girlfriend Deedee, but they fight quite a bit."

"What if it was Billy, Quinn?"

Quinn shook his head, his eyes darkening. "No, it couldn't be."

"You won't even discuss it?"

Quinn flattened his hand against the bar. "No, I won't talk about it. Billy couldn't kill anyone. He might have a temper, but he would never seriously hurt Joe."

"What if Joe was surprised in the dark, and didn't know it was Billy?"

"Jill, people were at Joe's all the time. He wouldn't have been surprised into a struggle with anyone unless it was someone who had no place being there, or someone who was obviously there for a strange reason."

Jill deflated, sank into the long john pastry with a sigh. "Who could have killed him?"

"I think you're looking at this the wrong way."

Jill perked up, waited.

"You should figure out *why* he was killed. The *who* will follow."

"But why would anyone target Joe? He rented that trailer, according to you was a slob until four or five days ago, and was..." Jill searched for the right word.

"Normal?" Quinn supplied.

Jill nodded. "What makes him different? All he owned besides clothing was a piece of shit truck that he was hoping to get four hundred out of."

Quinn shrugged. "I don't know, Jill."

Frustrated, Jill made a decision. "Well, I'm going to try and figure this out."

He raised an eyebrow. "Why? The police will handle this, Jill."

"I cared for him, Quinn." Jill studied her hands to avoid his searching gaze. "And everyone I've ever cared about has died. It doesn't make any sense, so I need it to make sense. I need to prove that he didn't die just because... just because he maybe loved me a little bit. I know it's stupid, but... I need to know it wasn't my fault. Do you understand?"

Quinn's heart broke for her. "Jill, you didn't have anything to do with Joe's death. It wasn't your fault."

Jill pasted a small smile on her face, continued with false enthusiasm. "I know, but it will make me feel better if I can help figure this out."

Quinn stared her down until she met his eyes. He touched her cheek lightly in an offer of support.

"It would make me feel even better if you would help me with this."

Quinn groaned. "What do you want me to do?"

"Let's start with information gathering."

"I'll talk to Marci. Maybe she can shed some more light on this Dick character. She knows all the seedy shit about everyone, and will have the killer all but figured out."

Fifty-Five

The bar opened with Jill still perched on a bar stool and Quinn regretting the decision not to clean up at her house that morning. Of course, other than a few workers in for lunch, it had been pretty quiet. There was never much traffic on Drummond in May. The tourist season didn't seriously pick up until late June. Jill bought a pad of paper at the Dry Goods and was now formulating a list of potentials. Quinn called Marci earlier, but she didn't answer the phone. Jill was antsy for more information. Soon enough, Quinn speculated, information would just come strolling into the bar. People who enjoyed gossiping usually partook in some kind of coffee clutch in the morning or gathered at the bar in the evening. Quinn studied Jill as he leaned against the bar and enjoyed her deductive reasoning. He was annoyed that he had allowed himself to be talked into helping her. In the back of his mind, he recognized that butting into the investigation was definitely illegal. With a start, he realized he should have called Alice. Quinn knew he'd find messages from her on his answering machine when he got home. Jill cut off her words in mid sentence when she realized Quinn wasn't paying attention.

"What's on your mind?"

Quinn urged her to continue.

"Oh come on. What is it?"

Sighing, he wiped down the bar. "I never gave Alice a thought last night."

"She was probably with her family, right?" Jill was puzzled, the realization dawning slowly. "Oh. You and Alice are close?"

"We've dated on and off. Not recently," Quinn shrugged. "Not since she moved away last fall. I just feel bad that I didn't try to call her, or offer my support."

"You couldn't have been both places at once, and honestly... I'm really glad you were with me. I know it sucks, and I shouldn't be selfish, but I can't join you in feeling guilty about that one. Being alone last night would have been tough." Jill looked into his eyes. "I know Alice probably needed you, and *I am* being selfish... but thanks."

Quinn nodded, accepting. Jill had been a wreck the day before. Alice wouldn't have begrudged him that. "She did have her family with her. I'm sure Jesse's probably here now, too."

"Who's Jesse?"

"The older sister: Jesse, Joe, Alice."

Jill's response was cut off by the front door swinging open. Both of their eyes were drawn to the medium framed, oval faced, tidy blond who walked with purpose. She marched straight up to the bar, and waited for Quinn to greet her.

"Can I help you?"

Beth nodded, weariness beginning to outline her features. "I'm hoping you can help me with something. I got onto the island this morning, and stopped at the party store, where they directed me to the Fort Drummond Marina. But the guy I talked to there didn't know anything, and directed me here."

Quinn shared a look with Jill. "Know anything about what?"

"Oh, I'm looking for my brother: Richard DeForge."

Jill's mouth dropped open, she shot a look to Quinn then turned back to the woman. Talk about information strolling in, she thought. "I work with Dick."

Beth shook her head, confused. "Work with him? Are you sure? Because my brother doesn't go by Dick."

"I'm Jill Traynor." She held out her hand for Beth to shake.

"Beth DeForge," Beth replied, smiling.

Quinn pointed to a table. "I think you should both sit and talk. Would you like something to drink?"

Beth nodded, grateful. "Do you have hot tea?"

Quinn nodded, rolled his eyes when she turned her back. "What would you like, Jill?"

"I still have some coffee in here, but thanks." Jill smiled, and turned back to Beth. "Beth, I am actually hoping that we can help each other."

Beth raised an eyebrow, confused. "How can *I help you*?"

"Well, it's a long story—but let's start with why you're here, and why you're looking for your brother." Jill leaned forward, placed her notebook on the table as she sat down.

Beth's neck tingled, and she decided to be honest with this woman. She accepted her tea from the bartender and started the story with her grandmother's diary and her grandfather's disappearance at the lighthouse. She explained that her father had died, and that she believed her brother might come to close the chapter in his mind, to see the lighthouse for himself. Her journey had led her to DeTour and now here. She left out the paranormal experiences, the visions of blood and her worries. When she finally finished her story, Jill looked slightly crestfallen.

"Did I say the wrong thing?"

Jill shook her head, disgusted that she was so transparent. "No, not at all. Let me tell you what I know. Dick asked for a job working with the construction crew renovating the lighthouse. I've never heard anything about his grandfather. I heard this second hand, through one of the guys, but I know that Dick told Pete that he wanted to move up to Drummond and needed some funds to start a life here."

"That's just preposterous. Richard's a real estate sales person and has never done physical labor in his life. Why didn't he just tell this Pete guy the truth?"

Jill hesitated. "Beth, it seems like a mighty big effort to drive here all the way from New York just to close a chapter. It seems like an even bigger effort for you to follow your brother here. Is there something you're not telling me?"

Leaning forward, Beth looked into Jill's eyes. "You seem quite interested in why I would come here."

Jill lifted the corner of her mouth lightly, inclined her head. "You first."

Resigned, Beth admitted the truth. "I get feelings."

"Go on."

"Usually, it's just a twinge at the back of my neck. When I get these sparks, it's about something specific. I found a letter from the DeTour Reef Lighthouse that mentioned an accompanying logbook. The logbook was gone, but the letter said the book contained a letter from my grandfather. When I found these things, and read my grandmother's diary, I felt as if Richard had come here and I was worried about him. So, I had to come." Beth pondered whether to tell her about the visions of blood but hesitated.

"I'm interested in your brother because a coworker of ours was killed yesterday morning." Jill's voice broke as the image flashed in her mind. She cleared her throat and continued. "That kind of thing just doesn't happen here and your brother didn't show up for work yesterday. He's new, so naturally I wondered about him."

Beth's mouth fell open, her face drained of color. "Oh, God."

Jill's eyes widened as the other woman grasped the edge of the table, moaned low in her throat. "How can I help? Quinn! Get me some water!"

"No, no. I'm fine." Beth willed herself to calm, to breathe. "Do you know where my brother is?"

Jill wanted to learn more and made the decision not to let Beth slip away: There was more to the story than Beth was sharing. "No, but I can drive you to the people who should." Jill spoke decisively, not allowing Beth any room to wriggle out of the offer of help. "Just let me tell Quinn where we're going."

Fifty-Six

Marci was treated to a double take when she slid into the bar, devoid of her usual perfectly styled hair, heavy make-up, and lack of clothing. Unfortunately, she was in no state to appreciate the achievement of her long sought goal. Her eyes were red rimmed, and Quinn assessed that she was taking Joe's death just as hard as everyone else. Her white blond hair hung freely around her face, which looked tired and run down.

"Hey, Marz."

"Hi, Quinn. Grab me a Pepsi, hey?" She fumbled inside her handbag for cigarettes, finally whipped out the soft pack and a lighter.

"How are you doing?" inquired Quinn.

Marci rocked her head from side to side. "I just can't believe he's gone. It's not right. How much can one family take? First the accident, the struggle to get through it, and now this." She paused to light the smoke. "How's his gal pal doing?"

Quinn shook his head. "You know, she's the one who found him."

Marci nodded, searching his face. "You must have had a long night."

"Yep." Quinn slid the drink across the bar. "Can I ask you something?"

"Go ahead."

"You took that new guy on Pete's crew home the other night, right?"

Marci offered a winsome smile. "You haven't developed a sudden interest in my activities have you?" She chuckled at Quinn's pained expression. "Never mind. Yes, I took him home and treated him to a good time. What do you want to know?"

"Anything strike you as odd?"

Marci raised an eyebrow.

"No, not that way. I mean… just that night in general. Did he tell you anything about himself that seemed unusual?"

Marci shrugged, considered. "When we were here, he spent most of his time talking to Bobby, not me."

"Bob? What about, do you know?"

"Just the lighthouse job, in general." She inhaled, furrowed her brow. "I don't really remember anything else, Quinn. Why do you want to know?"

"Jill's trying to figure out who killed Joe. We don't really know anything about this Dick guy, except that his sister came in here today. Apparently, they're from some little town in New York and their grandfather died out near the lighthouse."

Marci picked up her head. "Really? Do you think she needs help? I'm pretty good at digging stuff up," she offered.

He looked at her skeptically.

She held up her hands in defense. "Hey, don't look at me like that. Joe was a friend."

Quinn nodded. "I'll mention it to her."

"Actually, I did hear that Sheriff Cole has been checking up on Pete's financial status. Apparently, he's asking people to volunteer to be fingerprinted. The word is that they pulled three sets of fingerprints off the murder weapon, although I haven't heard what the weapon is yet."

"Where did you hear this?"

The Marci that Quinn was familiar with showed on her face with her feline smirk. "Let's just say I was having a good time when the person I was with got a phone call."

"Hey, that person could be a suspect. Spill it."

"No. The person I was with heard it from someone who heard it from Cole, so it's not a good link—but it is good information."

Quinn nodded, "Alright."

The phone rang, and Quinn swiveled to answer. When the conversation ended, he shook his head. "The phone has been ringing off the hook with people wanting to know when the funeral is."

"I heard that people have been calling around from college to college, planning to pick each other up to come home for the funeral."

The front door opened, catching Quinn's attention when Alice stumbled through it. She looked somewhat dead inside, certainly exhausted. She made her way to the bar, where he met her before she sat down. "Quinn," she breathed.

He pulled her into his arms and hugged her strongly. "I am so sorry, Alice."

Alice nodded, sniffed. "I just had to get out of the house for a little while. Dad's trying to keep Mom together, and Mom's just..." To Quinn's distress, tears filled Alice's eyes. "She's just broken, Quinn. It's so horrible. She only stops crying when she's too exhausted."

"Did Jesse get home today?"

Alice wiped at her face with a pocket sized Kleenex. "Yes, thank God. Jesse's the strong one. She's been a big help. I called you last night. I figured you'd be here, but they told me you were with Jill."

"I'm sorry…"

"No, I'm glad you were with her, Quinn. She needed someone with her, and I know our family would have been worse since she didn't know any of us, really. In fact, the only thing Mom has asked about since Cole told us was how Jill was doing."

Quinn shook his head, emotionally moved. "Only your mom in her darkest hour, would worry about someone she didn't even know."

The phone rang, so Marci stepped around the counter to grab it, while Quinn hugged Alice once more.

"Alice, it's Jesse. Your mom's collapsed."

Fifty-Seven

It was late afternoon before Cole returned to his home office, exhausted. Normally, he worked a twenty-hour week keeping the peace, dealing with car accidents, and handling small licensing problems. Since yesterday morning, he had worked non-stop on the murder, answered calls and assured islanders that they would find the person responsible. He knew that the first twenty-four hour period in any murder investigation provided the best leads, the best chance for finding the perpetrator. Like many, he had moved to Drummond to get away from city life. Until yesterday, his life was nothing like his eighteen years as a Toledo detective. His answering machine blinked erratically. Stifling a yawn, he hit the play button.

"Hey, Cole. This is Hank down at the Marathon. I didn't want to call and bother Tom and Mary about this, but I have Joe Barber's truck here. I'm not real sure what to do with it. There's no rush, I just thought I'd let you know."

Cole scratched a note onto the pad beside the phone and waited. The recording beeped and moved to the next message. "Cole, this is Bishop. The autopsy results are in. I'm just scanning them now. Death was definitely caused by the head wound but besides a few scrapes and abrasions there wasn't anything else of interest. The scrapes are defensive wounds, which support our theory that there was indeed a struggle. The body has been released, and I believe the funeral home has already put an inquiry in. I'll be down tomorrow. We need to get the rest of that list fingerprinted as soon as possible." The machine beeped again, signifying the last message had played.

Cole reached to pick up the phone and make a call when it rang. "Deputy Sheriff Cole," he answered.

"Sheriff, this is Jill Traynor." Jill's voice was strained, edgy.

Cole raised an eyebrow. "Yes, Ms. Traynor. How can I help you?"

"I just got home, and someone has ransacked my house."

"Are they still there? Are you in danger?" Cole pulled out his cell phone with his other hand, dialed Bishop's number.

"Uhm… I don't think so, no. But I don't feel safe…" Her voice started to fall apart, crack with panic.

Cole kept his voice calm as he gave her specific instructions to keep her mind busy and keep her safe. "Jill, go outside and get in your car. Lock the doors and drive out to the main road. Don't touch anything else in the house, just go. Go right now, Jill. Don't open your car for anyone but me. When I get there, I'll go with you. I'll get there as soon as I can."

"Okay. Thanks."

"Hello?" Bishop was yelling from the cell phone.

Cole brought it to his ear as he headed out the door. "I think the murderer has resurfaced. Jill Traynor just reported a break in. I'm on my way there now, but I want you to get here as soon as you can. It's too coincidental to not be related."

"How does she know? People who see bodies sometimes panic, Cole."

"Dammit, Bishop. Just get down here. If I'm wrong, you can tell me all about it later."

"I'm on my way. Get her fingerprints, this time, Cole. She's still a suspect."

Cole sighed into the phone. "Okay."

Fifty-Eight

The sun dipped just beyond the tree line as Jill flipped the radio off, annoyed with the selection. She hugged her arms around her chest and squeezed against the leather seat, mentally berating herself for being so panicked, and yet jumping as a car slowed around Pigeon Cove and drove by. She had left her car in Drive with her foot firmly pressed against the brake pedal. If anyone suspicious came along she could speed away, or if she was feeling brave... she could speed after them. Honestly, she doubted that was an option. She drummed her fingers against the steering wheel and peered down the road. It had easily been fifteen minutes since she had placed the call. Jill ran her hands through her hair, turned the inside light on to look for something to do while she waited.

Right now, she'd give anything for a cell phone. Carly could be calming her with the latest Knock Out story. She could call Uncle Dave and bug him for a few minutes, after all she hadn't called him since she had moved to Drummond. She could even call Quinn. Instead, she was stuck all alone in her Tracker as her house lay in chaos. *Why would anyone be looking in my house?* Jill rolled her eyes, the answer unpleasant but obvious. She had seen a similar ransacking yesterday morning. The same person who had killed Joe, had been looking for something. Obviously, the murderer hadn't found what he or she was looking for. *Why would anyone think that I had this object?* Again, the answer was obvious. Joe had told her how word traveled on Drummond, and Quinn had reiterated it. Once someone knows something, everyone knows. Everyone certainly knew that the two of them were dating. Maybe the killer assumed that their relationship had gone on longer or that Joe might have brought whatever the killer thought he had to Jill's. The only thing she had of Joe's was a sweater. *It couldn't be the sweater, could it?* No. *Stop it, Jill,* she told herself. *No one gets killed over a sweater.*

Finally, Cole pulled his 4 by 4 off the road, parallel to Jill's vehicle. He rolled down his window. "I'm going to go check out your place. You can either come with me and leave your car here, or you can stay in your car and follow me in. You can even stay right here, and I'll drive back out and get you."

"I'll follow you in."

Cole nodded, rolled up his window, and led the way. Jill followed, breathing easier now that he was here. When they reached her driveway, she parked beside him and waited for him. Stepping out, Cole swung his flashlight beam out along the grounds. The beam landed on the shattered glass pane at the back door. He indicated for her to follow him. Jill mimicked his careful footsteps and said nothing as he quietly stepped up to the door, used a gloved hand to pull it open, and stepped in.

Dishes throughout the kitchen were turned over, cans and baskets tipped or spilled. A coffee can's plastic lid was removed, grounds spilled onto the kitchen counter. Papers that rested on the dining table were now scattered. Drawers were emptied onto the floor, silverware haphazardly tossed out of the bin. In the living area, drawers in the entertainment center were treated the same way. The bottles from the previous night's drunken fest were overturned in spots, shattered in others. Her TV, DVD, and stereo were all still nestled comfortably on the shelves. Her computer still sat safely on her desk. The intruder had been after something specific, just as Jill had suspected. A new thought entered her mind slowly. Perhaps, someone was trying to scare her. *But why?*

When Cole finished checking the bathroom and bedrooms, he carefully stepped around debris and questioned Jill. "Jill, do you notice anything missing?"

Careful not to touch anything with her hands, Jill evaluated the rooms critically. Wrinkling her face, she shook her head. "I don't think so Sheriff, but let me check the bedrooms." She eased through the open door, dismayed at the havoc in her closet. The spare room, which didn't have much in it to begin with, was treated the same way. In both rooms, the chest of drawers, just like the ones in the living room and kitchen, were excavated thoroughly. Relief poured through her as she saw that her cameras were safe. Shaking her head, she turned to Cole, who was behind her in the hallway. "What a mess. Why would anyone do this?"

"That's something we need to talk about. I need to ask you some questions. Detective Bishop is on his way down. We'll want to dust for prints and take pictures. I don't have my camera with me."

"I have cameras here, if you'd like me to do it," she offered, dully.

Cole nodded, remembering her experience in forensics. "Okay, good."

Jill stepped toward the coffee, reached her hand inside the cupboard, pausing in mid-air. Sheepishly, she looked over her shoulder. "I guess I shouldn't make coffee, should I?

Cole shook his head. "No. You better wait for the fingerprinting to be done. Do you mind if I ask you some questions?" Jill shook her head. "When was the last time you were here?"

Jill bit her lower lip, pondered the question, bringing her thoughts together. "This morning. I think we may have left here at 11 AM-ish."

Cole raised an eyebrow. "We? Who was with you?"

"Quinn... uhm, I'm not sure what his last name is, actually. The bartender at the Northwood," she waited for Cole to show that he knew who she was referring to.

"Quinn McCord," Cole supplied.

"Neither of us were doing very well, so we grabbed some bottles and got drunk together."

"Can you retrace your steps of the day for me?"

Jill chewed on her lower lip, mentally retracing her steps before she spoke. "Sure. Quinn and I woke up here, and we drove to the Island Bakery. He went in and bought donuts and coffees. We took them back to the Northwood bar, ate them and talked. He had to work in a few hours, and said the place would be quiet and empty. I stayed there for a long time." She hesitated, debating. "Honestly, I was trying to put together notes on who could have killed Joe."

Cole raised an eyebrow, fascinated. "Go on."

"I sat at the bar and sipped coffee for hours. Then Dick's sister, Beth came in and wanted help finding her brother."

"Dick DeForge?"

"Yes. Dick's sister followed me over to Pete and Kate's. Beth got the information she needed and ended up staying for a little while, but then left to find her brother. Kate and I got to talking about Joe while she was cooking dinner.

"Pete wasn't there?"

"No. Kate told me that since Pete couldn't work on the lighthouse, he needed to work on something. Sitting around was driving him insane, so he went out to the Hillers to work on the deck Joe and I started. Kate told me that they needed money, and she didn't really expect him for dinner. Pete's taking this really hard." She paused, reflecting. "Anyway, I just drove here. I was going to stop at the Northwood and talk to

Quinn, but it looked pretty busy. We agreed to call each other after he got off work anyway. After I got here, I noticed the broken glass pane. I rushed right in to use the phone to call you."

"Was there any sign that the intruder was still here when you came in?"

Jill considered it for a moment, replayed the scene in her mind. "I didn't notice any if there was."

Cole nodded. "Jill, I'm going to level with you."

Recognizing the hard edge in his tone, Jill braced herself.

"I can't find any reason why someone would want to hurt Joe or steal something from him. I think I may have been looking in the wrong direction. You may be the key to this."

"Sheriff, if you think I had something to do with Joe's…"

Cole held up a hand, stopping her. "No, I don't think you are responsible for Joe's murder. What I'm saying is that someone may have been looking to shake you or scare you. Joe's death may have been unintentional." He observed her features carefully, looking for a reaction.

"I can't imagine who would have anything to gain from scaring me. I associate with a very small group of friends, and no enemies that come to mind. Honestly, I can count them on one hand. I have an uncle in Florida, a friend in Detroit, and an agent. Here, I knew Joe before he passed, and I'm friends with Quinn." Embarrassed, she thought carefully, as if trying to come up with more friends. "Oh, yeah. The Eby's next door, my closest neighbors."

"Do you have any enemies at all? Is there anyone that you've testified against concerning your forensic photographs that could be related to this?"

Jill leaned back against the counter. "I have testified a few times, but none of the cases involved people that would come after me about it. Sheriff…"

"Most people call me Cole."

Jill nodded. "Cole, Joe's trailer looked like it had been searched." She gestured widely encompassing her home. "This place looks like it has been searched."

"Sometimes ransacking appears specific, but is intended as a scare tactic," Cole pointed out.

Jill conceded. "Okay, that's possible. But why? I don't have any enemies and from what I knew about Joe—he didn't have any either."

The sound of crunching gravel had Cole rushing to the door. "Are you expecting anyone?"

Jill shook her head and then reconsidered. "I was supposed to call Quinn earlier, it might be him."

"What the hell happened here?" Quinn whistled from the back porch. He stepped through the door, his mouth dropping open. "Holy shit! Jill, are you okay?" Rushing to her side, he pulled her against him, offering comfort.

Jill sighed into his chest, glad to have him there. "I'm okay."

"What happened?"

Cole answered. "It looks like whoever killed Joe was probably in this house."

She pulled away from Quinn. "They're going to dust for prints tonight."

"Well, I hope you know you're not staying here alone." Quinn stated, receiving no complaint from Jill. "In fact, should she stay here at all?"

"Once the place is dusted, it shouldn't be a problem if you're comfortable with it." Cole looked worriedly from Quinn to Jill. "Jill, I need to get your fingerprints."

"Is she being treated as a suspect?" Quinn questioned mildly.

"Everyone with any connection to Joe is being printed. Also, we need Jill's prints to discern which ones aren't hers within this house."

Quinn nodded. "You should fingerprint me too then. I was a friend of Joe's and have been in his trailer. I've also spent time here."

Cole raised an eyebrow. "I appreciate you volunteering. To be honest, your name was already on my list. Who else has been in here recently, Jill?"

"Joe, Quinn and I have. Oh, the telephone guy hooked my phone line up but I'm not sure if he came in to do that or not." Jill shrugged.

Cole asked a few more questions before heading back to his vehicle to retrieve the materials needed for fingerprinting. Within the hour, Detective Bishop and another investigator arrived. Jill took pictures of the scene and provided them with the rolls she exposed. Bishop repeated questions about Joe's murder and their relationship. Before the men finally left, Cole assured Jill that he would be back early the next morning to reevaluate the scene and to check the outside grounds thoroughly for clues.

Fifty-Nine

Beth leaned against the open door, waiting for her brother's car to drive past the lodge into the parking lot. She talked the clerk at the front desk into renting her the room right next to Richard's. She had been there for hours contemplating the murder and its implications. When Jill told her about the tragedy, Beth was overwhelmed with feeling. The sick ache in her stomach intensified with each hour that she waited. Avoiding the thought that her brother could somehow be involved in someone's murder just wasn't working. Worse, the body Jill and Kate discussed seemed like the body in her visions. She knew her brother was involved.

The muffled ring of her cell phone interrupted her thoughts. Beth left her perch at the window to grab it out of her coat pocket and flip it open. "Beth DeForge."

"Hey, how's it going?" Lisa's familiar voice comforted her.

Beth sighed. "Well, I've hunted down my brother..."

"So he is okay?"

"I haven't actually seen him yet. I'm in a motel room waiting for him. It's bad. There was a murder here a few days ago. I ran into a girl who is already suspicious of him."

"Why would someone be suspicious of him?"

"He took a job at that lighthouse, Li. He... oh, goodness. He just drove in. I don't know what to say to him."

"Don't start out blaming him, Beth. Ask him why he's here, why he didn't tell you he was coming. Start small," Lisa advised.

"Good idea. Here he comes. I gotta go, Li."

"Bye, Beth."

Beth clicked the phone shut, watching Richard approach. He seemed disoriented. She stepped out of her room, and smiled. "Hey, there."

Startled speechless, Richard snapped his head up, looked into his younger sister's eyes. "Beth... what are you doing here?"

"I should ask you the same question." She scrutinized his appearance, his eyes.

"Well, let's not stand outside." He moved past her, gestured awkwardly toward the door. "Come on in."

Beth followed him in. Her worries increased as she noted his pale face, fatigued eyes, slumped stature. "Why are you here, Richard? And why didn't you tell me you were leaving?"

"Since when are you my mother, Beth?" he snapped, leaving Beth with a wounded expression. He immediately backed up. "I'm sorry, Sis. I'm just tired."

"It's okay." Beth sat on the edge of the bed, waiting.

Richard took off his tan jacket, tossed it onto a chair, and sat beside her. "You know, I didn't really take too much of an interest in all that family stuff that Dad used to go on and on about." Richard paused, exhaled slowly. "And I wasn't there for you when Dad died, I know that."

Beth nodded, silently urging him to continue.

"When we were cleaning the house something changed in me. I had…" He fumbled for the right words. "Regrets, I guess. Did you feel that way?"

"Yeah, I felt that way."

Richard nodded, placed his hand over his sister's smaller one. "I began to think that maybe Mom had been wrong. I began to see him as something more than just a drunk. I visited him for a while before he passed. Did I tell you that?"

Surprised, Beth raised her eyebrows, shook her head.

"I did." Richard nodded, lost in the memory. "Even though the doctor told him not to drink anymore, he wasn't willing to stop. He moaned on and on about Grandpa Lee. It was the unsolved mystery that haunted him. He wished he had done more in his youth to find out what had happened to him. He wanted to know why Lee was in the plane in the first place, what he was doing leaving his wife when she was sick. I mean there must have been a reason…" Richard's voice trailed off, as if caught up in the same unending questions. He peered over his shoulder, gauging her wide-eyed expression, and pushed forward. "Honestly, at that point I didn't think too much of it. He was so sad, Sis. I mean, he wasn't sad… just the situation was, do you know what I mean? But now that he's gone, I can't get it out of my mind. It's like… I need to do this for him."

Beth rolled her hand over his, and squeezed. She didn't know that her brother spent time with their father in the last days. "I had to do an internship at a nursing home. I know just what you mean."

"When I was cleaning out the attic, I found this chest in a cupboard. On the top there was an unopened envelope." Richard furrowed his brow in thought. "I can't figure out why it wasn't opened. Our great-grandmother, Lenora, must have just tossed Grandma's stuff into a box after she died. Maybe she was tired of all the death, or wanted to move on or something. Maybe our great-grandfather put it up there. I don't know who did, and at this point we'll never know." Richard shook off the wonder. "Anyway, there was this unopened envelope. I found a logbook and letter. Inside the logbook was an entry written by Grandpa. The letter explained that the Coast Guard believed him to have died after writing it. I guess Grandpa crashed in a plane at this lighthouse." Richard gestured vaguely. "So I had to come see it, Sis. I had to know where Grandpa spent his last days, just because it meant so much to Dad. All that time the answers were in the attic, and he never knew."

Beth wrapped an arm around her brother, supportively. The twinge she felt through her spine was so low that she almost missed it, but she raised an eyebrow and continued to hug her brother. In her stomach, worry unfolded: her brother was not telling the whole truth.

Suddenly, her brother looked up. "How did you find me here?"

"I saw the envelope and letter that had been with the logbook in the dumpster. I called around. I talked to Jean, who told me you were in Michigan and have some important meeting on Friday." Richard frowned at the reminder, but continued to listen. Unless he found the pennies soon, he'd never make the meeting. But, if he found the pennies, he wouldn't have to, Richard reasoned.

Beth recognized the look on her brother's face when he became lost in his own thoughts. She paused until he shook his head and refocused. "Go on," he mumbled.

"I put two and two together and figured you must have come searching for the lighthouse. Once I got to DeTour Village, someone directed me here. I found someone who knew the Dombrowski's." Beth raised her voice an octave, still dumbfounded. "Speaking of which, why did you ever take a job in construction?"

"I had to get out to the lighthouse, and I heard at the party store in town that they were looking for workers. When I went to talk to Pete, I sized him up as someone who would think a bystander would be in the way and I just had to get out there and see it for myself. So I asked for a job, what other choice did I have?" It was Richard's turn to be curious. "Why did you come all this way?"

"Why didn't you tell me you were coming?" Beth countered.

"I thought you'd disapprove."

Beth rolled her eyes, stood up and paced away from him. "Honestly, Richard. It's not like I am our mother."

"More like her than you know," he muttered, watching her walk toward the window. "Why did you come here?"

Beth allowed that comment to pass. "I was worried about you."

Smartly, Richard said nothing.

Beth pivoted on her heel, stared him down. "You must have stopped looking through the chest as soon as you found the logbook, hey?"

"Yeah. I was so overwhelmed by the logbook..." Richard's voice trailed off as he leaned back and looked at her. Richard sensed there was more to this, looked into Beth's eyes. "What else did you find?"

"Grandma had a diary."

His head tilted forward, eyes narrowed. "You're kidding me, right?"

"No, I'm not kidding. She started it right after Grandpa disappeared."

"No shit." For a second, the mask of emotion that had shown on Richard's face slipped with his genuine surprise. "Richard," Beth began, keeping her voice calm. "Lee wasn't our grandfather."

"What?!" Richard pulled away. "Of course he was our grandfather. Dad remembered him, loved him. It was his dying regret that he hadn't looked for more information. He *was* our grandfather." His voice was emphatic, he reached down to rub his leg while glaring at Beth.

"Grandma says it plainly in the diary. She had an affair."

"With who?"

"She doesn't say. At least, not yet."

"What do you mean? *Not yet?*"

"I couldn't bring myself to finish it."

Richard's eyes widened. "Have you lost your mind? Why the hell not? You've read *just part of it?*" He sputtered, incredulous. "Why on earth would you stop?"

Beth's face reddened. She escalated her voice to match her brother's. "No, I haven't lost my mind! You're really one to talk. Leaving without word to anyone on some huge mission to track down a memory for someone you couldn't have cared less about? That's insane!"

Richard glared into her eyes. "Why did you come here?"

"Because I was worried…"

"You've been worried before. Why, Beth? What's so different about this trip?"

"Because I saw blood, okay?! I saw your hands covered in it!" The color drained from his face and he backed up, against the wall. Beth attacked. "Tell me about Joe, Richard."

He shook his head weakly.

"Look me in the eyes and tell me you didn't have anything to do with his death."

Shocked, he fumbled for words. "How…" He gulped loudly. "How could you think that?"

"Tell me," her voice pleaded.

"I didn't even know the kid!" he roared.

"Tell me!"

"Hell, Beth! We didn't even work on the same job. He was never at the lighthouse when I was there. He was working with some girl on a deck job. I met him on my first day, and I saw him in the bar the night before he died. That's all I know. It's just a coincidence that he was murdered while I'm here. I didn't have anything to do with it."

Beth's eyes filled with tears, as she collapsed onto the edge of the bed.

"You have to believe me." Richard kneeled before her pleading. Kneeling made him grimace and roll onto his side, favoring his leg.

She nodded, desperate. "Okay," she whispered. "I want to see the logbook."

Richard started to argue, but stared into her determined eyes, and gave in. "Okay."

Sixty

DeTour Reef Lighthouse Logbook Entry, February 22nd, 1959

To Whom It May Concern:

At 1707 (5:07 PM) my plane went down about 2 to 2.5 miles south by southeast of the DeTour Passage. I was flying at 5000 ft when my engine quit. I tried to make it in, but landed in the water, as close to this lighthouse as my plane would take me. At that time, there were large open areas of water. I did not try to land on ice for two reasons: first, I did not think the ice would hold the plane and second, the area surrounding the lighthouse was largely open water.

The plane went down in about two minutes after it hit the water. Before it sank, it floated close enough to an ice floe for me to jump off the plane. The ice was not over two inches thick. I stayed in the center and laid down to disperse my weight, so the ice wouldn't tip me into the water. There was a large open area between me and the lighthouse so I waited. The wind shifted to the north and the ice slowly moved. Over three hours passed and the sun had set while I waited for the ice to move closer to the lighthouse. Before the ice chunk reached the edge, it began to break into smaller pieces. I made a run for it, and ended up swimming the final distance to the ladder that brought me up the side of the lighthouse.

My clothing froze before I broke in. I used towels, blankets, and clothing to keep me from freezing. A little after 2100 (9 PM), I was able to light the stove. My body shook from the cold. I suffered from hypothermia. I took all the blankets and towels and wrapped myself in them. I do not remember how long I was like that. When I woke it was still dark outside, but I had stopped shaking.

When daylight came, the clothing I had spread out was now dry, except for my shoes and coat. I spent several hours evaluating my surroundings. Land is close by. I believe it's less than a mile away. I saw a boat cross between Drummond Island and what I believe is the town of DeTour. I jumped up and down on the deck and waved my hands to get someone's attention. The boat is very small and I would guess it is at least three miles away, maybe further. I took note of the time it crossed to find out how often it made the trip. It seems to run every two hours or so. I searched the place for food, but found none. I tied a rope to a bucket and climbed back down the ladder to get water. I found a radio receiver, which works but I couldn't get it to send. I do not know enough about it to make it work. It's overcast, with no sign of the sun. According to the radio, it's going to start warming, day after tomorrow it will be above freezing. Looking northwest, I can see open water in places but I can also see ice. I believe the ice reaches all the way to land. I have broken a mirror out of the bathroom and will watch for a chance to reflect light. My best chance is to aim at the bridge of the boat that crosses.

There is little sign of life here. I took the batteries and hooked them to the light, which worked. I will turn it on tonight and tap out SOS.

Day 2

I stayed up till after midnight tapping out SOS with the light. The batteries started to dim so I stopped. I hoped to see flashing headlights or some sign that someone had seen the signal. None came. Someone, maybe many must have seen the light on and flashing. It's possible that they don't know how to read Morse code. Surely, they don't realize I'm here. In the last 48 hours, I have had only one candy bar. I ate that in Saginaw when I stopped to refuel. There will be no talk of me missing for days since I never filed a flight plan. The weather will start to change tomorrow afternoon. The radio calls for temperature above 40 degrees. I have decided to turn the light on and tap out SOS until the batteries die. If there is still no sign that someone saw me, I will leave for shore at first light.

Day 3

Hunger and warming weather have made my decision for me. The batteries lasted only 50 minutes before going dead last night and there was no sign anyone noticed. Like a fool, I didn't wait until I saw the running lights from the boat that crosses to start signaling. I guess hunger has made me lightheaded. It's been 72 hours since I last ate. I have a very bad headache. When I make it to shore, I will replace the items I have used and destroyed here at the lighthouse.

Capt. Lee DeForge

United States Air Force

Batavia, New York

Sixty-One

FRIDAY MORNING

Jill smiled at Quinn over the corner table of the Bear Track Inn, allowed her gaze to follow the bear track border across the top of the wall. They had a hard enough time sleeping the night before, and Jill was in no mood to start the clean up. Talking about the murder last night would have added to her fear, so they let it go till this morning. Today, she insisted that they discuss what they knew about the murder, and what they had each found out. "Goodness, they give you a lot of food here."

Quinn laughed as the waitress sat the giant blueberry pancakes in front of them. "I told you they were big."

Jill poured syrup over the leviathan pancakes. "I still can't get over what is happening. To think that someone killed Joe... and now, that same person was probably in my house. It's a big link, if I can only put it together." Jill squinted contemplatively.

"If we figured out the connection between Joe's murder and your break-in, I'm sure it wouldn't take much more to figure out the murderer. The only thing connecting Joe's trailer to your home, is that you had been dating, right?" Quinn spoke between bites.

"That's the only obvious connection, yes. But I can't see that translating into a motive." Jill rubbed her temples, attempting to ease a headache.

"Neither can I. Let's move on for now. Maybe if we talk about what else we have learned, something will click."

Jill sipped her coffee with her left hand, as she flipped her notebook open with the right. "Just that Richard called in, told Kate that he had slept in. He asked her if she thought Pete would give him another chance. Kate told him that she had just learned that Joe was killed, so the crew wouldn't be working anyway."

Quinn frowned. "No help there. What did you think of his sister?"

Jill shrugged, frowned thoughtfully. "She seemed… genuinely nice. Honestly, what motive would some stranger have to kill him? It must be someone closer."

Quinn's eyes moved to the doorway as Bob sauntered in. Quinn waved him over. Bob waved back and held up his hand to indicate he would join them in a moment. He placed his order with a waitress and grabbed himself a cup of coffee.

"Hey Quinn, Jill." Bob nodded, greeted them somberly.

"Have you heard anything, Bob?" Jill asked.

Bob shrugged. "Kate told me that everyone's off work till at least Monday. It's a damned shame, isn't it? How are you doing, honey?"

Jill met his eyes, shrugged sadly.

Bob nodded, sipped his coffee. "Damn Cole woke me up this morning. In fact…" Bob rubbed at his thumb, which was smudged with ink. "He got my fingerprints this morning. Word is, he's asking everyone on the crew to volunteer their prints."

Quinn nodded. "Jill and I were printed last night."

"Is that right?" Bob nodded. "I went to his home office to do the ink thing and he got a call from Mary, Joe's mama. I guess they got Joe's truck back and his big jug of money is missing from it. They wouldn't have even thought of it, but they knew that Joe was using the jug of money for a down payment on a new truck. Hell, I think the whole island knew about that water jug. Shit, everyone he knew tried to help him with it. We even found change at work the other day."

Quinn raised an eyebrow. "No kidding?"

Bob nodded. "Yeah. It was a pretty funny thing to find out there, but what the hell, right? He offered to split it with me, but what do I want with seventy-five cents? Joe needed a new truck." Bob shook his ahead again, sadly. "Damn, we used to give him such a hard time about that change jug. It was our standing joke around the crew..."

Beside Quinn, Jill gasped, then coughed.

Quinn and Bob turned to her. "Are you okay?"

Jill nodded, covering. "Oh yeah, just fine. My coffee went down the wrong tube."

From a table surrounded with coffee drinkers, someone signaled for Bob's attention. As soon as Bob made his excuses, Jill grabbed Quinn's arm. "We need to go. Right now."

He grabbed his jacket from a hanger and took a final bite of his breakfast. He tossed enough money onto the table to cover the bill plus tip and headed out after Jill. When they had reached his vehicle, he turned to her expectantly.

"Quinn, that's what the killer has to be looking for."

"What are you talking about?"

Jill trembled, met his eyes. "I have Joe's change jug."

"You do? Why haven't you said anything about it?"

"Joe and I moved it from his truck to my Tracker and I forgot all about it. I'm sure he did too. Bob says that they found change. Joe told me that it was a buck fifty." Jill smiled as another puzzle piece slid into place. "It fits."

Completely lost, Quinn asked, "What fits?"

"Whoever was in my house was looking for something modestly small. It wouldn't have been the actual change jug, but it could have been inside the jug."

"How could you possibly know that?"

"Whoever searched through my house took the plastic lid off of a one pound coffee can and actually looked through it. Not much will fit in a one pound coffee can."

Quinn shook his head, bewildered. Neither he nor Cole had picked up on the coffee can at all, but she had. "What does one thing have to do with the other? Even if the item is small, who would give a shit about one dollar and fifty cents, Jill?"

She shook her head at him, pointed to the road. "Let's just go look at the jug. Maybe there's something about it that's strange or off... who knows..."

Quinn engaged the automobile, but still thought the idea was preposterous. "Jill, that's a little on the thin side. Who would have known you had them? You just said you even forgot about them."

"You're the one that said everyone knows everything about everybody. If the killer believed Joe spent a substantial amount of time at my house, he may have thought Joe left the change there. Hell, maybe he didn't even know that Joe's truck was in the garage. He could have thought that Joe was at my house, when in fact, his truck was missing." Jill shook her head. "That part doesn't really matter. The bottom line is that the killer must have figured if it wasn't at Joe's place, it must be at mine."

"I knew about the jug, but I have no idea where he kept it."

"Yeah, but all the guys on the crew would have known." Jill pulled her thoughts together, her mind spinning. "So would any of his family members, which leads us to the possibility that whoever killed Joe didn't know him that well."

"Well, I should hope not."

"Actually, Quinn, most murder victims know their killers."

Quinn shook his head. "Yeah, but that just doesn't apply to Drummond. People here aren't like that." Quinn argued, turning onto Pike Bay road, headed for Cream City Point. "Let me just get this straight, because I think I am still missing something."

"Shoot."

"You think that this change or whatever the hell Joe and Bob found out at the lighthouse could be what the killer is looking for?"

Jill shook her head. "At this point, I'm not thinking anything. But you and I both know that Joe didn't own anything of real value and didn't really have any enemies. I'll never believe that Joe was having an affair with Kate at any time, so I think that rules out Pete. Of course, that doesn't rule out Billy."

Quinn shot her a dangerous look. "It's *not* Billy."

Jill held up her hands, defensively. "Let's say I agree with you for a minute. It's not Billy. What would anyone else have to gain by hurting him?"

Quinn considered, agreed. "Nothing. The only thing Joe had that was worth anything was that jug."

"Hell, Quinn. The killer wouldn't be looking in a coffee can for Joe's change pile. Trust me on this. Whatever he or she is looking for has to be pretty small."

"But… if Joe had recently acquired something of value… Hell, if Bob didn't know about it, Joe wouldn't have known either. Who would have known?"

"That's exactly the question." Jill quieted, thoughtfully considering individuals. "It's probably a ridiculous idea."

Quinn pulled into her drive. "What the hell?" Cole's SUV blocked the path to the house.

"Shit, I forgot that Cole was going to come over this morning." Jill swung her legs out of the vehicle, and hurried ahead of Quinn.

Cole waved from the back deck. "Hey, how are you doing?"

"I am so sorry I wasn't here. Quinn took me to breakfast."

Cole waved it off. "No problem. I just got here myself. I thought I would give you a chance to sleep in, if that was possible. I know you've had a rough time of it." Cole nodded to Quinn as he stepped up beside her. "I've been walking around, and I want to show you something."

Cole led them around to the front of the house, facing the water. He stopped at the edge of the deck. "Last night when I walked out here, I remember you warning me about the holes in the deck. Jill, I think I've stumbled onto something." He pointed at one of the holes. Quinn looked where he pointed with a blank expression.

Jill's face however changed dramatically. "My God, look at that."

"Look at what?"

"Blood," Jill pointed.

Cole nodded, pleased that she noticed. Barely noticeable, small red spots stained one of the boards. By her expression he knew the answer, but he asked anyway. "Have you had an accident out here recently?"

"No."

"I think it is possible that whoever was in your house, parked in the neighbor's drive last night. The next house is owned by summer residents who aren't here yet and there's a straight shot over from the shore. The intruder heard you, rushed through the sliding door, slipped through this hole and scraped his leg." Cole looked to Jill for confirmation. "Do you remember hearing anything?"

Jill thought back. "No, but there was a song on the radio that I liked at the time. I stayed in the car for an extra minute to hear the end of it." She frowned to herself. "If I hadn't waited, I might have seen him."

"Be thankful that you waited. If it was Joe's killer, there's no doubt in my mind that he would have attacked you as well." Cole gazed at his watch. "I have to meet with Gary and get his fingerprints. I'll pick up Bishop and come back. Don't touch this deck area. We'll be able to get a DNA sample from the blood. I'll be back in an hour. Don't talk to anybody about this. This is a real break," Cole called over his shoulder already headed back toward his vehicle.

As soon as Cole left the drive, Jill nodded toward the Tracker. "Let's get that jug."

Sixty-Two

Beth turned the logbook over in her hands, considering the ironies of having some of the last writing of both of her grandparents. Her father lived in that house so long and never knew that the logbook and journal existed. Judging from her brother's habit of sleeping in, Beth knew her brother must still be in the next room, which she was thankful for. Richard looked exhausted. Was it his fatigue and seeming lack of health that made her so concerned, or was it something else? Beth hated to believe that Richard had anything to do with his co-worker's death. He couldn't possibly have been involved. How could he? He had only been on this island for a few days. Even if they worked together, it really wasn't enough time to be provoked into murdering someone. Beth shook her head at the terrible turn her thoughts were taking. She couldn't deny what she saw when she closed her eyes; what she felt when she looked into the older eyes of her brother. He was stained with blood in her visions, but why?

Idly, Beth flipped through the pages of the lighthouse logbook, looking for something more meaningful in her grandfather's entries. The words read the same way they had the night before, giving nothing new for her to go on. She flipped the blank pages, amused by the irony of her mind being a blank page when she saw a lightly written inscription six or seven pages back from the last entry.

Carol- If I don't make it back, know that I love you.
Everything I have is yours. Where your mother lost her
wedding ring, you will find your father's gift in the lighthouse.
Lee

Startled, Beth looked up. *The drain pipe.* The solution
she was looking for flooded her mind. Their father, Raymond,
always talked about how his grandfather said his future would
be taken care of. When Raymond was old enough, his
grandfather promised to show him his 'future': the fortune that
would remove any and all financial stress for life. His
grandfather died in a car accident before he ever got around to
coming through on his promise. Beth's father searched through
the house for years, looking for this mysterious valuable that he
had been promised. He was still looking for it when he married
Beth's mother. Beth's mother claimed that if he spent as much
time with her as he did searching for some investment, or
safety deposit box, they could save their marriage. When he
finally gave up, his wife was cynically relieved and anything
but sympathetic. Instead of turning to her, he turned to the
bottle. Beth reflected that her father's obsession with this
promised fortune had derailed his life.

If what this said was true, Lee took the future and hid it.
Beth had known the story of the lost engagement ring like she
knew the back of her hand. Her father told them the story so
many times it was one of the few links she had to her family's
past. It was passed down from her grandmother's parents.
Great-Grandma Lenora lost the ring, which Great-Grandpa
Howard later found in the drain pipe. The very next day, she
did it again. Grandpa Lee must have thought it terribly ironic to
place this item in the drainpipe at the lighthouse. *But why*
would Lee have it? Did Howard and Lenora never notice that
the future was missing? It didn't make sense. But this small
inscription shed a great deal of light onto her brother's urge to
get in the lighthouse. He was searching for something with
value, not a memory for their father. The same greed that

plagued Raymond, plagued Richard. *He lied, and he knew exactly where to look.*

She leapt from the bed, and rushed out of her motel room, barefoot. Furious, she pounded on Richard's door continually. She stopped as she became aware of the pain in her fist. Richard didn't answer. *Where was he, now?*

There was only one place to gather more information. Not knowing what else to do, Beth decided it was time to finish the diary and face whatever it revealed.

Sixty-Three

THE LAST DIARY OF CAROL LENORA DEFORGE, THIRD ENTRY

Dad is acting so strange. All these years, he has told me that he was leaving me something of great value. Now that I am in my last days, he hasn't said a word about it. He's told me not to worry about Raymond. He says he and Mother will take care of him. I am worried, though. I guess I should just trust that it will work out, but it is so hard. Why would my father tell me our future was taken care of, and then not tell me how? I brought it up to him yesterday, and he changed the subject. What kind of a man would do something like that? Did he lose it? Or sell it? I don't understand him. It's late for me and I'm tired of all this. If it is true, it would be so comforting to know that Raymond's future will be taken care of, and that he will be able to go to college.

Ray and I have moved in with Mom and Dad. I thought it would be an easier transition for Ray if he was already here when I passed. It's also nicer for me. I get to spend time with my parents and my son, and Mom does all the cooking and house chores. I don't want to be a burden... but I know that sooner or later, I will be. I am so thankful that Mom and Dad moved here and have been such a big part of Ray's life. Lee was never close to his family, and now that Ray will be living with Mom and Dad... it just seems for the best. His bedroom here is bigger and he seems to like that.

I have decided not to tell Raymond who his father is. I want Mom and Dad to raise him. I don't really know what his real father would think. This way, my former lover will never be burdened and he will never be given the chance to hurt little Ray. He made a decision when he allowed me to pretend the baby was my husband's. Mom and Dad will take good care of him.

I wake up in the morning and I am so thankful that I'm alive one more day. When I go to sleep at night I pray that I'll get to see my son in the morning, get to listen to him chatter, watch him play. When I was young, I spent so much time dreaming of traveling. Lee told me once that he was drawn to service out of duty, not the exciting places that service would take him. I wonder what Raymond will do when he grows up. Will he like to travel? Or maybe he'll go into the service like his father?

I have grown so weak. Writing is even becoming such a chore...

Please God, take good care of Ray.

Sixty-Four

Jill leaned against the counter top strewn with the debris left by the intruder. She took a deep breath. "Damn, that thing is heavy."

Quinn grunted. "How should we do this?"

She put her hands on her thighs, exhaled. "Dump the jug out onto the floor?"

Quinn looked appalled. "Do you have any idea how much money is in here?"

"Well, how else should we do it then? We don't even know what we're looking for?"

Quinn thought about it, found no other option. "Why don't we pour it into a cardboard box, so we'll at least contain it?"

"Good idea. I have some left over from moving." Jill grabbed an empty box from the spare bedroom and brought it back near the dining table. They each grabbed an end and turned the jug over until coins began to pour out of its mouth. Every few seconds something would block the opening, so they'd have to rock the jug back and shake it a bit. Each time it happened Jill ran her hand through the coins, looking for anything unusual or different. When the first round tube shook out, Jill shouted. "Oh! That's it!"

"What?! How could you possibly know that?" He heaved his end up, but she insisted.

"Friday afternoon, when I saw Joe for the second time, he was covered in that green shit, and there was orange stuff all over him." She pointed to the substance that coated the roll. She dropped her end of the bucket, fetched the roll. "It looks like pennies."

"Pennies? I say it's not what the killer is looking for. It must be something else. Let's dump the rest of the jug in the box. It might be really obvious to us," Quinn argued.

"It wasn't obvious to Bob and Joe," Jill muttered, but heaved her end once again. When another roll slid out, covered by the same substance, Jill groaned but continued to shake the coins out of the jug. The third roll of pennies confirmed her suspicions. "A buck fifty. One hundred and fifty pennies, Quinn! That has to be it!"

She tore the paper open and spilled fifty pennies onto the dining table. They clunked onto the table like dead weight, causing Jill to meet Quinn's eyes. She realized by his expression that he noticed the sound difference as well.

Quinn reached into the box and scooped up a handful of pennies. On the opposite end of the table he dropped them onto the wood in the same manner that Jill had. "Did you hear that?"

Jill nodded. "The sound is different, isn't it? And why are they dark brown?"

Quinn scrunched his face, puzzled. "I have dealt with thousands of pennies, and I know that I have never heard coins that sound like these, but the color comes from moisture. They're just tarnished copper."

She picked one up, examined it closely. "They look like plain old 1943 copper pennies. Do you think they are actually something else?"

Quinn mirrored Jill's movements, examined one on his own. Finally, he shook his head. "No, they're definitely pennies."

"They're wheat pennies which might make them worth a few cents a piece, but I can't think of any other reason why they would be worth anything."

"Oh, no shit! They are *all* 1943 pennies."

Raising her eyebrows, she scanned through the pennies. She returned the penny she was holding to the table. "Would you like some lemonade?"

"What?" The invitation had come out of nowhere, and he treated her with a surprised expression.

"I guess I'm not thinking straight." Jill shrugged. "Lemonade might help. I'm going to make some."

"Sure," he said absently while contemplating the coins.

"I just don't get it," Jill began as she moved over to the cupboard and found the glass pitcher. "Maybe I'm just clinging to this change jug idea, but those pennies sound off. I feel like it's gotta be the link... but I can't see how."

"Mm-hmm," Quinn said, uttering the listening noises mindlessly, as he dropped a few of them onto the table again. "Are you hooked to the net?"

"What? Oh, yep. Who isn't? Actually, I don't use it much. I just use the E-mail." Jill stuck her head into a cupboard, retrieving a lemonade mix packet.

"Well, there we go. We'll look them up. We'll go online and run a search on 1943 pennies."

"Yeah, and the information will just pop up," Jill said, slightly sarcastic.

"That's right." Quinn headed toward Jill's computer. "Do you want me to wait for you?"

"No, go ahead. You find the pennies, I'll finish the lemonade."

The computer dialed onto to the internet, while Quinn fingered a penny in his left hand and watched Jill mix the ingredients together.

Jill turned the tap water to cold and waited until it reached the right temperature, then filled the pitcher. Quinn's clicking fingers caught her attention. "You couldn't have found information that quickly."

"What can I say? Computers and I just get along. I'm going to put this website in your favorites, that way we can find the information again if we need to, okay?"

Jill placed two glasses on the counter. "Okay. What did you find?"

"It is just coming up now."

Turning her back on him, she didn't see Quinn's jaw drop, but his long whistle drew her attention. "$112,500.00."

"For 150 copper pennies?" Jill's eyebrows lifted. "No way," she muttered, shaking her head, rolling the idea over in her mind.

"Jill."

"Shit, that's a lot of money… what makes them so special?"

"Jill!"

Jill met his eyes, saw the darkened grey that bored into hers. "What?"

"It's not $112,500.00 for 150 pennies."

"Okay, because that's a lot of money…"

"It's that much for one penny. And they're not copper, they're bronze. According to this website, a 1943 bronze penny was sold at auction for $112,500.00 in 1997."

"Oh, God." Jill sat on the edge of the chair beside him, suddenly breathless. "So how much would they... how ah..."

"Right. Give me a second." He paused, calculating in his head. He pulled a piece of paper from Jill's printer and scratched numbers onto the surface. He muttered under his breath as he computed the number. "Uhm... if my numbers are right, we're looking at $16,875,000."

Jill sputtered. "Quinn... that's not... that's..." She gulped the lemonade from her glass then coughed.

"Listen." Quinn read through the website, astounded. "In 1943, pennies were made from steel and coated with zinc because bronze was needed for the war..." His voice trailed off as he skimmed the page. "The bronze pennies were minted by accident. Bronze blanks were left in the press hopper when they started making the new pennies. They only used the zinc coated steel for a year or two, but there shouldn't have been any 1943 bronze pennies, so the ones that exist are really valuable. This website claims they know of twelve in existence, but they have no idea how many are actually out there."

"Twelve? There are 150, right here."

Quinn nodded slowly. "Apparently, the website needs to be updated."

"Oh my God, Quinn..."

Quinn leaned back in his chair, sipped the lemonade quietly. "I guess Joe did have something of value. We've got motive."

Jill raised her eyes to Quinn's, overwhelmed. "We have more than that."

"What?"

"The blood, Quinn. P-E was written in blood. The attacker must have asked Joe if he had the pennies. Maybe Joe inadvertently told the killer I had them and that's why my house was searched. It's P-E for pennies, not Pete."

Quinn exhaled deeply, thinking it through. "But who knew about this? Who knew the pennies were worth anything?"

Jill bit her lower lip. "It seems like I'm missing something. I know someone mentioned something about this, but I don't remember."

"Someone mentioned something about what? Pennies?" Quinn asked, trying to help her sort through her thoughts.

Jill shook her head. "It's close. It will come to me eventually. I'm incapable of forgetting these things long term."

Quinn nodded. "If someone knows these things exist, we need to get rid of them. We won't be safe until we do." Gravel crunching under a vehicle had Quinn swiveling around in his chair to peer out the window.

Sixty-Five

Cole and Bishop swung out of the SUV, nodded to Quinn who met them at the back door. Another police car pulled in behind Cole, filling the driveway. Cole introduced Bishop and the officer to Quinn, and led them around the house. When Cole finished with the instructions, Quinn gestured toward the door.

"Cole, there's something you need to see."

When the men entered the house, Cole's eyes darted from the empty water jug and mammoth pile of change heaped in a cardboard box to Jill and back. He recognized it immediately. "How long have you had that? And why didn't you tell me you had it?"

Jill met his eyes. "Oh, you're going to have many more questions than that by the time we're done explaining what we've really got. You might want to sit down, guys."

Bishop shrugged and pulled a seat back. Jill began the explanation with how she received the coin jug in the beginning and walked the men through their findings and suspicions.

When they were finished, Cole whistled, turned to the detective. "Well, that's what we were looking for."

Nodding, Bishop agreed. "Motive."

"I'd really appreciate it if you guys took those as soon as possible. It's not healthy for us to have them," Quinn said.

Bishop raised an eyebrow. "Who else knew that you had the jug, Ms. Traynor?"

Jill frowned. "I didn't even think about having it. I certainly didn't mention it to anybody. It was just no big deal. Nobody else knew."

Bishop scratched his head. "How did you forget about it? There must be seven hundred dollars in that pile."

"I didn't really forget about it, I just didn't think about it."

Cole leaned back, eyed her thoroughly. "You said you thought about it when you talked to Bob at the restaurant this morning. If I'm not mistaken, I was here when you came home from breakfast. Why didn't you just tell me you had the jug then?"

Quinn looked to Jill and chose to remain silent. It had been Jill's direction to let it go until they had checked it out themselves. Jill glanced to the ground, sheepish. "Well, I have been trying to figure this out."

Cole stared her down. "Sometimes, it doesn't hurt to trust the local authority. We can get more done if we work together. You should remember that you're messing with a murder investigation."

Jill met his eyes, nodded. "I'll remember that."

Bishop used a plastic glove to examine the roll more closely. "Cole, take a look at this." He held the roll up. "It looks like they were somewhere wet. The paper has decomposed in spots, and it's covered with this green material. These rolls must have been in the back of a toilet or in some area exposed to the weather or something. Quite the thing, isn't it? Finding 16 million in a lighthouse, I mean—unreal. If I was a betting man, I'd say they've been in there a long *long* time."

"Yeah. I can see hiding them somewhere, but why in a lighthouse? And who put them there? Is the person still around, still planning on retrieving them?" Cole questioned.

Bishop shrugged. "We may never know."

Quinn glanced up at the wall clock. "I have to go to work," he said, standing.

"Can you get out? Or did I block you in?"

Quinn squinted through the window. "I think I can slide past you."

Jill stood. "I'll walk you out."

When they reached his Jeep, he paused. "Do you want me to come back tonight?" *Say yes*, he willed.

Jill hesitated, shook her head. She wanted him to stay, but she couldn't allow Quinn to get the wrong idea. "No. I can't imagine anyone will come back. I'll be fine."

Quinn hid his disappointment behind a yawn. "Do you want me to pick you up for the funeral tomorrow?"

"I'll meet you. I'll just leave my car at the bar and we can ride from there, if that's okay with you."

"Yeah, that's fine. I'll call you tonight and if you need anything, or change your mind, just call me at the bar."

"Okay. Thanks, Quinn."

Quinn softened. "He was my friend too. I don't mind helping."

Jill grimaced, looked back toward the house. "I feel a bit bad about keeping information from Cole."

Quinn shrugged it off, climbed into the Jeep. "Don't worry about it. Cole wants this solved, Jill. He was impressed with your theory. Deep down, he's probably glad that you're trying to find answers. Take care, okay? I'll talk to you later."

Sixty-Six

Jill set the phone down with a smile. Quinn had called her twice to make sure she was okay and now that he was getting off work for the night he wanted to make absolutely sure that she didn't need him to come over. Obviously, he hadn't thought waking her up at 2:00 AM was such a bad thing. If she told him the truth, he would know that she hadn't slept. Her confidence on the phone was definitely an exaggeration, but she stayed firm to her convictions and repeated that she was fine by herself. When she talked to him earlier she felt better about it than she did now.

Crawling out of bed, she walked out into the living room. Surveying the living, dining and kitchen areas, she nodded to herself satisfied. After Cole left, she went right to work putting her house back in order. She righted drawers and refilled them, reorganized her papers into stacks on her dining room table, put dishes away and cleaned her floors and countertops. It helped to stay busy and the resulting organization comforted her.

The change jug and all of its remnants, including the three rolls of pennies, had been taken by Sheriff Cole, but she could call the picture up in her mind as clearly as if they still lay scattered before her. Furrowing her brow, she puzzled over the day. The sound of the pennies spilling onto the table replayed in her mind. That afternoon, she learned that pennies had returned to bronze when the war ended. In other words, the pennies that she had in her own piggy banks would undoubtedly be made from bronze, and were the same pennies that she was familiar with. Those that they dumped from the roll should have sounded just like any other penny. But they didn't. Quinn and Jill both recognized the difference between sounds.

Jill moved the kitchen chair away from the French door and unlocked it. She stepped onto her front deck, careful to avoid the unfinished section. Above her, stars shimmered and sparkled clearly in the night sky. Attempting to clear her mind, she focused on the water, on the barely discernible trees, the sliver of moon. None of the images were able to block the reoccurring thought that cycled in her mind. *The pennies didn't sound right.* She had tried to stop thinking about the pennies, but if she was thinking about solving the case she wasn't reliving Wednesday morning. *Anything was better than that.*

Resigned, she stepped back into her house and locked the door, dragged the chair back in front of it. Somewhat paranoid, she dragged chairs in front of every door, checked and rechecked the locks. She didn't really believe that the intruder would return, and she certainly didn't worry about enjoying the outdoors, but she decided to be cautious. Chuckling, she realized her actions were somewhat counter-productive, but felt comforted by the barrier. The glass pane hadn't been replaced yet, but she was sure she could get Bob or Pete to help her with it. For the time being, she covered it with plastic and taped some stray jingle bells she found in a craft box of her grandmother's to the bottom. Sitting down at her computer, she booted it up and waited for the internet connection to verify her password.

When the website that Quinn had saved in her computer came up, she searched until she found statistics for Lincoln pennies. The information made little sense or had little relevance until she spotted the weight readings for each type. To her surprise, she read that there were basically three

different types of Lincoln pennies. From 1909 to 1942, and
again from 1944 to 1958 pennies were bronze, weighing 3.11
grams each. In 1943 pennies were made from zinc coated steel
and weighed 2.7 grams per penny. From 1959, with one slight
change that didn't affect the weight or color, pennies were
considered to be made from copper and weighed 2.5 grams
each. The real physical make-up, however, was 99.2% zinc,
.8% copper, with a plating of real copper.

Pondering the statistics, Jill leaned back in her chair and
stared at the computer screen. *What relevance did this
information have to what she knew?* She was sure of one thing,
the 1943 pennies they had found did not sound like current day
pennies. Using her calculator she figured out that 150 steel
pennies would weigh 405 grams. 150 bronze pennies, however,
would weigh 466.5 grams. She clicked off the website, and
searched for a conversion chart. After finding one, she learned
that approximately 28.35 grams equals one ounce. The
difference in weight would equal a little over 2 full ounces.
That much weight distinction would be easily detected with any
postal scale.

*But was it the weight difference or the type of metal
used in making the penny that changed the sound?* She needed
a handful of bronze wheat pennies to prove or disprove her
theory. Ironically, she knew right where to find them. She had
come across a tin can of change in her grandfather's closet
while cleaning, and Jill was sure it would be full of bronze
wheat pennies for comparison. Locating the can and searching
through it only produced four bronze pennies. After dropping
them as a group, and then one at a time, she knew in her gut
that the rolls of 1943 pennies and these were not the same.

Pennies made since 1959, or Lincoln Memorial pennies
weighed 2.5 grams, which would make them even lighter then
the steel pennies. Getting lost in the numbers, Jill shook her
head against the data swirling through her thoughts and realized
that it would be easy to figure out. It didn't matter if one penny
was heavier then another. If the valuable pennies were real, 150

of them would weigh 466.5 grams, which could be easily
measured. Suspicions clouded her thoughts and made her doubt
that the pennies they found were actually valuable. But why
would anyone go to the trouble of gathering 150 virtually
worthless pennies? Further, why would anyone be looking for
them if they weren't real?

Someone would have intentionally had to color or
change the pennies to make them seem like a serious fortune.
Jill shook her head, scolding herself. Of course, someone had
done it deliberately. No one would gather 150 pennies that
happened to be from 1943 unless it was a specific purposeful
action.

Jill allowed the ramifications to take shape in her mind
slowly. If Jill's suspicions were right, the pennies were fake.
Overwhelmed by the direction of her thoughts, Jill printed out
the sheets with the weight information and turned off the
computer. Whoever had searched Joe's trailer and her own
house had to have been looking for the pennies, which meant
that the intruder believed the pennies were actually worth the
16 million. *I can't be right, can I?* If she was right, she realized,
Joe hadn't been murdered for 16 million, but for $1.50.
Irrevocably saddened, Jill blinked away the tears that
threatened to fall and attempted to block his curled and battered
body from her mind. Tormented and emotionally exhausted, Jill
tried to sleep.

Sixty-Seven

Poignant chords of *Amazing Grace* stretched outward from the organ and filled the sanctuary. Islanders stood shoulder to shoulder along the edges of the packed pews, sat in extra chairs set up along the aisle, filled every available space. Children's faces pressed against the glass of the cry room, and parishioners leaned against the walls of the staircase allowing their tears to fall freely. Haunting notes of the age old song mingled with sobs and whimpers of grief and pain. Darkly dressed mourners spilled out of the doors and took turns moving up to the closed casket of their beloved to say goodbye. Surrounding the casket on all sides was a jungle of crosses, wreaths, and bouquets. Live plants of all sizes, shapes, and kinds intermingled with brightly colored flowers, somehow making death more bearable. Loving messages flowed from cards of friends and family members offering their condolences and their prayers. The choir joined their voices with the organ's haunting melody as they wordlessly hummed the chords everyone knew so well.

Seated next to Quinn, Jill was struck by the contrast of darkly clothed mourners with the endless wall of flowers. Since childhood, Jill had used her keen ability to observe life, to distance herself from pain – she observed the displays of others, rather than feel pain herself. She captured the actions and poses of the mourners' in her mind, as if she was taking pictures of someone else's life. The trick didn't work to completely block the experience from her heart. As scenes repeated, Jill was brought back to her grandmother's funeral a few months before. She sat there, as she sat here, somewhat dry eyed, but dying internally as friends approached the casket and said their goodbyes. Today, people she barely knew were allowing this event to provide closure for them. Within Jill's mind, Joe would live just as he lived for the five days that she had known him; just as her parents still lived within the walls of her soul. She had faced funerals of the four most important people in her life before this day and because she lost everyone dear, she was numbed to most of the grief surrounding her.

As the minister spoke, his words were interrupted by great wracking sobs of a woman Jill could only presume to be Mary Barber. Jill's calm façade erupted into her own tears, her lip quivering, and her hands shaking as she watched this woman give up any shred of composure and hug the mahogany box that held her son's body. Achingly genuine and terribly heartbreaking, the love that Mary had shared with Joe was something Jill couldn't recall experiencing with her own parents. The joy that blossomed daily in their relationship was now replaced by something dark and horrible. Jill watched through her tears and remembered what her grandmother told her after her husband's death. She said that although she grieved deeply over the loss of the man she loved her entire adult life, the pain she held in her heart was little compared to the day they had buried her daughter. Burying a child was the worse possible thing and watching Mary react violently, passionately, Jill accepted that she had no idea what this woman was going through. Jill turned her head away, no longer able to distance herself from this woman's pain and allowed herself to weep against Quinn.

Quinn wrapped his arm around her and held her silently. He didn't realize just how different Jill's behavior was for her character, how much she gave up of her own control, when she allowed the sounds of her grief to accompany the tears around her. Several minutes later, Jill brought her smudged face away from Quinn and attempted to focus on what was happening.

She had attended many funerals, but she had never seen anything quite like what was happening here. So many faces: young, old, relatives and friends tormented by the grief that surrounded them, sadly wept into each other, leaned on each other. In the end, she didn't have any idea what the minister spoke about. She slowly relived the nightmare of the last few days that she blocked until now. Comforted by the unexpected presence of Quinn in her life, she realized that he had been a stable force that helped her to get through the strongest grief by focusing on something else. She glanced to her side, noted the tears that fell from his eyes; fell from the eyes of everyone she looked at. The church fell silent, save for the sniffles and tears that were wiped up and cried out again. After moments of silence, the organ player began notes of another song, and pall bearers took their places around the casket.

The strong young men were at such odds with the death for which they gathered. Mere days before, Joe had been very much one of them: strong and full of the carefree exuberance of youth and liveliness that characterized the group. Now, each one of these young men would grow a little wiser, a little less carefree as they carried the burden of their friend forward. Jill found herself tear stricken as the men carried the casket between the rows of mourners, down the length of the church and into the bright early summer sunshine. Islanders slowly filed out of the pews and followed the casket outdoors.

"Jill, I need to talk to Alice," Quinn whispered beside her. He slid past Jill and across the aisle to the front of the church where the family leaned on each other, in shared grief.

Jill nodded but remained seated, unable to move as she watched the woman that was so obviously Joe's mother grasp her husband's shoulders and weep into his chest. Inside Jill's chest, her heart broke again as Joe's father's face streamed with tears of his own. Alice's eyes were red rimmed but she held onto what Jill presumed to be her older sister. Quinn's strong arms pulled the small blond against him and whispered into her ear, talked to her quietly. The older sister followed the other mourners out of the church. An older man with stiffly held upright posture placed his hand on Mary's shoulder, and Mary turned tearfully to embrace him. His face wrinkled with his own sadness, and Jill was blown away by the generations of misery present, the many lives that Joe's death touched so deeply. She realized the level of grief must be directly related to the sense of community and shared experience the residents had on this island. Everyone loved him. Jill wondered if Joe ever understood just how amazing that kind of love was.

Jill had lost almost everyone she ever loved but she knew at this moment, she had never experienced the horror that Mary must be dealing with. Jill's heart thumped solidly against the wall of her chest, as tears flowed freely from her eyes and down her face. Mary pulled away from the older man; her hand clasped firmly with her husband's and took deep calming breaths. Solidly supportive, Quinn shook Tom Barber's hand, leaned in and kissed Mary's cheek.

When Quinn returned to her side, Jill turned her gold filled eyes to his and shook her head sadly. "Poor Mary," she whispered.

Quinn nodded heavily. "Joe was her life, he really was." They watched the family slowly pull away from one another and walk down the aisle, oblivious to the sympathetic looks from mourners still milling in the church.

"I never expected them to look so much like him. I mean," Jill paused to sniff lightly, "I knew Joe would look like his parents but he really looks *just like* his parents. Even that older guy…" Jill tilted her head, gesturing.

Quinn found a small smile. Always observant, he thought. "That's Mary's father."

"I figured he was a grandfather," Jill nodded. "I don't think I ever looked that much like my parents... of course, I'll never know, but..." Jill shook her head, realized she was rambling.

He turned his attention to Jill, concerned. "How are you holding up?"

Jill rubbed the tears away from her eyes, wiped them on her black linen pants. "I didn't think I had any tears left," she mumbled. "I guess I was wrong. I've never cried this much in my life."

Undone, Quinn pulled her against him and hugged her, kissed the top of her head. "Should we go?"

Jill nodded, silently standing and allowing him to lead her out of the church. When they made their way through the crowd to Quinn's Jeep, she spoke. "Is Mary doing any better? She looked really bad in there but the funeral is always tough."

Quinn shrugged. "I think it'll take her a long while to recover, if she ever really does." Quinn paused, lost in his thoughts. "The whole family is in pretty deep trouble. I've never seen Jesse so undone by anything before. She's usually unshakable."

Surprised, Jill turned her head back toward him. "She looked better than the others."

"Yeah, but for Jesse..." He shook his head and, allowed the thought to trail away. "Joe's sister told me that Mary keeps saying she is so thankful that his last days were good ones. You were the cause of that, Jill. Mary is getting through this because she knows you made her son so happy, so thrilled to be alive in his last days."

Jill leaned back against the leather seat and looked out the window silently. "I didn't really do anything special Quinn, but I'm glad she's comforted." Jill brought her hands to her face, allowed the tears she had valiantly attempted to keep at bay to flood her dampened face. Quinn brought the car to a stop in the line of funeral attendants, and walked around the Jeep, opened Jill's door and pulled her into him.

"God, Jill. I am so sorry," he whispered, as he wrapped his arms tighter around her. Jill leaned against him and cried freely for a moment, before she struggled to regain her composure.

Sobbing into his chest, she said the truth that had burdened her just below the surface. "It's just that... like you said, you know? They're getting through this because he was so much happier in his last days or something. Quinn, I'm not anything special. I don't want them to look at me and know me and then be disappointed. I mean, I only knew him for five days." Her voice carried her words sketchily, breaking on sobs, choking over tears. "What if they get to know me and they don't feel that way anymore? If they figure out who I am, they might have bad feelings about Joe's death. They might think I wasn't good enough to spend his final days with him. It's all a big misconception. Right now, they think I'm special because they don't know me. What if they learn about my family being dead and they think his meeting me caused this or something... I don't want their grief to be any worse then it is... it's just so sad, Quinn."

Amazed, Quinn shook his head, looking at her through new eyes. She constantly changed and surprised him. "Jill?"

She continued to bury her head against him, as if ashamed to be admitting her fears, ashamed that Quinn might think her thoughts were selfish or worse that she was right.

"Jill, look at me." He waited until she brought her eyes up to his. He wiped the ruined mascara off of her cheek and held her head lightly in his hands. "Joe's family doesn't think you're anything more than you are: the woman he liked, the woman he was excited about. Jill, *you are* a special, interesting person. They are getting through this or not getting through this... not because of you, it really doesn't have anything to do with you. It has to do with him. *He was happy.* That's why they are relieved. That's all. Don't worry about meeting them, just be yourself. You're not going to hurt their image of Joe."

Jill nodded sadly, hugged him once more.

The friends, family, and residents that packed into the church were not all present at the cemetery. Those that were there spread out, allowing Jill a better chance to recognize people she knew. Solemnly, Pete, Kate and their children stood near the gravesite, Kate crying softly as her husband's arm wrapped around her. Standing next to them was Bob, whose eyes were red, and next to him Gary, with a woman who must be his wife. Billy and a young woman stood surrounded by a group of other similar aged people. Jill avoided eye contact with the young man but moved her eyes to study others. Dick stood by his sister Beth, about ten feet away from them. Cole nodded to Jill from beside the detective. It seemed to Jill as if they had just arrived when they lowered the casket into the ground and the minister closed his Bible. Quinn was pulled away to speak with friends, leaving Jill to observe others. Cole spoke quietly to Tom and Mary Barber, offered his respects. Jill made a small hand signal to him when he looked her way and he nodded that he understood.

Cole made his way through the gathering to Jill, the detective close on his heels. Bishop opened his mouth before Jill had a chance to speak. "Ms. Traynor, I'd like to congratulate you on solving this matter."

Jill's eyes widened with surprise, shot to Cole in question.

"Well, all but solved. Once Cole tracks down the last three sets of fingerprints from this list, I'm sure it will be over. There are only three people left on the list, two friends and the last of the construction workers Cole hasn't had a chance to see yet. With both the fingerprints on the hammer and the DNA from your deck, we'll have the killer cold when it goes to court. The County Sheriff has already spoken with a treasury agent. The standard is to give you a ten percent finder's fee on the auctioned value of the pennies."

Jill's eyes widened further. "Unfortunately, Detective Bishop, I don't think the government will be paying me anything."

It was Bishop's turn to look dumbfounded. Cole raised his eyebrows.

She reached into her handbag and pulled out the folded papers that she had printed the night before. "I believe the pennies are fake. I found this on the internet. When Quinn and I spilled them on the table, they sounded strange. I couldn't get it out of my mind, so I looked them up. I'm pretty confident that those pennies are just regular 1943 pennies, that are colored or something. By regular, I mean steel, not bronze."

Cole leaned back on his heels, looked over the sheets Jill handed him.

Jill continued. "We can prove it easily by weighing them, but I'm pretty confident."

"Ms. Traynor, this doesn't make any sense. Why would anyone go to all the trouble..."

Jill raised a hand for him to stop. "Detective, I know exactly what you mean. That's why we need to weigh them immediately and see if I'm right or not."

Bishop arched an eyebrow. "The manager of the credit union is right over there. Why don't we meet there in," Cole paused while glancing at his watch. "One hour. I'll get the manager to open up so we can check your hunch."

Jill nodded, glanced at her own watch. "I'll grab Quinn." She turned noticing that Beth had looked toward her, seemed to want to speak with her. Something had clicked in her mind the night before and she needed to confirm it with Beth before she said anything. Intuitively, Jill felt she could trust her.

From behind Jill, Richard DeForge's mouth dropped open and the color rushed from his face. He lurked just within earshot. He knew that he was the only construction worker that hadn't been printed. He had first been staggered to know the pennies were recovered and flabbergasted to think they weren't real. *How could the pennies possibly be fake? After all these years, how could they be worthless?* She must be wrong and yet after hearing her, he knew somehow she was right. He faltered in his step, leaned against another tombstone to regain his breath, unnoticed. Jill turned to move closer to Beth, surprised to see Mary's father approach the young woman.

Jill steeled herself against the reality that she would have to speak with Joe's mother, express her sorrow over their loss. She attempted to come up with the right thing to say when someone tapped her shoulder. Jill turned to face the grieving eyes of Mary Barber.

Mary stared into Jill's eyes, searching, her own eyes still leaking tears. "I would know you anywhere, Jill."

An uncharacteristic gesture, Jill felt compelled to wrap her arms around Joe's mother and embrace her. "He loved you so much, Mrs. Barber."

"Oh, dear girl," Mary whispered, returning Jill's warm hug. "I can see why you brought him such joy." After a long moment, Mary pulled away from her but kept her close by. "You really made him..." Mary's voice trailed off, searching. "Jill. I will always love you for that, for giving me the comfort of knowing he was happy. He was growing up and changing so much in the last few days. I hadn't seen him so joyful since his days on the football field." Mary clasped Jill's hand in hers, met the younger girl's eyes and in a voice so quiet it was almost inaudible, whispered. "Thank you."

"I wish I could have known him longer."

Mary sniffled. "Please come visit me sometime soon." Mary's light smile broadened to encompass Quinn who had approached from Jill's side. "And I don't want you to be a stranger either, Quinn. If Tom becomes a handful, I'm going to send him to the bar to see you."

Quinn returned the smile. "I'll be there. If you need anything, Mrs. Barber... don't hesitate to call, okay?"

Mary nodded sadly. "Okay, dear."

Sixty-Eight

Beth watched her brother from a distance, absently pondering the difference in this funeral from the one she had attended for her father weeks before. From across the casket an elderly man kept glancing toward her during the service. He looked uneasily familiar, but when Beth looked his way, he looked away quickly. She brought her eyes back to where he had been standing, surprised to find the space filled by someone else. From the corner of her eye, she saw her brother step closer to her from the side. A light tap on her shoulder, brought her attention around, and she felt an intense wave of sensation ripple through her body.

"Carol?" The older man questioned, his eyes alive and wondering.

Beth's eyes held the man's. Very slowly and kindly she reached out and touched his arm, needing the contact.

The man shook his head after a moment and attempted to step back.

"No, wait. My grandmother's name was Carol. I'm Beth DeForge." When his cheeks paled, his eyes brimmed with tears, she knew she had found him. She extended her hand, urged him with her eyes to take it. When their hands connected, Beth's eyes widened at the strong sensation pulsing through her arm, her spine. "You're my grandfather, aren't you?"

Shock played across the man's face. Silently, he stood and looked her over, considered what to tell her. Finally, he decided on the truth. "I'm Cal Johansen, and yes, I'm your grandfather."

"We have many things to talk about." Beth took both of his hands in hers, leaned forward and kissed his cheek.

Cal stood back, overwhelmed after all these years. "When I first saw you, I thought I had seen a ghost... my God, how is Carol? Is she still..."

Beth shook her head. "She passed on before I was even born. My father, your son, was only a boy. He passed on weeks ago, himself."

The heavy burden that had been Cal's life weighed on his shoulders, in his eyes. "God, I didn't know. My son is gone?" He had never known him and yet the pain struck him like a fist in the gut. Tears fell onto his wrinkled cheeks.

Richard chose that moment to step forward. "Sis?" he questioned while he studied the older man.

"Oh, Richard. I'd like you to meet our grandfather."

His eyebrow shot up, his eyes burned into hers. "What?"

"I told you about Grandma's diary. This is our grandfather, Richard."

Cal stuck out his hand, disappointed when Richard remained motionless. Cal dropped his hand, nodded and sighed. "I'm not proud of myself, son. I've carried the guilt of what happened with me all my life."

Beth's face wrinkled up. She should have expected her brother to be mutinous to this man and she couldn't bring herself to blame him. Comfortingly, she placed her hand on her brother's shoulder. Suddenly, her eyes snapped up to Cal's. "Why are you here?"

With a motion that showed his age, Cal's shoulders slumped and he gestured, defeated, toward the lowering coffin. As if an explanation would help, Cal continued, using his right arm to point west. "I was stationed at Kincheloe Air Force Base before it was closed, which is about 45 miles from here. I married a local girl and had a daughter." He stopped, realized he should get back to her. Beth's eyes were the same shade as Carol's, the uncanny similarity in their features held him transfixed.. "Mary, my daughter married a young man from Drummond. They decided to make their home here, raise their three children here. Fine young adults, all." Tears welled in his eyes. In a small gesture, he pointed at the hole in the ground where the casket had been lowered. In a whisper, he added. "Joe was one of them, my grandson."

Beth's hand jumped from her brother's shoulder as the shock shook him. She replaced the hand, concerned. She noted the loss of color in her brother's face, his trembling lower lip, and suddenly shaking hands. She had felt this emotion from her brother before: guilt. The dreaded feeling coursed through her body, sparked at her neck just as other sensations hovered there. Within Beth's chest, a fist clenched around her heart. Her brother had killed Joe. As she knew anything in life to be true, she knew the nightmare unfolding around her was real.

Cal seemed oblivious to the moment that passed between siblings. "Joe was your cousin, Beth. His mother is my daughter. It was a terrible tragedy…"

Richard's eyes clouded, and he looked as if he was about to be sick. "Excuse me, Beth. I'm not feeling well," he murmured, breaking away from his sister.

Cal reached into his pocket for his wallet and pulled out a card. "Beth, this is my address and phone number. It would be an honor to get together and talk with you. I really need to be with my daughter now, if you'll excuse me."

Beth accepted the card. "Of course." Her mind had already turned back to her brother as she replayed the events

that took place. She knew in her heart that her brother had
come looking for their "future." When she confronted him
about it, he had denied it again, claimed ignorance about the
passage in the back of the logbook and she had wanted so
desperately to believe him. But she couldn't. Beth couldn't
deny what she felt, what she knew instinctively to be the truth.
Her brother killed her cousin. Richard must be falling apart.

Beth walked toward Richard's car and when she cleared
the crowd, she hurried into a jog. She had to find him, make
him turn himself in. It was the only option. As she approached
the cars she saw Richard's back out onto the road and speed
away. Crestfallen, Beth leaned against the car next to her,
breathless.

Jill approached with a calm pace and determined
manner. Again, she had withheld her thoughts from Cole and
the detective but she needed to put it together in her own mind
before she shared it with them. *She needed to be sure*.

"Beth, are you okay?" Close to her now, Jill could see
that Beth was exhausted.

"Hello, Jill." Even in her own grief and terror, Beth
remembered that Jill had buried a friend and was sympathetic.

"Can we talk?"

"I really need to talk to my…"

"It's really important. It concerns your brother."

Reluctantly, Beth nodded.

Jill gestured with her head, led the way for them to
walk. "I remember you telling me something, and I need to ask
you about it."

"Go ahead," Beth braced herself.

"I'm not sure if I conjured this up in my imagination
but I think you told me that your great grandfather worked for
the Philadelphia Mint. Did he?"

Beth raised an eyebrow at the unexpected turn. "Yes, he did."

"You also told me that your grandfather crashed in a plane out by the lighthouse?"

"That's correct."

Jill inserted the new information into the puzzle, gaining confidence in her theory. "Beth, what I'm about to tell you needs to stay with you."

"Okay."

Jill gave it one last moment of hesitation before she gambled. "Three rolls of 1943 bronze pennies were found in the lighthouse. I believe that your grandfather somehow got these pennies from your great grandfather and hid them in the lighthouse."

Beth maintained her outer calm. "So what?"

"If they really are bronze, the estimated worth is above 16 million."

Beth gaped and then recoiled. "Your tone suggests something else."

"I believe they're fake."

Beth's mind raced over the diary entries, remembered that Carol had questioned her father's behavior. *Why would Howard give fake pennies to Lee? He wouldn't. Why would he have them in the first place?* "Why would my grandfather get fake pennies from my great grandfather and then hide them in the lighthouse?"

Jill stumbled over that exact question. "I can't imagine why your grandfather would hide them if he knew they're fake. Maybe he thought they were real, and planned to go back and get them."

Beth remained silent for a moment. "This connects to Joe's murder, doesn't it?"

"Joe is the one who originally found the pennies in the lighthouse."

"Oh, God." Beth gasped, hugged her arms to her chest. "You don't have to tell me you suspect my brother, Jill. I can see it in your face."

"I know what I'm suggesting is hard, Beth. But Joe…" Jill's voice hitched, but she continued. "Joe didn't have anything. The only thing I can figure is Dick or maybe someone else knew about these pennies and searched for them. Maybe the intruder didn't expect Joe to be there, or maybe… honestly, I don't know what happened. "And there's more," Jill forced the words out. "We have the killer's blood and fingerprints. Richard hasn't been fingerprinted but he's on the Sheriff's list. He needs to come in. I might be making a terrible mistake and if I am, he's the only person that can clear it up. Richard is the only person I know that really could have understood their worth."

Beth shook her head. "Jill, there's a logbook. In the logbook, my grandfather says that he left something at the lighthouse, but Richard couldn't have known what to look for."

Taken aback, Jill frowned. "Are you sure?"

"He knew that whatever was there was in a drainpipe, but he couldn't have known what it was."

"A drain pipe?" Jill questioned. *The green slime had to have come from some place moist or damp.*

"Yes. There was a hint that I recognized as soon as I read it." Beth's voice was rushed, her hands shaky.

"Beth, can you bring that logbook to me?"

Beth hesitated, nodded. "Yes. Where?"

"I'm going to be at the credit union in…" She glanced at her watch. "Forty minutes." Jill furrowed her brow.

"I'll have to go straight there and come back." Beth hesitated, considering. "If my brother did this thing…" She shuddered involuntarily. "He might admit it to me, he might even admit it to the Sheriff, but I won't be able to get him to turn himself in. The Sheriff will need to be right there when he's ready to talk."

"What should we do?"

"Why don't you bring the Sheriff out to Richard?" Beth suggested.

"Will he still be at the motel?" Jill inquired.

Beth nodded, gave her the room number. "Yes, I'm confident that's where he went. I don't think he'd try to leave the island yet. I'll go out there, talk to him. Maybe, I can get him to admit to it. You go ahead with the credit union thing, but bring the Sheriff right out with you. Okay?"

Jill found a pen and slip of paper in her handbag. She scrawled the Sheriff's cell phone number from memory. "I don't have a cell phone, but this is the Sheriff's number just in case anything goes wrong."

"Okay."

"Beth... I'm sorry."

Beth met Jill's eyes. "So am I."

Sixty-Nine

Jill leaned against Quinn's Jeep, her forehead beading with perspiration in the bright sun. She drummed her fingers against her folded arms, and watched Quinn ponder what she had told him. He had been modestly shocked to learn Jill's thoughts, the conclusions that she had drawn, and her conversation with Beth; modestly insulted that she hadn't shared her ideas with him earlier.

"What if Beth goes to Richard and tells him your thoughts, Jill? What if he runs?"

Jill shook her head, moved to sit beside Quinn. "I wouldn't have talked to her unless I knew she wouldn't let him go. We need to end this, Quinn."

Reluctantly, Quinn nodded. "Okay. I just..." His voice trailed off as the Credit Union manager's car pulled in next to them.

A middle aged, darkly dressed woman slid gracefully out of the car. "Hello."

Jill nodded in greeting. "We're still waiting for Sheriff Cole and the detective."

The woman nodded. "No problem."

"I'm sorry to drag you here like this."

"Don't worry about it. Cole explained why he needed to get in, and it's no trouble. The sooner this is solved, the better." The manager was more than willing to comply with the special request.

Finally, Cole's SUV pulled alongside the car. At Cole's nod, the manager unlocked the door and flipped on the lights. The pennies were in the Credit Union vault for safe keeping, so she, accompanied by Cole, went into the next room to get them.

Typically, evidence relating to a crime scene is taken to the Chippewa County Sheriff's Department, in the Soo, and placed into lock-up, thus completing the chain of evidence. Cole first took possession of the pennies Friday afternoon, and called the Sheriff's office to make arrangements to take them to the Soo. The County Sheriff, however, gave him permission to leave them in a lock box on Drummond, rather than make the trip up. Chain of evidence could be preserved by Bishop holding one key and Cole having the other. Since Bishop was also staying on Drummond until after the funeral, this worked out efficiently.

Although unusual, the sergeant responsible for checking evidence in had a personal emergency and there wasn't personnel to complete the paperwork or come and retrieve the pennies. The Sheriff volunteered to call the Treasury Department in Grand Rapids to find out exactly what they wanted done with them.

Quinn and Jill stood beside Bishop, silently. After several minutes, they reappeared with the pennies. Jill explained, "If the pennies are real they are going to weigh just a bit over 16 ounces. If they're fake, they will probably weigh a little over 14 ounces."

"Should we unroll them?" The manager questioned.

Cole agreed. "Good idea."

The manager removed the wrapper with painstaking care and placed the pennies on the scale. After a moment, Cole announced. "14.3 ounces."

Jill let out a breath she had been holding. "I knew it."

The Sheriff's eyes met Bishop's across the room. "With your agreement Bishop, I'd like to scratch the end of one."

Bishop raised an eyebrow, turned to Jill. "Are you absolutely sure these are fake?"

Jill knew the numbers, but for the benefit of everyone's eyes trained on her, awaiting the response, she looked at the sheets she had printed the night before. "They are fake, Detective."

At her word, Bishop gave his assent. "Scratch one."

Cole reached into his pocket, grabbed a knife and opened the blade. Carefully, he nicked the edge of the coin. "Son of a bitch," he exclaimed. "It's steel. Jill's theory was right."

Jill interrupted Cole's thoughts, by changing mental gears. She knew they were running out of time. "Sheriff, I need you to come with me."

"Jill, I have calls..."

Jill continued, "I believe I have also figured out who the killer is. I know where he is. We need to go get him now."

Everyone expected her to say something more, but she remained silent. "Well, who is it?"

"Richard DeForge."

"Who?" Bishop croaked.

Cole raised an eyebrow. "He's one of the three left on the list—he's listed as Dick DeForge. Let's go."

Bishop held up his hands. "Wait just a damned minute. You can't just accuse someone of murder, without something behind it, Miss. I need a better explanation."

"There isn't time, Detective. I'll explain what I've learned along the way. Quinn can follow us down and take me home afterward," Jill implored, as Bishop looked like he was about to retort. "*Please.*"

Something changed in the detective's face and he relented.

Seventy

"Richard?" Beth called tentatively as she pushed open the motel room door and walked into the room. Richard's suitcase lay open, clothing tossed into it haphazardly. She paused a moment to allow her eyes to adjust to the dim light. She heard him before she saw him hunched over on the edge of the bed. Rushing to his side, she knelt on the floor at his feet and looked up into his face. Tears streamed from his eyes, down his cheeks, landed on his clenched hands. "Oh God, Richard. Talk to me. Please, talk to me."

Richard rocked gently back and forth. "Bethy," his voice choked on the grief and guilt that welled up within him. "Don't look at me, Beth. I don't want you to see me like this."

Beth's worst suspicions were confirmed as the physical pain that started at her neck slid down her body, her mind, rebelling against the new reality that was her brother. No longer could her memories of her brother as the boy who had looked out for her while growing up exist in her mind without the person that he was today clouding over the image. "Oh, Richard. How could you? Why did you?"

"I didn't mean to Beth, I swear it. I never meant to hurt him. He shouldn't have even been there. He should have been at work already. I went in, looking for Grandpa's future, you know? There wasn't a car in his yard. There wasn't any indication that anyone was there. I was going through one of his drawers when he came out of the bathroom."

Tears streamed down Beth's face; she held her brother's hands in her own as she listened to his story. The ramifications of this tragedy overwhelmed her. His greed led to the death of their cousin... but Beth couldn't help but wonder if their father's life search for a fortune had seeped into Richard's bones, his mind. Of course, Beth considered, if Richard wanted to blame someone else for his behavior, he could go as far back as their Great Grandfather, who originally started all the talk of a 'fortune.' Shaking her head at her thoughts, she forced herself to hear her brother out. Now was not the time to defend her brother. "What happened?" She choked out the words, hating to hear it, but needing to confirm the truth.

"I asked him about the pennies..."

"How did you even know that it was pennies? I don't understand."

"I knew from the logbook that whatever it was had to be in the drainpipe. I asked the construction guys if they found anything. At his birthday party, Bob told me Joe found 150 pennies in the lighthouse. After the party, I went home with a girl from the bar. She was drunk, and I got her to tell me where Joe lived." Richard shook his head, the endless stream of tears not yet quieting. "I went to Joe's the next morning. I didn't go to work. I figured that he would already be at work on the deck job. He should have been. This never should have happened, Beth. It really wasn't my fault. When he came out of the bathroom, he demanded to know why I was there and like a fool, I told him. After I realized what I said, I figured I'd just sort of scare him or threaten him into remaining quiet but he jumped me and knocked me over. I reached back, and the only thing I found was that damned hammer. So... I swung at him."

Beth sobbed as she leaned against the bed at Richard's side. For several moments, she gave herself over to the pain, unable to think of anything but the despair that had swallowed her brother whole. Finally able to calm herself, she pleaded. "Richard, you have to turn yourself in."

Shock colored his face. "Beth, I can't. I'll go to prison and this wasn't really my fault, it's just a horrible accident."

Beth fought for control, leaning forward against his leg. His pained yelp had her recoiling.

"I fell and hurt my leg a few days ago," he explained. When Beth gestured that she should look at it, he brushed her off. "It's fine, Beth."

"You need to turn yourself in," she repeated.

"I can't... its not my..."

"The moment you walked into Joe's trailer, it became your fault. You have to come forward." Beth's voice was stronger than she felt.

"I can't. We're close to Canada, Beth. I can cross the border and hide."

Beth wanted so much to let him go. She shook her head. "They'll find you."

Richard slid off the side of the bed onto the floor and faced her. "If I turn myself in, I'll lose. How will I defend myself? I'll spend the rest of my life in prison."

"If you turn yourself in, it'll show good character. And we'll use the money from Dad's house to defend you."

Hope lit his eyes. "You would do that?"

"Richard, you're my brother."

"Beth, I won't survive in prison."

"Maybe we can get you a low security facility or something... but we can't do that unless you make a show of good faith. If you run, they'll throw the book at you." Beth pushed her brother's head up, forcing him to look her in the eyes. "Richard, you have to."

"No, Beth, I can't. It wasn't my fault."

"Dammit, you can't stick your head under the covers and pretend this was just an accident. Joe was someone's son, Richard. He was our cousin. You killed our cousin. Do you get that? Do you understand what you've done?!" Beth demanded.

"Maybe they won't have enough evidence. Maybe the DNA test will be inconclusive." It was a futile hope and they both knew it. He had already given up. "You know the terrible thing?" asked Richard.

Beth raised an eyebrow. *What wasn't terrible?*

"They're not even real. The pennies, I mean. Mom was right. All those years, Beth. Just think of how many years Dad held on to that story. I was just trying to do the right thing by Dad. He needed that mystery to be solved. Why would his grandfather do such a thing?"

In the back of Beth's mind, she wondered if her brother had a chance at an insanity plea. His life would irrevocably change from this point forward, and he was concerned about the pennies. Maybe it *was* in his blood, she thought. She needed to keep him calm until the Sheriff arrived. Just as she concluded her thought, she heard a knock on the door.

"Come in," Beth called out, before her brother could say anything.

"Did you turn me in?"

"No." Beth shook her head. "That's what you're going to do right now."

Sheriff Cole and Detective Bishop stepped through the door, followed by Jill and Quinn. No one said anything for a moment. Above Richard's head, Beth's eyes met Jill's and held them. Beth gently pulled away from her brother. "Richard, Sheriff Cole is here. Sheriff, my brother has something he needs to tell you."

Shaking his head, with tears streaming down his face Richard stood up. "I didn't mean to do this. I didn't mean to kill Joe. He wasn't supposed to be there." He turned around and held his arms behind him for them to cuff. Detective Bishop recited Richard's Miranda Rights and cuffed him.

Beth didn't try to stop the tears that rolled down her cheeks. She turned to Cole. "Where will you take him?"

"We'll take him up to the jail in the Soo. That's where we'll fingerprint him and we'll have to take a blood sample for comparison," Cole informed. "Ms. DeForge, I'll need the logbook and diary that Jill told me about."

Beth nodded, turned away from her brother. "Both books are in my room, next door."

"I'll take him down to the 4 by 4, Cole," Bishop said.

Beth stepped forward, touched her brother's face. "I'll make arrangements, Richard."

Richard sobbed, cooperating wordlessly. He turned with Bishop, followed him out the door. Behind them, Beth accepted the comforting arm that Jill wrapped around her. The day couldn't have been any darker.

Seventy-One

Jill held Beth tightly, determined to keep her eyes from burning into Richard's back as the men left her view. It was almost impossible not to hate him. Richard had stolen so much when he killed Joe. Yet, as Jill awkwardly comforted Beth, she knew that loss existed on both sides. As much as she wanted to believe that Joe was the victim of intentional malice, she knew that he wasn't. She could see guilt and remorse within Richard, which however absurdly, made Jill feel sorry for him.

As Beth regained her composure, Jill felt Quinn's hand squeeze her shoulder lightly. Cole stood in the doorway, observing and waiting silently.

Gently, Jill spoke. "Beth, Cole needs those books."

Beth nodded, finding the door key in her pocket. She held out the key to Cole, who met her eyes with sympathy.

"Miss DeForge, I appreciate your help," Cole said.

Beth sniffed. "The logbook and journal are on the bedside table."

"Thank you," Cole fished a card out of his pocket. "Here is my card. I'll be in the Soo for a few hours, but then I can answer any questions you might have. I have to go now. Beth, you can follow me up if you'd like to, but I can't let you ride with us."

Beth shook her head. "I need some time, Sheriff."

Cole exhaled, seemingly relieved. "I understand. Call me anytime." Cole turned swiftly and moved to Beth's motel room.

"Thank you, Jill."

"God, Beth. For what?"

"For not hating me and for helping... just, thanks. I know it will never be enough but... I'm sorry."

Jill frowned. "It's not your fault, Beth."

"I need to be by myself for awhile. Do you mind?"

"No, of course not," Quinn responded.

"Call me if you need anything." Jill followed Quinn out the motel room door, peeking her head into the room Cole occupied.

"Jill, I need to talk to you for a moment." Cole said, books in hand as he shut the motel door behind him. "Let me just give Beth her key back, and I'll be with you."

Quinn and Jill made their way to Cole's vehicle, where Bishop and Richard were already secured. Cole was beside them quickly.

"Jill, I want to thank you for your help in solving this case. Without you, it certainly would have taken a great deal longer—if we had ever found him."

"Well, I had a lot of help, Cole." Jill smiled at Quinn in appreciation.

Cole's eyes took them both in, and begrudgingly he asked for more help. "Listen, I know this is a bad day, but I need a favor."

"Name it." Jill didn't hesitate.

"You know how the rumor mill is around here. I would hate for Mary and Tom to hear that the killer was caught from someone else. Would you go and tell them? I'll understand if it's too difficult."

Jill's eyes widened at the request, but she agreed.

"Thank you, Jill." Cole reached his hand out, which Jill met with a firm clasp. He shook Quinn's hand before moving on.

After the Sheriff's vehicle had swung out of the driveway, Jill turned to Quinn. "Come with me?"

"Of course," Quinn said, wondering why she even asked.

Jill offered him a small smile. "What would I have done without you this week?"

"You would have survived, I'm sure."

Jill bit her lower lip in thought. "I'm not so sure."

"Let's get this over with, hey?" Quinn suggested.

"Yeah." Jill took his offered hand and walked with him to his jeep. Lost in thought, she remained silent until they pulled out of the driveway. "God, I wonder what next week will bring."

"You'll probably go back to work on Monday, and things will go back to some state of normal."

"Will they?" Jill questioned, softly.

Quinn narrowed his eyes at her, speculating on her strange expression. "The world never stops turning, Jill. Not even here. Not for anyone. You just need to pick yourself up and keep going."

Jill laid her head back against the seat and looked at him, knowing the truth in what he said all too well. Moments passed before she spoke again, carrying her to a memory that seemed to have taken place so long ago. "You know, Joe was the first person..."

"The first person to what?" Quinn prodded.

A small smile broke across her lips, but she shook her

head. "Never mind, it's silly." Jill turned her head to gaze at the passing trees.

"Jill."

She relented. "Joe was the first person to welcome me to Drummond."

"He must have seen that look about you," Quinn said. "Well, I'm not sure if it's a look so much as a feeling."

She turned her head back to face him and without speech, urged him to continue.

Meeting her eyes, Quinn struggled to find the right words. "You're *home*, Jill. Drummond is a part of you, just like it is for me... like it was for Joe."

Seventy-Two

SEVERAL WEEKS LATER, ITHACA, NEW YORK

Beth set her tea cup back on the dining table; glad to be done with the retelling of the story.

Lisa shook her head sadly. "It's just so hard to believe, you know? I never would have thought Richard could be driven to kill someone. It's so terrible."

"It was hard for me at first too. After a few weeks, the truth just sort of settled."

"When do you go back?"

"I'm not sure. I have to find another job, and yet I need to be there for Richard. I'm going to fly when I do go, but I'm not going back for at least another week. I hate to leave him there alone. He's fallen apart, Li. He's just... he's just, not anything like he was. The realtor can't list the house until it passes the inspection. Of course, that's almost done... but it's just a nightmare."

Lisa couldn't help but dwell on the thoughts coursing through her mind. "First, Great Grandpa Howard must have gotten the pennies and then dipped them in bronze. But why? And let's say there was some reason for that? Why would he give them to Lee?"

"I can't tell you how many hours I have contemplated

the exact same thoughts. I can only come up with one possible idea that works in my mind." Beth sipped her tea.

"You mean you have an answer to this and you haven't told me?"

"Well, we'll never know the truth, but I have a theory. There's only one part of this that I am not sure of. I believe this started with Great-Grandpa Howard who worked at the mint in 1943. He either stole 150 bronze pennies, as he hinted to Grandma Carol and Dad, or he was ashamed of himself and felt inadequate for not building any sort of wealth to leave his children and he made up this story. I never knew the man, and since he died just weeks after Grandma Carol died, Dad never passed down much information about him. In reading the diaries and letters that were left in the house, I believe my great grandfather knew that my dad was illegitimate. He probably had a great deal of respect for Lee for staying with Grandma Carol, even though she hadn't been faithful." Beth fumbled with her thoughts, feeling better about her ideas as she verbalized them.

"I think he gave the pennies to Lee as a way of showing his gratitude. Again, there are two possibilities. He either gave him real pennies and stole them back or just gave him the fake pennies in the beginning. The only reason that I can figure he stole them back is because Carol came down with cancer and Great Grandpa wanted the pennies for Raymond's future." She tilted the corners of her mouth up sardonically amused that she had chosen that word. "Maybe he even just became greedy and kept the originals for himself…" She allowed her voice to quiet, cupped her hands around the steaming mug. "You know, it could drive me insane. But they definitely came from him, and no matter what actually happened—he must have led Lee to believe that they were real. One thing I am sure of – I wish Great Grandpa Howard never took those damn pennies, real or fake. Look at all the misery they have caused our family. Richard's 'future' is prison."

"It's just incredible when you think about it, isn't it?" Lisa stared off, dazed. "First Great Grandpa Howard was slick enough to get the pennies..."

"Assuming the real pennies ever existed," Beth piped in.

"Then Lee was given them, or maybe even stole the pennies from Howard... causing your father and your brother to be haunted by this terrible..." Lisa searched for the right word.

"Greed?" Beth supplied.

"Exactly."

"Thank God, you're not the same way. It must just be the men in your family that are all screwed up."

Beth shook her head. "Not just the men, Li. Grandma Carol betrayed her husband by having a child by another man." Beth quieted for a moment, thoughts spinning through her mind. "Who knows if that didn't have something to do with Lee taking the pennies and leaving?"

"Here's the 16 million dollar question." Lisa grinned. "Do the real pennies exist?"

"That's a real coin toss," Beth retorted, unwilling to pass up the corny wit. She laughed with Lisa for a moment before responding. "On one side is the fact that twelve 1943 bronze pennies have actually showed up in circulation, which leads me to believe that the real pennies could exist. If Great Grandpa Howard knew about them back then, it seems reasonable that he had access to them. What else would have given him the idea to make the fakes? On the other side, if they don't exist, why would he have made the fakes in the first place?" Beth shrugged, rubbing the back of her neck. "I guess, Lisa, we'll never know."

Seventy-Two

The DeForge House, Batavia, New York

George Henson pulled the cast iron remnants out from under the sink with a groan. "Can you believe this shit, Phil?"

The other man raised an eyebrow. "Are you talking about that nasty old plumbing?" When George nodded, Phil continued. "The whole damned house is like that. No one's done any work on this place in a long time."

"At least, it's been cleaned." George frowned at the crumbled pipes, shook one loose. "Hey, there's something in there."

"What?"

Slowly, three tubes slid out of the busted pipe. "I'll be damned."

"What'd you find, George?" Phil looked over his shoulder.

"It looks like three rolls of pennies and some sort of note."

"Open it up."

George unwrapped a layer of plastic and rolled open the piece of paper. *"Carol, this is your inheritance, Dad."* George snorted. "Who's Carol?"

"I don't know. The house belongs to a... oh what is her name...uh, Betsy... no, Beth? Yeah, that's it." Phil frowned. "What kind of a sick bastard would leave $1.50..."

"Actually Phil, this roll isn't even full."

"Odd." Phil shook his head. "He couldn't even leave his daughter three rolls of pennies? He had to use some?"

"Must be a cruel joke, hey?" George countered.

"Damn. I'm glad my old man wasn't like that."

"What should I do with them?"

"Shit, take 'em home and put them in your kid's piggy bank," Phil suggested.

"You think I should? Isn't that like... stealing?"

"Leave them on the counter if it bothers you, but it's only pennies. No one's gonna miss 'em."

Epilogue

The black and white four-by-five told the story.

The man sitting on the edge of the bed turned the worn picture over in his hands, yearning for the days when the group first formed, when innocence had still shown in his own eyes. He served his country for thirty years and was the veteran of two wars. The uniform that still fit snugly against his chest was decorated with seventeen ribbons above his left breast pocket: four of them earned for outstanding service and valor. Although retired, he still held the conviction of an officer: he would die and be buried in uniform. Through the years, he had become a husband, father, and grandfather, subscribing to a code of honor few understood or believed in. Raising his children with solid values of right and wrong, he taught them a strong code of morality. In the back of his mind, he had believed that if he behaved with rigid dignity, the judgment he had feared throughout life would pass him by.

Beside him on the bed, another picture told the tale of his downfall. Carol smiled from the black and white photograph, held the baby boy on her lap, joyfully. Lee stood behind the pair. Lee had eventually mailed him the picture in a Christmas card. Cal had always believed fate, or life, or the circle that eventually forces persons to face the demons in their closets would face him directly. Instead, the grandson of his infidelity had murdered the grandson of his morality. Now, his daughter whom he loved with all his being could barely look at him, refused to speak with him. Mary had been horrified to learn the truth.

Tears that were normally held rigidly in check, streamed down his tired, wrinkled face. In his right hand, a 44 Colt was clenched tightly. Justice should be swift and certain. After all, he *deserved* to die. His betrayal was total.

Authors' Notes

If you're familiar with KAFB, you may be aware that Kincheloe Air Force Base was originally named Kinross Air Force Base and later changed. Because it was called Kincheloe until it closed, we chose to keep the name consistent throughout the book, rather than confuse the reader. Also, if you're familiar with historical events from the eastern Upper Peninsula, pieces of this story may sound vaguely familiar.

Although the story we have told is completely a work of fiction, and in no way reflects actual events that have taken place or real people, we did find our inspiration for this story from historical events. In November of 1953, an F-89C Interceptor was launched from KAFB in search of an unidentified target and went missing. More information can be found about this incident in The UFO Casebook; The Encyclopedia of Extraterrestrial Encounters; and The Sault Evening News.

Similarly, in the winter of 1959 an airman crashed near Spectacle Reef Lighthouse, and left a letter behind. The airman's disappearance resulted in one of the largest searches in Michigan's history. The Sault Evening News follows the original report of the airman's disappearance in February, 1959 and reports the findings of the letter at the lighthouse in April

of the same year. The character and the story following this
event are completely fictitious. In no way, are we implying that
this character and the airman that actually crashed have any
similarities whatsoever. For your interest, and with the
permission of *The Sault Evening News*, we have reprinted the
letter that was found at the lighthouse at the end of the book.
Names have been omitted from the letter.

Drummond Island is also a real place, located just off
the tip of Michigan's eastern Upper Peninsula. Off Drummond
Island's coast, sits the DeTour Reef Lighthouse. Currently
leased to the DeTour Reef Light Preservation Society, the
lighthouse is under renovation. The names of the businesses
included within the novel are also real businesses, though the
characters in the scenes are completely fictitious.

D. Ann Kelley

James G. Kelley

Drummond Island, MI

References

Randle, Kevin D. The UFO Casebook. *November 23, 1953: The Kinross Disappearance.* P 77-81.

Story, Ronald D. The Encyclopedia of Extraterrestrial Encounters. *Kinross (Michigan) Jet Chase.* P 299, 300.

Articles from the Sault Evening News:

Search Superior for Missing Jet: Interceptor from Kinross Missing Since Last Night, November 24, 1953

Abandon Search for Missing Aircraft, November 30, 1953

Search for Missing Airman: Presumed Headed to Kinross, February 25, 1959

Search for Missing Airman One of the Biggest in State's History, February, 1959

Final Sweep Made, February, 1959

Letter Found at Huron Light Gives Clue to Missing Airman, April 9, 1959

Airman May Have Been Saved by Flight Plan, April 10, 1959

To Whom It May Concern:

At 1705 hours (5:05 PM) my plane went down 400 kilometers
out at 035 to 050 degrees. I was one mile north, northeast of
here at 5,000 feet when my engine quit dead. I tried to make it
in, but landed in the water. At that time there were, large open
areas of water. I did not try to land on the ice as it did not look
thick enough. Also I wanted to get as close to this light as
possible.

The plane went down in about two minutes after it landed.
Before it did it floated close enough to a floe for me to jump.
The ice was not over two inches thick. Another large body of
water separated me from the light, so I waited.

Suddenly the wind shifted to the northeast. The ice I was on
started to move. At the very last moment one quarter of the ice
grounded against the ice packed around the light. My ice floe
broke up fast so I ran for the light. I got ashore but was wet
from falling in. My clothes froze before I could get the door
open.

Once inside I used your towels and overshoes to keep from
freezing. About 2100 (9pm) I got your stove lit. I hooked up the
batteries and lit your warning lamp. The radio receiver worked
but the transmitter was dead. I don't know enough about it to
make it work. I have used the batteries until they are going
dead.

I sat up last night sending out SOS calls by blinking the main
light.

Right now I am deliberating whether to stay here or cross the ice. From the chart I will have 11 miles to travel. There are large water holes, thin ice which has been broken into pieces by the wind yesterday. There is hardly any wind today. We have had two freezing nights, so I ought to make it in about four hours. I want to go now because it is nice weather.

Also did not file a flight plan so no one will look for me another two or three days. The weather may be bad again.

I have made a mess of your building. I hope you will forgive me. I am going to take some equipment with me, binoculars, coat, hat, blankets, etc. I will turn them into the United States Coast Guard as soon as I get ashore.

Signed,

M.Sgt. *
USAF

About the Authors

D. Ann Kelley

D. Ann has spent the last year working for one of her parents' businesses on Drummond Island and writing the novel with her father. After achieving a Bachelor of Science degree in Interpersonal Communication, she is currently in graduate school. D. Ann is a prolific reader, and an avid movie watcher. She has enjoyed a variety of unique life encounters from political involvement to various creative endeavors that have given her the benefit of a life's worth of experiences in a relatively short time.

James G. Kelley

From Great Grandparents who homesteaded on Drummond Island in the 1800's, James has always called Drummond home except for one year in 1976/77 when he helped build the Alaskan Pipeline. He has traveled extensively in the National Park system, visiting 106 National Parks, Monuments, and Historic Sites. For over 10 years, James worked as a professional photographer and today he and his wife own multiple businesses in Northern Michigan. In his spare time, he wri   novels with his daughter, D. Ann.

D. Ann and James Kelley are members of the DeTour Light Preservation Society and the National Writers :iation.